THE DIVORCE;

OR, THE

MYSTERY OF THE WRECK.

A Novel.

> " O, I have suffer'd
> With those that I saw suffer! a brave vessel,
> Who had no doubt some noble creatures in her,
> Dash'd all to pieces. O, the cry did knock
> Against my very heart! Poor souls! they perish'd.
> Had I been any god of power, I would
> Have sunk the sea within the earth, or e'er
> It should the good ship so have swallowed, and
> The freighting souls within her."—SHAKSPERE.

LONDON:

PRINTED AND PUBLISHED BY E. LLOYD, 12, SALISBURY SQUARE,
FLEET STREET.

1847.

PREFACE.

———

THE heartlessness and frivolity of fashionable life have never, perhaps, been depicted in more truthful colours than by the author of "The Divorce." This fact has been acknowledged by various journals during the passage of the work through the press ; and public attention has been likewise called to the many well-drawn characters which abound in the tale. The resignation under suffering of Colonel Lessley and his lady—the profligate selfishness of the Newland family and their vicious associates—the unyielding probity of Montague—and the too easy temperament of Lord Millford, whose happiness is nearly wrecked through his inability to resist ordinary temptation, all are equally well described. Our sympathies are from the first enlisted on behalf of the gentle, much-enduring Caroline, and her amiable friend Lady Emma ; and the reader must be gratified at the retributive justice which at length restores the young heiress to her friends, and overwhelms her persecutors ith confusion.

The thanks of the Publisher are due for such hearty commendations, which will continue to act as an additional incentive to the production of other works of sterling merit.

London, September, 1847.

THE DIVORCE.
A Novel.

INTRODUCTION.

"ANOTHER novel!" cried a sage erudite, glancing his eye with a look of contempt, on a small volume which lay half open on the breakfast-table; "when," he continued, "will this inundation of nonsense cease? I wish, with all my heart, the society for the suppression of vice would turn their thoughts towards these volumes of demoralising trash, that fill the minds of youth with vain hopes, false fears, and romantic expectations."

"Dear grandpapa," exclaimed a blooming girl, that was sitting beside him, "how can you be so very severe? What should we do in the country without books of amusement?"

No 1.

"Do," he replied, peevishly, " what your grandmamma used to do; gather herbs pickle vegetables, and preserve fruits."

"Or get up early in the morning to dip cambric handkerchiefs in dew, to improve your complexion," cried Mrs. Modish, sneeringly, as she turned over the leaves of a new comedy.

"Well," retorted the erudite, "the morning air would brace her nerves, and the dew clear her complexion, much better than all the cosmetics and perfumes that load your toilet."

"Deriding, as usual, everything that approaches refinement," said the lady; " now what objection can you possibly make to a well-written novel? "

"Only," said he, drily, "that so few of them are well-written; they paint life in false colours, and represent scenes that never occurred, except in the inane imaginations of their puerile authors; it is such writings," he added, "that make our present generation of girls vain, foolish, and contemptible."

"Your censure, my good sir, is too general," said Mr. Manly, raising his eyes from a morning paper that he had been attentively perusing; "there must be books for all stages of life; in infancy, the mind is instructed with fables and amused with fiction. It has always been admitted that the drama, under proper regulations, may be made conducive to morality and virtue; and a novel is only a drama of larger dimensions. I have frequently been much entertained by the perusal of one; I like to trace the train of an author's thoughts through those effusions of fancy; an original thinker will seldom fail in producing, at least, an interesting work."

"I have seldom heard of a novel having any claim to originality," replied the erudite; "love, hatred, joy, sorrow, deaths, courtships, and marriages are the ingredients of which they are all composed."

"And if we exclude the horrors of war, and the awful devastations and visitations of nature, what other ingredients are there in the history of human life?" said Mr. Manly.

"I never before thought you an advocate for nonsense," replied his opponent.

"Nor am I now," answered he, mildly; "there are many novels as well as many other books, that I should think time lost in reading, but it is not candid to condemn all because some may be objected to. I think on this subject, that even the good and justly-admired Cowper was rather too severe, especially when it is considered how feelingly alive he was to the success of his own productions; and when exclaiming,—

"None but an author knows an author's cares,
Or fancies fondness for the child she bears,"

should he not have thought how many were, and how many would be, labouring under similar anxieties? "

The erudite did not reply; the ladies rose from the table; the younger one taking up her book, thanked Mr. Manly with a sweet smile for his defence of her favourite amusement.

I wished them good morning, and on returning home, penned down this short dialogue, when it occurred to me that it would be an appropriate introduction to the following pages, and as such I present it to my readers.

CHAPTER I.

Fast to the driving winds the marshall'd clouds
 Sweep discontinuous o'er th' etherial plain;
Another still upon another crowds,
 All hastening downward to their native main.
Thus passes o'er, thro' varied life's career,
 Man's fleeting age: the seasons, as they fly,
Snatch from us in their course, year after year,
 Some sweet connection—some endearing tie.
The parent, ever honoured, ever dear,
 Claims from the filial breast the pious sigh,
A brother's urn demands the kindred tear,
 And gentle sorrows gush from friendship's eye;
To-day we frolic in the rosy bloom
Of jocund youth—the morrow knells us to the tomb!—EMILY.

In a romantic part of the luxuriant county of Surrey was situated the ancient and venerable structure of Millford Priory, whose extensive grounds were fertilised and enlivened by the meanderings of the silent Mole, rendered familiar to every poetical ear, by the numbers of Pope. At the commencement of our pages, it was the residence of the earl of that name, a widower with two children, a son and daughter; the son, in his twentieth year, had not left the university, and Lady Emma, two years younger, was completing her education under a lady, celebrated both for her virtues and accomplishments, the principal of an elegant establishment in the metropolis.

In the vicinity of the priory was Firr Grove, the seat of Sir Timothy Acrimony, with whom the earl had been long acquainted. Lady Acrimony was a truly feminine character—mild, affectionate, and forbearing; and with the baronet, it must be acknowledged, she had frequent occasion to exert the latter qualification. She had been the mother of several children, but only one son had survived, who was at once the sole prop of an ancient family, the hope of his father, and the delight of his fond and excellent mother. The death of a daughter, in her sixteenth year, had given so severe a shock to the maternal heart of that lady, as to occasion a long fit of illness, from which she had never entirely recovered. Her sorrow was deep, though silent, and more poignant from having no one to whom she could apply for consolation. Her son was then absent, being a resident at the house of a Dr. Maxwell, who had superintended his education, and Sir Timothy would not hear of his studies being interrupted; and though he felt most keenly the loss of his lovely daughter, yet it did not leave that deep impression on his mind that it had fixed on his lady's. To add to the severity of her sufferings, about the same time she had to mourn the loss of Lady Millford, who died at Lisbon, to which place she had been ordered for the improvement of her health.

At the accustomed time Montague Acrimony returned home; and Dr. Maxwell, having acquired a handsome independence, retired from his arduous profession, and at the request of Sir Timothy, became an inmate at the grove; and in his society and that of her son, Lady Acrimony found her spirits revive, though her health did not sensibly improve. Within a few months after their arrival, Lord Millford (who had buried his lady but two years preceding) paid the debt of nature, and left Sir Timothy one of his executors and trustees for his son and daughter during the remainder of their minorities, and a Mr. Newland, an eminent conveyancer, was associated with him. This gentleman, of whom we shall have frequent occasion to speak, had risen by slow gradations to a very great degree of opulence. He had long conducted Lord Millford's money transactions in a very satisfactory manner. The baronet's secluded habits and love of retirement made him reluctant to undertake the part assigned him, but from the mandate of a deceased friend there was no appeal upon this melancholy occasion. Lady Acrimony, who had not visited London for several years, set out for that place in order to conduct Sir Timothy's interesting ward to the grove. at which place Lord Millford was hourly expected, an express having been forwarded to him prior to her ladyship's departure, who on her arrival at the capital found her beautiful charge (whom she had known from childhood) overwhelmed with affliction, the news of the earl's almost sudden death having been incautiously disclosed to her by a young lady who had heard it from Miss Newland, with whom she was on terms of particular intimacy. After the first emotions of sorrow were subsided, Lady Acrimony imparted the motive of her journey, and found her companion much soothed at the prospect of meeting her brother.

"Oh," said she, with great feeling, turning towards Mrs. Bellamy (the lady whose care she had been under), "that poor Caroline would but go with me!"

"And who is Caroline?" said her ladyship.

"Oh," cried Lady Emma, with great earnestness, while the glow of hope flushed on her before colourless cheeks, "I am sure if your ladyship knew her, you would soon love her almost as well as I do."

"Youth is the season for ardent affections," replied her ladyship, "and the friendships contracted at that period are not easily forgotten. I hope, my dear girl, that your selections will be fortunate to both."

"You cannot think what pleasure it would give me, at least how it would relieve my spirits, to have her with me at this melancholy period," said the young mourner.

"What is your opinion, madam," said Lady Acrimony, addressing Mrs. Bellamy, " of Lady Emma's request ?"

"It is very considerate and kind of Lady Emma," she replied, " to think of this truly estimable young woman ; but she is to recollect that, even if the proposal met with your ladyship's acquiescence, as Caroline is situated, I could not admit of her absence, unless sanctioned by Mrs. Newland's approbation."

"Is the young lady under the care of Mrs. Newland?" was the next inquiry. To which Mrs. Bellamy replied,—

"She understood Miss Melbourne was an orphan, entirely dependent on Mrs. Newland, who had placed her there."

On Lady Acrimony expressing her surprise at Mrs. Newland's generosity in placing her at so elegant an establishment as Mrs. Bellamy's, that lady replied,

"It is on a very economical plan, for, Miss Melbourne is only a half boarder; she came here, indeed," she added, " rather as an attendant on Miss Newland than a scholar; and I know not from what motive she has been left here so long after that young lady's departure."

"I have," said Lady Acrimony, " a slight knowledge of Mrs. Newland, and it is most likely we shall now, on account of these young people, meet more frequently. Do you think, if I apply to her that she will oblige Lady Emma with the company of her friend for a few weeks?"

Mrs. Bellamy shook her head, saying,—

"I have received strict charge to keep her at a distance from ladies of superior rank."

This charge was rendered unnecessary, for Miss Newland's neglect of her had been followed by most of the other ladies, and no one paid any attention to her, except Lady Emma.

A long conversation ensued between the two elder ladies, principally relating to the young ones, Lady Emma having left the room in search of Caroline, at Mr. Bellamy's request. Lady Acrimony agreed to continue with her during her stay in town, which would be no longer than to give the necessary orders for her own and Lady Emma's mourning, to oblige whom, she made a visit to Mrs. Newland, for the purpose of obtaining her permission for Caroline's journey to the grove, having previously seen and conversed with that amiable and neglected young female, on her arrival at Mr. Newland's splendid mansion in Grosvenor-square. She was received with real surprise and well-affected pleasure by Mrs. Newland and her daughter ; and, as Lady Acrimony did not wish to protract her visit, she availed herself of the first pause in the conversation that the recent death of the earl had given rise to, to name the earnest wish Lady Emma had expressed for the company of Miss Mellbourne. Mrs. Newland expressed herself much obliged by the condescension of Lady Emma and the kindness of her visitor, and protested that she was extremely sorry to refuse any request that Lady Acrimony would make, but that she had unanswerable reasons for the line of conduct she had adopted towards Caroline, who could not, under any circumstances, be deemed a proper companion for Lady Emma Millford.

"I sent her," she continued, "to Mrs. Bellamy's as an attendant on Miss Newland, who had, I am sorry to say, frequent occasions to complain both of her pride and ingratitude. I am sensible that on the least encouragement she would be very insolent. I intend keeping her where she is, till I can hear of some lady to whom she may be useful, either as a companion, or amanuensis; therefore, it is necessary that she should consider herself destined to occupy a subordinate rank in society."

"Mrs. Bellamy gives the young lady a most amiable character," replied her ladyship.

"Mrs. Bellamy is a very good-natured woman," said Mrs. Newland, "and one very easily imposed on."

"This disappointment will be most severely felt by Lady Emma," returned her visitor.

"But I am sure," answered Mrs. Newland, "it will be properly appreciated by your ladyship.

And so indeed it was; for she saw in it all the meanness of a narrow mind; the subject was dropped, and her ladyship soon after concluded her unsatisfactory visit. It is needless to account the vexation of Lady Emma when informed that her application had been rejected by Mrs. Newland. To her, who had been accustomed to unlimited indulgence, every disappointment appeared an imaginary misfortune; more so, perhaps, at that time, as her spirits were particularly depressed, while poor Caroline who, in opposition to experience, had ventured to indulge the fond hope of accompanying the ladies to the grove, felt most severely the bitterness of the disappointment. During Lady Acrimony's short stay at Mrs. Bellamy's. Caroline was permitted to spend all the time she could spare from her usual avocations with Lady Emma, and had hourly improved in the good opinion and esteem of Lady Acrimony who could not discover any indications of that insolence and ingratitude that Mrs. Newland had depicted; on the contrary, she appeared affectionate, interesting, and unassuming. When the time for their departure arrived, Lady Emma, from various causes, wept bitterly; but Caroline assumed a calm though dejected air; she kissed the cheek of her friend and the offered hand of Lady Acrimony, but could not trust herself to speak. She, however, followed them to the carriage, watched till it was out of sight, and then hurrying to her chamber, indulged in a luxury of tears. Here she was joined by Mrs. Bellamy, whose affection for her was almost maternal; but prudence prevented her from betraying her partiality towards her.

"Dry up your tears, my dear girl," said that worthy woman, "and reassume your composure; for be assured any appearance of sorrow for this disappointment will be reported by some of the ladies to Miss Newland, and be, perhaps, construed to your disadvantage. They may call it anger, wounded pride, resentment; and such misrepresentations can scarce fail making unfavourable impressions on the mind of Mrs. Newland, who generally adopts the opinions of her daughter, however erroneous. The truth of these observations were evident to Caroline, and profiting by the advice of her real friend, she endeavoured to conquer, at least to conceal, the effects of her late mortification. When our travellers had completed their journey, which was nearly a silent one, they were met at the gate by the young earl and Montague Acrimony. The meeting between the brother and sister was truly fraternal, and their natural grief for their irreparable loss was felt and respected by their surrounding friends. The entrance of a servant with the tea-tray produced something like composure, and then it was that Montague, advancing towards Lady Emma, inquired if she would not honour an old playfellow with one look of recollection."

"Indeed, Mr. Montague," said she, presenting her hand, and smiling through her tears, "I think I should not have known you in any other place."

"That to me," he answered, "is a most mortifying confession, as it seems to imply that during our long separation, you have seldom honoured me with a single thought."

"You are greatly mistaken," she replied, with enchanting simplicity, "for I have frequently inquired of my brother, if you were taller than him—if you were as merry as you used to be—if," She paused, and coloured deeply.

"If what?" he inquired, regarding her with deep interest.

"Oh!" she replied, with quickness, "one is not obliged to confess all ones impertinent inquiries."

"I should think them kind, not impertinent," was the answer, "and am proud of being honoured with a place in your memory, whatever might be the subject that recalled me to it." To this no answer was returned: and during tea, the conversation was languid, for all were occupied in melancholy reflections. In the evening Mr. Newland arrived at the grove, accompanied by Meanwell, the steward of the late earl, a most worthy and respectable character; they came to inform Sir Timothy that the funeral would take place the following day. On their entrance, Lady Acrimony took the opportunity of conducting her lovely guest to the chamber that had been prepared for her.

"Oh," said she, looking round the large and lofty room, "in such a spacious place now rests the mortal remains of my dear and honoured parent; how small a spot will he occupy to-morrow?" She wept bitterly, and Lady Acrimony could not restrain her tears, as she said,—

"My dear girl, Amelia's resting place is quite as small; our families have lived in friendship, and we shall rest together; our vaults join each other." After settling a few necessary arrangements for the conveniency of her visitor, and directing her own woman to Emma's bell, they ascended to the supper-room and found their visitors were departed. It seemd more from form than appetite that they sat down to supper—all were spiritless, and Sir Timothy very peevish. He did not like Mr. Newland; they had differed on some points of little importance, in which the latter pertinaciously maintained his own opinions: this had offended the baronet, who never yielded quietly to contradiction. We have before observed that the earl died almost suddenly after being taken with a fit in the morning, out of which he partially recovered, and being perfectly sensible, directed Meanwell to pen down what he should dictate, and to send for Sir Timothy, if another fit attacked him.

"The baronet and Mr. Newland," he said, "are any executors; send for my son and daughter; I have settled everything between them fairly and, I hope, satisfactorily. Let my will be read after the funeral. You will find it in my escritoir."

While dictating, the spasms returned. Sir Timothy was sent for, but before he arrived, the last struggle was over. Just before he died, he said,—

"I have neglected to name the bond; but Newland will find it with some other papers in——"

Death arrested the half-finished sentence. He sank back and expired. This circumstance Meanwell repeated to the parties. Sir Timothy said he knew nothing of any bond; and Mr. Newland said, if such a thing existed, it was most likely deposited with the will; it had been settled between them that the baronet and the earl should go over to the priory the following morning, where they were to be met by Mr. Newland, who had a seat near it. Accordingly, they set out soon after breakfast, in the baronet's carriage, accompanied by Montague. Before the funeral procession commenced, the will was sought for and found in the place mentioned; but no bond was discovered, although every place was searched in which it was thought likely such a document might be deposited. It was then given up, and supposed that it was only the wanderings of imagination in the last moments of nature's trial. After the funeral was over, and the last solemn duties performed, the party dined together at the priory, and in the evening returned with the will.

The day at the grove had been particularly cheerless. Lady Emma languid, and by turns much agitated, begged to be left alone, saying she was unfit for company.

" And still less so for solitude," said her considerate hostess.

" I feel, my dearest girl," she continued, "that I am not exactly a suitable companion for you ; yet I would endeavour to divert your thoughts from dwelling too intensely on the melancholy subject that at present occupies them."

" Oh, you are so very good, so very indulgent," said the weeping, grateful Lady Emma, " that I am ashamed of seeming inattentive to your kindness, even for a moment ; but this day, this awful day, quite unnerves me."

" Not to feel severely your recent loss would betray a cold and unfeeling heart ; but to indulge in unavailing sorrow would be injurious to your health, and distressing to your friends," replied her ladyship.

A walk in the grounds was then agreed upon. It was one of those fine autumnal mornings so frequent in our climate ; the heat of the sun, though near meridian, was not oppressive ; and the foliage, though tinged with the brown and yellow vesture of decay, was still luxuriant ; many flowers and shrubs yet blossomed in the borders, and scattered their perfumes in reviving profusion. Their walk was long, during which Lady Emma, related many anecdotes of the Newlands' consequence, nor was Caroline forgotten by either of the ladies. Lady Emma described her character with fidelity and feeling, and her sensible friend listened to it with pleasure and satisfaction, as it proved to her that the mind of her young companion was generous, as her person was lovely. The violent perturbations of grief that Lady Emma had experienced in the morning were by degrees abated ; yet still the sigh was heaved, and tears flowed plentifully : these her considerate friend did not attempt to interrupt, for she well knew how little effect common-place condolence has on a wounded heart.

In the evening they were joined by Mr. Newland and Meanwell, in addition to their other friends ; the will was then read. The estate of course was annexed to the title, as was another purchased by the deceased, on which Mr. Newland occupied a country seat ; the furniture at the priory, all of it costly, and much of it modern, was left as heir-looms ; the valuable lease of a noble mansion in Bedford-square, with furniture, books, paintings, &c., &c., was bequeathed to Lady Emma, with funded property, to the amount of five-and-twenty thousand pounds. There were likewise legacies of five hundred pounds each, to Sir Timothy, Newland, Meanwell, and Mrs. Pembroke, sister of the late countess, and Wilson, a favourite valet (who had recently left his service through ill health, and retired to a small estate, in the North of England, which had devolved to him by heirship ;) and many other smaller donations to servants.

He recommended his son to make the tour of Europe as soon as it should be practicable, and left to Sir Timothy the choice of a suitable companion. Lady Emma was to continue at Mrs. Bellamy's till she had completed her eighteenth year, of which some months were unexpired ; the money in hand, and arrears due on the estate, were set apart for the funeral expenses, payment of legacies, &c., &c. ; and whatever the surplus might be, was to be divided between his son and daughter for their immediate use. Some valuable jewels were also assigned to Lady Emma, but with a restrictive clause, that they should be placed in Sir Timothy's hands till she had completed her one and twentieth year ; neither was she to contract any matrimonial engagement till that period, without the full consent of both her guardians and the present earl, under the penalty of forfeiting half her fortune to her brother. Lady Acrimony was requested to superintend her minority, to regulate her expenses, and allow her to become an inmate at Firr Grove, after she left Mrs. Bellamy's, till she was of age to act for herself. The motive for this request was known to Lady Acrimony ; she had heard the earl express his fears of Mrs. Pembrooke (who was quite a fashionable woman) obtaining any influence over the mind of his daughter, should he not live to see her properly placed in life. The will had not been made many months ; it was written in the earl's own hand, and witnessed by a friend, and the rector of the parish. The establishment at the priory was also to continue on its present foundation, under the direction of

Meanwell. As the plans for the future were so clearly defined, there remained but little for the executors to do, but to follow the directions left them. Sir Timothy, after attending to all the most important arrangements, willingly resigned the pecuniary ones to Meanwell and Mr. Newland. He, however, directed the plan for Lord Millford's tour, which was to be undertaken in company with his son Montague, accompanied by Dr. Maxwell. The restraints that had so long impeded the intercourse between this country and the continent no longer existed; the decisive battle of Waterloo had been fought the preceding summer, and it was already inundated with British visitors.

As soon as the necessary arrangements were completed, the gentlemen proceeded to Dover, and Lady Emma returned to Mrs. Bellamy's, where she was received with unfeigned pleasure, both by that lady and her friend Caroline, who had severely felt the loss of her society. Lady Acrimony parted with regret from her young friend, in whose affectionate tenderness she had found a solace for her former loss.

Shortly after, letters arrived from the travellers, announcing their safe arrival at Paris.

Here, then, for the present we leave them, and hasten to introduce our readers to the no less (at least in their own opinion) important family of the Newlands.

CHAPTER II.

> Placed for his trial on this bustling stage,
> From thoughtless youth to ruminating age,
> Free in his will to choose or to refuse,
> Man may improve the crisis or abuse;
> Else, on the fatalist's unrighteous plan,
> Say to what bar amenable were man.—COWPER.

THE now opulent and consequential Mr. Newland was the son of a poor country shopkeeper, whose young and increasing family he with great difficulty and persevering industry contrived to supply with the mere necessaries of life—its comforts and conveniences were both beyond his reach. George, the subject of our present memoir, was the eldest of nine children, and being a very quick and intelligent lad, he, fortunately for himself, attracted the attention of Sir John Lofty, who was candidate for the borough of Moneyfield, in the vicinity of his father's humble habitation. Pleased with the shrewd answers of the lad, whom he met with at an inn, in the humble station of helper to the ostler, Sir John engaged him in his service during the election, and found him on many occasions a very useful auxiliary. His dexterity in delivering a note, and secrecy in presenting a few small but fashionable presents among the females of the town, together with a peculiar quick way that he had of giving meaning to a message, greatly facilitated the knight's election, on which occasion he became domesticated in the family, and soon after accompanied it to London, where he attained the high honour of cleaning the knives, blacking the shoes, and waiting at the second table, in which employment he soon improved his manners at the expense of his morals. In place of his native simple archness, he acquired a competent share of knavery, and cunning. He would very adroitly procure wine for the housekeeper, without being suspected by the butler; and purloin tea and sugar for the cook, without being detected by the housekeeper; in short, he soon became too quick for his employers, who in some degree feared, yet continued to profit by, his dexterity. At length some of his exploits were detected by a second hand, Mrs. Slipslop, and reported to her lady. He had also been heard to make some observations on the election at Moneyfield, which being fully brought home to him, was thought a sufficient motive for his dismissal ; he was in consequence stripped of his gaudy livery, branded with the name of an ungrateful slanderer, and dismissed in disgrace. His whole stock of clothes were tied up in a pocket handkerchief, and his money amounted only to nine shillings and sixpence, being a seven shilling piece sent him by Sir John, and half-a-crown he forgot to give the cook out of some change he had of hers. This was all he had to face the world with. Those who had initiated him into the mysteries of knavery secretly rejoiced that he was about to depart quietly, without any very minute inquiry being made into his conduct, which certainly would have led to their own exposure. Each loaded him with favours, it may be supposed. No such thing. They loaded him with advice that, like the friar's blessing, cost them nothing. The cook and housekeeper, in particular, charged him to be sober and honest ; and the butler, who had elicited from him the offensive truths that had occasioned his disgrace, bade him be sure to keep a civil tongue in his head, and never, in future, speak disrespectfully of his betters, thus endeavouring to gloss over the foundation they had been laying in his mind for future derelictions from truth and morality.

After leaving Sir John's he wandered about till towards evening, uncertain what to do or where to apply for a lodging. At last an office for hiring servants attracted his attention ; and as he stood gazing at the bills in the window, he was accosted by a young man at the door, who inquired if he wanted a place.

George replied in the affirmative.

"Can you pay for being recommended to a good one ?"

" I do not know," was the answer; " how much money do you want ?"

" Only half-a-crown," was the reply.

George produced his half-crown, and was ushered into the office, and there interrogated as to where he came from and what he could do.

" I be comed from the country," he answered, with great simplicity. "I can black shoes, clean knives, take care of a horse, and drive plough."

This last qualification occasioned a laugh at what was thought the lad's ignorance of London.

" But if the gentleman to whom I am going to recommend you should require a character, to whom can you refer ?"

This was a stroke some persons would have thought very difficult to parry, but our young adventurer was not to be intimidated by trifles, and he therefore replied, in a very natural manner,—

" That if they know'd anybody at Canterbury, they might hear of father, who would tell all about him, for he was but just come from the country."

The idea of sending to Canterbury for a character occasioned another laugh at his simplicity, which they at last agreed to trust to for his future honesty.

George deposited his half-crown ; a few lines were written by way of recommendation, and George was about to depart, when another difficulty occurred : he did not know the way.

"I can get a boy to go with you for threepence," said the young man that had first accosted him.

" I have only three halfpence," said George, feeling in his pocket, and unwilling to show his seven shilling piece.

"Well, there are three more," said the young man, presenting them ; " you shall not lose the chance of a good place for a few coppers."

A boy was then called, who seemed a kind of assistant, who conducted him to the house of an eminent solicitor, in Chancery-lane. Here his apparent simplicity again befriended him, and without any further inquiry he was admitted into the house of Mr. Goosequill, as the servant of the family, where his natural archness and good humour made him a favourite among the servants in general, and more particularly with a young gentleman that was articled to Mr. Goosequill.

No. 2.

As George was one day employed in sweeping the office, young Egerton entered. Some conversation ensued, in which he inquired of George if he could write.

The answer was in the negative.

"Should you like to learn?"

The lad's countenance brightened as he answered in the affirmative.

"Then," replied the other, good naturedly, "come into the office whenever you can make it convenient, and I will instruct you."

George was punctual, assiduous, and tractable; in short, his improvement both surprised and pleased his instructor, to whom, after a few months' application, he became very serviceable.

Young Egerton was of good family, and heir to a genteel fortune, which a prudent father proposed he should increase by the practice of a lucrative profession. With this view he had been placed with Mr. Goosequill. Egerton, with high spirits, a fund of good nature, and no great stock of self-denial, was given to indulge too largely in the amusements of the metropolis. Mr. Goosequill was very particular in the conduct of his family, and, one instance excepted, set them a moral example. He was very punctual as to hours, and always expected his doors to be closed by eleven, unless a reason was given why any part of his family should be out later. On this point George was particularly useful to Egerton, who frequently wished for more liberty than that early hour allowed him to have. On such occasions he had only to apprise George of his intentions, who, sleeping in the kitchen, on a signal being given, could admit him down the area and into the house without suspicion.

Things went on in this way for nearly three years, in which time George had grown manly, and had improved greatly in his person; was become a good accountant and a clear engrosser—a qualification very servicable, as it enabled him to assist his friend in the office, which was under his care, having the key of it, that it might be ready for the clerks in the morning. This he availed himself of, and frequently wrote part of the nights, unknown to any one but Egerton, who liberally rewarded him for his services. He also, through the interest of his friend, obtained an advance in his wages, with a new livery once a year. It is but justice to observe that he acquitted himself well, for neither his civility nor industry was lessened by these advantages; and having no inclination for anything but gain, he continued to plod patiently on. It must be allowed, however, that he felt his consequence a little increased, and no longer considered either the cook or housemaid his betters; with the housekeeper he had nothing to do, except to execute the orders she gave from the parlour; for, being the companion of Mr. Goosequill, she presided at his table, and directed the family with unlimited authority. Of course no ladies visited at the house.

The familiarity with which Egerton treated George opened his eyes to the lucrative profession of the law. He heard with astonishment the ease by which fortunes had been acquired by many whose best assistants had been effrontery and good fortune. Then it was that enterprise began to dawn upon his mind, and one evening, when they were alone in the office, and the subject renewed, he ventured to express a wish of being initiated into the mysteries of the profession. After the pause of a few minutes, Egerton replied,—

"There is but one way that I can serve you in, and if I do, it will require great application on your part to acquire a necessary share of legal knowledge."

This George professed his willingness to undertake.

In reply Egerton observed,—

"You must be articled to some regular attorney. It will require some money."

"I have but little," said George.

"I will make up the deficiency," replied the other. "And I know a poor scribe that I think will oblige me in the business, but it must be done privately. I shall see him to-morrow morning, and we will talk it over."

The usual good fortune of George prevailed, and all was concluded to his entire satisfaction.

Much about the same time, Mr. Goosequill's favourite companion, *terrore devote*, having by chance heard a high Calvinistic preacher violently declaim against the deadly sin of fornication, she determined to turn from the evil of her ways, in order to avoid the dreadful lake of fire and brimstone that he had so forcibly described.

This resolution was, after some inward struggles, imparted to Mr. Goosequill, with a modest hint that he might quiet her conscience, and promote his own salvation, by only submitting to the solemn ordinances of the Church.

"Never!" said the blunt old lawyer. "I have been married once, and I think I must have worked my way to salvation, for I was in purgatory full fourteen years."

Yet it must be confessed he was vexed at her determination; for long habit had made her society necessary to him, and having, as he thought, liberally rewarded her for the attentions she had paid to him, he left her to settle the matter with her conscience in the way most agreeable to herself. He tried the force both of reason and ridicule to induce her continuance on with him, but to no effect.

She was determined to be married, and if he would not marry her, she had some reason to think the maledictory preacher would.

At length, finding his quiet much interrupted by her frequent exhortations to repentance and amendment of life, he agreed to allow her fifty pounds a year for her life, and desired her to leave him, and repent by herself.

She took the money, but not the advice, for shortly after she married the preacher, and retired to a distant part of the kingdom.

The chasm in the family was soon filled up.

Egerton, at the request of Mr. Goosequill, sent an advertisement to a morning paper, stating the qualifications necessary for the important situation, and where an answer might be addressed.

In the course of the day one was received, well written and cautiously worded, in which the writer said enough to procure an interview, without appearing to understand the full meaning of the advertisement.

"This is a woman of intellect," said Mr. Goosequill, as he gave the letter to Egerton. "I hope if we agree she will not turn methodist, and leave me as her predecessor has done."

In short, through the agency of Egerton, the parties met, clearly understood each other, and in the course of a few days, a fine woman, of about five-and-twenty years of age, dressed in deep mourning, was at the head of Mr. Goosequill's family; and as she will frequently make her appearance in the following pages, it may not be amiss, in this place, to introduce her to the notice of our readers.

Harriet Newport was the daughter of a country apothecary, who, viewing with parental partiality the rising beauties of his only daughter, resolved that the advantages of education should be added to the gifts of nature; frequently indulging himself in the expectation that her beauty and accomplishments would procure for her an eligible station in society. Comformable to these views, she was placed at a fashionable and expensive school, where she acquired with facility the usual accomplishments taught there. At eighteen, she returned to take upon herself the arrangement of her father's house, he having recently become a widower. In the following autumn, she danced at a race-ball with an officer in a regiment of infantry, then in barracks, near the town. In short, the acquaintance thus commenced soon ripened into an intimacy. Parties were formed, balls were given, and the winter passed away in continual diversions. During which, Captain Nettelby had all the opportunities he could wish for of making an impression on the heart of the volatile Harriet, whose indulgent father, proud of the visitors her attractions drew to his house, seldom interfered in her amusements. She was passionately fond of the drama, so was the captain, who frequently attended her to a theatre that was recently opened at the next town. He was, in fact, become a supposed lover, and certainly a constant admirer.

Mr. Newport was not very well pleased that he made no direct proposal for his daughter, but contented himself with thinking that it was all in good time, and that an explanation would, of course, precede his quitting the barracks. In this, however, he was mistaken, for the captain had no explanation to make, but such as would have injured his interest with Harriet; and his principal aim was to avoid all opportunities of being asked for any.

When the orders arrived for these sons of Mars to march to another part of the kingdom, it was proposed that they should engage the theatre (it was then closed or the season), and get up a play, the profits of which were to be distributed among the wives and children of the soldiers, and for the relief of such as were sick. The motive was laudable, and met with general approbation. What drama should be performed, was for some days an object of consideration ; at length *The Confederacy* was fixed on ; but the female characters were hawked about in vain,—no ladies of delicacy would disgrace themselves by appearing in such immoral scenes In this dilemma, recourse was had to some itinerant children of Thespis that were then performing in a neighbouring barn, and, at the earnest request of the captain, Harriet consented to play Flippanta to his Brass.

Her father made some forcible objections, but they were soon silenced, and his better judgment yielded to the volubility of his daughter, not the arguments she advanced in support of her Thespian *debut*.

Her friends remonstrated against her appearing in public with women of doubtful character; to this she gaily answered,—

"It was only for an evening's amuse-ment."

Those who wished her well were sorry for her folly ; while those who envied her wit, vivacity, and spirit, secretly rejoiced that she was about to make herself ridiculous, if not contemptible.

The play was well got up, and received with loud applause. Harriet seemed to tread on air ; while the plaudits that were bestowed on her performance, when the curtain dropped, completed her infatuation.

An elegant supper was provided at a tavern, which she thoughtlessly consented to partake of, though she had faithfully promised her father that she would return home as soon as the performance was over. There she continued till the morning was far advanced, regaling with women without character, and most of them without principle.

In the midst of a duet which she was singing with Nettelby, her father entered the room. Anxious for her return, he had not retired to rest, but sat patiently waiting for her till the clock struck one. He then sent his assistant to the theatre, all there was silent, but a person that he met by chance told him the players were all gone to sup at the Lion. With this intelligence, he returned to his master, who, dreading the scandal this piece of folly would give rise to, as it respected his daughter, instantly determined to fetch her home.

On his entrance, the surprise and vexation of Harriet could not be concealed. Wine was offered him, which he declined taking, and peremptorily insisted on Harriet's returning home.

"One more hour," cried the captain.

"Not another minute by my consent," said the father, in a tone that silenced solicitation ; and Harriet, somewhat crest-fallen, retired with him.

The distance they had to walk was not more than a quarter of a mile ; and neither of them spoke. The captain followed at a distance, and overtook them just as the door was opened. The apothecary held the door in his hand ; after putting his daughter forward, and wishing the captain a good morning, the door was shut, and Nettelby returned to his companions.

When Harriet entered the parlour, she was followed by her father, who, addressing her in a mild but firm tone, said,—

"For the follies that are past I condemn myself; I have been too indulgent. I might have foreseen that the incaution and vivacity of your temper would lead you into indiscretions; and I might still have trusted you to your own guidance if a ircumstance which has occurred since we parted had not made me tremble for our safety."

Harriet was silent through vexation.

"You want rest," said her father, "so do I. Only one thing more I have to ay : Captain Nettelby visits here no more."

After saying this he left the astonished Harriet to muse on the prohibition.

"What can he mean?" said she, while in the act of taking her taper and etiring to her room, in no very pleasant state of mind; when, turning hastily ound, she perceived that she had left the key in her writing desk. She opened it, nd found all her letters gone. "Oh, very pretty!" she cried, indignantly. 'The mystery is unravelled. But what meanness to search my desk. Well, rom this time forward I will act as I please."

So saying, this ungrateful girl retired to rest; though she had planted a thorn n her father's pillow that prevented his repose.

Here it may be proper to acquaint our readers that, soon after Harriet had left iome for the theatre, an old friend of her father's called on him, and, after some ndifferent conversation had passed between them, informed him that Nettelby was , married man.

Surprise at first made the apothecary incredulous; but at last he was convinced f the truth by a letter which his friend produced from his sister at Glasgow, vhere Mrs. Nettelby then resided with her mother and an infant girl.

"I saw," continued his friend, "the influence this man was gaining over the mind f your daughter; I did not like him; and, with a wish to serve you, made some nquiries of a person who had known him before he entered the regiment he now erves in; from him I heard that he had been stationed at Glasgow; thither I vrote, and this is my answer."

It is needless to say how grateful the apothecary was for this proof of riendship.

"What shall I do ?" said he, in great agitation.

"Do ?" said his friend. "Why, break off all intercourse with him directly, and 1ever suffer the acquaintance to be renewed on any account whatever." So saying 1e took his leave.

When left to himself the thought of his daughter's danger overpowered every ither consideration. He rang for the servant maid, and bade her bring down Miss Newport's writing-desk, intending to force the lock, in order to discover how ar the correspondence between them had proceeded, and if she was acquainted vith his real situation. The key, as we have before observed, was in it; and, to lis great satisfaction, it did not appear that she knew anything of his legal :onnections.

The captain's letters breathed the very soul of passion; he raved of honour, of levotion, of the jealousy of love, but not one word of marriage. Indignant, he :hrew the whole mass of folly into the fire, and bade the servant replace the desk n his daughter's room.

In strict justice to Harriet we are bound to assert that she was unacquainted with his marriage, and never harboured a doubt of either his honour or affection. A love of admiration and a certain levity of conduct had led to his first advances, which, being favourably received, flattered his vanity, and induced him to proceed n the accomplishment of his libertine designs. She was, in his opinion, a dashing girl of spirit, whom he intended to persuade that a life of liberty was far preferable :o a life of bondage; and it was not difficult to discover that Harriet's principles were not of the most rigid description.

It was late before Mr. Newport and his daughter met at breakfast. He then :old her again that Captain Nettelby should never again enter his house.

"What has he done, sir," demanded Harriet, colouring, "to merit so positive a prohibition?"

"He has shamefully abused my confidence, and imposed upon your credulity," was the reply.

"I am not so easily imposed on as you may imagine," said she, with a toss of the head.

"Then you are more culpable than I thought," replied her agitated father.

"I do not understand you, sir," was the answer.

"Then, to speak so as not to be misunderstood, did you know that you were corresponding with a married man?" replied her father.

"A married man!" she exclaimed, in a mixed tone between surprise and mortification. But with another toss of the head she added, "What is it to any one whom I correspond with?"

To this she received no answer; her father was too much hurt to reply. Finding him silent, she continued,—

"As you have satisfied a mean curiosity by inspecting my letters, I suppose, sir, you can make no objection to giving them back to me."

"That I cannot do," he replied; "and if I could, under the present circumstances, it would disgrace you to receive them."

"I see no disgrace attached to it," she answered. "Why cannot you restore them?"

"Because I have destroyed them, and with them I hope every vestige of your recent folly."

Harriet bit her lips, but after a pause, asked who had reported that the captain was married.

"My intelligence is certain," her father replied; "but I will not give up my author."

"Then I am at liberty to doubt the truth of your assertion," said she, contemptuously.

"Harriet," replied her father, mildly, without noticing her last sally, "will you do one thing to oblige me?"

"It depends, sir, on what you may require of me."

"Go to your aunt's, at Bexley, and continue there till the officers and the players have left the neighbourhood. I will drive you there in the chaise after tea."

"And back again, sir, if you please. I have no inclination for being shut up in a rookery, with a cross, moralising old woman, and her notable daughters."

"Then you will not go?" cried her father.

"I cannot, sir. I have an engagement for the evening."

"With whom?" was the inquiry.

"With the ladies I left so abruptly, last night."

"You shall not receive them here," said her father, firmly; "and I think you will scarce have the temerity to hazard my displeasure by meeting them elsewhere."

"This is very strange," she answered. "You never before, sir, interfered with my engagements."

"I never before considered them disgraceful ones."

Many more arguments were advanced by the anxious father, in favour of his plan, and all evaded or rejected by the incorrigible Harriet. Finding it was hopeless to expect compliance from his self-willed daughter, the disappointed apothecary left, and prepared to attend on his patients. But before he left the house, he gave strict orders that none of the parties should be admitted into it.

CHAPTER III.

————She may feel,
How sharper than a serpent's tooth it is
To have a thankless child.—SHAKSPERE.

IN the course of the day the captain called, but was refused admittance by the shopman. Harriet heard the man say,—

" I was desired by my master, sir, to inform you that he has forbidden Miss Newport to receive any visitors during his absence."

" Very unaccountable," said the captain, haughtily, "but I shall call again in the evening for an explanation.

Harriet retired to her room to pen a note.

" Some very unpleasant suspicions," she said, " have been infused into the head of my fantastical father. I know not the Marplot who has been so busy here. My endeavours to elicit information have been ineffectual; the servants either do not know or will not tell me. I have had a smart skirmish with him this morning, which ended rather abruptly, in consequence I must decline my engagement for this evening : make my apologies, ladies, and tell them to expect me to-morrow at the usual place, at the usual time."

The servant maid, who was in her confidence, was despatched with the note. Mr. Newport, on his return, was pleased to find his daughter tranquil, and employed at her needle. The next day was the one usually devoted to distant patients; and no sooner was the little low chaise that the confiding father drove out of sight, than his unthinking daughter prepared to meet her libertine lover. He was punctual to the time, and with seeming anxiety entreated an explanation. It was soon given; but not without sighs, tears, and regrets at the bare possibility of a prior engagement.

He let the first burst of anger subside before he ventured on reply; then, in a tone of anguish, cried,—

" We must part, Harriet ; you have been prejudiced, I see, against me ; you condemn me unheard."

" Not so," she cried, " I came to hear a refutation from your own lips of this, I hope false, calumny."

" It is not false," he answered; " would to God it was !"

" Oh," cried the imprudent girl, "why did you not confide in me? I would have been your friend, your confident, and taught myself to give up all claims to your affections, but such as the most scrupulous delicacy would have allowed me to retain."

" The fear of losing your society, my dear, my idolised Harriet," said he, "drove me to what I hate—dissimulation. I hoped to secure a place in your heart, before I ventured to disclose my state of bondage. I thought, presumptuously perhaps, that affection would induce you to forgive a little deviation from candour, occasioned only by an attachment as ardent as ever warmed the heart of man. Oh, Harriet," he continued, " what are the vulgar ties that marriage imposes on us, when compared with the rosy bands that love wreathes for her chosen votaries ?"

" Then you are married ?" she replied, with a deep-drawn sigh, while a plentiful flood of tears bedewed her face.

" I am," he answered ; " but, if I have an interest in your dear heart, and those precious tears almost confirm my, perhaps, too aspiring hopes, speak, ease my tortured soul, but do not, by cruelty, drive me to despair."

Harriet was silent. He repeated professions of eternal love, in short, she listened, wept, upbraided, and forgave him. In his own vindication, he told an artful tale of an early marriage with a worthless woman, whose dissipated conduct had ruined his fortune, and destroyed his peace. Mutual dislike had caused a separation, which had led to his entering the army.

"Never having felt," said he, "the irresistible power of love, I laughed at those who languished under its influence, and exulted in my own freedom. But it was reserved for you, my charming girl, to punish my temerity."

The interview was long protracted, and a future plan of correspondence was agreed on. Their meeting's were to be held at the same place, during the captain's continuance in the neighbourhood, and, finally, their love was to end but with their lives ; and, like Petrach's and Laura's, be pure as the mountain snow. When they separated, Harriet returned home, secretly pleased with the arrangements she had consented to, and almost convinced, by Nettelby's argument's, that their love was mutual, and that there could be no crime in indulging it. Such are the sophisms with which passion misleads its votaries. The captain was exulting in the power he had obtained over the affections of a vain and thoughtless girl. Their meetings were continued, but, in spite of the precautions taken by both parties, they were detected and published ; and, as is usually the case, the worst constructions were fixed on the character of Harriet, and she had the mortification of finding herself shunned by many of her former acquaintances. To this she paid but little attention, while her lover was on the spot ; but, when he left it, her solitary situation struck forcibly on her mind. Then it was that she endeavoured to renew some former friendships, but without success. She was not admitted into families where there were daughters, without their mothers betraying evident marks of dissatisfaction ; and some few that did receive her, on her father's account, never returned her visits. Thus, by her own folly, shut out from all genteel society, she had no resources to rest on but Nettelby's letter. To him she complained that the world had forsaken her, and he advised her to despise the opinions of those that could not know the purity of her affections. While her father, finding too late, that his accomplished daughter was neither happy herself, nor endeavoured to make him so, consoled himself out, for want of society at home, and, in a few months after these transactions, brought home another wife, to the mortification and annoyance of Harriet. Mrs. Newport was a complete Mrs. Bustle, and delighted in nothing more than displaying her notability. Closets and cupboards, that had been long unsearched, were now ransacked, old clothes and rags sold or changed, the mattresses were beat, the blankets scoured, carpets cleaned, and the house painted ; in short, to use Mrs. Newport's own expresssions, she had turned everything topsy-turvy. One day when employed in rummaging, as she called it, she called out to the honest apothecary, (who by the way was nearly as much annoyed by his notable wife, as he had before been by his careless daughter), I think I have pretty well done routing out the holes and corners, but when the things will be got to rights God knows : the linen is shamefully out of repair, the furniture eat up with dirt, and all the china covered with dust ; aye, it is well Harriet is not my daughter, if she was I would soon let her know that it would not spoil her white hands to help wash it ; but Harriet was very differently employed. Accustomed to control, she could not contentedly yield her place at table, nor her control over the domestic affairs to her father's wife. She determined therefore on leaving her home with what little money she could get together (and small indeed was the same), and endeavour to procure an engagement at a provincial theatre ; she apprised Nettelby by letter of her intentions, and he warmly applauded her spirit, and promised to obtain leave of absence, and meet her on the road. As her father was frequently from home, and his wife always busy, she had time to complete her packages unsuspected. The servant that had been her confident had been dismissed soon after Mrs. Newport's arrival because she would not get up in the morning without calling, and was in many respects unfit for a family, where a mistress looked after her own affairs. To her Harriet applied for assistance ; she was then living with her mother (a poor woman) in a cottage in the town——, who for a trifling gratuity undertook to facilitate her departure ; while the undutiful Harriet, without one feeling of compunction, prepared to leave the abode of her childhood and the roof of her fond but mistaken father, and by so doing plant in the bosom that had cherished her, a thousand agonising cares for her future safety; while regardless of future consequences she was about to throw herself in the power of an artful libertine, on whose principles she could have no reliance, and who had himself confessed he could give her no legal claim to his protection. Her elopement completed, she was met at the place appointed by her base seducer, who conveyed her to a lodging he had provided, where he introduced her to the mistress of the house as his wife; for this she was not prepared, she looked confused and angry, but was so situated she could not contradict him. He seized the moment of surprise and vexation to lead her into another room, where he implored her to excuse the necessary artifice circumstances had compelled him to resort to; he slipped a ring on her finger, and saluted her by the name of Westcote; it is needless to say more than that passion and adulation silenced the few scruples she raised, and she consented to appear his nominal wife; for some time the life of love, as it was called, seemed a life of happiness, but everything in nature changes, and even rapture and admiration are palsied by the hand of time.

The captain's leave of absence was expired, their money nearly expended, and no plan decided on for their future support. The company Harriet had expected to join had no vacancies, but the manager, hearing her recite several difficult characters, gave her a letter of recommendation to another theatre, at the distance of thirty miles. Thither she went, and was fortunate in procuring an engagement for the season, though at a very low salary. Nettelby on his return to his regiment, was harassed with debts which he had before contracted; to avoid the importunities of his creditors, he privately disposed of his commission, and joined Harriet at Norwich, where she was then performing with a very necessary supply of money, which while it lasted steeped their senses in forgetfulness. Neither of them knew how to practice economy, and both had a very superior contempt for the vulgar computation of pounds, shillings, and pence; again embarrassments crowded on them, the season was over, and Harriet left without an engagement. In this dilemma they resolved on decamping to London, where Mrs. Westcote, as she was called, hoped through the interest of some theatrical friends to gain an introduction to one of the London managers. After some weeks spent in unsuccessful applications, she at last obtained an audience with a celebrated manager, to whom she recited some of her most favoured parts. To her severe mortification, he heard her with apathy, and at the conclusion told her that her declamation was provincial, her tones monotonous, and her gestures not sufficiently varied to please a London audience. He advised her to try Bath, and cultivate her taste under some of the female performers there, who were many of them excellent patterns. Vexed and disgusted at the thought of being a copyist—for in her diction she had aimed at originality—she returned dispirited to her lodgings, where the first thing that met her eye was a letter from Nettelby It was short and laconic; he informed her that some of his vigilant creditors had discovered him, and that there was no alternative for him but imprisonment or emigration.

"I prefer the latter," he said, "which I have had for some time in contemplation. My route," he continued, "is resolved on; it is a private engagement, and all inquiries after me will be fruitless. You possess sufficient attractions to procure yourself a lucrative establishment, and the only advice I can give you, is to make the best possible use of them."

"Wretch!" she cried, in tones of undissembled passion. "Why have I devoted one hour of my existence to so complete a villain?"

A severe fit of weeping followed, after which she became more composed. Her first employment was to examine the strength of her purse, which finding very light—for Nettelby had taken all the cash he knew of—she then determined on taking a less expensive lodging. To account for her sudden removal, she said Mr. Westcote had been suddenly called into the country, and that during his

No. 3.

absence she should board in a family. The landlady recommended her to a person that took in single ladies, and thither she went. But previous to her departure, by pledging a few ornaments, she settled with her hostess, and on the evening on which she quitted apartments, burnt all Nettelby's letters, his plaited hair, and miniature.

"And now," said she, "I will convince the wretch that I can live without him."

Soon after her removal, she had reason to discover that the morals of her new hostess were not of the most rigid description.

At first she employed herself at her needle ; but finding a sedentary life very irksome, she mixed with the girls of the house, and devoted herself to a life of irregular gaiety, which continued a considerable time.

It is not our intention to follow her through her imprudent progress, to which she at last fell nearly a victim. A long fit of illness reduced her to the most pitiable state of distress. Her clothes and ornaments were one by one disposed of to support her during her long illness, and nothing remained for her to do, but to implore the forgiveness and assistance of her father, of whom she intreated a small supply of money, to rescue her from her inevitable misery.

Her letter was answered by Mrs. Newport, who in very warm language informed her that her father had never recovered the shock of her unexpected elopement, had long lingered in a declining state, and been dead near a twelvemonth—that he had bequeathed her thirty pounds for mourning, which she might receive at a solicitor's office in Lincoln's Inn ; at which place she would also find a letter from her brother, who had been long stationed on the medical staff in the East Indies.

In a very few days she called at the appointed place, and on producing Mrs. Newport's order, received ten pounds on account, with her brother's letter ; and was desired to call in a fortnight for the remainder. With this sum she satisfied the claims of her landlady, and attended only to the restoration of her health ; and having a good constitution and excellent spirits, without any alloy of what she termed fine feelings, her efforts were speedily crowned with success.

At the expiration of the time she called again in Lincoln's Inn, and while waiting in the office she saw in a morning paper the identical advertisement we have before spoken of, which she asked permission to answer. The young man in the office was too polite to refuse her request ; and having supplied her with materials, she wrote a few lines. And after her business there was concluded, she left the letter at the appointed place

She then hurried to her old friend, the milliner, with whom she had always kept up her acquaintance ; and gave her directions for the character that would, she hoped, be sent for, to the milliner. Egerton replied the character was satisfactory ; and as we have before seen, she was soon after domesticated in the house of Mr. Goosequill ; and to him she devoted the whole of her attention, and he found her an obliging and amusing companion. She conversed with fluency, having acquired a general knowledge of the world. She knew more of what is termed high life than she chose to reveal, and more of low manners than it was prudent to name. She warily steered a middle course, and rarely spoke of any one above or below the rank she wished him to think she herself occupied in society. Her love of the drama she did not try to conceal, and she frequently entertained him with reading new and popular productions ; but it must be confessed that it required all her address to ward off the questions he frequently proposed to her concerning her real connections in life. At last, the fear of being entangled in her own web induced her to tell him something like the truth, but cautiously concealing her real situation with Westcote, whom she always spoke of as her husband.

She said close application to her needle had so much injured her health that she was compelled to abandon it for a less sedentary engagement; and having said thus much, she expressed a wish that the subject might never be renewed.

Mr. Goosequill was satisfied, and never after importuned her on the subject; her brother's letter proved that he had been made acquainted with her undutiful and ungrateful behaviour to their father. This she answered in terms of affected sorrow, and assured him that her conduct had been greatly and cruelly exaggerated and entreated him to believe that her future conduct should be strictly irreproachable : to this she signed the name of Westcote.

It may be inquired how a young woman that had lived—to use a modern term—so gay a life, could all at once conform to sober and domestic habits. To this we are prepared to answer (for the character is not fictious), that she had suffered so severely in her profligate course, that her present situation seemed a happy asylum from debasement and misery; besides, she was ambitious, and the liberality of Mr. Goosequill towards her gave her hopes of receiving at some future time more substantial proofs of his munificence. He had passed the sear and yellow leaf of autumn, and his early and indefatigable attention to business had carried him prematurely towards the broken arches of Mirza's-bridge, while increasing infirmities confined him more closely at home.

Then it was that he more than ever admired the constant ood-humour and vivacity of his companion, whose pleasant sallies often diverted him in the midst of pain, With the approach of winter his languor increased; he gave up all concerns in the profession to Egerton, except such as he could inspect or transact in his own chamber. He usually took his breakfast in bed; this occasioned a more familiar intercourse between Egerton and the lady, who generally made breakfast in the parlour; and though they had always dined together, it was mostly in the presence of Mr. Goosequill, till his late confinement; and seeing him, as she thought, near his end, she had some thoughts of making a conquest of his successor; and to accomplish this, no art was left untried. But all was ineffectual, for Egerton was honourably attached to a woman of virtue; and though a man of the world, he would have scorned any favours a woman so situated as Mrs. Westcote could have conferred. Still, his behaviour towards her was always that of a gentleman, strictly within the rules of good breeding.

"You seem," said he one morning, with an air of gaiety, "to want amusement. Will you, to fill up your vacant time, take under your tuition a young man I wish to see a little polished?"

"Who is he?" was the natural inquiry.

"What do you say to the young man in the kitchen?" The lady frowned. "Nay, do not be angry," said Egerton, laughing; "I assure you he is a very promising subject."

"But a very rough one," she replied.

"Then the more credit will be due to you if you polish the diamond; for I assure you, he is one. But, seriously, you could much improve his situation here, by forwarding a little plan I have long projected for his advancement, and, by so doing, you will infinitely oblige me."

"To that," she answered, "I can have no objection; only inform me what I am to do."

"Only," said he, "now and then say that you have seen him writing late in the office, and that will lead to an inquiry of how he is employed there : leave the rest to me."

The lady bowed her assent, and did as Egerton requested her, who soon took occasion to observe that he wanted another assistant in the office, and was told to engage one; he then said,—

"He thought he could make George very useful: I have taught him already to engross "

Mrs. Westcote then observed, "I have more than once, s'r, told you that I have seen him writing in the office at night."

"So you have," was the answer.

"Well, then, you must get some one in his place, and do the best you can with him, I leave the terms to you ; if he has merit, he shall not go unrewarded."

"He has good abilities," said Egerton, "and is made of sound persevering materials. I think he will make in time an excellent lawyer."

"I hope he will be an honest one," replied Mr. Goosequil; "for there are already too my rogues in the profession."

"If I thought otherwise of him," answered the other, "I would not have recommended him to your notice."

There it rested ; in a very little time George left the kitchen for the office, and was soon of no small importance there. A salary superior to his expectations was allowed him, and he emerged rapidly from his former obscurity; his exterior appearance was not disagreeable ; he was short in stature, but well made ; his countenance was pleasing, without being handsome ; his eyes were rather sunk, small, but lively ; and there was an archness about his mouth that gave the whole face a peculiar expression. He sometimes visited the theatres, and mixed occasionally with young men in his own station, in whose society the rusticity of his early manners by degrees disappeared. His acquaintance, for he was looked upon as a rising young man was courted by many of his brother scribes, who had sisters they wished married, or daughters to dispose of ; but George, or as we must in future call him Newland, was wary and looked only to the main chance. In short, money was his idol, and he determined to get what he could and keep what he got.

Things went on so for several months, and as Mr. Goosequill was, at the time we are speaking of, entirely confined to his room, Newland was admitted to the parlour, to take his meals with Mrs. Westcote and his friend Egerton. After languishing some weeks, totally unable to leave his bed, Mr. Goosequill, finding his end approaching, sent for Egerton to his bed side, and gave him directions for making his will.

"There is the outline," said he, giving a paper, "I have written it with difficulty, see it properly executed, and send for my nephew who is my only heir. "One thing," said he, "I particularly wish." Egerton bent attentively. "Inquire of the housekeeper if Westcote is her real name ; I have nothing to do with anything she may wish to conceal, only these things are not to be trifled with. I mean to make her a handsome remuneration for the time she has devoted to me, and it must be done securely ; I intend to settle on her two hundred a year for her natural life, and one hundred pounds by way of legacy, to be paid soon after my demise."

"Perhaps," said Egerton, "a sum paid at once would be more agreeable."

"It might be so," replied the other, "and then some needy fellow would marry her for the money, and she would be a beggar when it was spent : this I mean to guard against, my nephew will be rich enough, besides the principal will devolve to his children after her decease."

"I did not mean, sir, to interfere with your arrangements, nor presume to limit your generosity. I thought as Mrs. Westcote is only in the summer of life——"

He paused. "I understand you," replied Mr. Goosequill, "you think she might marry better with a fortune than an annuity."

"Exactly so, sir, as it could be secured to her by settlement·"

"Tush !" replied Mr. Goosequill, "you, a limb of the law, and talk such nonsense ; a woman may be coaxed or kicked out of a settlement at any time ; mind, she is not to have the power of disposing of it in any way whatever. Make it secure ; I have seen women in my time do so many foolish things, that I think no man of understanding should give them the power of injuring themselves. I feel fatigued ; go and see it executed as soon as possible ; I wish it completed, for I am convinced I shall not last long."

"Oh ! sir," said Egerton, with feeling, "you may yet live many years."

"No, Egerton," he replied, calmly, "my frame never promised protracted life; none of my family ever exceeded the age I am arrived at, and as death is a debt due to nature, I do not see why an old man should wish to procrastinate the payment of it."

"Few persons meet it with such fortitude," said Egerton.

"A clear conscience," replied Mr. Goosequill, laying his hand on Egerton's, " is the best defence against its terrors. I am not without my faults. Who is ?"

" None, sir," said Egerton.

"But believe me," he continued, "when I tell you that I have been an honest lawyer. I never wronged the orphan, nor defrauded the widow ; to every one I have done justice, as far as lay in my power ; and frequently have allayed, by argument and reason, differences I might have fomented to my own advantage. The law," he added, "is a profession in which a man, if so disposed, may do much good ; but at the same time it must be confessed, he can be a knave with impunity." The entrance of Mrs. Westcote ended the conference, and Egerton retired.

In the course of the day, he made the inquiry Mr. Goosequill had required of him. At first Mrs. Westcote hesitated, and wished to evade the question, but after hearing from what motive the inquiry arose, she owned her real name, and said she had no legal right to any other.

Mr. Goosequill's predictions were well founded. His will was executed to his satisfaction, after which he continued in a dozing kind of stupor for some hours, and at last expired without a groan, resting his head on the arm of Mrs. Westcote, who on this occasion seemed much affected ; but sorrow seldom makes any lasting impressions on a selfish heart, and her tears were soon dried up at the prospects that opened before her. She was still under thirty, handsome, and independent, and she thought with these advantages, she might yet make, as her father used to term it, a figure in life. With Egerton she knew she stood no chance ; but Newland was unconnected, and aspiring ; he had no relations to inquire who she was, or what she had been ; this was a consideration not to be overlooked.

Mr. Goosequill had directed the housekeeping to be continued for six months, in order that his servants might have time to suit themselves with other situations. His nephew was generous ; he extended it to twelve under the directions of Mrs. Westcote, and commissioned Egerton to supply her with the necessary funds and place them to his account.

The situation of the parties introduced a familiarity not disagreeable to either. Mr. Egerton was seldom at home after dinner, and the evenings were devoted to amusement. Newland introduced several of his acquaintances to Mrs. Westcote, with whom she formed frequent parties both at home and abroad, and not having occasion to practice rigid economy, she displayed her taste both in her dress and entertainments. During this time Mr. Egerton was united to the lady we have before alluded to, and intending to reside principally in the country, proposed to Newland his taking a share in the business, as it was necessary for some one interested in so important a concern to be always in London. We should before have observed that Egerton had acquired the whole on the death of Mr. Goosequill.

A proposal so liberal was gladly accepted—his articles were expired, and he was at liberty to act as a regular solicitor. At the expiration of the twelvemonth the lease of the house, with the furniture, was purchased for him by his invaluable friend Egerton, and soon after, Mrs. Westcote was the mistress of the house in Chancery-lane. Fortune continued to smile upon her favourites, and within a very few years Mr. Newland was considered a very safe and able solicitor. Two children—a son and daughter—were the only fruits of this marriage. It is not to be supposed that Mrs. Newland lived so retired as Mrs. Westcote had done— quite the contrary, she had parties at home, and excursions abroad ; her trips to Tunbridge, Brighton, or Margate were annual. Besides these indulgences, she had a pretty villa at Hammersmith, with the gardens sloping to the Thames , and at this place she exercised the versatility of her genius—she gave rural *fetes* and public breakfasts, interspersed with private theatricals and public assemblies ; in the former, she always took a principal part—the *Lady Teazle* of the play and the *Nell* of the farce ; equally at ease either as the high-bred lady of town, or the humble cobbler's wife. She was said to equal the elegant Farren in the one, and the unfortunate Jordan in the other. But how, my readers will naturally inquire, was this profusion of expense supported? We will endeavour to explain it. In the first place, Mr. Egerton had retired with a competent fortune from business, and the whole concern was in the hands of Newland, who was indefatigable in it. He took but little share in the amusements of Mrs. Newland, who, on her part, seldom let pleasure interfere with interest. Among her numerous visitors she had frequent opportunities of selecting profitable clients for her husband—settlements, mortgages, and conveyances passed from his office with a celerity not often known among the professors of law. And thus in a few years, through the misfortunes of some, and misconduct of others, he had claims on the estates or property of half their acquaintance. Mrs. Newland's brother had arrived from India, with a tolerable share of eastern treasures; some part acquired by industry and application, but more, it was said, left him by a friend that had died in India. On his return, the ship foundered in sight of land, and it was supposed every one on board had perished; fortunately, he had not much property on board; for, having heard long before of the favourable turn in his sister's fortune, he trusted her husband with considerable remittances, which he had employed to great advantage. On his arrival in Chancery-lane, very weak and much emaciated, he had with him a little girl, about four years of age, that he had saved from the wreck; the child, he said, was much attached to him during the voyage (she was coming to England with her aunt), and clung to him for safety in the terrors of the storm. The spirits of this little interesting creature had received so severe a shock, that it was some weeks before she recollected Mr. Newport; and when she did, her frequent inquiries after her aunt both distressed and agitated him. He himself continued very weak, and, for change of air, and change of scene, Mrs. Newland accompanied him to the villa, where she gave up much of her time to attend on him; and after some months he was partially restored to health. The little girl, too, recovered her spirits, and played about him; but as the sight of her gave him inquietude, from bringing the wreck to his recollection, Mrs. Newland proposed placing her at a school in the vicinity; this he consented to; and there she continued till, as they conjectured, she was fourteen years old. Her holidays were spent at Mr. Newland's, where she was left to the care of the housekeeper, and being considered a dependent in the family, was taken little notice of by any part of it. Mr. Newport resided with them; they managed his fortune, and governed him at their pleasure. A nervous affliction had followed his illness, which it was by some thought had injured his intellects. He seldom saw Caroline, but frequently inquired after her, and desired no expense might be spared for her education or appearance; this Mrs. Newland thought extremely ridiculous; she heard his orders without contradiction, but complied with them as suited her own inclination. At the time we are speaking of, Mr. George Newland was twenty, and his sister eighteen; the last twelvemonth that Miss Newland passed at Mrs. Bellamy's she had Caroline for an attendant; for, having observed to her mother that some of the ladies had abigails allowed them who were paid for as half-boarders, Mrs. Newland determined that Caroline should attend her in that capacity. And there it was, that she attracted the attentions of Lady Emma, whose sweetness of temper, and unaffected goodness of heart, induced her to pity her neglected and, as it respected the haughty Miss Newland, uncomfortable situation.

George Newland had too much spirit to drudge in an office; he despised the droning profession of the law, and preferred the army; a commission was in consequence purchased for him in a troop of horse, that was usually in service at home, he soon became a person of importance in the vicinity of St. James's, drank free, played deep, and drove four-in-hand; to these accomplishments, were added a passable person, and a purse liberally supplied. Our readers will not wonder that under such favourable circumstances, his acquaintance was courted by many who would at a former period have looked down with contempt on his plebeian origin, well versed in the Chesterfield school. He could smile on those he detested, and flatter those he despised. Miss Newland, too, had, as the term is, been brought out. She was reckoned handsome, with a good figure, which she well knew how to display, and a fortune in expectation that she anticipated the enjoyment of, when it should, as was intended, procure her a title; for which her mother was anxiously looking out. It may be supposed that so fashionable a *belle*, had many admirers, especially when the fortune she was expected to have, was taken into consideration; but as her father was too wary to throw away his money on a mere title, she was disengaged at the period we have been writing of; but it was rumoured that she was privately engaged to a gay colonel, who was an intimate of her brother's.

CHAPTER IV.

The man of wealth and pride
Takes up a space that many poor supplied—
Space for his lake, his parks intended bounds;
Space for his horses, equipage, and hounds.
The robe that wraps his limbs in silken cloth
Has rob'd the neighbouring fields of half their growth.
His seat—where solitary sports are seen—
Indignant spurns the cottage from the green.
Around the world each needful product flies,
For all the luxuries the world supplies;
While thus the land adorn'd for pleasure all,
In barren splendour feebly waits the fall.—GOLDSMITH.

WE have before observed that the late Earl of Millford had purchased an estate contiguous to his own; it was of considerable extent, and consisted of several farms, the leases of which were nearly expired.

An old-fashioned mansion, in a state of decay, for it had been long uninhabited, stood in the centre of a well-wooded though not extensive park.

When on a visit of business to the earl, Mr. Newland expressed a wish of having a residence in that part of the country; as Mrs. Newland intended to spend her summers further from London, on which the earl observed that he might have the house in the park, if it was such as Mrs. Newland would choose to occupy.

Mr. Newland embraced the proposal. Workmen were instantly employed, and, urged forward by extra pay, it was soon rendered commodious and convenient; and the family took possession of it the summer preceding the earl's decease.

The rich scenery that surrounded the house rendered it so romantic that Mrs. Newland, her daughter, and friends expressed themselves delighted with it. And Mr. Newland, to oblige them, promised that if he could obtain a lease of the estate, he would build a new house on a more elevated site. This was in agitation at the earl's death, and probably would have been accomplished if that event had not intervened.

Mr. Newland knew that the earl had by deed annexed it to the title; yet thought, and indeed knew, that it would be possible to hold it on that tenure in perpetuity to his family.

Till this was effected, Mrs. Newland contented herself with the old mansion, which, during the time she spent there, was generally full of company, to the great annoyance of Mr. Newport, whose melancholy seemed to increase more and more, as the wealth and consequence of his family advanced.

At length he determined on removing from scenes that afforded him no pleasure, and seek for that repose in retirement that he could not obtain in either of the residences of the opulent Mr. Newland, whose lady did not oppose the removal of her brother, for his eccentricities were become troublesome, and his admonitions, particularly to the young people, disagreeable.

Accordingly he was soon fixed with a genteel family in a neighbouring village, where he enjoyed himself in his own way. He gathered herbs; prepared medicines; spread plaisters; and became gratuitously the apothecary of the village, or such part of it as chose to apply for his assistance.

We should have observed that before he left Mr. Newland's, he stipulated that he should, for the present, content himself with four hundred per annum, out of which they were to deduct the expenses incurred for Miss Melbourne, whom he always spoke of with affection, though he had not seen her for years.

It was during this period that Lady Acrimony had become acquainted with Mrs. Newland—they had occasionally met at the priory, but never were on terms of intimacy. There was a certain something in Mrs. Newland's manner that did not please Lady Acrimony, while the haughty and supercilious Augusta was still less agreeable to her.

While these events were passing, Mr. Newland was advancing rapidly in his fortunate career. A seat in Parliament, to which he was nominated through the interest of a peer, who could not refuse any favour he thought proper to ask, gratified at once his interest and his vanity, for he did not, like Sir Francis Wronghead, say ay, when he should say no.

The house in Chancery-lane was occupied by the clerks belonging to the office, and Mr. Newland's town-house was in Grosvenor-square; about the same time a banking-house was opened in the city under the firm of Newland, Golding, Newport, and company: this was the situation of the parties at the decease of the late earl.

Before the young earl left England, he had promised Mr. Newland that the lease he required should be executed on his return, stipulating at the same time that no alteration should take place with respect to those who had small farms upon it; in consequence the new building was commenced and carried on with such rapidity that in two years it was quite completed and fit for the reception of the family; the old mansion was pulled down and the new one became the admiration of the surrounding country. All that art or ingenuity could devise was called in to aid the advantages of situation, and the house at Newland Manor was pronounced by the amateurs in architectural beauties one of the most elegant buildings of modern date. Green-houses stocked with the choicest exotics, orangeries diffusing fragrance, plantations tastefully designed, vistas cut through luxuriant woods, and water brought at great expense from the river, that watered the grounds at the priory, formed a part of the beauties of this delightful residence.

After the usual time devoted to a continental tour was expired, our travellers returned home with hearts unsophisticated by foreign manners, in perfect health and high spirits. Their first visit was to the grove, where they found Lady Emma happy with her sensible and affectionate friend, in all the bloom of youth and beauty. The meeting between them was a mixture of tenderness and affection that may be easily imagined by every reader of sensibility.

Lord Millford had acquired a little dash of Parisian manners, but Montague retained all the equability of his character. Caroline still continued at Mrs. Bellamy's, and though twice invited, had not been permitted to accept the offer of spending a short time at the grove. Lady Acrimony, disgusted with the *hauteur* of Mrs. and Miss Newland, forbore making any further application on the subject. Lord Millford spent the following season in London, where he formed an intimacy with Captain Newland, and in consequence was a frequent visitor in Grosvenor-square, where he was always received with particular marks of attention by the whole family; their pursuits were in unison with his own, and he dashed with them into all the fashionable follies of the day.

At the request of Miss Newland, Lord Millford had promised to give a *fete* at the priory, on the return of the Newland's to the manor.

His aunt, Mrs. Pembroke, who was one of Mrs. Newland's intimate acquaint-ances, was delighted at the thoughts of such a delectable entertainment, and offered her assistance in the necessary preparations. This was accepted, and in conse-quence, she accompanied that family to the mansion, who late in July prepared to spend the summer in the country. On their arrival there, she paid an early visit to the grove, where Lady Acrimony received her with the politeness natural to her,

Lady Emma with tenderness, and Sir Timothy with reserve, for with him she was no favourite.

In the course of conversation, Lady Emma inquired if Miss Newland ever mentioned Caroline.

"I have heard the girl spoken of as a *protegee* of old Newport's, and was thinking, as we shall want some hands in fancy-work, that she might be made useful at the priory," said Mrs. Pembroke.

No. 4.

"Good Heavens, madam!" cried Lady Emma, "you would not so degrade her."

"Nonsense, child," replied Sir Timothy, fidgeting in his chair; "how can any one be degraded by being made useful? It is more than some people are all their lives."

"You wish her to come, I presume?" said Mrs. Pembroke, letting the baronet's observation pass without notice.

"Certainly," she answered, "but not as an assistant."

"Well," replied the lady, in answer to her niece, "I will see what I can do for you; but I think Miss Newland will object to her coming as a visitor. I suppose," she continued, turning to Lady Acrimony, "your ladyship visits at the manor?"

"Sometimes," was the answer; "but only since Lady Emma has resided with me. My health will not admit of trifling; late hours and crowded rooms would soon destroy me, and Mrs. Newland's house is always full of company; besides," she added, "Sir Timothy would not like me to live as they live."

"I certainly," said he, bluntly, "should not like to see you make such a fool of yourself as some old women do."

"Why, my good knight," replied Mrs. Pembroke, "you seem to forget that the term, old woman, is quite obsolete in the gay world; there is no such thing to be met with; it is erased from all modern dictionaries."

"But they cannot erase it from the book of nature," retorted the baronet.

"Well," replied the lady, "as the season of youth is allowed to be the season of pleasure, you cannot surely condemn the women for procrastinating it to the latest possible period."

"Roses will not bloom in December," he replied.

"Oh, I beg your pardon there," cried the lady; "they are produced early and preserved late."

"Yes," said he, sarcastically, "by the effects of art, but nature has nothing to do with it."

"I must return," said Mrs. Pembroke, looking at her watch; "we are going to have a concert in the evening, and a rehearsal before dinner. But what of this *protegee* of Newport's, is she handsome?"

"Very," replied Lady Acrimony.

"And so, let me add, amiable and accomplished," said Lady Emma.

"Ay, that is the very reason why she is in the background of the picture," returned Mrs. Pembroke; "if suffered to come forward she might rival the daughter or captivate the son. Upon my word, the airs of this Fungus family is very diverting."

"Do you not like them?" inquired Sir Timothy.

"Not exactly," she answered.

"Why, then, do you associate with them?" said the baronet.

"Oh, everybody visits them," she answered. "I declare that twice last season while Mrs. Newland's rooms were crowded to suffocation, my concerts, falling unfortunately on the same night, were quite deserted. I never will forgive her, for I am sure it was done on purpose to distress me."

"Perhaps," said Sir Timothy, "Mrs. Newland's entertainments were more substantial than yours, for there are persons so downright material as to prefer the wines of Burgundy to the nectar of Helicon."

"Oh, all is profusion, I assure you, there," replied Mrs. Pembroke. "Besides, Mrs. Newland plays scientifically on an exquisite piano; and miss displays all the graces of attitude as she bends over her harp; and on the last evening it was understood that some novelty was to be exhibited after twelve: this thinned my rooms most unmercifully, for no one could imagine what it was to be. Some thought the vaulting lady was to exhibit her wonderful feats, but then there was no place fit for the exhibition; others that the royal progeny from Exeter-change would form the *dramatis personæ*, or Mathews' imitations, or the Indian conjuror."

"And what, after all, was it?" inquired Sir Timothy.

"Why, the lady of the mansion dressed as the Tragic Muse, who, in true Siddonian tones, recited to an applauding audience, Collins's Ode on the Passions."

"It is no wonder, then," said Sir Timothy, "that against so brilliant a competition, your musicians played to empty chairs."

"Oh, it was done on purpose," cried Mrs. Pembroke, colouring with vexation at the recollection; "but if I live till next season, I will have my revenge."

"Bravely resolved," cried her nephew, who just then entered the room with his friend Montague. They had been out for a ride, and understanding that Mrs. Pembroke was at the grove, he called to escort her back to the manor.

"What, you still continue to brave Miss Newland's penetrating glances?" said Montague, addressing Lord Millford.

"True," replied Mrs. Pembroke, "she levels them at him without mercy."

"At him or his coronet?" asked Sir Timothy.

"At both, most likely," said Montague.

"She dances delightfully," cried Millford.

"Ay," replied Lady Acrimony; "but you have, I trust, my lord, too much good sense not to perceive that the partner for a ball and the partner for life require very different qualifications."

"Millford," said Mrs. Pembroke, colouring above her rouge, "must not contaminate the fluid of his progenitors with such plebeian alloy."

Lord Millford laughed. Mrs. Pembroke was offended with him, and rather abruptly departed.

The next day had been appointed for a meeting at the priory, and at the particular request of her young friend, Lady Acrimony agreed to go thither with her. They set out, accompanied by Montague on horseback, and on the road met Mr. Newport, driving his one-horse chaise. To Montague he was well known, who accosted him without ceremony. The chaise stopped, and they were some time in conversation. He had bowed to Lady Acrimony as her carriage passed.

"Oh, that I could but have spoke to him," said Lady Emma, on hearing from her friend who it was; perhaps he would have obliged me with Caroline's company, if only for one short month."

"Do not wish it, my dear Emma," said her ladyship, "for perhaps Mrs. Newland may have motives for her seclusion that we are unacquainted with. You know my invitations have been twice declined, and Sir Timothy would be offended if I repeated them. At the manor, what pleasure could this interesting young woman experience? Pained she must be by the pride of Mrs. Newland, and mortified by the envy and contempt of her daughter, to say nothing of the neglect she would experience from the company when it was known she was only a dependent in the family, or the insulting advances that might be made to her by Captain Newland's gay associates. Trust me, she is better where she is."

Lady Emma's judgment was convinced, and the subject dropped. On arriving at the priory, they found the party all assembled; and as that antique building was a novelty to many of them, they separated to promenade over it. Lady Acrimony and her young friend sought the picture gallery, a place Lady Emma never failed to visit, on her occasional calls at the priory. In the gallery were two full-length portraits of her parents, by the masterly and chaste hand of the admired and lamented Opie.

"Oh," said Lady Emma, "so mild, so benignant, did my dear father look when last I saw him. Of the countess, my mother, I have not so perfect a recollection."

"It is a very good likeness," said Mrs. Pembroke, advancing, "only I do not like the drapery—it is so stiff and formal."

"I never think of the drapery when I look at the face," replied her niece.

"Dear me," cried Mrs. Pembroke, "if here is not Mr. Newport, Mrs. Newland's brother. How I should like to mortify him, by asking him to let your favourite make one amongst us at the fete. She has quite offended me this morning."

"In what manner?" inquired Lady Emma.

"Oh, by objecting to the primrose draperies that I had ordered for the drawing-room, to relieve the heavy velvet hangings."

"A most important subject, indeed, to differ on," replied the niece; "but that was not all; she said velvet coverings suited old walls and old women."

"Oh, she could not mean you, my dear madam," replied Lady Emma; "the company we speak in is always excepted."

As she was speaking, Lady Acrimony called her attention towards a painting, ying,—

"I never before saw that painting to so much advantage. As the light now falls on it, it shows every shade. I am chilled with looking at it."

"Which?" was the inquiry of Mrs. Pembroke.

"The shipwreck," answered her ladyship; "I could almost fancy I see the billows roll, and hear the tempest roar." A deep groan caused her to turn round, and behind her stood Mr. Newport, the very image of despair—his complexion was livid, his lips trembled, and his eyes, though fixed on the painting, seemed to glare with the quick motion of insanity, rather than to notice the object they were so intensely placed on.

Montague perceiving his agitation, offered his arm, and they quitted the gallery together.

"This is vastly odd," cried Mrs. Pembroke; "I'll go and see what is the matter with the poor man."

"Not for the world," said Lady Acrimony. "It was my inadvertently pointing to the painting that disturbed him. I have before heard how much he is affected by the subject."

"It is so many years ago," answered Mrs. Pembroke, "that I wonder he has not forgot it. I am sure his sister would not have remembered it half so long."

At this moment Montague returned to say Sir Timothy was come.

As this was quite unexpected, it required some explanation, which Montague gave in a few words.

"When I met Mr. Newport," said he, "he was going to the grove on business with Sir Timothy. The fact was, that the former had been for some time out on a rambling excursion, which was not uncommon with him, and on his return home, found his landlord involved in a perplexing dispute with the rector concerning his tithes; and having a dislike to litigation, particularly in cases where the plaintiff is so seldom remunerated for the trouble he sustains, he offered his services to procure an adjustment of their differences; and knowing Sir Timothy was well with both parties, he hoped to prevail on him to be the arbitrator between them. The baronet, on being consulted, proposed referring it to Meanwell, whom he knew to be on terms of intimacy with the rector. Newport then prevailed on him to go with him to the priory: this the other did not object to. As the carriage was there with the ladies, it rendered his return home convenient and agreeable. When the different parties met to partake of a cold collation, Mr. Newport was among them: Mrs. Pembroke, who had not forgotten the fancied insult of the morning, told him her niece had a favour to ask of him. He appeared surprised, Lady Emma embarrassed, and Mrs. Newland offended, for she anticipated what it was. When addressing Mrs. Pembroke, she said,—

"I would have wished, madam, after witnessing Mr. Newport's recent indisposition, that you would not have renewed his agitation by adverting to the subject of it."

"To what do you allude, ladies?" said Mr. Newport.

"I do not wish to distress you, sir," replied Mrs. Pembroke, "and, as you appear rather nervous to-day, I think we may as well drop the conversation."

"I think not," cried Sir Timothy; "and as I despise needless mystery, when a few plain words will do, I therefore request the young lady to speak for herself."

Lady Emma hesitated, as she called to mind the conversation of the morning, and the recent distress of Mr. Newport; when Mrs. Pembroke, encouraged by the manner in which Sir Timothy spoke, and enjoying the mortification Mrs. Newland could not conceal, explained the favour it was in his power to confer on her niece.

"We understand," she added, "that the young lady is a *protegee* of yours, and therefore conclude that your consent will ensure Mrs. Newland's approbation."

"I have no objection," he answered; "and, indeed, have often wondered that Mrs. Newland has so long secluded her from the world."

"I have had," she answered, "particular reasons for it, and have before explained them to Lady Acrimony, and I must still oppose her introduction into the gay world. Besides, I have another motive for not sending for her at the present time: the Duchess of Montcreiff has requested me to select her a well-educated young woman as a companion; I have named Caroline, and, in short, the whole affair is agreed on, and I think she will require her immediate attendance. It is a desirable and will be an eligible situation for her."

"Much," said Lady Acrimony, "will depend on what kind of person the duchess is."

"Oh, she is," cried Miss Newland, who had not spoken before, "very poor, at least for a duchess, and very proud—in short, a walking vocabulary of history and heraldry; she is, too, well skilled in the legendary lore of the north, and, I believe, has it in contemplation to present the world with some choice scraps of Scottish history. I have heard her say that she has in her possession traditional poems as ancient as those of Ossian; and most likely it will be part of Caroline's employment to transcribe them for public inspection. It will be charming amusement for a Highland writer."

"Is Caroline then going to the Highlands?" asked Lady Emma.

"We expect so," Mrs. Newland replied; "the duchess purposes returning to her castle in the autumn."

"From whence I hope she will never more emerge," cried Miss Newland, "for she is much too learned for us humble southerns. She was disputing the other day with a celebrated linguist on the antiquity of languages, and insisted that the Erse was equal to the Greek in harmony, and superior to the Latin in energy."

"Very astonishing indeed," said Mrs. Pembroke, "for a woman of her rank to trouble her head about languages."

"It is," said Sir Timothy, "strange in these days for ladies to trouble their heads about anything but the decoration of their persons, the wasting their time, and dissipating their fortunes. The lady in question seems to have laid up a store of intellectual treasures on which she can draw for amusement in the winter of life; it will then throw the sunbeams of cheerfulness round her antique hearth, when many who are glittering beneath wax-lights and resplendent chandeliers may feel the want of tranquillity."

No one answered, when Miss Newland broke silence by addressing Lady Emma.

"You know," she said, "how romantically fond Caroline affects to be of the country, and in the Highlands she may admire the beautiful, and study the sublime."

The conversation then turned on the projected *fete.*

Sir Timothy objected to it on account of the expenses that would be incurred.

Mrs. Pembroke defended it as indispensably necessary. It was keeping up the consequence of the privileged orders, and the means of attaching the peasantry to their lord.

"We have happily," said Sir Timothy, "outlived the days of feudal tyranny; the lords of the soil can no longer summon their vassals to storm castles, or desolate tracts that they would have been much better employed in cultivating; the aristocracy are now considered only as a portion of society to which power has been delegated, and to obtain respect they must endeavour to deserve it."

Mrs. Pembroke was silenced. The younger part of the company had retired to the music-room, when

Lady Acrimony observed that she thought the expense excusable, as it enabled the wealthy to employ the poor.

"Oh, I have nothing to do with it," replied Sir Timothy; "only I conceive it is not exactly the way in which my deceased friend would have spent his money."

"Perhaps not," said Mrs. Pembroke, "for he was *outré* in his notions, but I presume Lord Millford can afford the expenditure of a few hundreds."

"Thousands," replied Sir Timothy, "if he pleases; it will not be my money, but his own, that is squandered."

A servant just then entered with a letter for Mrs. Newland. She retired to read it, and on returning to the company, said,—

"It is from the duchess; she has the gout in her right hand, and wants Caroline immediately as her amanuensis; the letter is written by a friend; her grace also intimates that she is weary of London, and shall accept of my invitation to the manor."

"Horrible! most horrible!" cried Miss Newland, who had just entered the room, leaning on the arm of Lord Millford. "We shall absolutely be bored to death with verse and history."

"She will at least be an original," cried Sir Timothy; "something to wonder at in these days of insipidity."

"La! Sir Timothy," replied Miss Newland, "do you approve of women studying history?"

"What study is more necessary?" replied the baronet. "It is a whole sheet map of human nature, from which every thinking being may glean both instruction and amusement."

"It is very tiresome," cried Mrs. Pembroke, "for it requires both attention and memory; I never liked it in my life."

"If life was to be estimated by improvement instead of time," said Sir Timothy, "we should have a great many grey-headed babies among our present ladies of fashion; but the carriage is waiting, we must take leave."

Montague took the hand of Lady Emma, and Lord Millford conducted Lady Acrimony to the carriage, while Mrs. Pembroke, who on Lady Emma's account had been invited to spend a few days at the grove, and was to return with them, followed down stairs alone.

"What Vandals!" she exclaimed to Miss Newland, as she passed her in the hall; "how glad I shall be when the humdrum visit is over."

Lord Millford on returning took her hand, and placed her in the carriage.

Before Sir Timothy joined the company, he had put the business which had brought him and Mr. Newport to the priory, into the hands of Meanwell, who had willingly consented to become an arbitrator between the parties; and Mrs. Newland and her party returned to the manor, the ladies not a little discomposed at the unexpected turn things had taken with respect to Caroline; but as it would now be altered, she wrote to Mrs. Bellamy, desiring her to see Caroline properly provided with suitable necessaries, and place it to her account, but strictly prohibiting everything superfluous, particularly ornaments; this was an unnecessary precaution, for Caroline neither wanted nor wished for them.

Miss Newland insisted that Caroline should not be admitted as a visitor, but treated as a kind of upper servant.

To this Mrs. Newland replied that, as the companion of the duchess, it would be impossible to treat her otherwise than a visitor, though it might be possible to throw her to a very great distance, which would perhaps induce her to spend much of her time alone. This plan of behaviour was finally resolved on; in the meantime, the duchess caused the necessary inquiries to be made of Mrs. Bellamy respecting Caroline's temper, manners, and qualifications; and having received an answer perfectly satisfactory, she a few days afterwards sent the carriage to fetch her to Portland-place.

In the meantime, Mrs. Pembroke had completed the time she intended spending at the grove, and set out for the manor in Sir Timothy's carriage, and as the evening was remarkably fine, Lady Acrimony and her young friend accompanied her thither. The ladies did not intend to alight, but the pressing invitation of Mrs. Newland could not well be refused.

Scarcely were they seated in the drawing-room before the duchess's carriage drove up to the door, when the delighted Lady Emma sprang forward to receive her friend, and Mrs. Newland had thrice announced her noble visitor, before she had sufficiently recovered her self-possession to return the necessary compliments that etiquette demanded on the occasion ; her grace seated herself on the sofa with Lady Acrimony.

"Aye, this," she cried, " is pure nature and as such I honour it," presenting her hand at the same time to Lady Emma.

" I have heard much of you, my dear young lady, from this interesting creature, and do not wonder at your attachment to each other."

Lady Acrimony was charmed with the air of real dignity that adorned the duchess, while Mrs. Pembroke, who soon after entered with Miss Newland, and was introduced in form to her grace, was surprised at the ease and elegance of Caroline's manner.

After a short time Lady Acrimony rose to depart ; but not before Lady Emma had requested the duchess to indulge her with Caroline's company the next day at the grove, which was acceded to with a smile of good humour. Lady Acrimony politely included Miss Newland in the invitation, who replied that she did not wish to interrupt the soft intercourse of soul that must be expected to flow between such friends after so long a separation. Mrs. Newland observed that herself and friends were going the next day to dine with General Westlake, and that the carriages would all be wanted.

" Except mine !" cried the duchess, " and that can convey Miss Melbourne to Sir Timothy's."

This was agreed on, and the ladies departed.

" That is really an uncommonly fine girl," said Mrs. Pembroke, as they quitted the room. " And there is none of that *mauvais honte* about her that I expected to have seen."

" On the contrary," replied the duchess, " her lady-like appearance prepossessed me in her favour, the first moment I saw her."

" Her features are very pensive," returned Mrs. Pembroke, who, looking at Mrs. Newland, and perceiving she was vexed at the subject, was therefore determined to pursue it.

" But very beautiful !" replied the duchess.

" It is a pity she is so totally unconnected," continued the mischievous Mrs. Pembroke, who had not forgotten the velvet hangings and primrose drapery.

" Did you never, madam," said the duchess, addressing Mrs. Newland, " make any inquiries after her family ?"

" Every possible inquiry that could be made," replied that lady ; " but without success. Not a creature was supposed to have escaped the wreck, except Mr. Newport and the child. There were many passengers, I have heard him say, on board, and a lady among them, that she called her aunt ; and right or wrong, it is by that lady's name we called her."

" Then, by that name I would have advertised her," said Mrs. Pembroke.

" My dear friend," replied Mrs. Newland, " you must recollect that I told you what were my surmises, and the subject so unnerved my poor brother, that I dreaded to distress his feelings by pursuing it."

" But justice should not be sacrificed to feelings," said the duchess, with energy.

" But there is another motive which has prevented me from pressing it so forcibly as I otherwise should," returned Mrs. Newland ; " it is a point so delicate that I do not like to touch on it."

" I wonder, madam," cried Miss Newland, addressing her mother, " that you should make a mystery of your opinion, particularly among friends."

" Oh," said Mrs. Pembroke, " I know now what you allude to—you think she is the natural child of your brother ; it is very likely ; but she bears no resemblance either to him or you. And why should he conceal such a thing from you ?"

"There is no accounting for his eccentricities," replied Mrs. Newland; "and I am weary of attempting to solve the problem."

"Well, then," said Mrs. Pembroke, "we will designate her a Venus sprung from the sea."

"One of the Graces, I think, would be a more apt similitude, for she has exactly the fine outline of countenance and elegance of form that both poets and statuaries give to those imaginative beings," said the duchess; "and she is a most lovely and instructing creature, be her origin what it may."

"I am weary of this provoking conversation," whispered Miss Newland to Mrs. Pembroke; so was his mother, who never, if it could be avoided, would have entered into it; and frequently did she regret that it had ever been known by what means Caroline was placed under her protection; but as it had gone forth to the world, it could not be contradicted.

In the morning, Caroline set out in the duchess's carriage for the grove, where she was received with an affected pleasure by the ladies, and with more feeling than he usually evinced by Sir Timothy. At dinner they were joined by Lord Millford, who informed them he had pleaded business at the priory in order to disengage himself from the party that was formed for the general; for he was, in fact, wearied out with the continual repetition of draperies, fringes, and decorations. He was an agreeable addition to their party, for his lively sallies and constant good humour diverted even Sir Timothy, who laughed heartily at the description Lord Millford gave of the motley group at the manor, which it was expected would soon be augmented with other arrivals. The day appeared short to the young people, who were all in perfect harmony with themselves and each other; in the evening, the carriage came for Caroline, who was accompanied back by Lord Millford, on horseback. After their departure, Sir Timothy, addressing Lady Emma, said,—

"I am very much pleased with your friend—it is rarely we see young women at once handsome and unaffected!"

"There is something about her that steals strangely on the affections," said Lady Acrimony.

"She has all the ease of a French woman," said Montague, "with the modesty of an English one." He said nothing of her beauty, for in his opinion she was not near so lovely as Lady Emma; it was fortunate for Caroline that they reached the manor before the family returned from the general's; for she feared Mrs. Newland would feel offended at Lord Millford having paid her the compliment of attending her home. After handing her from the carriage, he remounted his horse and rode to the general's, where the party, with the exception of the duchess, whose carriage had been ordered at eleven, continued till the morning broke in upon their revels. The following days were wholly employed in arranging preparations for the fete, which was fixed for Tuesday in the ensuing week and deciding on the important article of dress.

All that fancy could devise was called in to aid the appearance of Miss Newland, Mrs. Pembroke, and the lady of the mansion; on the evening of their arrival, the whole paraphernalia was opened for the admiration of the ladies.

"And what, lassie, is to be your dress," said the duchess, turning to Caroline, who looked confused and remained silent.

"Oh! I had forgotten," said Mrs. Newland, "that Caroline had no ball dress. Well, child, as the time is so short, we must make up the dresses as well as we can. Miss Newland, I think, can accommodate you with one: a muslin robe and straw hat will be quite sufficient for the morning promenade, as we are to breakfast in the gardens. The duchess looked displeased, and Mrs. Newland quitted the room, and was soon followed by her particular friends. When the duchess was alone with Caroline, she observed that if she had thought it possible for Mrs. Newland so to have neglected her, that she would have sent to London for a ball dress for her.

Tears trembled in the eyes of Caroline, but she did not, could not reply; and it cannot be concealed that she felt severely the neglect it implied; and spite of the condescension of the duchess, who honoured her with particular attention, and the unabated friendship of Lady Emma, there were moments in which she wished herself again under the roof of Mrs. Bellamy."

Mrs. Newland and her daughter soon returned, when the former, addressing Caroline, said,—"In Miss Newland's dressing-room, you will find the dress I was speaking of; alter it to your own fancy, and consider it your own."

Caroline curtsied, and thinking it an order to retire, left the room.

"There," cried Miss Newland, "such are the airs of indifference with which that girl receives every favour conferred on her." "There is," said the duchess "as much difference in the manner of conferring as in receiving a favour."

Mrs. Pembroke, who had met Caroline on the stairs, and having heard of Miss Newland's present, had the curiosity to inspect it. Taking it from the sofa, and holding it up, she cried,—

"La! child, you cannot wear this tawdry thing; it is dirty and torn.'

No. 5.

"Well," cried Miss Newland, who just then entered, "I suppose it can be cleaned and mended."

"Impossible," said Mrs. Pembroke, in reply, "why, it is only fit for the wardrobe of a strolling actress."

"If that is not worth wearing," cried Miss Newland, in a pet, "the young lady must suit herself elsewhere, for I have no other that I choose to part with."

Caroline took it from Mrs. Pembroke, and replaced it on the sofa, secretly resolving to invent some excuse for not joining the festive party; and to Miss Newland nothing could have been more agreeable. It is said that an insult is more forcibly felt than an injury, and at that moment poor Caroline thought so. She quitted the dressing-room, and left the present behind her.

"Pretty insolent behaviour indeed," cried Miss Newland; "the next present I offer her shall be more gratefully received."

Caroline retired to the apartments of the duchess, and vented her vexation in a flood of tears. That good-humoured lady surprised her before she had recovered her serenity, and kindly inquired the cause of her distress. On hearing it, she said, "There is a strange mixture of pride and meanness about these people that I cannot reconcile; but you must not give up the *fete*."

"I cannot wear that dress," said Caroline, "I should be an object of ridicule to the whole company."

"You shall not wear it, lassie. If you can make one for yourself, I think I have materials with me that will answer the purpose very well."

"But Mrs. Newland will be offended if I wear any other, madam."

"I will take that upon myself," replied the duchess, "so ring the bell for my woman."

On her entrance she received directions what to fetch, and soon returned with an elegant plaid sarsenet.

"It will look heavy," said her grace, "for this season of the year, but you must contrive to relieve it with silver crape, and trimmings. Morton," she continued, "I think there is both among my things, that I purchased for Lady Randolph. Did it go in the last package?"

Morton replied in the negative, but added, "not thinking it would be wanted, she had left it in London," and then inquired if she was to make that dress up for her grace.

"No," replied her ladyship, "but I shall want you to assist in making it up for Miss Mellbourne, if these good people here will give you time, for they seem to employ every one."

As she was speaking, a rather large parcel was brought in by a servant, directed to Miss Mellbourne, which on opening was found to contain the very thing in question, an elegant ball dress, with white satin slippers, gloves, and a necklace of pearl.

The present was from Lady Emma, who, thinking her friend would be neglected, though she had not named it to her, had, with the approbation of Lady Acrimony, ordered it with her own. They had both come from London, that morning, and her ladyship sent it as an agreeable surprise. It was accompanied with a most affectionate note.

"How kind, how considerate," she exclaimed, "how shall I ever reward this dear, generous friend. Oh! I would rather wear this than one trimmed with diamonds from the hands of——"

"Hush!" said the duchess. "Morton, you may retire. My dear lassie," she then said, "your gratitude might have been misconstrued. You have here, I plainly perceive, a delicate part to play; I would not wish you to offend Mrs. Newland, that would have the appearance of ingratitude, yet I am pleased that you had the spirit to refuse the tawdry present offered by her daughter. Make up the tartan, I will send for the trimmings; and say it is my whim that you should wear plaid. Lady Emma will excuse it when she hears your motives, and no one will presume to interfere with any present I choose to make you. Lady Emma' will be useful another time, for in all probability, there will be more public doings. The Newlands will not be outdone by Lord Millford."

Caroline thanked the generous duchess in grateful language, both for her present and advice, and on the following morning Morton was sent to London, and returned laden with such things as were thought necessary for the occasion. The duchess did not attend the breakfast-table the next morning, being rather indisposed; in consequence Caroline continued with her during that repast. Mrs. Pembroke took occasion to say it was a great pity the poor girl should be deprived of being present at the ball. Mrs. Newland replied that she would breakfast at the priory, and if she was too proud to be obliged, she must submit to the mortification she had brought upon herself.

"Oh, her pride has for once," said Miss Newland, "prevented her being ridiculous, for I do not think she can dance well enough to figure in a public assembly," secretly rejoiced that there was no chance of her appearing there. But she was soon deprived of that pleasing hope, for on retiring to dress for dinner, she was informed by her officious attendant that the duchess's woman was gone to London for trimmings and feathers, and many other things for the *fete*; the trimmings might be for her grace, but the feathers could only be for Caroline. The mortified Miss Newland could scarcely breathe; at last she exclaimed, "Nelson, you may take that yellow dress, and be sure make it very smart, and wear it when you attend me to the priory. I will tell all my acquaintance of her ingratitude, and convince Mrs. Pembroke that it was fit for something better than being in the wardrobe of a travelling actress. I wish to my heart, Caroline, she, and the duchess were in the Highlands together."

"So do I, miss," replied the obsequious abigail; "they give a great deal [of trouble here."

CHAPTER V.

A few short years, and then these sounds shall hail
The day again, and gladness fill the vale;
So soon, the child a youth, the youth a man,
Eager to run the race his fathers ran;
Then the huge ox shall yield the broad sirloin,
The ale now brewed in floods of amber shine,
And basking in the chimney's ample blaze,
'Mid many a tale told of his boyish days,
The nurse shall cry, of all her cares beguiled,
" 'Twas on these knees he sat so oft and smil'd."—ROGERS.

AT length the expected morning arrived, and it seemed as if nature was in unison with the wishes of the company. The manor was crowded with visitors some days before, all eager to enjoy the expected scene. Among them was Lady Lucy O'Leary, a friend of Mrs. Pembroke's, and the widow of an Irish baronet, Colonel Dinever, Captain Newland, Miss Dinever, and many others of *haut ton*. Their presence, by occupying the attention of the ladies, had spared Caroline many little mortifications, and gave her time to complete her work. Lady Emma had twice paid a morning visit, and was delighted to find her friend in such high estimation with the duchess, and entirely coincided in her grace's opinion respecting the dresses. We shall not enter into a minute description of this splendid entertainment, being sensible that anything we could say would convey but a faint idea of its superlative elegance. The lawn and avenues were filled with tents, in which musicians were placed, who played during breakfast the most exhilarating tunes. In the park a space was allotted for a rural fair, which, amid the shade afforded by the lofty trees, formed a most picturesque appearance. From a booth of considerable dimensions was suspended the Milford Arms, from which provisions were distributed to such as were allowed admittance, consisting principally of the tenantry and peasantry connected with the estate. The ale brewed at the birth of the present earl sparkled in goblets, or foamed in tankards of massive weight, from which long life to Lord Millford and his lovely sister was drunk with enthusiasm. Over this part of the festival Meanwell presided; he had occupied the same station at the birth of the earl. After breakfast the company repaired to the fair, and most of them seemed to enjoy the rustic scene. Many little elegant trinkets were presented as fairings to the ladies, and even Sir Timothy displayed his gallantry on the joyful occasion. The duchess, leaning on the arm of her youthful host, stopped at the Millford Arms to enjoy the festivity of the scene.

"I delight," said she to Sir Timothy, who was standing near her, "in this display of old English hospitality."

"So should I, my lady duchess," he answered, "if it ended here; but the frippery within doors is too refined for my vulgar feelings; for I suppose we shall have to show the wonderful effects of tinsel and tiffinany, and dine by candle-light in the middle of August."

"Fashion," replied her grace, "is generally in extremes; in the reign of our Mary and your Elizabeth the hours were inconveniently early. But we must take the world as it is, Timothy: we cannot alter it."

"The world would be well enough," he answered, "if we could shuffle the knaves and fools out of it; then youth might stand a chance of being artless, and age respectable."

In the midst of this scene of pleasure, Caroline kept close to the duchess, and Montague conducted Lady Emma. Lady Acrimony finding herself fatigued, looked from the window of the priory on the varied groups that were passing in all directions beneath her view. The important duties of the toilet occupied the company till dinner, which consisted of every luxury that wealth could produce. In the evening the avenues were lit with coloured lamps, the music continued to play till eleven, when an appointed signal was given for the company in the park to disperse. The ball-room was beginning to fill, but as the evening was very warm, Lady Emma proposed a turn in the garden before she joined those who longed to trip upon the light fantastic toe. She was joined by Caroline, and followed by Montague, who placed himself between them. They had proceeded but a few paces, when a tall figure, leaning on a stick, stood before them; a large hat shaded his countenance, but from the reflection thrown by the moon on his figure, Montague penetrated the disguise. Caroline started.

"Lady," said he, in a low voice, "be not alarmed; I came not here to injure you."

"That is not feared, sir," said Montague, who was convinced by his voice that it was Newport; though, thinking that it was an eccentric whim in which he chose to be concealed, he forbore addressing him by name; he was soon convinced that it was so by the manner in which he spoke to Caroline.

"I should like, young lady," he said, "to tell your fortune."

"Tell mine first," said Lady Emma, presenting her delicate and finely-formed hand; "but I think by this light you cannot see the lines."

"That is of no consequence," he answered; "for I possess prescience that neither light can increase, nor darkness diminish. I watched the moon last night, and the bright luminary of day this morning, as it threw its radiance around thy native spires.

"You know me, then," she cried.

"And me too, perhaps," said Caroline.

He sighed, but did not answer.

"And I," said Montague, "am not unknown to you."

The old man (at least so he appeared) bowed.

"But I wish not to interfere with your destiny　my peculiar province is to guard the young and fair."

"These young ladies need not your attention," replied Montague, "for the are happy in having many friends."

"The mask of friendship is often assumed," he replied, "for purposes of self interest, or motives of delusion."

" Farewell," said he ; " I will not intrude. The sounds of harmony summon you to scenes of gaiety; but, when there—beware !"

" Of what ?" said Caroline.

" Of the allurements of pleasure, the design of artifice, and the professions of love. Beneath the fragrant foliage lurks the adder, and near the rosebush grows the noisome nettle. So envy lurks unseen near youth and beauty, to mildew with its envenomed breath the spring of life. May neither of you feel its influence. Yet envy," he said, "you must excite, for you are young and lovely ; and love you must expect to hear of, but shun its power, for it too often leads to misery and sorrow."

" Oh, do not chill us with such sad presages," said Lady Emma, leaning a little heavier on the arm of Montague, as if to trust to him for protection from every future evil.

His heart felt the appeal, and he pressed closer the arm that was within his. The music sounded louder.

" We must return," said Montague. " Another time we will listen to your admonitory councils."

" Another time," said he, " you may not hear them."

He passed on, and they returned to the house, where they found that Lord Millford and Miss Newland had just ended the first country dance.

Lord Harry Hazard solicited the hand of Caroline, and Montague before had secured Lady Emma's. Country dances over, waltzing commenced, when Lady Emma and Caroline seated themselves beside the duchess and Lady Acrimony.

" Do you not waltz, ladies ?" said Colonel Dinever, advancing.

A negative was the answer.

" How cruel," he cried, " to deny us the pleasure of seeing too such exquisite forms in the most captivating attitudes."

" I will teach you to waltz," said Captain Newland, rudely seizing the hand of Caroline, whom he before scarcely noticed.

" I have no ambition to learn, sir," was the answer he received.

" But I have set my mind on teaching you," he replied.

" Then you will certainly be disappointed," she answered, colouring with vexation.

" I have won my bet, Hazard," he cried; " here is not paint. But come, fair lady, waltz you must, if only to show how attractive nature can be without the aid of art."

" Waltz she shall not, captain," said Sir Timothy, advancing, "unless by her own consent, and that I think you will find it difficult to obtain."

" Everybody waltzes, now," cried Mrs. Pembroke, who had just heard Caroline decline the amusement.

" No, not every one," retorted Sir Timothy, " for sure you will not ?"

" I am just come to look for a companion," she answered, " and, colonel, putting her hand on Dinever's arm,——

" I have the honour, madam," said he, " of being engaged to waltz with Miss Newland. I am now waiting for her."

The lady looked displeased, and seemed thinking who else she should select, when Sir Timothy called out,—

" Will no one bring the cap and bells? Here is the goddess of Folly waiting for them."

" I think," she cried, " there are other heads here quite as fit for them as mine.

" But, by precedence," said he, " they shall be yours first, and we will see what other heads they will fit when you have done with them."

" If these ladies will oblige me," said the duchess, " they will reel to one of my national tunes."

" Then reels let it be," cried the captain, retaining the hand of Caroline, and giving her a quick turn. As she rose from her seat, the comb that confined her hair fell, and with it her luxuriant tresses; they floated from her neck to her waist.

"A very Godiva. Now for a reel," said the unfeeling captain; and so saying, he whirled her in a moment into the middle of the room.

Mortified and confused, she struggled to disengage herself, when Sir Timothy, advancing, interposed, saying,—

"I see, Captain Newland, neither wit nor good breeding in this exploit of yours. Allow me, Miss Mellbourne, to conduct you to a seat."

She gratefully accepted his offered hand, and was again seated by her friends, but not before she had excited the observation of many who enjoyed her confusion; though, had the same disaster happened to themselves, they might have lost their tresses as well as broke their combs, which was the fate of Caroline's.

"Do let me retire," she said to Lady Emma, who instantly complied with her request. Her hair was soon adjusted, and they returned to the ball-room.

Caroline had all the evening excited general attention. The gentlemen admired her person, and the ladies criticised her dress, to which Miss Newland directed their attention, describing, at the same time, her insolence, as she termed it, in refusing the one she offered her.

"She is dressed to please the duchess," she added. "See what a quantity of Vandyke there is round her petticoat. I suppose it is a copy from some old grandmother's dress, worked in tapestry at Moncrief Castle."

"But not a single jewel," observed Miss Dinever. "Her ear-rings and necklace are only paste."

This delectable conversation was broke up by a summons to the supper-rooms, soon after which the duchess's carriage was announced. She was conducted to it by Lord Millford, while Lord Harry Hazard took the hand of Caroline. Sir Timothy's was the next in rotation, and Lady Emma, giving her hand to the delighted Montague, followed Sir Timothy and his lady.

We have said Montague was delighted, and in fact he was so, for Lady Emma's return to the grove was unexpected, as she had accepted of an invitation from her brother to continue there some days, in order to assist Mrs. Pembroke in entertaining the friends he had had invited there, who were to continue the remainder of the week; among whom was Captain and Miss Newland, whose treatment of Caroline had so offended her, that she determined on returning to the grove, and leaving Mrs. Pembroke to act alone.

Their departure was very agreeable to most of the company, and to none more than Mrs. Pembroke and Miss Newland. The former dreaded the baronet; the latter affected to laugh at the country gentleman, his son; while she certainly envied Lady Emma and Caroline the admiration they had attracted.

Lord Millford warmly commended Caroline's ease in dancing; and Lord Harry Hazard declared she was not excelled by any dancer that he had ever seen.

Again the company repaired to the ball-room, and before the revels concluded, the car of Aurora had long been launched in the eastern horizon, as the duchess had anticipated.

Mrs. Newland proposed outdoing her usual entertainments at the manor. Another breakfast and *fete* would have been no novelty; she therefore determined on a theatrical exhibition. All then was hurry and confusion again, and the ladies were most delightfully employed in studying characters and practising attitudes. There was but a short time to get up the pieces, as the company were on the wing for different watering-places.

After much demur, the *West Indian* was fixed on for the play, and *Rosina* for the afterpiece. Workmen were employed to erect a temporary theatre, in the gardens, and scenery was procured from London.

Mrs. Newland undertook to arrange the characters. She found it very difficult to please her company. After many alterations, however, she accomplished her purpose. She wished Lord Millford to play Charles Dudly to her daughter's Charlotte Ruspont; but he objected to the military character, when there were others who could support it with more propriety. She then offered him Belcour, and entreated her daughter to take that of Louisa Dudly; this Miss Newland declared was so monkish a character, that she would have nothing to do with it; and being offended with Lord Millford for refusing his part, she proposed that it should be given to Colonel Dinever. The colonel having more gallantry than the peer, accepted the proposal with apparent pleasure.

Now, then, how was Louisa to be disposed of? Mrs. Pembroke and Lady Lucy were both too old to personate the youthful beauty; and, of the young ladies, none remained that could be prevailed on to perform, except Miss Dinever; but she, after one rehearsal, declared herself too fatigued to proceed in the study.

Mrs. Newland, vexed at being so disappointed, proposed to the duchess that Caroline should take the part. That lady, who had frequently admired the sweet plaintive tones of Caroline's voice, warmly seconded Mrs. Newland's proposal. Thus situated, she at length agreed, and having consented, she determined on exerting herself to be perfect in her part, while the duchess, who was a great admirer of the drama, assisted her, by her observations, in the study of her character; and, after two rehearsals, she was declared to be mistress of her part, but was advised by Mrs. Newland to divest herself of prudery, and play with more ease.

Nearly the same party that had been at the *fete* were invited. Mrs. Newland undertook to play Lady Rusport, her son to be Major O'Flarty, and Lord Harry Hazard was the Varland; Mrs. Fullmore was assigned to Lady Lucy, and never were characters more appropriately appointed. Montague was the Stockwell, and he made a most excellent old man. As Miss Newland would have all the advantages of dress that were denied the humble Louisa, she did not oppose her playing the character, secretly determining on mortifying Lord Millford by playing in a very spirited style to the colonel. The remainder of the characters were easily appointed.

The duchess with Sir Timothy and Lady Acrimony sat in the centre box; Lady Emma and Miss Dinever on the right hand of them, and the rest of the company seated themselves as chance or fancy dictated.

Mrs. Newland looked, spoke, and moved as if she had been born purposely to display the consequence of a citizen's widow. And it was remarked that her daughter was peculiarly poignant when scrutinising her mother's affectation. Lord Milford played Belcour with great animation; but it is difficult to say, when Caroline appeared, timid, trembling, and embarrassed, which was most agitated, Lady Emma or herself.

"She will faint—I know she will. Do, dear duchess, go to her."

"No, no," cried that lady, "she will recover her self-possession. I know she will."

Her predictions were verified, for she sustained the character with ease, propriety, and elegance. And Miss Newland, though very correct, would have appeared more amiable if she had sweetened her raillery with a little more good nature of manner, when playing to Caroline; but she fully atoned for that deficiency by the spirit she displayed in the remainder of the part. And even Sir Timothy, with whom she was no favourite, confessed her excellence. But the most difficult part for Caroline still remained in the scene, in which [Belcour offers himself as her honourable lover, and a sense of propriety induces her to reject his hand. The pathos of her voice thrilled every heart; and when she uttered, " Poor like myself, but not so well protected," the actress was lost in the woman; and she would have sunk to the ground overpowered by her own feelings, if the supporting arm of Lord Millford had not saved her from falling. A long and loud clap restored her; and the little that remained for her to say was uttered with feeling and propriety. The curtain dropped amidst long and loud plaudits.

The after-piece was deferred till some other time.

When the performers retired to change their dresses, Caroline was followed by her friend Lady Emma, who, as a dress ball was to conclude the entertainment, had accepted Mrs. Newland's invitation of continuing at the manor till the next morning, when Lady Acrimony promised to fetch her home and soon after took leave of the company; Sir Timothy did the same; but Montague remained till morning.

A little difference of opinion existed between the duchess and Lady Emma, the latter wishing Caroline to appear in her new dress, which the former opposed.

"Enough of admiration, my dear girl," she said, "has our favourite excited to-night; more might rouse Miss Newland's envy, which prudence should teach her to avoid. There will be more opportunities than this for Miss Mellbourne to appear in the dress you presented her with."

Vanity has been said by Lavater to be the first and last passion of a woman's heart; and pleased as we are, and hope our readers will be, with the character of Caroline, we must ingenuously confess she was not without a small portion of it. She certainly would willingly have complied with the wishes of her friend, had not the sensible observation of the duchess, to whose opinion she paid implicit deference; prevented her, nearly then, as she appeared at the priory, she returned to the company.

The scenery being removed, the whole stage formed the dancing floor. A full band still occupied the orchestra; the centre boxes remained for such as did not partake of the amusement; and from the side ones, the domestics distributed the most choice wines and luxuriant viands; for, at the request of the company, supper was dispensed with.

Lord Millford solicited the hand of Caroline for the two first country dances, Montague took Lady Emma, and the colonel, Miss Newland; after the country dances were over, quadrilles and waltzing followed, in the latter of which Miss Newland displayed both her figure and science. She waltzed both with Lord Millford and the colonel; the former, however, soon returned to the side of Caroline, from which all the coquetry of Miss Newland could not divert him; and it must be confessed that, many times during the entertainment, Caroline had occasion to recal to her recollection the caution given by Newport, "Beware of the professions of love." The admonition was serviceable, for it enabled her to hear his compliments without betraying the embarrassment she would some time before have experienced from similar conversations; she called to mind, too, that his lordship had recently returned from a land where flattery is considered a mark of good-breeding, which all ladies expect to receive, and which they estimate at its exact value, namely, a desire to make them pleased with themselves, and so Caroline thought she would receive the incense thus offered her.

Miss Newland, in revenge for his lordship's neglect, flirted immoderately with the colonel, to whom, but for one reason, if her father would have given a hundred thousand pounds, she certainly would have honoured with her hand: only his coronet was in reversion, Lord Millford's in possession; besides one was an earl, the other would only be a viscount, and his uncle might marry again, and should an heir make its appearance, why there would be no coronet for the colonel. All these things taken into consideration, Miss Newland determined to try for the Millford coronet if she could obtain it, and her vexation at finding the wearer of it could not be drawn from the side of Caroline was such as she found it difficult to conceal. To her very great relief, the duchess rose to retire, and was followed by Caroline; Lady Emma soon after left the company, and Montague, whose groom had been some time in waiting with his horse, made a slight alteration in his dress, slipped on his boots, and rode home by daylight.

The next day the theatre disappeared, and, within a week, the company, most of them on the wing for other scenes of amusement; some to Brighton, others to Cheltenham, and Mrs. Pembroke, for a few weeks, to her villa at old Windsor, to which place she was followed by Lady Lucy, Miss Newland, Miss Dinever, and the colonel. Lord Millford, too, promised to join them the ensuing week, and of all the party, none remained but the duchess and Caroline, and their company Mrs. Newland would willingly have dispensed with. The continuance of the duchess was owing to having business with Mr. Newland, and though we have not lately spoken of him, our readers will suppose that he was frequently among the gay circles that visited his lady. Much of his time, however, was occupied in London, in attending to the various concerns he was connected with; and the lawsuit he had undertaken to conduct for the duchess now claimed his particular attention; it had been some years depending, and she had come from the north to hasten its decision The object in question was an estate in Northumberland, which she claimed a being sole heiress to Lord Macdonald. It had hitherto been conducted at great ex

pense, which had, as Miss Newland observed, made her poor for a duchess; and by the advice of her friends, she had come to England in hopes of accelerating its conclusion. Mr. Newland had been recommended to her as a person of great abilities, and to him she had applied for professional assistance. Aware of the advantages that ought to arise to himself from serving his dignified client, Mr. Newland exerted himself in the cause which soon bore a very favourable appearance. Mrs. Newland's introduction followed, which led to the circumstances we
No. 6.

have related ; the duchess had proposed returning to Scotland in the autumn, but this she had the vexation to find would not be accomplished. Mr. Newland observed that in the state the suit was then in, many consultations would be necessary; he therefore entreated her grace to continue another month at the manor, which for mutual conveniency was acceded to by her.

Dr. Maxwell, whom we have not for some time spoken of, had purchased a very pretty cottage and grounds in Westmoreland, in the neighbourhood of his old residence ; and had written to request that Montague and Lord Millford would spend the autumn with him. Montague availed himself of the invitation, but the latter was embarrassed with the promise he had made of joining the party at old Windsor, which he had heard was augmented by several new arrivals ; and that a trip to the Isle of Wight was in contemplation among them. His lordship hesitated, he had no particular business in the country, yet still he lingered there. Though his nominal residence was at the priory, he frequently spent whole days at the manor. This was not unnoticed by either of the ladies, and to Mrs. Newland it was anything but agreeable; though she was too much a woman of the world to let her vexation be visible.

At length, to her very great satisfaction, Lord Millford determined for the lakes, and entreated Mrs. Newland, when she wrote, to make his apologies to the party at Mrs. Pembrokes. That lady had much rather he had gone thither himself, but at all events anything was better than his hovering round Caroline, walking with her, and the Highland chieftess, as Miss Newland had named the duchess, in the garden, or driving them occasionally to the grove.

Lady Acrimony, on Lady Emma's account, frequently visited at the manor, and a most friendly intercourse was formed between herself and the duchess, cemented by the interest they both felt for the welfare of their mutual young favourites.

Lord Millford and Montague departed. Soon after they left the grove, Lady Acrimony became seriously ill. We have before observed she had been long declining, and at last her malady was by the faculty pronounced consumptive ; indeed it had every appearance of that fatal complaint; but as no immediate danger was apprehended, she would not suffer her son's pleasurable tour to be interrupted by any notice being sent to him of her illness.

Lady Emma confined herself at home, where she devoted her whole time to her suffering friend but there was seldom a day passed without her seeing Caroline ; for the duchess's airings were always to the grove. These were generally made without Mrs. Newland, who did not conceal the dislike she had long entertained for the sarcastic manners of the baronet.

On one occasion, when the young ladies were absent, the duchess spoke of the conversation that had passed between herself and Mrs. Newland, and the strange account she had heard Mrs. Newland give for not letting Mr. Newport see Caroline.

" But he did see her," replied Sir Timothy, " and on the night of the *fete*."

"So I was informed by Mr. Montague," she answered, " and the whole seems to me a mystery I cannot easily comprehend." She added, " that it must be unpleasant to see a person we have injured, but how anything disagreeable can attach to the presence of one we have benefited I am unable to discover."

" So, too, am I," replied the baronet, " and am fully persuaded that in this affair, more is meant than meets the ear."

" I have," said Lady Acrimony, " frequently had my doubts ; time perhaps may discover the truth."

" Never," cried Sir Timothy. " if it is Newland's interest to conceal it,"

The return of Lady Emma and her friend ended the conversation.

Mrs. Newland was quite lost in the calm of quiet life, and thought every day a week till the month was expired, when she understood the duchess intended removing to Bath, on a visit to an old friend, and as the gout had entirely left her hand, she feared Caroline would not be wanted, especially as her return to Scotland would not take place till the following spring. But on this point the duchess had not explained herself, and she was left to conjecture; one thing she resolved on, and that was that she should not spend the winter in Grosvenor-square.

In the meantime Caroline continued to improve in the estimation of the duchess, whose partiality for her increased as her sweetness of temper and sincerity of heart became better known to her; not a moment passed heavily in her society. She read, sang, played on the piano, and in short conformed so entirely to the taste of the duchess as led Mrs. Newland to hope she would be a necessary appendage in her suite.

With her grace the poems of Ossian were standing favourites, and Caroline in reading the powerful effusions of the Highland bard seemed frequently to have caught a portion of his melancholy enthusiasm. The tones of her voice were soft and melodious, and her variations were rapid, sweet, and appropriate, while her countenance now glowed with animation, now sank in sadness, and at such times her grace would mentally sigh, "Oh, this exquisitely gifted creature is neither the offspring of guilty love, nor the child of obscure parents."

One day while employed at her needle, she sang at the request of her grace the favourite ballad of Auld Robin Gray, when suddenly raising her eyes, she perceived the countenance of the duchess softened into an expression of extreme tenderness: tears stood in her eyes, and the colour had forsaken her lips.

"Your grace is indisposed," she said, rising and advancing towards her.

"No, dear lassie," she said, "only overcome by powerful reflections under the illusions of imagination. I could almost have fancied Lady M'Gregorie herself had been singing to me."

"Am I so much like her ladyship?" said Caroline, timidly.

"She has been long dead," replied the duchess, "but I have not forgotten her: she was my only sister. You are like her, and not like her, for I cannot describe the resemblance, though I frequently trace it. It flashes over your countenance like a sunbeam on the water, and instantly disappears; but it is not so much in your person as in your voice that I discover the similitude, and I love you for it," she continued, drawing her towards her and kissing her cheek; "for it blends painful recollections with sweet remembrances."

The minstrel of Beattie, and the beautiful poetry of poor neglected Burns, sometimes formed part of their mornings' amusement, when the duchess would direct her in the pronunciation of the Scottish dialect, and explain its idioms. History and heraldry were, as Miss Newland had said, favourite subjects with the duchess.

To these Caroline listened with polite attention, and heard recounted the pedigrees and intermarriages of half the Scottish nobility.

The duchess was proud of her descent, and could trace it distinctly to a very remote period. One day after talking some time on these, to her, interesting subjects, she rather abruptly inquired of Caroline, if she would copy a manuscript for her.

"With pleasure, madam," was the reply.

"It is rather long," said the duchess, "and will beguile you of your tears; I have long promised it to the friend I am about to visit at Bath, but have not had sufficient resolution to perform it."

The next morning the papers were given to Caroline, who commenced the pleasing task, and shortly accomplished it to the satisfaction of the duchess, who told her the original was written by herself, and if it interested her, she might take another copy for her own amusement; the offer was thankfully accepted, and speedily executed.

During the time the duchess continued at the priory, Captain Newland frequently appeared there, generally with a party of military friends; these parties were very unpleasant to Caroline, for the captain was either rude or familiar, as it suited the whim of the minute. If he was in a grave humour, he treated her with rudeness or neglect; if in a gay one, she was sure to be made the subject of his boisterous mirth. It is but justice to his companions to say that his conduct was neither approved nor copied by them. On the first night of her appearance, they had seen and admired her, but the interest she excited was considerably abated by the general buzz circulated by Miss Newland that she was friendles and portionless, and about to become toadeater to the Highland duchess.

At length the period so long desired by Mrs. Newland arrived, when the duchess announced her intention of leaving the manor, Mr. Newland having informed her that the business must rest as it was till January.

One thing distressed her, it was where to place Caroline till she returned to London; for she perceived Mrs. Newland would not make the offer of her continuing with her, and the lady to whom she was going was an invalid of narrow fortune and small establishment. She, therefore, intended that her carriage and servants, except her own woman, should return to London, but she could not with propriety send Caroline there without some one as a companion; in this perplexity she applied to Lady Acrimony, when to her great relief the baronet proposed sending for her to the grove. "This poor girl will have a sad time of it when you are gone; and let Caroline come to keep her company."

" The very thing to make me happy in leaving her," answered the duchess; " but perhaps Mrs. Newland may object to it."

" I do not see how that is possible," replied Lady Acrimony, " but yet I think she had better be consulted."

" It will at least," said Sir Timothy, " compel her to say, whether she thinks herself freed from all further care of this interesting girl." To Mrs. Newland then the duchess applied, who, rather thrown off her guard, hesitated in her reply, but at length answered, " That she was going to join her daughter and some friends at the Isle of Wight, and as she could not take Caroline with her, she had no objection to her accepting Lady Acrimony's invitation."

Things thus settled, Caroline prepared for her visit to the grove, and the duchess for her journey to Bath. The day previous to its commencement, she called on Lady Acrimony and left Caroline behind her, saying as soon as she was fixed for the winter, that she should expect her in London; then slipping a small purse into her hand, bade her an affectionate adieu.

The pleasure this visit would have afforded to all parties was considerably lessened by the increasing languor of Lady Acrimony, who was evidently worse; the young ladies alternately sat with her, for she seldom left her own apartment, and when one retired, the other took her place.

Thus were they situated when Montague and Lord Millford returned from their journey. The former was alarmed at seeing the alteration a few weeks had made in the appearance of his mother, and anxiously implored her to call in more medical aid.

" It is useless," she replied; " all that medicine could effect has been tried, and do not distress me by useless anxiety. I think I have been worse than I now am; if I feel any fresh symptoms, I will consent to try other experiments; but, believe me, for my complaint there is no cure."

It was then the beginning of a fine October, and Lord Millford proposed passing the shooting season at the priory, to which place he gave numerous invitations.

Montague frequently partook of their morning amusements, but, owing to Lady Acrimony's ill-health, he seldom dined from home. Lord Millford called several times during his continuance at the priory; but, after a few weeks, he became tired of the country, and returned with his friends to London, where he pursued the career of pleasure with all the avidity of a young heir possessed of good health, good spirits, and a handsome fortune. The duchess wrote frequently and friendly to Caroline, and hoped to receive her in London about the end of January, at which time she expected the town would begin to fill. Mrs. Newland and her friends intended passing the Christmas at the manor, but the melancholy situation of Lady Acrimony prevented the ladies there from taking any interest in the festivities that were expected to follow their arrival.

CHAPTER VI.

The man how blest, who, sick of gaudy scenes—
Scenes apt to thrust between us and ourselves—
Is led by choice to take his favourite walk
Beneath death's gloomy, silent, cypress shapes,
Unpierc'd by vanity's fantastic ray,
To read his monuments, to weigh his dust,
Visit his vaults, and dwell among the tombs.—YOUNG.

LADY ACRIMONY's complaint increased rapidly, and again her son importuned her to call in more assistance.

"It will be useless," she replied. "My dear Montague, the mandate of dissolution is gone forth : it is the fiat of my Creator, and I humbly bow to His decree."

The firm though mild tone with which this sentence was uttered silenced him. He left her, and applied to Sir Timothy, who instantly complied with his request, and, on the following day, two physicians of eminence were summoned from London. Montague, on entering her room, to prepare her for their arrival, found her free from pain. Emma was reading to her, and Caroline was employed in writing to the duchess.

"What is your subject this morning?" he inquired, drawing a chair near the sofa on which his mother reclined.

"The Pleasures of Hope," Lady Emma replied.

"Campbell is a consolatory poet," said her suffering friend. "Do, my dea. Emma, read that passage again. Your voice models it to harmony."

She complied, and read with great feeling, the following beautiful lines :—

" Cold in the dust this perished heart must lie,
But that which warmed it once shall never die.
That spark unburied in its mortal frame,
With living light eternal and the same,
Shall beam on joys interminable years,
Unveiled by darkness, unassuaged by tears."

She closed the book, when Lady Acrimony, looking at her son, said,—

"You have something, I think, to communicate ; what is it?"

He briefly explained that the physicians were hourly expected.

"I hope," he added, "that their presence will not hurry you."

"Not at all," she answered, "nor did I need this proof of affection from you, for your whole life has been one of love and duty. I will certainly abide by any rules that may be prescribed to abate my disorder ; but do not, I entreat you, flatter yourself that it can ever be removed."

"Do not say so, my more than mother," said Lady Emma, while tears, that she could not restrain, flowed down her pallid cheeks.

"Child of my fondest love," cried the patient sufferer, "dear to me as my lost Amelia, whose place you have so well supplied, for your sake I have prayed that my span of life might be protracted, if only for a few short years. My prayers, doubtless, for wise purposes, have been rejected ; and I wait, not unresigned, nor, I trust, unprepared, for that awful hour which, closing the gates of time, will open the portals of eternity. An opportunity like the present I have long wished for, yet wanted resolution to seek. Emma, may I probe your heart? Montague, yours has long been known to me."

The death-like paleness that had before shaded the countenance of Lady Emma was succeeded by the deepest vermillion, and her sweet face might have been poetically compared to a sunbeam obscured by a cloud : she rose from her seat, bent on one knee by the side of the sofa, and wept in agony.

"This is what I feared," said her ladyship, "my dear Emma, for my sake—for your own, be tranquillised, and hear with calmness the little I would say to you."

She arose, and endeavoured to restrain her tears.

"I have seen with pleasure, Montague," continued her ladyship, "the affection you entertain for this inestimable young creature, and I have thought—correct me, Emma, if I am wrong—that the prepossession was mutual, and that thought has afforded me indescribable satisfaction. Emma," she continued, "you may have more splendid offers, but, trust me, you will never find a heart more devoted to you, nor one you can trust to with more security."

Montague advanced, she gave him her hand, he raised it to his lips in silence.

"I will be yours, and only yours, Montague," she cried, "if you and your dear mother wish me so to be."

"Dear, generous, candid creature," cried Montague, deeply affected by the scene, "cold must that heart be that does not feel your power ; over mine, you are the unlimited mistress ; you will be mine, then, at the expiration of your minority? Promise me this, and I shall be as happy as I can be ;" his voice faltered—he paused.

"Exact no further promise, claim no pledge," said Lady Acrimony ; "be satisfied with Lady Emma's esteem, and deserve it, by placing implicit confidence in her stability. Promises frequently embarrass both the giver and receiver, and seldom add to the repose of the one or security of the other; cultivate each other's good opinion ; confide in each other's rectitude; then should any unforeseen circumstances —(for what is certain in this state of uncertainty?)—prevent your union, you may be friends through life, if no longer lovers; but should the affection you now feel for each other be strengthened by time and improved by reflection, then may Heaven sanctify your union with its choicest blessings, may your lives be long and happy, and at last, when full of years, may you calmly glide into the sleep of death, surrounded by your children's children, and may they deserve to be as dear to your hearts as you are both to mine."

Lady Emma sobbed violently. Montague, in great emotion, kissed a hand of each, and left the room.

The entrance of Caroline relieved Lady Emma, who took that opportunity of retiring to recover her serenity ; the opinions of the physicians accorded entirely with those expressed by their patient : they had nothing to recommend but change of air.

"It is too late for the experiment," said Lady Acrimony, with firmness ; "I will die at home ;" and finding her so determined, all further importunities on the subject were spared her ; one wish only she expressed, and that was for the presence of Dr. Maxwell. "Often," she said, "has that worthy man's conversation, under former trials, raised my thoughts from earth to heaven, and it would afford consolation to my heart, in the last hour of nature's struggles, to be assisted with his prayers."

It is scarcely necessary to add that the request was instantly complied with, and that the doctor arrived in less time than could have been expected ; her ladyship lingered some weeks longer, free from pain, and able frequently to converse calmly with those about her : she entreated Sir Timothy to watch over her darling Emma, and to afford Caroline his protection, should future circumstances render it necessary.

The baronet, too much affected to answer, bowed an assent; the attachment that existed between their son and Lady Emma she did not name, thinking as all parties were situated, that it would be premature to her son. She was explicit, and advised him to make no public declaration of his sentiments, till Lady Emma had completed her minority. With Lady Emma she held long and frequent conferences, and the advice given her was never obliterated from the heart of that excellent young woman; one day, in speaking of the probable consequences that would follow her dissolution, she said,—

" You may, my dearest girl, be thrown into the gay world, and separated from Montague. If that should be the case, suffer no artifices to cloud your better judgment. There may be those who would willingly deprive him of your good opinion—always remember that his dying mother assures you that you might rely on his affectionate and firm regards; continue to cultivate the esteem of Sir Timothy, and on no account marry without his consent. I know the irritability of his temper would induce him to consider such a measure an insult to him."

During this melancholy season at the grove, the gay party had arrived to commence their Christmas revels at the manor. Mrs. Pembroke was among them; she made an early visit to her niece. Lady Acrimony was too ill to admit her. Lord Millford called frequently, but seldom saw Caroline, as she was usually in the sick chamber. Mrs. Newland contented herself with inquiries, saying the dismals did not suit her. Mr. Newland had recently given Sir Timothy great offence by ejecting out many of the tenants on the estate he held under Lord Millford ; having, before he gained his lease, given a verbal promise that he would not disturb them. This Sir Timothy resented, who, spite of all his eccentricities, was the poor man's friend ; and being a conscientious observer of his own words, he rarely forgave the deviation in another. Meanwell, too, was hurt at the distress he could not relieve ; and at his request Sir Timothy condescended to write to Mr. Newland on the subject. The comfortable residences of many were levelled with the ground, which was enclosed to extend the park. Some few, more remote from the manor, were suffered to remain, though at very advanced rents Lord Millford remonstrated, but Mr. Newland assured him the ground he had enclosed was considered by his surveyor indispensably necessary for the completion of his plan. Besides, he added,—

"As it will be well planted, the advantage to the estate will be very considerable, as your lordship will recollect that I am not to have the liberty of felling the timber."

Lord Millford did not reply, and the improvements, as they were termed, went on. To the baronet he wrote that the plan he had laid down for the enlargement of the park could not now be deviated from. " The old people and children," he added, " will find refuge in the poorhouse, while the young and able can labour as well on any other soil as on mine."

The contents of this letter received severe animadversion, particularly from Sir Timothy.

"Lady Emma," said Dr. Maxwell, " I have often heard you censure the Duchess of Moncrieff's pride of ancestry. Do you not now think it less destructive than that displayed by the votaries of wealth ?"

" I like neither in the extreme, doctor," was the reply.

" Nor do I," said Montague ; " but I think it must be admitted that the one is much less objectionable than the other. The pride of ancestry," he continued, " is a harmless vapour, it neither mildews the poor man's comforts, nor snatches from him the fruits of honest industry; while the other, with the dreadful force of tornado, sweeps all before it, and expels him from the habitation of his youth, and the abode of his forefathers."

A summons to the chamber of Lady Acrimony interrupted the conversation. Lady Emma was first there, where she found her maternal friend expiring on the arm of Caroline ; the patient sufferer was sensible ; she extended her cold hand to Lady Emma, who bathed it with her tears.

A few minutes passed in silence, when it was evident the last, the final stroke was struck, and life extinguished. Lady Emma sank nearly lifeless on the shoulder of Dr. Maxwell, who instantly supported, or rather carried, her from the awful scene. Sir Timothy and his son retired, while Caroline joined Lady Emma, whom he found overwhelmed with sorrow. A medical gentleman who was present, and

had witnessed that young lady's devotion to her friend, followed her to her apartment, and, after much entreaty, prevailed on her to take a pacific draught (for her
nerves were much affected), and endeavour to obtain a few hours' repose. She
complied, and Caroline prepared to sit beside her. Sir Timothy sought the solitude of his own chamber, and after some time Montague returned to the scene of
death, where his sainted mother lay as if fallen into a peaceful slumber. He kissed
her cold cheek and retired. Dinner was served, but no one attended. In the
evening all except Lady Emma met at the tea-table, where Caroline presided.
No conversation was attempted, and as soon as the repast was over, each retired.
Lady Emma was sleeping, and her friend again seated herself beside her; on the
following morning she was more composed. The melancholy news having reached
the priory, Lord Millford early in the day made his appearance at the grove, and
his presence gave real pleasure to the sensitive Lady Emma, who, unable to take
any part in the necessary preparations, requested Caroline to act for her. This
she did, assisted by the housekeeper, and by the time appointed for the funeral,
everything was in readiness that appertained to the female part of the family. On
the second morning after the decease of Lady Acrimony, the ladies entered the
breakfast parlour together; Montague met them, and taking the passive hand of
Lady Emma, placed her next to the baronet.

"You have lost an excellent friend, my poor girl," said he, laying his hand on
hers; "but what is your loss compared to mine?"

Lady Emma attempted an answer, but her words died inaudibly away. Caroline
exerted herself to arouse the attention of her friend; she introduced subjects that
she thought would lead to general conversation, but without effect. Some short
sentences were elicited from Lady Emma, and all again was silent. Dr. Maxwell
and Sir Timothy left the room; Montague remained, who endeavoured, by every
argument that affection could suggest, to soothe the heartfelt grief of one so truly
dear to him. After some time she abruptly quitted the room.

"Follow her, my dear Miss Mellbourne," cried Montague, "she is not fit to be
alone; grief will destroy her."

"Not so, I hope, Mr. Montague," she replied; "I think we had better let her
indulge it without restraint. The draught she took was powerful, and the sleep
that it produced, though long, was not refreshing; her head is confused; if she
could weep, tears would relieve her."

"Do not," he cried, with great emotion, "leave her one moment alone; do
seek her."

Caroline did as he requested, and found her leaning over the coffin of her
maternal friend, and weeping in agony. She stood on the opposite side, but did
not interrupt her. They were soon joined by Montague, who likewise remained
silent. After some time she looked up, and perceiving them, left the coffin and
retired to the further part of the room, where she continued for some time undis-
turbed. At length, making an effort to recover her self-possession, she rose, and
giving a hand to each, said,—

"I give you both a great deal of trouble; I am better now. The weight
here," drawing her hand from Caroline's, and placing it on her heart, "is not
near so heavy as it was, and I will endeavour to be all my friends can wish
me to be."

"Oh, you are all that is lovely and interesting in woman," thought Montague,
as he raised her hand to his lips, and conducted her from the melancholy scene.

On the day appointed for the funeral, Sir Timothy proposed that Mrs. Pembroke
should be invited, to help to support the spirits of her niece, and that lady arrived
in the morning, accompanied by Lord Millford.

Lady Emma exerted herself beyond what was expected of her on the solemn
occasion; while Caroline, calm, attentive, and considerate, seemed to inspire those
around her with a portion of her own serenity. It was not insensibility, for none
had felt more acutely than herself through all the trying scenes that had preceded
that awful hour: it was fortitude that enabled her to conceal her own emotions,

the better to support her suffering friend. The doctor observed her with admiration, Montague with gratitude, and Sir Timothy with feelings bordering on affection.

About noon the solemn ceremony commenced, when the ladies retired to a distant apartment. Sir Timothy, too ill to attend, sought the solitude of his own chamber. Montague, Lord Millford, Dr. Maxwell, and the rector, were the princi-

pal mourners. Meanwell and the medical attendant, and two gentlemen, friends of Sir Timothy, were in the second coach ; that with the domestics followed. On their return from the place appointed for all that live, Sir Timothy was waiting their return, and then the ladies joined them. The party was increased by the arrival of Miss Lewson, the rector's sister. Dinner passed in silence, every one seemed too much affected for conversation, and the vacant chair at the head of the table renewed all the sorrow of Lady Emma ; and Caroline, no longer able to conceal

No. 7.

her emotions, was unequal to the task of supporting her friends. The melancholy meal over, the ladies withdrew.

"That poor girl," said Sir Timothy, " would be lost without Miss Mellbourne."

"Lady Emma's feelings are very acute," replied the doctor. "It is a pity they are not more under the control of reason, for there is no passing through life without meeting frequent causes for mental energy. I honour sensibility in the female character, and, when allied with fortitude, like Miss Mellbourne's, it becomes irresistible."

"But strength of mind, or fortitude, call it which you please," replied Montague, "has been said to be only strength of nerve, and, if nature has denied one, how is the other to be acquired?"

"By resisting, as much as possible, all violent emotions, of either joy or sorrow," replied the former; " for all extremes begin with irritating the nerves, and end with destroying them."

Montague did not reply, and the conversation ended.

Soon after tea, the party separated, and for some days after the family only met at meals. Within the week, a letter arrived from the duchess to Caroline. It contained the usual compliments of condolence, after which, her grace stated that she should be in Portland-place at the time she had before named; "but," she added, " as other changes may, perhaps, take place, in consequence of Lady Emma's recent loss, I leave it to yourself to settle the time when I may expect to receive you." Other changes were at that very time in agitation. The Newlands were preparing to quit the manor. Mrs. Newland, before she left, made a morning call at Firr Grove, and warmly entreated Lady Emma to take up her abode with them for the winter. This she declined, but, in a few days, was induced to consent to another arrangement. Mrs. Pembroke proposed to her that, as the house in Bedford-square was unoccupied, and, as she had no regular town residence herself, having usually hired a private house for the season, that Lord Millford and his sister should, under her superintendance fix their residence there, during the remainder of Lady Emma's minority. Lord Millford warmly seconded the proposal, nor did Sir Timothy object to it; he only stipulated that his ward should not be subject to any unnecessary expenses, and proposed a certain sum for her board and of her servants, of whom she had only two—a female attendant and footman.

Montague contemplated this change with feelings of intense anxiety, yet he could start no reasonable objections; he saw the spirits of Lady Emma deeply distressed, and he felt that everything at the grove, even inanimate objects, recalled her loss to her memory, and he could but acknowledge that change of scene was necessary for the restoration of her serenity. In the course of the conversation Lady Emma said,—

"Sir Timothy, I am fearful you will be very dull when we are gone."

" Never think of that," he replied; " I am not a fit companion for young people. I hope you will share the pleasures of the world without being contaminated by its frivolities. The doctor has consented to continue the winter with me, and early in the next month Montague must go on business of importance to Ireland."

This intelligence struck cold on the heart of Lady Emma. It was the first time she had heard it named, though she knew that in that part of the kingdom Sir Timothy had extensive possessions.

"In about a month, then," said Mrs. Pembroke, " I shall be prepared to receive you, and shall in a few days commence the necessary preparations."

"What will be wanting?" asked Lady Emma; " the house s elegantly furnished."

"Oh, child, many things will be wanting in way of decoration," said Mrs Pembroke."

" Add what you like at your own expense," replied Sir Timothy; " it is a noble house, and I do not think needs any alteration; but that Lord Millford and you can settle between yourselves."

That point agreed on, the lady departed the following day; the Newlands and Mrs. Pembroke departed for London. Lord Millford and some friends of his took up their residence at the priory; and the time at the grove was spent by the young ladies in lamenting the past, and anticipating the future. Lady Emma frequently thought on Lady Acrimony's, as it should seem, prophetic words—"You may be thrown into the gay world, and separated from Montague." "From my heart," she would say, "his image can never be removed."

To Caroline every wish and thought of that pure heart was known, who secretly prayed that no intervening evil might separate two persons so deserving of each other. Montague sometimes looked forward with apprehension, yet forbore to express a single doubt of her stability. He treated her with affectionate confidence and unceasing attention, while she, on her part, looked forward with pleasure to the time when she should depend on him only for every ray of future happiness.

Lord Millford, during his continuance at the priory, made frequent calls at Firr Grove, where Sir Timothy and the doctor were usually together, either in the library or at the chess board. This left the young people at liberty to pursue their own amusements.

Montague's attachment to Lady Emma had not escaped the observation of Lord Millford, who frequently found himself engaged with Caroline, while Montague was entertaining his sister; and it must be confessed that he exerted himself to the utmost to amuse her. His frequent absences occasioned much raillery among the friends he had at the priory, who were often left to amuse themselves. Certain it is, that while Lord Millford was securing for himself a great interest in the heart of Caroline, he never once inquired of himself to what purpose he meant to convert her preference, if he should succeed in obtaining it.

"Caroline," he once said to Montague, "is everything that could be wished or expected in woman; yet she is so equivocally situated that few men of family would think of making honourable proposals."

"I hope the monster does not live that would insult her with any other," replied Montague."

"I hope the same," said the other, "and heartily wish these Newlands had not insinuated her illegitimacy; it will be an obstacle to her advancement. Mrs. Pembroke believes her to be Newport's daughter, and Lady Lucy has very successfully circulated the report, and what is worse, none but himself can contradict it."

"Perhaps," replied Montague, "he will be the last person to hear it."

Still Lord Millford continued his visits till Mrs. Pembroke announced by letter that the house was ready for their reception. We pass over the ceremony of taking leave; it was both melancholy and affectionate. Sir Timothy's carriage conveyed them to London. Montague accompanied them to Bedford-square, from whence Caroline sent Lady Emma's servant with a note to the duchess, whose carriage was announced in the evening, waiting for Miss Mellbourne.

Lady Emma parted with her friend with real reluctance, yet secretly pleased that she was now placed beyond the reach of the Newlands' insolence.

Montague, who had business to transact, accepted Mrs. Pembroke's invitation of making his home in Bedford-square during his continuance in London. While there, he prevailed on Lady Emma to promise that she would be a regular correspondent during their separation, which, from the intelligence he obtained from the gentlemen of the long robe, he conjectured would be some months. With Lady Emma he twice visited the duchess, who received them with the freedom of an old friend; his mornings were necessarily devoted to business but in the evenings he entered into the amusements that the fertile genius of Mrs. Pembroke was continually projecting; one thing excited some uneasiness, he found Lady Lucy O'Leary was expected in Bedford-square, and he had heard she was passionately addicted to the gaming-table.

CHAPTER VII.

Faults in the life breed errors in the brain,
And these reciprocally those again ;
The mind and conduct mutually imprint,
And stamp their image on each other's mint,
With caution taste the sweet Circean cup,
He that sips often, at last drinks it up.—Cowper.

WHEN Montague returned to the grove, Sir Timothy inquired how he had left his ward, and on being informed that Lady Lucy was expected to pass the winter season in Bedford-square, he expressed both surprise and vexation.

"Mrs. Pembroke," said he, "is vain, noisy, and thoughtless ; but the other is, I think, a mixture of artifice and treachery, a Mrs. Fullmore in real life. I hope our poor girl will, as much as possible, shun her society."

"That cannot be expected," replied Montague, with a sigh; "situated as she is, she must mix in their parties, and partake of their amusements."

"Well," replied the baronet, "she wanted amusement; what could she find here to divert her? I really was apprehensive that she would fret herself into a decline ; and, in short, she renewed my trouble every time I looked at her. Millford, I hope, will caution her against deep play, and in a few months she will be at liberty to act for herself. Probably, her brother will marry, and then she can reside with him; or, perhaps—but no matter, we must now trust her to her own discretion."

Montague did not reply, for he perceived the subject was not agreeable.

The baronet then spoke of the business that would take him to Ireland, and proposed that he should commence his journey to Holyhead early in the ensuing week; this was assented to, for Montague wished the business concluded as early as possible, in order that he might be in England when Lady Emma's minority expired, which would be near the time when the mourning would (as far as related to appearance,) be over for his lamented mother. At the time appointed he set out, continued in London a few days, and had the pleasure to find Lady Emma in better spirits than he left her, though she complained much of late hours, and the dissipated life of her aunt. Every attempt made by Montague to obtain an hour's conversation alone with Lady Emma was prevented either by the influx of visitors, or the interruptions of Lady Lucy, who seemed to penetrate his design, and resolved on preventing it ; while Lady Emma, fearful of exciting her raillery, carefully guarded her behaviour, so as not to give rise to it ; yet the soft melody of her voice when she spoke to him—the pleasure that beamed in her bright blue eyes when he approached her, could not pass unnoticed by so vigilant and experienced an observer as Lady Lucy. Montague called in Portland-place, and in a conversation he held with Caroline, found her equally uneasy with himself for the future happiness of Lady Emma.

"I will send," said the duchess, "and request her company to dinner Mr. Montague," she added. "I give no splendid entertainments, but if you will partake of my homely fare, you shall have a plain dinner and a hearty welcome." It is needless to say the invitation was accepted with pleasure.

"Miss Mellbourne write a note, and to avoid any appearance of singularity, include Lord Millford in the invitation ; you may not all meet again for some time, and I think friendly farewells sweeten separation."

"So they do," said Montague, in reply, "and I leave London to-morrow."

Caroline retired to execute her pleasing task, and wondered if Lord Millford should accept the invitation. It must be confessed she took more than usual time at her toilet ,and adjusted her glossy ringlets in the manner that Lord Millford had frequently admired while she was with Lady Emma at the grove.

During her absence, the duchess and Montague held a long conversation, in which she fully understood the particular interest he felt for the fair ward of the baronet.

"I will cultivate her acquaintance," she said, "as much as I can, without being annoyed by her trifling aunt and the despicable Lady Lucy, who, while she ridicules the foibles of Mrs. Pembroke, is playing on her good nature."

The heart of Montague was on his lips, and he thanked her with a warmth of feeling that indicated his gratitude.

When the carriage drove to the door, the colour mounted to the cheek of Caroline, and before she could recover herself their guests were announced. It was to them all a day of perfect harmony; in the evening, a few friends who visited in Portland-place, *sans ceremonie*, dropped in. A party to the theatre was proposed. Kean was to play one of his most admired characters. To Lady Emma his performance was not new; but Caroline had never seen him before. She sat all mute attention, fearing to lose a word he uttered, or miss a gesture he assumed. The play was *Othello*, and the fate of the innocent Desdemona beguiled the ladies of their tears.

"Ah, this indeed is acting," said Caroline, as the curtain dropped. "I never could have supposed the scenic art had arrived at such superlative perfection."

"I have enjoyed your distress, young ladies," said a gentleman present, "because I perceived you properly appreciated both the powers of the actor and the beauties of the bard."

The time between the play and the after-piece was passed in conversation; Lord Millford entertained Caroline, and Montague availed himself of the opportunity to caution Lady Emma against the parties that were likely to be formed at Mrs. Pembroke's. Their plan of correspondence, too, was settled. As all parties were differently situated to what they were at the death of Lady Acrimony, he thought it prudent to acquaint Lord Millford, in confidence, that his sister had promised him to be a regular correspondent. This Lady Emma did not object to.

After sitting out the first act, they returned to Portland-place. Lord Millford's carriage set Montague down at the hotel where he had lodged since his arrival in London, Mrs. Pembroke not having offered him a residence in Bedford-square. Before they separated, Montague pressed Lord Millford to breakfast with him in the morning. This was agreed to.

"I shall see you once more, my dear Emma, before I quit London, which I intend doing to-morrow evening by the mail," said Montague.

She heaved a gentle sigh at the thoughts of his departure, and the carriage drove on. Neither the brother nor sister were inclined for conversation: she was thinking of Montague, and probably his lordship's thoughts were in Portland-place.

Lord Millford was punctual to his engagement, and Montague without reserve entered on the subject nearest his heart. Lord Millford was gratified at the confidence reposed in him, but observed that he had long ago penetrated their secret; and added,—

"I know no man living to whom I should so willingly resign my too sensitive sister. As you wish," he continued, "to keep your sentiments private till your return, I think it better that your letters to her should come enclosed to me; it will prevent the raillery she would otherwise be exposed to from Lady Lucy and the Newlands."

So considerate a proposal was thankfully acceded to by Montague. Lord Millford soon after departed for a morning ride, and his friend to the chambers of Sir Timothy's solicitor.

The visit to the duchess afforded matter for animadversion at Mrs. Pembroke's, principally as related to Lord Millford's acceptance of an invitation to such a dull party. This was Mrs. Pembroke's observation; but Lady Lucy shrewdly remarked, that it had doubtless been planned to oblige Lady Emma, who most likely met young Acrimony there.

"I meant to have invited him here to-day," said Mrs. Pembroke, "but he is so distant and formal, that really I do not know what to do with him."

"Nor anybody else but Millford and Lady Emma," rejoined her companion. "And really I think it very strange that your niece should allow him to be so constantly at her side, as he has not declared himself in form, I have been told, either to Mr. Newland or her brother; it may prevent her from receiving offers much superior to any he can propose making. I wonder you do not point out to her the impropriety of encouraging him. I think he is always here."

"But he is going to Ireland, you know," said Mrs. Pembroke; "and during his absence it is likely that Lady Emma may be some one else's that we may persuade her to accept; for I really neither like the baronet nor his son."

"And I am much mistaken," replied Lady Lucy, "if they have any regard for you."

The entrance of Lady Emma ended the dialogue. A large party was expected in the evening, and the two elder ladies were engaged in much important conversation connected with it, in which Lady Emma took no part; but the entrance of Montague, dressed for his journey, aroused her attention. Forgetful of forms, she arose and met him with an open palm, saying,—

"Then you are going, Montague."

He took the offered hand, and, conducting her to a chair, seated himself beside her.

"Where is Millford, I wonder," cried Mrs. Pembroke. "I suppose you wish to see him as well as Lady Emma?"

"Certainly," he replied; "I came to bid adieu to both my friends."

Lady Lucy looked angry. Mrs. Pembroke was not pleased, and pettishly answered,—

"Then you do not include me in the number."

"I did not know, madam, that you would allow me to do so," was the reply to this. No answer was returned. Lord Millford soon after made his appearance, Montague then bade the ladies good morning. A gentle pressure of the hand accompanied his adieu to Lady Emma. A tear started from her eye as it followed him from the drawing-room. As the door closed, Lady Lucy cried,—

"He is gone, child; don't fret; he will come back, no doubt, a true and faithful Corydon, to confer on you the high honour of being nurse extraordinary to the old peevish baronet at the grove."

"I wish for no higher honour," said Lady Emma, "however ridiculous such a wish may appear to your ladyship; and, if Sir Timothy would accept of my company, I would return to the grove, and continue with him during his son's absence."

"And for life too, perhaps," returned her ladyship.

"That is an unfair inference, Lady Lucy."

"But a very natural one," was the answer, "for it is not possible you can love that old man but for his own sake."

"It is time to dress for dinner," said Mrs. Pembroke, "I am weary of so much prosing; Emma, you must study the graces at the toilet, or you will be eclipsed to-night by a brilliant luminary: the dowager Countess of Maybank has accepted an invitation I sent her only this morning, though she has a hundred invitations on her hands."

"I aim at no competition," replied her ladyship; "the countess may shine unenvied by me." So saying, she retired.

"The girl is certainly in love," cried Lady Lucy, "she must be diverted from such a childish attachment."

"She is so romantic," replied Mrs. Pembroke, "that I absolutely despair of ever seeing her a woman of fashion; and so fascinated with that girl in Portland-place, that I really think I had better get the duchess to take her with her into the Highlands."

"No, no," replied Lady Lucy, "we must contrive to divert her from such ridiculous notions of friendship as those she has imbibed at the grove. If Lady Acrimony had lived, I dare say, she would have been Montague's wife; but, as it is, something better may be done for her."

The evening was a very brilliant one, and everybody but Lady Emma in high spirits. The countess paid particular attention to her, and she could not but confess that she possessed, to a very high degree, the power of pleasing.

The Newlands, too, were there, and Mrs. Pembroke had the pleasure to see her rooms delightfully crowded. Lord Millford was in high spirits; he had always admired the countess, but had never before enjoyed the pleasure of her society. Her person was commanding, her manners elegant, and her face without being regularly beautiful, was unique and pleasing; this, with a certain archness in her eye, that seemed to denote at once vivacity and good-humour, rendered her an object of attraction whenever she appeared. Lord Millford was charmed with her, and we are not certain that Caroline was not for a time forgotten.

Captain Newland singled out Lady Emma, whom he greatly distressed by his unmeaning professions and unnecessary compliments; to avoid listening to his voluble effusions she sat down to cards; the stake was high, and she lost considerably, nor did she leave the table till her purse was nearly empty. Colonel Diniver and the countess were the winners.

"You shall take your revenge another evening," said the countess. "I never play but for amusement, and seldom win. This is all Diniver's luck, I have nothing to do with it."

This was the first time Lady Emma had lost any sum sufficient to make her uneasy; she had forfeited her word to Montague the first night of his departure; for she had promised him not to play deep. Lord Harry Hazard had been her partner, and, in spite of her incautious nature, she more than once observed him look very suspicious towards the countess, yet she thought it was impossible that a woman of her rank could take any advantage in play. As soon as the rooms cleared, she hurried to her own room, dissatisfied with the evening's amusement, and more so with herself.

To avoid prolixity, we shall briefly observe that, in the house where Mrs. Pembroke presided, it was impossible to avoid play. Lady Emma was cautious, at least she thought so, but ridicule and importunity frequently overcame her resolutions, and she became the dupe of those whose business it was to deceive.

Lord Millford, too, was constant at the club houses, and other fashionable places of resort, and seldom saw his sister but at breakfast, or in a crowd. Lady Emma's only solace was now and then passing a morning in Portland-place, where she had more than once unexpectedly met her brother. The first time he had called to invite the duchess and Caroline to the theatre, the next with tickets for a masquerade, and the third with some new music. It was singular, Lady Emma thought, he had not named to her his intention of calling there; but, at all events, she was happy to see him in such rational society. Her own unpleasant situation she slightly glanced at, and as the duchess was already acquainted with the exact situation she was in with Montague—for Lord Millford had confirmed, rather incautiously, in conversation, the surmises her grace had before entertained on that subject—she, therefore, delicately cautioned Lady Emma carefully to avoid any application for money being made to Sir Timothy.

"You know his eccentricities, my dear lady," she added, "and do not, for your own sake, and that of your absent friend, be drawn into any altercation with him."

"That is the very thing I fear," replied Lady Emma, "for I am sadly importuned, both by Mrs. Pembroke and Lady Lucy, to write to him for a thousand pounds."

"Assuredly," cried her grace, in evident surprise, "your debts of honour do not require so large a supply."

"Not exactly," she answered, "but my aunt is so embarrassed with the people that fitted up and almost new furnished her suite of rooms, that I have promised them some money to keep them quiet."

"Oh, this is what Mr. Acrimony feared," said Caroline ; "what a loss to you was his excellent mother."

"An irreparable one, indeed," she replied, with a heartfelt sigh. "But a very few months," she added, "will leave me at liberty to choose my own residence."

"I trust whatever the change may be," said the duchess, "that you will, as soon as possible, emancipate yourself from such a dangerous set. If I had the means," continued her grace, "I would advance you the money; but this long and expensive lawsuit has left me too poor to serve you ; but come to us whenever you can, without incurring the censure of Mrs. Pembroke for deserting her parties. I do not like," she continued, "this gay countess ; her character is not so unexceptionable as it should be : guard against her seeming artlessness ; it is only a mask ; on no account form any intimacy with her—she is a dangerous woman."

Lady Emma thanked the duchess for her friendly caution, and the visit ended.

If it had not been for Caroline's anxiety on her friend's account, she would have been more happy than at any former period of her life. Treated with unaffected kindness and good nature, she met with no proud display of superiority, as her grace supported her rank with real dignity ; and to those she valued, it was blended with so much ease and evenness of temper, as rendered every one she associated with happy in her society. Her establishment was small, but well regulated, her visitors few, but select ; for they consisted of men of sense, and women of character ; and her amusements were those of a firm and cultivated mind. With such a friend, the mind of Caroline expanded ; her talents were admired and cultivated. With the duchess she frequented the theatres, the opera, and public concerts, by which her taste in music was infinitely improved. As the duchess gave no public entertainments, she had not accepted the invitations sent her by either Mrs. Newland or Mrs. Pembroke, who were contending with each other for crowded rooms ; nor would she, on any account, have mixed with their parties, after finding her favourite entirely overlooked ; for no card came for Caroline. A few ceremonious visits, or rather calls, passed between them, when her grace could not miss observing the cold neglect with which Caroline was treated by Mrs Newland, and those who wished to flatter her prejudices, or court her favour. On such occasions, she invariably convinced them by her manner that she considered her companion their equal.

Mr. Newland was frequently in Portland-place, and as his visits were those of business only, Caroline was seldom present. In the course of their conversations, the duchess had named to him a wish she entertained, that the marquis, her son-in-law, might obtain the dormant title.

"It was the intention," she added, "of my dear husband, to have brought the business forward ; but death prevented him from doing it."

Mr. Newland, entered heartily into the business ; he knew the full importance of Scottish influence, and how many snug nominations might be annexed to a dukedom ; he, therefore, inquired minutely into the family genealogy, and listened with deep attention to her grace's account of the family tree, with all its bearings ; and, finding that the marquis was a collateral branch of it, he advised that the application should be made without delay ; part of the estates had escheated to the crown, as the late duke died without heirs male ; the remainder was vested in the marchioness. The castle and estate round it, which was of vast dimensions, would likewise be lost to the family at the decease of the duchess.

"These things do not admit of delay," he said ; "it is yet early in the session, the business may be brought forward immediately by petition to the upper house, where I have many friends, who I am sure would support it.'

The duchess was delighted ; she had always thought Mr. Newland a most able civilian ; but she then considered him as a friendly and sensible man. And why ? Because he supported her ruling passion, family pride ; and even her firm mind was not on this subject proof against his artifice. He suggested the necessity there would be for the marquis to be present, and secure all the interest he could in a certain quarter, before the question was brought forward.

" Such an appendage as an ancient dukedom," he observed, " should not be lost for want of exertion. Let the marquis come forward," he added, "his claim is undeniable ; and as he has a large family, he is in duty bound to obtain for them the possessions of their ancestors."

The duchess, by his advice, wrote immediately to the marquis, and offered to

No. 8.

provide him a furnished house against his arrival, as she supposed he would be accompanied by the marchioness and part of their family.

His answer threw her into great perplexity, for he signified his intentions of taking up his abode in Portland-place.

" I wish," he wrote, " to avoid all possible expense ; therefore, I shall leave my family at home under the care of my sister, Lady Matilda. The marchioness and Lady Rachel, with their woman, and my own valet, are all that will accompany me. I propose travelling in my own carriage, about fifty miles into England ; I shall then dismiss it, and come post to London."

This letter was received one morning while she was taking her chocolate with Caroline, who instantly observed the vexation on her countenance ; the duchess did not leave her long in suspense as to its cause.

" My dear lassie," she said, " this letter has sadly deranged my plans ; read it, and tell me where I shall place you during the residence of the marquis's family here. Lady Rachel is a maiden sister of the marquis's, very formal, and by no means amiable in her temper. I cannot propose to her the occupying a part of your apartment, and I have no other to offer her."

Caroline did read the letter, and replacing it on the table, remained silent.

" This is what I did not anticipate," said the duchess. " I thought the marquis would not have obtruded on my small establishment, yet so situated on my daughter's account, I can raise no objections." After a pause, she added, " Should you like to return to Mrs. Bellamy's for a few months? I will take upon myself to defray all the expenses attendant on your residence there."

Caroline looked her gratitude, and taking the hand of the duchess between both her own, said,—" Dispose of me, my dear madam, as you please, only do not let my presence either interfere with the harmony or comfort of your family."

" Well," said the duchess, " we have time enough on our hands to arrange this business, for you see they will not commence their journey till the latter end of May, so we have nearly a month good, and, I think, to avoid giving offence, Mrs. Newland must be consulted."

Caroline looked a little uneasy.

" Do not be alarmed," said the duchess, " she will not invite you to Grosvenor-square."

" I neither wish nor expect it," Caroline replied ; " but I am sorry to be any additional expense to your grace ; yet, except my dear Lady Emma, I would rather be under an obligation to you than any other person living."

" It will be no obligation, my dearest lassie," returned the duchess ; " and I grieve that there should be any necessity for our separation."

The entrance of Lord Millford, who was become a frequent visitor, ended the subject. He came with cards for a concert that was to be given at the Countess of Maybank's elegant villa at Highgate. The duchess declined the offer, saying she was engaged that night for a party to the Opera.

Lord Millford looked disappointed, but replied,—

" Perhaps Miss Mellbourne is not so engaged."

" In my parties," said the duchess, with strong emphasis, " she is always included."

He shortened his visit ; but not before he had inquired if they passed that evening at home.

The duchess answered that they were going to hear Miss Stephens sing in one of her most celebrated characters.

In the evening, soon after the curtain drew up, the duchess and Caroline, attended by a Scotch gentleman, were seated in a centre box ; and, within a quarter of an hour, Lord Millford, who was with a party on the other side of the theatre, joined them, and his attentions to Caroline were too particular to escape observation. The party he had quitted levelled their glasses without mercy at Caroline, and, among them, he pointed out to her the much-admired countess.

When the curtain dropped, the duchess retired. Lord Millford conducted her to the carriage, and almost at the moment, Lord Harry Hazard, who had sat in an adjoining box, offered his hand to Caroline.

During their ride home, the duchess seemed lost in thought; and Caroline was occupied in musing upon the occurr ...ces of the evening. On their arrival in Portland-place, Colonel Frazier, who had been their escort, produced something like conversation by his remarks on the performance of the evening, and observations on the company at the theatre.

"*Apropos*," said the duchess, "I think you know something of the old Earl of Maybank."

"Oh! I know him for a foolish old dotard," he replied; "he ought to have divorced that woman eleven years years ago; but he contented himself with a separation, that left her a handsome allowance. Since his decease, she has married an Irish officer, whose name covers her irregularities. It is well known that neither her jointure or his fortune could support the extravagant style they live in; and it is generally supposed play makes up the deficiencies. Lady O'Leary," he added, "is distantly related to the parties."

Caroline sighed as she thought of the dissipated set her friend could not avoid mixing with, and the duchess very severely commented on the imprudence of Lady Lucy, in introducing a woman of at least doubtful character into the parties at Mrs. Pembrook's.

The following morning Lord Millford again appeared in Portland-place; he continued during breakfast, which he partook of, and told them Lady Emma would call before dinner.

After he left them, the duchess rather abruptly inquired of Caroline if his lordship had ever made her any serious proposals.

Caroline coloured and trembled as she answered in the negative.

"He has never in any way explained himself then?" said the duchess.

"Never," replied Caroline.

"Then it is high time he did," returned her grace; "for his attentions have fixed the eyes of envy and curiosity upon you. He is too dangerous a man to be suffered thus to glide insensibly, as it seems, into your heart, to rob you of your peace. He is free to choose, has no one to consult, evidently prefers her to every other woman, and yet he is silent. I think he is superior to the meanness of male coquetting; and yet I have heard it whispered that he is much devoted to the countess."

"But the countess is a married lady," said Caroline.

"And therefore the more dangerous, if an imprudent one," replied the duchess; "and I assure you," she added, "my thoughts have been for these last few days occupied on this subject. Shall I speak to his lordship, and——"

"Not for worlds, dear duchess," cried Caroline, interrupting her. "I will go less into public; I will avoid him here if you think I should do so; but I am not so visionary as to suppose he entertains one serious thought of me."

"Then his behaviour is ill calculated to impress the same opinion on others," replied the duchess.

A long conversation followed, in which her grace delicately hinted that she thought family pride kept Lord Millford silent. "Fortune," she added, "is, to generous minds, only a secondary consideration; but the want of birth and family is rarely overlooked."

Caroline was silent, for she felt the full force of the duchess's observation, and mentally resolved to remove herself from the dangerous pinnacle on which she thought the caprice of fortune had so unexpectedly placed her.

Before dinner Lady Emma called. Letters had arrived from Ireland; Montague described the affairs there to be in such a state of derangement as to require his continuance there much longer than had been expected. "But this," she added, "is not the only piece of bad news. Mrs. Newland has received a most unexpected shock, though she carries it off admirably."

"Of what kind?" said the duchess.

Lady Emma then explained that Mr. Newport had been for some time privately married, and the birth of a son had been announced in the morning papers of that day.

"Does it affect their fortune?" inquired the duchess.

"Lady Lucy says not," replied her visitor; "but Lord Harry says otherwise; at all events it has wounded their pride, for fame reports the lady to be of low origin, and the marriage would never have been named if the birth of the child had not been announced. When Lady Lucy laid down the paper," continued Lady Emma, Aunt Pembroke said she must instantly go to Mrs. Newland's. 'To congratulate your dear friend on the birth of her nephew?' cried Millford. 'Assuredly not,' she answered, 'that would be to insult her, and you cannot suppose I wish to distress her; no, I should only inquire if the news were true and whom he had married.' 'I can satisfy your curiosity on those points,' said Lady Lucy. 'She was a tallow-chandler's widow, who left her, it is said, a tolerable income. The parties met at Margate last summer; they lodged in the same house; the lady was good-humoured; played a good game at cribbage, which the old man is very fond of; in short he wanted a companion, and she wanted a home, and so it was very natural that they should agree to live together. Newport sent Mrs. Newland a letter immediately after his nuptials, which I understand was very distantly answered, and since then there has been no intercourse between them.' 'Very odd,' replied Aunt Pembroke; 'but I think the old man has done right for he was strangely neglected among them, and as they have no pretensions to family themselves, I do not see how his marriage can disgrace them.' 'Not disgrace them!' replied Lady Lucy. 'It is impossible for Mrs. Newland to acknowledge such a low woman.' 'And why not?' answered the other. 'It is well known that Newland was only old Goosequill's clerk; and I have heard an old friend of mine say Mrs. Newland was once an actress. I never inquired the particulars, but people will talk.' 'Mrs. Newland is certainly a well-educated woman,' said Lady Lucy, who was determined not to give up the point. 'Superficial, I believe,' cried Mrs. Pembroke. 'Perfectly self-possessed at all times,' said the other.' 'Aye, that is all acquired by practice,' said Aunt Pembroke. 'She certainly is very ladylike in her manners,' retorted Lady Lucy. 'A perfect actress at all times,' cried Millford; 'but hitherto it must be admitted she has played her part well.' 'Sans doute,' said aunt; and 'adieu' said I, weary of the dialogue."

Lady Emma that morning was in particular good spirits, having received a most satisfactory letter from Ireland. Her visit concluded, the ladies retired to dress. Caroline had named to her friend that the arrival of the marquis and his lady would occasion her removal from Portland-place, and that she hoped to return, for a few months, to Mrs. Bellamy, if Mrs. Newland made no objection.

"I do not think that likely," replied her ladyship, "but I would rather you came to Bedford-square."

Caroline did not reply, but she perceived that if the invitation were given, which was very improbable, that it would be imprudent for her to accept it. When Caroline was alone, she fell into a very unpleasant train of thought. The attentions of Lord Millford, and the friendship of his sister, had given rise to some expectations—some hopes that had gained imperceptibly on her heart. These feelings she had never attempted to analyse, till the questions of the duchess, like the spear of Ithuriel, showed all things as they were. "I must," she said, mentally, "fly from his fascinating but dangerous society. Perhaps Lord Millford has already discovered the pleasure his presence inspires, and presuming on my partiality, is trifling with my peace. Oh, if the duchess had spoken to him on the subject, how contemptible must I have appeared in his opinion. He must have laughed at my folly, or ridiculed my presumption." The thought of either was painful. "True," said she, "was the observation made by the duchess, that men of rank seldom marry their inferiors."

Pale and languid, she joined the duchess at dinner. This change was not unobserved by one who had her interest so much at heart, and Caroline was too candid to conceal the cause of her inquietude.

"I aim," she said, "at no competition with the rich or great; and, though greatly obliged by your grace's condescension, I must feel moving in a sphere where I intrude on the pleasures of others, at the hazard of my own repose."

CHAPTER VIII.

Good name in man or woman dear, my lord,
Is the immediate jewel of their souls.
Who steals my purse steals trash, 'tis something, nothing.
'Twas mine, 'tis his, and has been slave to thousands;
But he that filches from me my good name,
Robs me of that which not enriches him,
And makes me poor indeed.—SHAKSPERE.

"With the permission of your grace," said Caroline, "if Mrs. Newland does not object to it, I will instantly retire to Mrs. Bellamy's."

The duchess looked uneasy, but after a pause, she added,—

"Much as I shall regret parting with you, my own dear lassie, I do not see anything at present so likely to insure tranquillity to you. The last time," she added, "that Mr. Newland was here, though generally taciturn on all subjects but those immediately under discussion, he hinted at Lord Millford's recent losses, both at play and on the turf, which he said nothing but a prudent marriage could repair. Thus, you may perceive, that his lordship's dissipation will prevent him from marrying any woman without fortune, however great her merit."

Caroline sighed.

"I will see Nrs. Newland," she continued, "and explain my reasons for our temporary separation, and tell her I mean to place you at Mrs. Bellamy's on my own account."

Tears of gratitude started to the eyes of Caroline, as she thanked her noble friend for all the consideration she had shown her.

In the evening Lord Millford called. He seemed out of spirits, but pressed Caroline to accept a ticket for a masquerade that was to be given at the Argyle Rooms.

"And who is Miss Mellbourne to go with?" said the duchess.

"With Mrs. Pembroke and my sister," he added.

"Before Miss Mellbourne decides on going, she must see Lady Emma," said her grace.

"Lord Millford did not reply, and shortly after took leave. Within a few days the duchess called on Mrs. Newland, and fortunately found her disengaged. The motive of her visit was instantly explained. Mrs. Newland appeared quite satisfied with the proposal of Caroline's returning to Mrs. Bellamy's, and said she would call on that lady, and prepare her for Caroline's return to her.

After the departure of her visitor, she sent for Lady Lucy, who was her principal confidante, and advised with her on the subject.

"On no account let her go to Bellamy's," said that wily woman; "the duchess will only place her there as a visitor, or parlour boarder; and she will, through Lady Emma and the duchess, be more seen than ever."

"That I was thinking of," replied the other; perhaps she may invited to Bedford-square."

"That I will guard against," said Lady Lucy, "and fortunately Mrs. Pembroke talks of spending a week or ten days at old Windsor. We will get Lady Emma out of town, while you dispose of Caroline in the best way you can."

"We must talk more on this subject another time," said Mrs. Newland, "I will see Mrs. Bellamy myself to-morrow, and give her my directions in what manner to act, should the duchess call on her."

"We have heard with surprise how very frequent Lord Millford's visits have been in Portland-place. I am quite surprised the duchess has not observed the impropriety of it ; nor has she, I am well informed, accepted an invitation the whole season to any party, where her favourite was not included."

"Oh, I know all that, and much more," replied the other.

"I really was fearful some time ago that he would have made the girl serious offers, which, no doubt, the old Highland dowager would gladly have promoted. I thought our dear Augusta would have fainted the other night when he left us at the Opera, to join the duchess's party of formal old quizzes ; but I rallied him the other morning so unmercifully, that I do not think he will be so ridiculous as to leave us again ; besides, I introduced the countess for no other purpose than to draw him off from Caroline."

"It may be a dangerous expedient," replied Mrs. Newland, "for if it should proceed further than is anticipated, the damages may be heavy ; and his lordship is already tolerably embarrassed."

"Pho !" replied Lady Lucy, "you startle at chimeras ; the general would get but a few thousands from him. I could whisper some anecdotes to the councillor that would make the damages comparatively nothing."

"But the countess is your relation," said Mrs. Newland.

"True ; but am I not your friend?" replied Lady Lucy, "and wish for nothing more than to see the forehead of our dear Augusta encircled with the Millford coronet on which I know she has set her heart."

"Well, I will leave it all to you," replied Mrs. Newland ; "he cannot marry the countess, and I will place Caroline out of his way."

"And I will tell the countess of the formal rivalship she has to encounter," said Lady Lucy, "and this will set her upon keeping Millford constantly engaged. She is the very woman to do it ; very tenacious of conquest ; and a perfect Cleopatra in art ; she can be, by turns, grave and gay, either prude or coquette, whichever character best suits her purpose ; and equally herself in all. I shall not tell that foolish woman, Mrs. Pembroke, that I have been here. You can call and hear if Lady Emma (who, doubtless, is acquainted with the movement expected,) has made any proposals for the girl's coming to Bedford-square ; ad I will say what I think necessary on the occasion."

On this the ladies parted ; and on the following morning, Mrs. Newland drove to Mrs. Bellamy's, and in a very plausible strain informed her of the duchess's intention respecting Caroline. "Now," she added, "nothing could afford me more pleasure than her return to you ; but perhaps it would in some degree affect the order of your establishment ; for I think the duchess would expect that she might be allowed to visit public places, or pay morning visits with her, when she chose to call here, or send for her to Portland-place ; and this is what I cannot approve. I have other reasons, too, that shall be nameless, for I do not wish to prejudice any one against her."

She paused, but Mrs. Bellamy did not reply, for she did not know what to say.

"I have," continued Mrs. Newland, "thought it would be better to send her out of town for a few months, you know she is fond of the country." Mrs. Belamy bowed her assent. "And not to offend the duchess, who is very partial to her, I must make use of your name on the occasion." Mrs. Bellamy looked surprised. "Do not be alarmed," said Mrs. Newland ; "I only mean to say that your establishment is full, but that as soon as you have a vacancy, you will let me know ; and, should the duchess either call or send here, I must request you will confirm what I have said. Observe, you must not deceive me."

It was not Mrs. Bellamy's interest to offend Mrs. Newland, who had, to gratify her own vanity, undertaken to patronise Mrs. Bellamy's establishment; and she had then several ladies of rank under her care, placed there by Mrs. Newland's recommendation. She, therefore, bowed an assent, and that lady returned to her carriage.

Her next visit was to Bedford-square; where, as if by chance, she mentioned the subject.

"Oh, I remember," said Mrs. Pembroke, "that my niece did say something to me about it the other morning; but I do not think she told me why the duchess wanted to part with her."

"Oh, she says it is because her son-in-law, the marquis, and his lady are coming to London," said Mrs. Newland; "it was not anticipated, when she took Caroline, but, I surmise, she finds that the girl has presumed too much on her condescension. She is very proud, though she conceals it under a great deal of artifice."

"Very likely," returned Mrs. Pembroke; "but Millford and his sister both think her the most artless of human beings. I cannot say I ever liked her after she refused to waltz. Such a girl should have exerted herself to have entertained the company whether she liked or disliked what was required."

"That is exactly my idea," said Mrs. Newland; "and, indeed, her coming there at all quite perplexed me, and vexed poor Augusta."

"Oh, I know that," cried Mrs. Pembroke; "but what do you mean to do with her?"—then, not waiting for an answer, she added,—"She is vastly admired, perhaps you may get her married in a short time."

"I know of no one," replied Mrs. Newland, "unless she can draw Lord Millford into her snares. You know how frequent a visitor he has been in Port-land-place."

"Lord Millford," cried Mrs. Pembroke, indignantly; "why, I am sure she cannot have the presumption to think he will make her a countess."

"I cannot answer for what she may presume on," replied the other. "I have heard many observations made on his attentions to her."

"Pho," cried Mrs. Pembroke, "he is only trifling with her; but, to prevent the poor girl from getting laughed at, I think you had better send her out of the way."

"Mrs. Bellamy's house is full," replied the other, "or I would have placed her there."

"Oh, that will never do," cried Mrs. Pembrooke, "for Lady Emma would desert me and go there too. Why don't you send her to Mr. Newport's? She might amuse his wife, and play with the child."

"Oh, such a proposal would distress Mr. Newport," replied Mrs. Newland "besides, he has lately taken no share in any expenses incurred on her account."

"Very strange," cried Mrs. Newport; "though not more so than his marriage, which I think must have been a great mortification to you."

To this observation Mrs. Newland did not reply, but said with an air of indifference, "If Lady Emma should invite her here, it would appear ill-natured in me to make any objection."

"Oh, I shall not sanction any such thing," cried the other; "besides Lady Lucy does not like her, and it would not be agreeable to my own feelings to offend her; but why not take her to Grosvenor-square?"

"Why, Augusta does not like her, and, in short, girls so situated are exposed to many dangers."

"Well," said Mrs. Newland, having effected all she wanted, "I think I will send her to the manor. There she will be safer; but I shall give strict orders that no company be admitted."

"Do so, by all means, and the sooner the better."

Mrs. Newland concluded her visit, and Mrs. Pembroke retired to her toilet.

At dinner Lady Lucy observed that the Scotch duchess was tired of her toad-eater.

"Oh, that I expected would be the case," cried an ill-natured old lady who was present : "these handsome girls, when noticed by the men, are so insufferably vain and presuming."

"But the duchess is not tired of her, if it is Miss Mellbourne that your lady-ship alludes to," replied Lady Emma.

"Who else should it be?" answered Mrs. Pembroke.

"I suppose they will take her to Grosvenor-square for the remainder of the season," said the old lady, who had spoken before."

"No, no," said Lady Lucy, sneeringly, "Mrs. Newland has had enough of her pride and ingratitude."

"She will not go there ; she is going to the manor," cried Mrs. Pembroke.

"To assist the housekeeper." added Lady Lucy.

"Contemptible meanness," cried Lord Millford, when raising his eyes, he met the reproving glance of the countess, who sat opposite him, and had observed the colour mount to his face as Caroline was spoken of.

"Well, what can Mrs. Newland do better than send her out of the way? for I think girls without either fortune or connections should not be allowed to obtrude on the society of their superiors," said Mrs. Pembroke.

"I do not know where Caroline's superiors are to be found," replied Lady Emma.

"Oh, in heaven, I suppose," retorted Lady Lucy. "They cannot be expected to exist among such mere mortals as we are."

Lord Millford looked uneasy.

"Do, my lord," said the countess, "oblige me with the wing of that chicken," pointing to one that stood near him, "and let me recommend a merry-thought to you ; you seem in want of one."

This sally completely roused Lord Millford, and the conversation took a different turn. A party to the play was proposed, and immediately agreed to. But Mrs. Pembroke stipulated that they should return, and spend the evening in Bedford-square.

On their arrival at the theatre, they found themselves in the next box to the duchess ; Caroline, and some other ladies recently arrived from the north, were with her, to whom an English theatre was a novelty, at least in dimensions and decorations. Their remarks on it were made in the dialect of their native country, which, being overheard by the countess and Lady Lucy, occasioned them infinite amusement. Indeed, those ladies did not restrain their mirth within the rules of good breeding; for they often laughed so loud as to disturb those who had met to hear others, and not be heard themselves. Caroline was uneasy, and the duchess looked displeased. To add to her vexation, she saw the Newlands in an opposite direction ; and the gentlemen of their party, among whom was the captain, and some other military heroes, without mercy directed their glasses towards the duchess's box.

Lady Emma was so much distressed at the observation the behaviour of her companions had excited—for all eyes were turned to that part of the house—that she sat languid and nearly silent during the representation of the play. To speak to either her grace or Caroline was impossible, for the countess and Lady Lucy had so placed themselves that they occupied the seats next to the duchess and her party. A friendly nod and a curtsey were, therefore, all that passed.

Lord Millford did not enjoy the mirth of his companions ; for he was evidently displeased at it. The play was that truly laughable comedy, *A Cure for the Heartache*. The character of Jessy gave scope for the ill-natured mirth of Lady Lady, who, at the conclusion, said loud enough to be overheard by those it was intended for—"So much for sentimentality—the toad-eater and the tailor are properly paired." Poor Caroline, who had endeavoured to be occupied with the piece, but had not been able to keep her thoughts from wandering to the next box, now turned sick at heart. She felt the insulting illusion, and, faint and giddy, would have fallen back, had not one of the ladies supported her while a gentleman of their party applied restoratives."

"Open the door," cried the duchess, in an angry tone, as she darted a look of scornful indignation towards the countess and Lady Lucy ; " the dear girl is dying for want of air."

The door was instantly opened by Lord Millford himself. Two gentlemen of the duchess's party had raised Caroline from her seat, and were supporting her against the side of the box, while the company behind separated as much as possible to admit a circulation of air. The house being crowded to excess, and the heat very oppressive, many ladies were about to retire, and the lobby was completely full. Lady Emma tried in vain to make her way to her friend ; in the meantime Lord Millford had taken the lovely and almost lifeless form of Caroline from the

No. 9.

gentleman nearest to him, and supported her in his arms. The duchess became extremely embarrassed; she could not let Caroline retire alone, and did not wish to break up her party, the ladies of which had promised themselves much pleasure, from hearing some favourite singers in the after-piece. As the air was admitted, Caroline gradually recovered; but on finding by whom she was supported, the deepest tints of vermillion flushed on her before colourless cheek; and with all the strength she could assume, she begged of the duchess leave to return home, and one of the elder gentlemen offered to attend her; this was gladly accepted. She took his offered arm, and assisted by Lord Millford was led or rather carried from the house. The Moncrieff carriage had not been ordered till eleven, but Lord Millford's chariot was already arrived; in that she was placed, while he in the hurry of the moment obeyed the impulse of inclination, and having placed her in the carriage with the gentleman on one side, and himself on the other, ordered it to Portland-place, where, having resigned her to the care of an attendant, with an "I shall see you in the morning," he hurried back to the theatre, where his absence had given rise to many ill-natured observations, particularly from Lady Lucy, who said loud enough to be heard by the duchess, "that the girl's fainting was all affectation, merely to excite attention."

Lord Millford, on his return, was very coolly received by the countess, who, addressing Mrs. Pembroke, expressed a wish of retiring.

Lady Emma, really indisposed through heat and vexation, warmly seconded the proposal; and the party, to the great relief of the duchess, quitted the theatre, but not before Lord Millford had informed the duchess that he should do himself the honour of calling in the morning to inquire after the health of Miss Millbourne. To this she only bowed an answer; angry as the countess had appeared to be, she allowed Lord Millford to hand her to his own carriage; and to the surprise of all but Lady Lucy, they did not arrive in Bedford-square till the card-tables were nearly full.

"Bless me," cried Mrs. Pembroke, on their entrance, "where can you have been?"

"Oh," returned the countess, with perfect *sang froid*, "the stupid coachman mistook the orders, and would actually have driven to Highgate, if my footman, who was behind, had not discovered the mistake."

Lord Millford, if he had chosen, could have given a better account of their absence, but he was silent; the lady was, or appeared to be, in perfect good humour, and Mrs. Pembroke, too much occupied with her cards to make any comment, dropped the subject.

Lady Lucy, who was engaged in another part of the room, took no notice of their entrance; nor was it till after supper that she exerted her satirical talents at the expense of the duchess and her party.

Lord Millford said but little, though he inwardly execrated her ill-nature; but Lady Emma, sensibly wounded at the sarcasms that were cast on the duchess and her party, could not restrain her indignation; the tears trembled in her eyes as she said,—

"I wish, Lady Lucy, that you would, when I am present, spare my friends."

"Wit," said Lord Millford, "is at all times a dangerous talent, and not unfrequently an ill-natured one."

"Pho," said the countess.

> " Let satire still go free ;
> To her 'tis pleasure, and no pain to me.
> Nor would I wish to stop that harmless dart
> Which plays around, but cannot wound the heart."—CHURCHILL.

All again was good humour; most of the ladies fell into the usual train of cards or scandal, while Lord Millford circulated the bottle briskly among the gentlemen, who called loudly for his toast. Finding it was not to be evaded, he gave, "Miss Newland." It was drunk in bumpers; in short, it was a night of revelry, from which Lady Emma hastily retired. When the party broke up, which was not till daybreak, Lord Millford, who had, by the help of wine, kept up his spirits, conducted the countess to the carriage that had long been waiting for her, and then without returning to the ladies, retired to his own apartment.

About twelve the next morning Mrs. Newland called in Portland-place. Her daughter had informed her of what had passed the preceding evening at the theatre; a note from Lady Lucy stated more particulars, and ended with,—"Get the girl out of the way as soon as possible."

In consequence, she sat out for Portland-place, where, finding the duchess alone, she began by lamenting that Mrs. Bellamy's house was too full to admit of any increase at the present; but, on the first vacancy that occurred, she would receive Miss Millbourne. The duchess looked distressed, but did not reply.

"I have been thinking," she continued, "as Caroline is fond of the country, that she shall spend a few weeks at the manor."

Still the duchess was silent.

"I would invite her to Grosvenor-square," she added, "but your grace must perceive the impropriety of placing her in the very face of danger; for, as society is now formed, it is next to an impossibility for a young and lovely woman, unprotected and portionless, to escape the snares of one, and the envy of the other."

"Merit usually excites that baneful passion," replied the duchess, "nor do I wonder that Miss Millbourne is so cruelly assailed by it; but unprotected," she added, "she could not be, while under your care; and I most sincerely regret that the expected arrival of my family should have rendered a separation necessary. It will be," she added, "but for a few months at most, and, if my favourite should wish to quit the manor before Mrs. Bellamy can receive her, I hope no objection will be made to my placing her in some other suitable establishment."

To this proposal Mrs. Newland made no objection; she only said she thought the next day she could spare her own woman to attend Miss Millbourne, if the duchess could make it convenient to part with her so early.

"I must part with her," said the duchess, "and so your time shall be ours."

Mrs. Newland then set out for Mrs. Pembroke's, where we shall for the present leave her. When the duchess was alone, she pondered on the conversation, and, upon the whole, was not displeased that Caroline was going from the parties that met both at Mrs. Pembroke's and the Newlands. With the exception of Lady Emma and Lord Millford, there was not one amongst them that she esteemed; and it was because she did see that a residence in Grosvenor-square would be the place of danger for Caroline, that she coincided with Mrs. Newland on the propriety of removing her from London.

Caroline, who had not quite recovered the shock of the last evening, did not see the duchess till dinner, and was then informed by her of Mrs. Newland's plan. It was gratefully acceded to by Caroline, who longed for solitude. While they were conversing in perfect confidence, a note was brought from Lady Emma. It was most affectionately written. She regretted that she could not see her Caroline for several days,—

"For these troublesome people," she added, "are hurrying me off with them to old Windsor, and I have scarce a moment to call my own. I hope you will not have left town before my return, for I have very much to say to you." The occurrences of the last evening were named, with a degree of sorrow and regret. "I long to be freed," she added, "from these trifling and ill-natured people, now more than ever disagreeable to me in having offended our dear duchess, through distressing you. My perplexities, too, increase daily; but more of this another time."

"Oh, these harpies," cried the duchess, "they will strip that dear creature of half her fortune."

"I fear it will be so," replied Caroline, "unless Lord Millford should detect their artifices."

"And he is at present, I think," said the duchess, "in as much danger as his sister."

Caroline answered only with a sigh.

"Had the excellent Lady Acrimony lived," said the duchess, "all would have been different; but now I tremble both for her fortune and repose, for Lady Emma will never be happy while pursuing a life of dissipation. She has not fortitude to bear up against the tide of custom, and the influence of example. None but Sir Timothy can rescue her from the dangers that assail her."

"And he," replied Caroline, "has resigned her, inexperienced as she is, to the care of a woman he despises, and a world he hates."

"As this will, probably, be the last evening we shall spend together for some time," said the duchess, "music will chase away melancholy ideas; we will go alone to the Opera."

Caroline did not object, but proposed answering Lady Emma's note.

The duchess advised her not to say when she expected to quit London. "It will," she added, "distress her to know you are going so soon, and you can write from the manor a letter, to meet her on her return; and if you write confidentially, which doubtless you will, let it come enclosed in one to me, for I fear every artifice that can be adopted will be put in practice to injure you."

Caroline thanked her noble friend for her considerate caution, and it was finally agreed that the note should remain unanswered for the present.

On entering the Opera-house rather early in the evening, they observed the countess, and some young men of quality in a distant box, and instantly perceived that Lord Millford was of the party.

Caroline felt her heart beat, and could not think how to reconcile his appearance with the countess, to the anxiety he had expressed on her account only on the evening before.

The duchess anxiously watched her countenance (they were alone), and seemed to read her thoughts.

"My dear Caroline," said she, "this is a painful but, I trust, an useful lesson. Do not let even a look escape that can betray your feelings."

Caroline obeyed. The music was soothing, and the hurry of her spirits subsided.

At the conclusion, Lord Millford entered their box (his manner was rather hurried); he apologised for not calling in the morning, and said he had been engaged with Hazard till the hour of dining, (which was early, as the ladies had left town afterwards for old Windsor) he complimented Caroline on having recovered from her indisposition, and inquired if she was really going alone to the manor.

She replied in the affirmative.

"And how will you contrive to exist in the country? at a time, too, when all the world are in London."

"I am partial to the country," she replied, "at all seasons."

"And when do you go?"

"That," she answered, "depends upon Mrs. Newland."

"Then your journey will soon commence," he answered.

He had taken her fan, and hastily twirling it, one of the sticks snapped.

"This, I think," said he, "was a token of friendship."

"It was Lady Emma's gift," she said, "and as such I value it." So saying, she put out her hand to receive it.

"No," said he, putting it into his bosom. "This I shall keep as a memorial of friendship; you must, you will allow me to replace it with an emblem of love."

Their eyes met, the expression in his lordship's could not be mistaken. The colour mounted to the cheek of Caroline, but she did not reply.

"I shall not wait the conclusion," said the duchess, fearing the conversation would distress Caroline, and surmising truly that Lord Millford's spirits had been elevated by wine then taking the arm of Caroline, she left the theatre. Lord Millford followed to the carriage, and, bidding them adieu, returned to the countess.

"Ay, lassie," said the duchess, "the sooner you are from this vile town the better. I wish we were both at the old castle."

"So do I, dear lady," said Caroline.

On their return they found a note from Mrs. Newland, signifying that a post-chaise would be at the door at three o'clock the following morning, and desiring Caroline would be ready for her departure.

At the appointed time the chaise appeared, and Caroline's grateful heart seemed bursting at the thought of leaving her noble friend. The duchess, too, was much affected.

"Is your writing-desk well stored," said her grace; "for I shall expect plenty of letters, so, too, no doubt, will Lady Emma." Then putting a small pocket-book into the hands of Caroline, she added,—"Under any emergency, apply to me, my dear lassie, for either advice or assistance."

Caroline offered to kiss the extended hand, but the duchess opened her arms, pressed her to her bosom, and imprinted a kiss, almost maternal, on her cheek. Caroline, unable to speak, hurried to the chaise, her packages having been previously disposed of.

At the moment she was seated, Lord Millford made his appearance (he had been riding). He placed his hand on the side of the chaise, saying at the same time,—

"I am indeed surprised at this very sudden movement; are you alone?"

"No, my lord;"—Caroline looked up, and saw the duchess leaning against the window—"we keep the duchess standing, my lord."

He looked up, kissed his hand, and rode instantly away; at the same moment the chaise drove on.

Not a little mortified was his lordship at finding Caroline so speedily disposed of. He, however, consoled himself with thinking that he could make short excursions to the priory, and perhaps contrive to see her unknown to her vigilant gaoler, as he thought Mrs. Newland was inclined to be. His lordship did not stop to inquire if this would be either prudent or delicate conduct. It soothed a little petulance of temper that her departure had occasioned, and that for the present satisfied him. His first impulse was to ride forward and meet the chaise at the usual place for changing horses. Happily for Caroline this plan was interrupted by his sudden recollection of an appointment he had made with the countess, whom he was that evening to escort to old Windsor.

No interruption occurred on their journey, and they arrived at the manor before the close of the evening. The housekeeper there was prepared for their appearance, and tea was waiting for Caroline in a small parlour adjoining the library, to which she led the way.

Matley, Mrs. Newland's maid, delivered a letter to Bennet, and another to Caroline, and then returned to attend to the unloading of the chaise in which she was to return to London, in consequence all possible despatch was used. She stayed no longer than to take tea, and set forward for her journey.

After her departure Caroline opened her letter, and Bennet retired to read hers. Both were on one subject, and both related to the rules Mrs. Newland expected Caroline to abide by during her residence at the manor. She was not to receive nor pay visits of any kind, should any one be foolish enough to wish it, nor to correspond with any one unless she first acquainted Mrs. Newland with the name of the person she wished to hear from or write to. The first prohibition she willingly assented to, for there was no one likely to intrude on her solitude; but to be prevented from writing to, or hearing from, the duchess and Lady Emma was what she could not easily submit to.

Whatever might be the consequence, she resolved on acquainting the duchess with the strange restrictions Mrs. Newland had imposed on her; but how, circumstanced as she was, could she get a letter conveyed to the post-office, which was some miles distant. In this dilemma, though much against her inclination, she was necessitated to consult Mrs. Bennet.

"The order," she answered, "miss, is a strange one; but I fear disobliging Mrs. Newland by letting any letter go from hence; my orders on the subject are peremptory. Yet," she added, "one way, I think I can serve you, Mr. Meanwell sometimes calls here on his way to Firr Grove; have a letter in readiness, and trust to him for having it safely delivered."

Caroline thanked her for the suggestion, and promised to avail herself of it, when Mrs. Bennet added,—

"I have yet to inform you, miss, that I am to intercept all letters that come to you, and send them, unopened, to Mrs. Newland."

Caroline had been at the manor some days when this conversation passed.

"Have any letters come for me?" she added, in a tremulous tone, fearing that Lady Emma might have written.

"None," was the reply; "but the sooner you guard against this mandate the better."

So Caroline thought, and instantly penned a letter to the duchess, stating implicitly the restraints she was placed under, and leaving it to her in what manner to caution her dear friend against writing to her. In the evening Mr. Meanwell came, and Caroline suspected by invitation, though it seemed by chance. They took tea together. For to avoid giving trouble, Caroline had always taken her meals in Mrs. Bennet's apartment, who was a sensible, intelligent woman, and, in birth, much superior to the proud woman she served. During their social meal, the subject nearest the heart of Caroline was introduced, and Mr. Meanwell offered freely to serve her. She retired to close her letter, and requested that her grace would honour her with an answer, under cover to Mr. Meanwell, at the priory. This, to her, important subject settled, she returned to the parlour, where the conversation turned on Mr. Newport.

"I was on a visit," said Mrs. Bennet, "at Mrs. Newland's when he arrived with you there," speaking to Caroline.

"And how old did you think I then was?"

"We conjectured about four years. I left for Ireland a few days after your arrival. You were in a high fever, and your life despaired of. Mr. Newport was very anxious for your recovery; and I understand that he afterwards had a violent nervous fever, which left his faculties much impaired."

"He still continues much afflicted with it," said Mr. Meanwell, "and is now taking the benefit of sea air; but, the last time I saw him, he was better than usual. The birth of a son seems to have charmed away the blue devils. Did you ever hear the name of the vessel he came home in?" he inquired.

Mrs. Bennet replied she might have heard it, but, if so, it had escaped her memory.

There the conversation ended, and he soon after took his leave. After this Caroline's time passed very tranquilly. The spring had been particularly fine, and the summer was rapidly approaching. She enjoyed the beautiful scenery that surrounded the splendid mansion she inhabited, and congratulated herself on the quiet she had obtained in it. She heard from Mrs. Bennet that Sir Timothy seldom went out, and Dr. Maxwell, whom she had once or twice seen, was, she believed, still at the grove.

"Ah," thought Caroline, "what a change has a few months made in all our prospects!"

The library was open to her, so was the music-room, and if Caroline was not happy, she was, at least, contented. Sometimes the thought of Lady Emma's perplexities would cloud her brow, and cause a tear of sympathy, perhaps not unmixed with solicitude, for the welfare of Lord Millford; but she carefully repressed every aspiring hope, and checked every fond recollection. Yet still some uneasy thoughts would rise connected with her future prospects. It was then late in May, and in July the family was expected to arrive at the manor; but, by that time, she hoped Mrs. Bellamy would have a vacancy open for her reception.

CHAPTER IX.

'Tis slander,
Whose edge is sharper than the sword, whose tongue,
Outvenoms all the worms of Nile, whose breath
Rides on the posting winds, and doth belie
All corners of the world.
Maids, matrons, nay, the secrets of the grave,
This viperous slander enters.—SHAKSPERE.

IN about a week after Mr. Meanwell's visit, he again made his appearance, and brought with him letters from Lady Emma and the duchess. Neither of them brought pleasing intelligence. The former, after expressing both surprise and indignation at Mrs. Newland's prohibitions, which seemed to imply that some impropriety in the conduct of Caroline had made such cautions necessary, said her family was in London, and that, much against her inclinations, the marchioness had formed an intimacy with the Newlands, and was frequently of their parties.

"This, in part," she added, "arose from the business in hand; but as I had almost broken off the acquaintance, I did not wish it renewed. To add to my perplexity it is thought adviseable that the marquis should reside in future at Moncrieff Castle, the better to support his title to the dukedom, his claims being in a train of forwardness, and very little doubt entertained of the issue. His family is large, and, I fear, it will not be thought prudent in me to make any addition to it, unless you, my dearest lassie, will condescend to go with us as governess to the young ladies. It would offend the ladies of the family if I introduced you as my companion, as it would seem to imply that their society was not agreeable to me. I have not yet named the subject to the marchioness, though I think she intends taking an English lady down with her; but she is so engaged in a continued round of visiting that I have little leisure for domestic conversation."

Her grace concluded with assuring Caroline of her sincere wishes to serve her, and lamented, with great sincerity, the loss of her society.

Lady Emma's communications were still less satisfactory, but we will give the letter as it was :—

"I cannot express how vexed I was on hearing from Millford that you had left London so very suddenly. I had hoped to have seen you in Portland-place before your departure. I called on the duchess, and found her late quiet home in as much hurry as Mrs. Pembroke's; it was with difficulty that I obtained half an hour's conversation with her. I do not like the marchioness near so well as I do the duchess; she has more pride, and less real dignity about her—Lady Rachel, her sister-in-law, is a formal piece of antiquity—very precise, very reserved, and, my aunt says, very disagreeable. The marquis appears a plain man, but tolerably well supplied with the family foible. The duchess seemed extremely mortified at Mrs. Newlands laying such unnecessary restraints on your correspondence, and rather unwilling to avail herself of any clandestine means of writing to you, she even advised me to send but this one letter, fearing that, by some means or other, Mrs. Newland might be made acquainted with the channel through which they were received. 'In that case,' she added, 'poor Caroline would meet with more mortifications, and, perhaps, the housekeeper lose both situation and character.'

"I could but coincide in the justness of her observation; yet I shall write as as frequently as I can, for I am sure I can depend on my old friend Meanwell; and I shall be careful that no other person is acquainted with my secret. And now I have nothing but disagreeables to relate. You already know how much I was distressed for money before you left London, and to my great mortification Millford could not assist me, having himself met with most severe losses. When we got to old Windsor, the weather was cold for the season; none of the party liked reading beyond a new comedy or a Scotch novel; music, too, was a bore, unless heard in a crowd; in short the billiard-room was the principal amusement of the gentlemen, and the card-table employed the ladies. I lost considerably, particularly when opposed to Lady Lucy and the countess, though the latter was more frequently with the gentleman than with us. The general her husband being gone to Bath for his health, to which place she did not choose to accompany him at this season of the year, his absence left her at liberty to accept of Mrs. Pembroke's invitation. Well, not to tire you with prolixity, on our return to London I was induced to accept the offer of two thousand pounds from Colonel Dinever, and understood from my aunt and Lady Lucy. that payment would not be required of me till I settled with Sir Timothy and Mr. Newland; but, to my surprise and vexation, I was soon informed by Lady Lucy that the colonel was in immediate want of the money, having himself sustained a severe loss at play, which he was compelled as a man of honour to settle without delay. In this dilemma I applied to Millford for advice; he knew of no way unless Mr. Newland would assist me with the money that must be in hand; to him I applied. Through the agency of Mr. Pembroke, he said the money or more might be had, but without the consent of Sir Timothy, he could not advance it. This I absolutely refused to solicit; but, for what reason I know not, Mr. Newland, unknown to me, wrote to the baronet; his answer was a positive refusal. On the following morning I received a friendly though rather admonitory letter from Dr. Maxwell, inclosing a draft on Sir Timothy's banker for two hundred pounds. This at Firr Grove, where I scarcely ever touched a card, would have been a tolerable sum, but what was it in Bedford-square? Actually nothing. Well, this refusal which transpired through Mr. Newland greatly enraged both my aunt and Lady Lucy; the latter insinuated that the baronet's parsimony proceeded from his fear of my fortune being injured before his son returned to receive my hand, and my aunt seemed of the same opinion. I neither contradicted nor assented to their opinions, indeed I was too much out of spirits to do either. 'Write yourself," cried Lady Lucy, ' write peremptorily, and tell the testy old baronet that you do not require his money, you only want the use of your own.' This I positively refused to do. ' I cannot, I will not,' said I, 'confirm Sir Timothy's opinion that I have lost the money at a card-table. This, you may perceive, is what he alludes to here (pointing to the letter). 'Oh, yes,' cried Mrs. Pembroke, ' and he insinuates, too, that I encourage deep play, when I am sure I have lost more money than any other person at my tables.' ' The colonel,' I said, ' must wait till I am of age, when I will settle with him; Millford will give him, if he requires it, a bond for the money.' ' Oh, these things do not admit of delay,' cried Lady Lucy; ' debts of honour are not to be trifled with.'

"At length worn out with importunity, I again consulted my brother, and he agreed, being himself in want of money, to negotiate with Mr. Newland for five thousand pounds, half of which I was to have the use of till I was twenty-one. I am somewhat easier since I know I shall soon be free from these encroaching people, and I am determined they never shall persuade me to play again. And now for a few words in perfect confidence—I do not like the countess, and I fear much for her influence over Millford; I am sure he does not, cannot respect her, yet he is almost always with her. Oh, how shocking are the levities of a married woman!—they set, as our dear Lady Acrimony used to say, delicacy and decorum at defiance. I have been sadly annoyed by a proposal made by Lord Fitz Albert to my brother; I need not say it was rejected. My aunt was very angry. ' What,' she said, ' can you expect more? he has two honours in possession, and a marquisate in reversion; besides, his proposals for settlements are most liberal.' ' I do not like him,' I replied, ' he is much too ostentatious for me, and would, if I mistake not, soon think more highly of the honours than the person he conferred them on. I, wish Montague would come, in him I should have a friend I could trust, and a heart I could rely on.''

A few days after the receipt of these letters, which had thrown a shade of sadness over the mind of Caroline, Mr. Meanwell again made a visit to the manor.

"I am the bearer, Miss Millbourne," said he, "of a message from Lord Millford and Mr. Acrimony, who both wish to inquire after your health in their way to Firr Grove."

"Is Mr. Montague Acrimony returned then?"

"He is," replied the other. "You know," she returned for answer, "that I must not see them, and if they are indeed my friends, they will not wish to injure me in the opinion of Mrs. Newland, for I have certainly no right to disobey her commands while taking the benefit of her protection."

"You are perfectly right," he replied, "but I was requested to inquire if you could not walk in the park, and give them the meeting?"

"Certainly not," she replied; "have the goodness to express my regret at not

No. 10.

being allowed to receive them, and say that under different circumstances I should have been proud of the honour they intended me."

He then gave her another letter from Lady Emma, and departed for the priory.

Her friend wrote in high spirits; the money had been advanced, and she was freed from pecuniary difficulties.

"I wish," she added, "that Sir Timothy would invite me to the grove, and I could be favoured with your company. In this there could be no inpropriety, as Montague must return again to Ireland, where he expects to be detained for some months longer."

"The wish is vain," thought Caroline, as she closed the letter and cast a melancholy look at her own insolated situation.

The next morning she amused herself with her embroidery, when, finding herself rather faint from the position she had sat in, she went into the garden to recover from so uneasy a sensation; and being lost in no very pleasant train of thought she had wandered some distance into the park, and gained a vista through which was a view of the spires at the priory. At that moment the duchess, Lady Emma, and perhaps Lord Millford, rushed upon her memory, she leaned her arm against a rustic seat, and stood lost in thought, when her attention was aroused by the barking of a little spaniel that was her usual companion; she looked towards the spot from whence the sound came, and saw Lord Millford advancing towards her; surprise fixed her motionless, a dizziness seized her, and she sank down on the seat.

Alarmed at seeing her almost fainting, without any means of recovering her, he raised her in his arms, and prevailed on her to endeavour to walk, thinking exercise would turn the faintness; and as he supported her tottering steps, and gazed on a form that nature had seldom equalled, and art never excelled, how did he execrate the pride of birth, the vanity of wealth, and the dominion of custom.

"Oh!" said he, encircling her waist with his arm, "that you would allow me to be through life, your friend, your protector, your eternally devoted Millford."

She started, the colour mounted to her face, while tears of wounded pride trembled in her eyes as she replied, struggling to disengage herself from his arms,—

"Lord Millford, how have I deserved this intrusion, you are acquainted with Mrs. Newland's orders."

"I am," he said, still detaining her, "and would, if you would honour me with your confidence, free you from these degrading trammels."

"Degrading, indeed!" she answered with spirit, "since they have exposed me to an insult like this."

A servant at that moment met them, saying, Mrs. Newland was arrived and expected Miss Millbourne in the house.

Lord Millford offered to attend her; she rather indignantly declined his aid, and followed the servant; he returned, remounted his horse, which he had left with his groom at the park-gate and galloped full speed to the house, where he arrived before Caroline entered it, and found Mrs. and Miss Newland, Lady Lucy, and Mrs. Pembroke seated in the drawing-room. An exclamation of surprise was uttered by the ladies, and Lady Lucy inquired what strange chance had conducted him there.

"I was on my way," he answered, "to the grove, when I saw your carriage (bowing to Mrs. Newland,) turn up and enter the gateway, and therefore did myself the honour of calling; then seating himself on a sofa by the side of Miss Newland, with whom he began trifling, to avoid any particular inquiries from the elder ladies, and was struggling with her for permisson to place a rose, which she held in her hand, in her bosom, when Caroline entered, pale and agitated; she curtsied to the ladies, who returned her compliment with a nod.

"You look pale, child, are you ill?" said Mrs. Newland.

"I have a slight head-ache," she answered, but might with more truth have said an heart-ache.

"Upon my honour," cried his lordship, "I am a most fortunate fellow, for it was only last evening that I was informed Miss Millbourne saw no company in the absence of Mrs. Newland."

"And how came you to make the inquiry?" said Mrs. Pembroke.

"Because Montague and myself intended calling on her in our way to the grove."

"But he is not with you," cried Miss Newland, in a languid tone.

"No," he answered, "Montague is an early riser, he set off before I had left my room. We settled it before that I should be at the grove by four to dinner."

"What an antediluvian hour," drawled Miss Newland; "but why are you not seated?"

He had risen at the entrance of Caroline.

"Because," said he, "a lady is standing."

"Oh, she can find a chair," cried Mrs. Newland.

Caroline seated herself near the window, and his lordship returned to the side of Miss Newland.

"We thought," said Lady Lucy, "that you had an engagement to-day at Highgate; the countess, I know, expects a large party, and you not there?"

He said, "Oh, the day was so fine, that we preferred a ride into the country."

Mrs. Newland replied, "But we shall return time enough to look in on them."

"Just so," cried Miss Newland, "so you may as well send an apology to the grove, and go back with us."

As nothing was further from Lord Millford's thoughts than dining at the grove, he readily assented to the proposal.

At that moment, the spaniel we have before mentioned, bounded into the room (it had been taught to fetch and carry,) with a small paper parcel, sealed and directed to Miss Millbourne.

"This is your writing, my lord," said Mrs. Pembroke, taking it from Juno, who till then held it in her mouth.

He bowed an assent.

Miss Newland bit her lips. Her lady mother looked both angry and inquisitive, while poor Caroline trembled with apprehensions.

"May I presume to inquire, my lord," she said, "how Caroline came to be honoured with such a particular proof of your lordship's attention."

"It is easily explained, madam," he replied, in a tone that seemed to imply indignation and resentment; "I by accident broke a fan of Miss Millbourne's at the Opera, which I beg leave to replace with another."

"But where did Juno find it?" cried Miss Newland.

"I left it," he answered carelessly, "in the hall, with my hat and gloves."

"Then Juno can read," cried Lady Lucy, who had till then been silent, "for she has brought the parcel and left the hat and gloves."

He looked confused, took the parcel from the hand of Mrs. Pembroke, broke the seal, and presented to Caroline a most elegant and costly fan.

"You may take it, child," said Mrs. Newland.

"I would rather have my own, my lord," said Caroline.

"Now for affectation," cried Miss Newland; "do not let your vanity be too much flattered by your present—for you are not the only person to whom his lordship makes them." Then turning towards Lord Millford, she added, "The reticule you gave the countess was particularly elegant."

"But the one I have ordered for you," said he, "will be superior to it."

The lady smiled graciously.

"Take your present, child," cried Mrs. Newland; "and as we came unexpectedly, perhaps Bennet may want your assistance in the store-room to help to prepare the dessert; you can make pastry, I suppose?"

Poor Caroline felt the insult, but did not reply.

"Observe, we must dine early, for we have to dress on our return to town for the countess's concert."

"If we are there by eleven it will be quite time enough," said Miss Newland.

As Caroline quitted the room, she heard Lord Millford inquire after his sister.

"She is gone to Portland-place, to pass the morning with the duchess," Mrs. Pembroke replied, "and our party was not formed before her departure."

"Am I to conclude," said Mrs. Newland, "that your lordship expected to see Caroline this morning in opposition to my orders?"

"Certainly not," he replied, "I did not expect a general rule to be broken through in compliment to me—but I certainly should have inquired after her health, and left a card with the fan."

Mrs. Newland seemed satisfied, but observed, that she should have felt herself much hurt, if he had seen Caroline unknown to her. "For," she added, "it was from the very best of motives that I sent her here; even the duchess acquiesced in the propriety of her being moved from the fascinating scenes of high life, in which she has no pretensions to figure; and, really, she was grown giddy with vanity and adulation."

"Positively," said Mrs. Pembroke, "Millford and his sister have quite spoiled her."

"For Heaven's sake," cried Lady Lucy, in a whining tone of pity not very natural to her, "think what you are doing; your attentions to this girl have been long obvious to every one, and may in the end injure both her peace and reputation.

"I will never intentionally injure either," he replied.

"The world," continued his hypocritical monitress, "may not place such implicit confidence in your explanations, as this company have done; and you must pardon me for saying that the whole of this morning's adventure has a very strange appearance."

"Both the world and yourself, Lady Lucy," he replied, "are at liberty to pass censure on my conduct, but do not insinuate any thing injurious against a young and amiable woman, whose only crime seems to be that nature has so liberally endowed her with its choicest favours."

"That of pride," cried Miss Newland, "has not been spared in her composition."

"It rests," he answered, "on the best of principles; those of conscious rectitude and self-approbation."

"Enough," answered the lady, "I am for a promenade. Let us leave these matronly ladies to settle this knotty point."

His lordship offered his arm, and they descended to the garden.

"It is very strange," escaped from every one at once.

"I must inquire of Bennet in what manner she conducts herself," cried Mrs. Newland, "and if I find she has in a single point disobeyed my orders, I will send her to some other place."

Caroline, to her very great relief, was not invited to the dining parlour; and she took as usual her meal in Mrs. Bennet's room. Spiritless and uneasy, she waited to hear if any further inquiries would be made respecting Lord Millford's visit; and determined, if interrogated, to tell without reserve, of his having surprised her in the park; and bear both reproof and ridicule, in preference to being entangled in a web of falsehood and equivocation. No inquiry, however, was made, except of Mrs. Bennet; and her account was perfectly satisfactory. Caroline was most happy when she heard the carriage roll from the door. Lord Millford rode beside it, and they arrived in Bedford-square before eight, where Lady Emma was already dressed for the concert, and waiting their return.

Lord Milford explained to her in part the occurrences of the morning, concealing only his meeting Caroline in the park. This, however, was not long a secret'; for the servant, who had been sent to look after her, on his return to London mentioned, among his fellow lacqueys, with whom he had found her. This intelligence reached the ears of Miss Newland's abigail, who soon conveyed it with some exaggerations of her own to her lady. Upon how slender a thread hangs the reputation of woman; for this incident, trifling as it was in itself, was most important in its consequences to the future fate of Caroline, as it was artfully manufactured into a secret correspondence with Lord Millford, which had led to a private assignation in the park.

As soon as this piece of scandal was told to Mrs. Newland, the servant was summoned to her presence. Lady Lucy happened to be one of the party, with a few more of her particular friends. The man was closely interrogated, and threatened with the loss of his place if it should be discovered that he deviated from the truth. His statement was short, but in the opinion of his hearers, quite conclusive; he said, when he met Miss Millbourne, she looked very pale, that Lord Millford was supporting her, with one of his arms around her waist, and that she struggled much to free herself.

"Not before she saw you, I dare say," cried Lady Lucy.

"But she did free herself, my lady, and followed me to the house; his lordship, at the same time, took the path that leads to the gate."

"Oh, it is as plain as the sun at noon," said Mrs. Newland.

"And this accounts for her pale looks and her head-ache," cried Lady Lucy; "besides, you know that Bennet said that she spent much of her time in walking about the grounds; ay, it is an intrigue, no doubt, and one of long standing."

The old Marquis of Quaver observed that appearances were much against her. "But," added he, "Lord Millford's time is too much occupied in another quarter to admit of many visits to the recluse of the manor."

"Oh, that is quite a different thing," cried Lady Lucy. "His lordship's engagements with my friend are of a public nature; he frequents her parties because they are principally formed of young people, men of his own age and rank, with whom it suits him to associate, and yet leaves him much time unoccupied for other pursuits."

In short, they determined to find poor Caroline guilty, and at once condemned her as such. This spiteful intelligence was repeated by Lady Lucy to Mrs. Pembroke, who took occasion in the course of the day to inform Lady Emma of it.

"You must," said Mrs. Pembroke, "absolutely give up the girl at the manor, and never for the future hold any correspondence with her."

"For why, madam?" said her niece, in unfeigned surprise.

"It is absolutely necessary," was the reply. "If you have any regard for your own reputation, you will cease to notice a person who has been carrying on a clandestine correspondence with your brother."

"Who can have asserted so injurious a slander?" cried Lady Emma, in great emotion.

"It is no slander," cried Lady Lucy; "the whole has been investigated and satisfactorily proved. Besides, what could be plainer than the fan? it was not likely that the spaniel found it in the hall—and, after all this, Lady Emma, what can you say in her defence?"

"It is useless to plead," she answered, "when a cause is prejudiced"

"That is right," said Lord Harry Hazard, who was present. "I never decide on presumptive evidence."

"Well, say what you please in her defence," said Lady Lucy, "the most candid must allow that the whole has a very suspicious appearance; his going to the priory, because his friend Montague was going to the grove looked very strange; then his staying there, and letting the other go without him, was equally odd; but the meeting is proof positive of the intrigue."

"I beg your pardon, Lady Lucy," replied Lady Emma, "I cannot and will not believe that Caroline had any previous knowledge of his being at the priory; the meeting, if it took place at all, must have been accidental."

"If it took place," retorted her opponent, "why, Lord Lavender and the Marquis of Quaver were both present when the servant was interrogated."

"Yes," said Lord Harry, "and they have widely circulated the report. For my part, I think nobody should have a licence for the promulgation of slander, but superannuated old maids and disappointed widows."

"And why would you allow it to them?" inquired Lady Emma.

"Because," he replied, "their reports would generally be thought the effects of envy, and therefore not believed."

A pause ensued, and Lady Emma left the room. In passing to her dressing-room she met her brother coming from his own.

"Five minutes' conversation," she said, "if you can spare as much time." He followed her, and the subject was immediately introduced.

"Oh, a mere bagatelle," said he, "why do you look so serious?"

"How can I look otherwise," was the answer, "when poor Caroline is become the victim of slander? Lord Lavender and the Marquis of Quaver have both given the affair credence and circulation."

"Then they shall answer it to me," said he, "or make an apology for their slander."

"No, no," said Lady Emma, fearing she had gone too far; "the marquis is only an old gossip, and the other a mere dandy? What can you do with either of them?"

"Beat the one," said he, "with his own fiddle-stick, and shake the other out of his stays. But seriously, Emma," he continued, "if any person, whom I can meet on equal terms, dares sully the purity of your friend's reputation, my arm shall avenge her."

"Do not talk so," said she. "Men of sense will be superior to the promulgation of scandal, and fops and fools must be laughed at and despised."

"What," said he, indignantly, "shall an inestimable young creature have her fair fame traduced on my account, and I not raise an arm to chastise the villain that dares calumniate her?"

"Well," replied she, "as you know it to be false, your contradiction of the report will set all right."

He shook his head, as he answered,—

"It is not all false. I did see her in the park. I saw her weak and trembling through surprise—I caught her in my arms—I pressed her to my heart."

"And was your meeting accidental on her part?"

"Entirely so," he answered. "Nor did I ever pen a line to her, or receive one from her in my life."

"And yet your incaution has given rise to insinuations that will, I fear, deeply injure the reputation of Caroline," replied Lady Emma.

He left his seat, and paced the room.

"It was foolish," he replied; "it was incautious. But who is wise at all times?"

"You used to be very different, Henry," she answered; "but the force of example has been too powerful for us both."

"Where do you spend your evening?" he inquired.

"By appointment at Portland-place," was the answer. "Lady Lucy and our aunt have other engagements. And where, may I ask, do you spend yours?"

"I do not know. It all depends on the party I meet with."

They then separated, his lordship to keep an assignation with the countess, and his sister set out for her visit, and fortunately found the duchess alone. She had, however, the mortification to discover that the tale of scandal had arrived there before her. The marchioness had heard it in the morning from Miss Newland.

When Lady Emma explained it to her grace, as it really was, she commented most severely on the conduct of Lady Lucy and the Newlands.

"It is nothing but envy," she added. "That base and malevolent passion has given rise to this cruel slander, which may, eventually, be most injurious to this good and persecuted young woman."

The duchess then mentioned the little plan she had formed of introducing Caroline to the marchioness, as a fit person for superintending the education of her daughters."

"I should by that means," she said, "have enjoyed much of her company, and have snatched her at once from danger and detraction. As it is," she continued, "I fear to press the subject, though I only yesterday thought it in a favourable train. At all events," she added "my dear lady, caution Caroline against walking far from the house, as no doubt some of Captain Newland's libertine companions will now think they have a licence to insult her."

The duchess regretted that, under existing circumstances, she could not write herself, but begged, through her ladyship, to inform Caroline that her purse, on any emergency, should be open for her.

The time passed rapidly, and on Lady Emma's return to Bedford-square, she found Lady Lucy and Mrs. Pembroke had arrived before her. Not choosing to enter into conversation with them, she retired.

The next morning, when they met at the breakfast table, Lady Emma, on glancing her eye over a morning paper, met with the following paragraph,—

"It is positively stated, in the fashionable circles, that a certain nobleman, whose name is the very essence of poignancy, will soon conduct that lovely *elegante*, the sylph of Bedford-square, to the hymeneal altar."

The paper dropped from her hand, as she exclaimed,—

"Then, Caroline, you are not the only one that slander throws its darts at."

"What is the matter, child?" cried Mrs. Pembroke.

Her niece pointed to the paragraph. Lady Lucy laughed.

"A great deal," said she, "to be angry about. Many ladies would be proud of the compliment it conveys."

"I think it a satire," replied Lady Emma.

"How, for Heaven's sake?" asked Mrs. Pembroke.

"Both on my taste and understanding," was the answer.

At this moment Lord Millford entered.

"Oh, I see by your looks, Emma," he cried, "that you have heard the news of the morning."

"Where did you meet it?" cried Mrs. Pembroke.

"At Hazard's," he replied, "where I have been on a little private business. I wish," he added, "that I knew its author. I have been to the office where the paper is published, and seen the editor, who produced the original article. The hand is disguised."

"To me it appears strange," said Lady Emma, "that men of talent should condescend to be the promulgators of private scandal."

"Money does everything in this mercenary age," replied her brother, "for even the insertion of this falsehood was paid for ; and the complaisant gentleman offered to contradict it to-morrow on similar terms."

"And will it be contradicted?" cried Lady Emma.

"Certainly," he replied ; "but adieu. I am going to take a ride to Harrow ; so leave you to receive the compliments of your exquisite admirer, who will, doubtless, soon make his appearance."

Lady Emma was vexed at the levity of her brother; and saw, with extreme concern that the dissipated set he was continually with had in some degree robbed him of that high sense of honour that she had so lately prided herself in seeing him possessed of.

Another severe mortification assailed her, when she reflected that this very paper was the one read at the grove. What would Sir Timothy—what would Montague think of it?

To conceal the secret anxiety of her mind, she left the room, and retired with the intention of writing to her friend ; but finding herself too much disturbed to put her thoughts on paper, she resolved on paying a morning visit to Mrs. Bellamy. On sending to inquire if she could have the carriage, the answer was, that the ladies were going to Mrs. Newland's. She then directed that a coach should be sent for, and attended by her own footman, set out for her ride.

Mrs. Bellamy's residence was at the extremity of the town ; and in going down Piccadilly, she distinctly saw her brother driving his barouch, in which was seated the Countess of Maybank, rapidly towards Hyde Park turnpike. They were alone, and no other carriage followed them. A heavy sigh burst from her bosom, when she reflected on the influence that insinuating woman had obtained over him, and on the probable consequences that would result foom it.

At Mrs. Bellamy's we shall, for the present, leave her, and return to the vicinity of the manor.

— — —

CHAPTER X.

The strange vicissitudes of human fate,
Still altering, never in a steady state.
Good after ill, and after pain delight,
Alternate like the scenes of day and night,
Since every man who lives is born to die,
And none can boast sincere felicity.—DRYDEN.

WE now call the attention of our readers to the situation in which we left Caroline at the manor. The hurry of her spirits for some time nearly overcame the powers of reflection ; but when her agitation was in some degree abated, how severe and painful her recollections were, we leave every reader of taste and delicacy to imagine.

The word protector still seemed to vibrate on her ear, and called, though alone, the blush of indignation on her faded cheek. Most severely did she tax her past behaviour, in order to discover if any impropriety on her part had given him liberty to suppose she could be so easily obtained ; but all was purity of heart—nor was there a single action that conveyed, what to a feeling mind is the bitterest anguish, self-reproach. Reason came to her assistance, and silenced, in some degree, the perturbation of wounded pride. She determined on concealing the mortifying secret both from the duchess and Lady Emma, as she would now only hear from the former through the latter.

For the two following days she confined herself entirely to the house, and resolved for the future never to venture into the park.

On the third day a letter arrived from Mrs. Newland, which conveyed an order for her quitting the manor as soon as possible, and taking up her residence at the rectory, where she would be for the present accommodated with board and lodging.

"Your duplicity," said Mrs. Newland, "does not merit this consideration from me, yet I cannot bring myself entirely to abandon you. Your intrigue with Lord Millford is perfectly understood, and you are consigned to that obscurity you ought never to have been taken from. Bennet has my directions how to proceed, and by this time Miss Lewson is prepared to receive you."

Tears gushed from her eyes, the letter fell from her hand, and, before she had recovered her self-possession, Mrs. Bennet entered with hers, which contained an account of what has before been related. She glanced her eye over the letter, and, in returning it, said,—

"Is it on so slight a charge as this that I am to be stigmatised with disgrace? I certainly did see Lord Millford in the park, but the meeting was, I think, accidental on both sides ; and surely Mrs. Newland might have heard my explanation before she condemned me. Lord Milford never wrote to me, and if he had, situated as I am, I should have disdained any private correspondence with him."

"I believe you, my dear Miss Millbourne," said Mrs. Bennet ; "but you are too good, and too handsome, to escape detraction. Will you permit me to speak to you as a friend ?"

Caroline bowed an assent.

"It did not escape my observation," said Mrs. Bennet, "that, during your residence here last season with the duchess, Lord Millford's attention to you excited the envy of Miss Newland, particularly after your very excellent performance of Louisa Dudley. You must recollect how abruptly the after-piece was dispensed with. That was because you should not play Rosina to his lordship's Belville. Miss Newland had chosen the part of William, in which her full form

would have been displayed to great advantage; but then there was no Rosina but yourself, and in consequence the piece was dropped. Miss Newland is, I believe, determined to be the Countess of Millford, and I fear the embarrassments his lordship is said to be involved in will hasten the completion of her wishes."

Caroline sighed, but was silent.

"I know," continued the other, "that Mr. Newport used to remunerate Mrs.

No. 11.

Newland for any expenses incurred on your account ; it is most likely he does so still.   Write to him, my dear young lady, and explain your real situation, a~~ ~~~ ~~~ him—you need not state particular reasons—that you wish to be freed from the control of Mrs. Newland, and be in some way enabled to provide for yourself."

" Would not such a proceeding have the appearance of ingratitude ?" said Caroline, in reply.

" I do not think it would be so construed," replied Mrs. Bennet, " for Mr. Newport is so well acquainted with the pride of his family, that he will feel no surprise on hearing you wish to withdraw yourself from this control.   Mr. Meanwell can give you his address, and also forward your letters."

Caroline agreed to follow her advice as soon as she had consulted Mr. Meanwell.

" That," replied Mrs. Bennet, " you will soon have an opportunity of doing, for he is intimate with the rector."

Mrs. Bennet then stated, confidentially, that she expected shortly to leave the manor.   An early marriage, she said, had plunged her into many difficulties.   Her husband's imprudence had estranged her from her family ; he squandered his fortune among sharpers and gamesters, and finally ended his fatal career with suicide.

Caroline shuddered, and Mrs. Bennet continued,—

" I was left in very indifferen. circumstances, with two boys to support.   A distant relation of their father's undertook to provide for them, and at a proper age placed them in a mercantile house of great respectability at Bristol, where they now are, and, I am informed, are in a air way of becoming sarers in the firm ; they are good and affectionate young men, and have expressed a desire for me to be nearer to them, but circumstances would not allow of their taking me entirely on their hands, nor did I wish they should ; unexpectedly their friend heard their wishes, and made a successful application to some of my own family, who have added to the little I have left, a sufficient sum to purchase a small annuity, which will enable me to live in independent retirement.   A small house is already taken for me near Bristol, to which place I shall retire as soon as my business is completed. My home will be an humble one," she added, " but such as it is, if Mr. Newport does not object to it, and Mrs. Newland, I think will not, you shall freely share it with me."

Caroline, with tearful eyes, thanked Mrs. Bennet for her friendly offer.

" Do not name it," said her kind friend ; " and let me intrude on your notice for a few moments longer, as I wish you to be fully acquainted with my past conduct and future prosperity.   After my sons were provided for, I determined to reserve the little that was left of a once considerable fortune, against any emergencies that might arise either to myself or children ; in order to accomplish this it was necessary that I should procure the means of living.   For this purpose I engaged to become an attendant on a superannuated dowager of quality, who contrived, by her peevishness and constant ill-humour, to make me eat the bitter bread of carefulness and sorrow ; yet I continued with her, for her family were kind to me, and as tney acted for her, I was not accountable to her for the expendiu re of the house, but to them.   Death at last released her from a life that was burdensome to herself, and useless to others.   I was remunerated handsomely, and quitted the house soon after the funeral.   I should have told you long before this, that I had met with Mrs. Newland at Tonbridge ; soon after her marriage she sought my acquaintance with great assiduity, for I moved in a circle she wished to be introduced to ; her plan succeeded—many of my intimates became hers, and as she advanced, I retrogaded, yet we always kept up an how-do-you-do acquaintance, and as I never wanted nor applied to her for assistance, she remained my friend.   After the decease of Lady G——, I called upon her, and she expressed a very great desire for me to undertake the management of the house in the country.   I agreed to her proposal, and have now been four years in this situation, of which I am now completely weary ; my eldest son is about to be married to a young lady of genteel fortune, part of the money I have in the funds will be advanced for his house, bearing interest, and the remainder laid out for my own annuity."

"Does Mrs. Newland suspect that you intend leaving the manor?" said Caroline.

"I have not yet informed her of my intentions," Mrs. Bennet replied, "but when I see her next, I shall be explicit on the subject. I could smile at their folly," she added, "if it was accompanied with less arrogance; and when the expected title is announced, it will be unbearable."

"Title!" exclaimed Caroline in surprise.

"Even so," replied the other; "a patent of nobility is expected at the next making of peers. And now," she continued, "I will assist you in preparing for your departure, which, according to my orders must take place to-morrow."

"I shall have but one regret, my kind friend," said Caroline, "and that is leaving you,"

"Our separation I hope will not be for long," Mrs. Bennet answered, "for as soon as I am settled, I will write to Mrs. Newland on the subject, and if Mr. Newport will allow you a sufficient stipend for clothes and pocket-money, I will take upon myself every other expense, and think myself amply repaid by enjoying your society."

"How kind, how good you are," said Caroline as she arose, "my things will soon be packed up, and let us do it immediately." This point settled, Caroline felt more at ease; she busied herself in sorting her clothes; she looked at the dress she had worn the last time she saw Lord Milford at the opera; it brought some painful recollections to her mind, which she strove hard to subdue. "There," said she, giving it to Mrs. Bennet, "lay that among the other useless finery, I dare say I shall never wear it again." Then came Lady Emma's presents. "And his too," she said, "I may lay by to look at for the giver's sake." In fine, every thing that was not likely to be wanted was packed by itself, and nothing but the simplest apparel set apart for use.

Mrs. Bennet was pleased to see the ease with which she disposed of several elegant dresses, as things no longer of any value, but as remembrances of her friends. The next morning a small caravan was ready, a seat was placed in it, and Caroline set out for the rectory. The novelty of such a conveyance was very-striking, when compared to the elegant carriage she had so lately been accustomed to.

"Time," thought Caroline, "will reconcile me to the change of scene, yet, when seated in the duchess's carriage, how little did I expect I should leave the manor in an humble caravan." Her train of reflections was interrupted by their arrival at the rectory, where she was received with studied civility by the doctor and his sister. Miss Lewson was a maiden lady, of about forty-eight, she was some years younger than her brother, a circumstance she frequently took occasion to remind him of.

"You are come to a sad dull place, Miss Melbourne," said she.

"It is very pleasantly situated," returned Caroline. "I have frequently admired it during our rides last summer."

"Pretty well at this time of the year," was the reply, "but shocking in winter."

The good lady then made many apologies for the smallness of the bed-room, saying, she was quite unprepared for company, but she would make it as comfortable as she could.

For this she was thanked by her visitor, who began unpacking a trunk that held her books. Miss Lewson then left her to her own reflections.

Mrs. Newland's letter to the rector had given directions for the restraints Caroline was to be under, and were similar to those before prescribed. The inmates at the rectory were left to conjecture the causes that had excluded her from society; Mrs. Newland only said she considered it a point of duty to place Miss Millbourne in retirement, till she could otherwise provide for her. Dr. Lewson did not trouble himself about the arrangements of the family; though he was no great admirer of female society, he behaved, at least, with civility to Caroline, for, in the first place, he thought her a very agreeable young woman, and in the next, he considered he was obliging Mrs. Newland by receiving her, a circumstance by no means to be overlooked, for, though verging fast towards another world, he was not indifferent to the good things of this, and Mr. Newland had promised him his interest with a certain bishop, for the next vacant prebendary in the diocese.

In a few days Caroline was quite at home. Doctor Lewson was a good-humoured quiet man. It was thought that he slept more than he read, and preached more sermons than he wrote. Nothing seemed to disturb his serenity so much as an ill-dressed dinner, and it often happened that he had one, for his sister frequently forgot what was going forward in the kitchen, while she was altering her own dresses, or drawing patterns for flounces; for, having in her youth been praised for her taste in dress, she could not easily resign her pretensions to it.

The family was small, and consisted only of two female servants, and a lad to mind the house, clean the chaise, &c. The rectory was three miles from a market town, and the same distance from the priory. After Caroline had been there about a week, she inquired when the lad would go to D——.

" My dear Miss Millbourne," replied Miss Lewson ; " I regret to inform you that no letters can go from hence, without Mrs. Newland's permission."

" I have none to send, madam," she answered.

" My dear girl," replied Miss Lewson, " I can easily conceive the severity of your feelings, in being deprived of the pleasure of hearing from a favoured object, doubly endeared to you, no doubt, by the persecutions you have endured on his account. I have heard a rumour, though the real reasons of your being placed here have not been fully explained, but if you will confide in my discretion, and trust me with your entire confidence, I will forward your letters secretly and safely."

An observation, once made to her by the duchess, instantly occurred ; it was " As you are situated, you cannot be too reserved."

She therefore politely thanked Miss Lewson for her offer, but declined accepting it. That lady was silent, but not satisfied ; she had expected that Caroline would have accepted her offer, and told her all the particulars, of what she was determined to think an affair of the heart. After this the subject was never renewed. In the meantime Caroline contrived to be continually employed—her mind naturally active found amusement in her needle, her pencil, and her small though well-chosen collection of books.

No sooner did Miss Lewson make the important discovery that her guest was fond of the needle, than she solicited her assistance in new modelling some of her dresses, according to the last new fashions in the " Ladies' Magazine."

Caroline smiled as she assented to the request, and secretly thought that they would not be worth the time or materials that must be bestowed on them ; but the time was seldom thought of by Miss Lewson, unless her glass reminded her how unpolitely he had stolen the roses from her cheeks, and made some little alterations in her form ; but as these observations were not of the most agreeable kind, they were speedily dismissed.

More than a fortnight had elapsed, and no Mr. Meanwell appeared. Caroline feared to inquire after him, lest it might give rise to unpleasant suspicions, and lead Miss Lewson to conjecture that through him she expected to hear of Lord Millford.

Our readers must now return with us to Mr. Montague, whom it may be recollected, we left at Firr Grove ; his return to England was sudden and unexpected, for he had been but a few weeks in the sister kingdom, before he found it necessary to return, and consult Sir Timothy on the sale of some estates that had long been in chancery, but were lately awarded to him. On his arrival he spent but a short time in London ; and then, as we have before seen, set out for the baronet's, whom he found ill and out of humour—even the presence of his only son could not chase from his countenance the gloom of melancholy that preyed upon his spirits ; nor was the intelligence which Montague had to impart at all calculated to enliven him. He detested law, and yet found himself involved, through the neglect or artifice of his agents, in a web of almost endless litigation.

"You must return, Montague," said he, "and I will invest you with full powers to sell all you can, unless you can lease the land off to good and sure tenants, free from those pests to that unfortunate country, the middlemen."

Montague made no objections he knew it was necessary he should return, and take London in his way, in order to consult with Sir Timothy's legal advisers on the intricate business he had to accomplish, and also to obtain a recommendation to some one of eminence at the Irish bar. When these arrangements were fully decided on, he consulted Dr. Maxwell on the propriety of speaking to Sir Timothy on the subject nearest his heart.

"I wish," said he, "to see Lady Emma removed from the dangerous society she is placed in before I leave England. Do you think if I could prevail on her to consent to a private marriage that Sir Timothy would receive her, and allow her to continue here during my absence?"

The doctor shook his head.

"The year of mourning," he observed, "is not yet expired; and, assuredly, you would not think of proposing such a thing at present."

"Nothing," replied the former, "but the necessity of the case would induce me to propose it."

This led to some explanations that both vexed and disconcerted him.

"The public prints," said the doctor, "frequently speak of this lady in very ambiguous terms—her gaiety, her losses at play, her numerous lovers. Besides, it is not many weeks since Sir Timothy was applied to by Newland for a considerable sum, who plainly stated the money was wanted to settle debts of honour. Sir Timothy refused the demand, and he has since been informed by an anonymous letter, that Lord Millford took the money of Newland, on bond for his sister."

"She must be snatched from this precipice of folly," cried Montague, with energy; "her genuine, unsuspecting nature must not be sacrificed to the nefarious views and treachery of designing women."

"What," said the doctor calmly, "can save a willing victim from immolation?"

"She is not the willing victim of error," cried Montague; "circumstances, on her part unavoidable, threw her into this vortex of dissipation, and she has not had sufficient fortitude to stem the torrent of custom, and stand alone and unaided amidst the whirlpool of modern deterioration."

"So it appears," replied the former; "but I assure you, Mr. Montague, that she has been advised to guard against the dangers with which she is surrounded."

"It would have been far better," he answered, "to have kept her from the force of overwhelming example. Had the dear creature been left to choose, she would have continued here till the time arrived when I could with propriety have claimed her hand."

"Perhaps it would have been better," said the doctor, "that she had not gone to London; but as it is, I do not see how any one can extricate her from the net she has allowed herself to be entangled in."

"You are severe, doctor, and make no allowance for youth, inexperience, and elevated rank."

"Not so much, certainly, as I should thirty years ago," was the answer.

"Yet I assure you, sir, no one feels more than I do for the future welfare of the lovely but flexible Lady Emma."

"You cannot suppose that your predilection in her favour was unobserved by Sir Timothy."

"Then why did he let her leave his protecting roof?" was the reply.

"Shall I speak to you with candour, Mr. Montague?"

"I should be sorry to hear you speak otherwise."

He was silent, and the doctor proceeded to state that Sir Timothy feared Lady Emma's very susceptible feelings were indicative of weakness of character; in short, he feared her stability, and wished it put to the proof.

"It was an experiment then upon her feelings," retorted Montague, "and as such, disgraceful to those that planned it."

"Do not judge rashly, sir, you may live to be grateful to those that projected it."

"Never," said Montague.

"Shall I advise you as a friend?"

He bowed, and the doctor proceeded, saying,—

"Go back to Ireland without delay; accelerate the business there. The deeds that are to invest you with the power of acting for Sir Timothy are expected here to-night for his signature."

"So I understand," returned the other.

"Well," continued the doctor, "when you next see Lady Emma, point out to her the precipice on which she stands—caution her against cards—against giving any occasion for her name to be so frequently blazoned in the fashionable papers."

"Oh, that is impossible," replied Montague; "the possession of youth, beauty, and fortune ever creates envy, and envy engenders slander."

"Well, caution her at all events," said the doctor, "but never propose marriage without the baronet's consent. Your absence will not, I should suppose, exceed the close of the year; soon after that time the mourning will expire, and Lady Emma will be twenty-one; besides, the restrictive clause in the late earl's will is a total barrier against a private marriage."

To this last suggestion Montague did not reply; to be brief, he left the grove without any explanation with Sir Timothy, and arrived in London a few days after Caroline had quitted it. The buzz of scandal was still afloat, and he heard the tale with all its various insinuations annexed to it, stating the manner in which she declined receiving Lord Millford and himself.

"Aye," cried Lady Lucy, "that was done to cover the intrigue. It was all by chance, I suppose, that Millford left his horse at the park gate; it was all by chance, too, that he met the lady; and certainly it was all by chance that the whole affair was discovered."

"Do call another subject," said Lord Harry Hazard, "for I am weary of hearing this poor girl's character so unmercifully dissected."

So, too, was Lady Emma, but she took no part in the conversation.

Montague and Lord Millford had both engaged to pass the evening with some gentlemen lately arrived from the continent, and in consequence left Mrs. Pembroke's early. The following morning, however, he made his appearance just as the family were seated at the breakfast-table. He took a seat by Lady Emma, and, taking her offered hand, felt it parched with fever; he for a moment threw an inquiring glance at her sylph-like form, as if to say, "What a melancholy change has a few months made!" when his attention was interrupted by Lady Lucy, who exclaimed,—

"I presume, Mr. Montague, you have taken up your diploma; pray let us hear what you prescribe for your patient."

"Change of air, change of company, and regular hours," he answered.

"All this can be obtained by going either to old Windsor or the priory," said Mrs. Pembroke.

"A little nautical excursion might be more agreeable," cried Lady Lucy, with a sneer.

"It rests solely with Lady Emma to decide the point in question," replied Montague; "but for the present," he added, "I would prescribe an airing in the park."

"I would rather walk," she answered, "to Portland-place, and if the duchess is disposed for an airing, we can ride with her."

This was assented to, and as she retired to make the necessary alteration in her dress, Lord Millford entered the room.

"One five minutes' conversation," said Montague, addressing him, "if you can spare so much time from more important occupations."

Lord Millford bowed an assent, and they left the room. The former led the way to an empty parlour.

"Now for your commands," said he, "but be brief, my good friend, for I am in haste."

Montague then repeated part of the conversation with Doctor Maxwell, and slightly touched on the money that it was said Mr. Newland had advanced.

"It was I that took up the money, and not Emma," replied his lordship; "but I think that Mrs. Pembroke has had money on her account since, of Captain Newland. By-the-by, I think that whiskered hero aspires to the honour of her hand."

"And rests his pretensions, perhaps, on having obliged her," retorted the other.

"So I have been thinking," said his lordship, yawning.

"Thinking!" replied Montague, vexed at his indifference. "I believe you never think at all."

"Oh, if you are angry, I am off. The fascinating countess has appointed me to attend her and some friends in a ride to Harrow. You cannot think how graceful she looks on horseback."

Montague looked grave, as he replied,—

"Beware, Millford—you stand on dangerous ground."

"Pho," cried the other, "you are too prudent by half; you would not, I dare say, have an intrigue on your hands for the world."

"Certainly not with a married woman, on any account," was the answer.

The conversation then became more serious, and Montague, in spite of Doctor Maxwell's advice, expressed an ardent desire of gaining Lady Emma's consent to a private marriage.

"You have my free consent," replied his lordship, "and I give you my word of honour that I will take no pecuniary advantage of the circumstance. Lady Emma is not happy—she is not well—and the sooner she is taken from this scene of folly the better; for, thoughtless as I am, it is not a house I should choose a wife of mine to remain in."

The dialogue was interrupted by the entrance o Lady Emma. Lord Millford wished them good morning, and they commenced their walk.

"Suppose," said Montague, "we ride to Kensington, and walk back through the gardens. I have much to say to you, and may not have another opportunity of seeing you alone."

Lady Emma did not object to the proposal, and they stepped into a hackney coach. Their ride was nearly a silent one, but on entering the gardens, Montague entered with great earnestness on the subject nearest his heart. His fair companion listened with attention to all he advanced, and condemned with sincerity the routine of dissipation that she was continually immersed in, and lamented Mrs. Pembroke's attachment to the card table, and her own folly in having been persuaded to partake of their amusements.

"Consent," he cried, "my dearest Emma; consent for your own sake to my proposals. I will continue near London while the banns are published. Your brother approves the plan—the season is remarkably fine—the sea air will improve your health, and from Holyhead I will write both to Sir Timothy and Mrs. Newland. By this measure, you will be extricated from many perplexities that now oppress you."

"There is so much of kindness and consideration in your proposal," she replied, "that I think if I was of age, and the mourning for your dear mother over, I should be inclined to consent; but you cannot have forgotten Lady Acrimony's admonition, of never marrying without Sir Timothy's consent; besides I do not like stolen weddings."

"Nor do I," he answered; "but circumstances render many things necessary that our judgment cannot entirely approve. If you were differently situated, I should not have distressed you by such an offer; but I am about to leave you for months. Beset by dangers, and surrounded by people in whom you can place no confidence, your health is injured, and your feelings sported with. A paper of this morning," said he, "insinuates that Captain Newland is at last selected from among your numerous admirers as the fortunate man that is to be honoured with your hand."

"Oh! these vile vendors of slander," said she, in tremulous agitation; "but you, Montague, I am sure, will not for a moment be uneasy at such ridiculous insinuations."

"I cannot be otherwise than uneasy," he replied, "when I think on the impressions these reports may make on the mind of Sir Timothy. I only speak of them to enforce the necessity of an immediate alteration. And I can but fear," said he, "that during my absence many events may occur to alter your present sentiments in my favour."

"Nothing," she answered, "can ever alter the high opinion I entertain of your sincerity, and it rests with yourself to confirm or annul it. I understand that we shall pass some time at the priory, and during my stay there, I will frequently visit Sir Timothy, and convince him by my conduct that I am not unworthy of his good opinion."

"You are all that is good and amiable in woman," he replied, "and on your rectitude my heart can repose in safety; but these wasps and butterflies that buzz about you——"

"They are," she answered, "tiresome insects, "but I can easily brush them off. My sentiments of the Marquis and Lord Lavender are well known—Hazard has ceased to importune me, and as for Captain Newland, he is a mere dangler."

"But certainly," he replied, "you must see the impropriety of encouraging mere danglers."

"I do not encourage him," she answered with quickness; "but to oblige me he has assisted Mrs. Pembroke, and freed her from some very perplexing difficulties."

"I dislike them all," he answered; "for to me they appear a heartless set, and the only bond that unites them is that of self-interest."

Again and again, he urged every argument that reason and affection could dictate to obtain her consent to an early union.

"I will leave London," said he, "till the necessary time is expired; and after the ceremony is over, we can set out immediately for Holyhead, and embark for Dublin. Then, and then only, shall I think myself secure of you."

Her heart yielded, but pride and propriety supported her in the resolution of not marrying without the baronet's consent. "He is, I well know, displeased with me," she said, "on account of the letter Mr. Newland wrote to him, and I should merit his censure if, availing myself of your partiality, I was to steal clandestinely into his family; perhaps, for you know his high notions of parental authority, he would never forgive you, and if so, I should never forgive myself."

Finding her so determined, he dropped the subject, but not before she had promised him that she would not answer for any more money being advanced by Mr. Pembroke, or incur any fresh obligation from the Newlands; he then proposed that Lord Millford should take the captain's debt on his own account, "and on my return" said he, "I will settle it, and by that means it may be kept from the knowledge of Sir Timothy." To this proposal, Lady Emma assented; she promised also to correspond with him as before, her letter inclosed by her brother, and his answer to be received through the same channel; with these arrangements he endeavoured to be satisfied, and having concluded their walk, they again entered the coach, called again in Portland-place (on their way to Bedford-square), where finding the marchioness surrounded by company and the duchess rather indisposed, they made but a short visit; on arriving at Mr. Pembroke's, they found the ladies were dressing for dinner. Montague returned to his hotel and Lady Emma retired to her dressing-room; he had promised to call again in the evening, but on his return to his lodging, he found a letter that required his attendance in the Temple at seven, and he instantly sent a short note by his servant explaining the nature of his engagement as an apology for his absence. When alone, Montague reflected seriously on the conversation of the morning, and deeply regretted that he could not effectually extricate from thraldom the being he loved more than he loved himself.

At dinner Lady Emma had to sustain the raillery of Lady Lucy, on the occurrences of the morning ; she bore it without any resentment, and only replied that Mr. Acrimony was one of the very few friends in whom she could confide, and one she hoped she should never lose. " Admirable," replied the other, " quite a platonic affair, I dare say." At that moment her own servant delivered a note, it was the one from Montague ; she put it in her bosom.

" A *billet doux,* and so near your heart too," said Lady Lucy.

This speech did not extract an answer. Mrs. Pembroke then inquired if they were to expect her company to Colonel Dinever's.

" It depends on circumstances," was the answer ; and soon as the cloth was removed, she retired to read her note, and finding she should not see Montague, she resolved to attend her aunt to Miss Dinever's party, though she felt it would

No. 12.

to her be productive of no pleasure; at the usual time she met them dressed for the occasion. On their arrival the rooms were nearly full, and Lord Millford was leaning over the chair of Miss Newland, who was seated at the same table with Colonel Dinever.

" Do, Millford," said she, " take my hand of cards? I am really weary of play."

" Really I cannot oblige you," he answered, " for I have an indispensable engagement."

Miss Newland looked offended.

Mrs. Newland, who was seated at the next table, said, " I have to complain that of late, my lord, you sadly neglect your old friends."

" Oh," he replied carelessly, " one cannot be everywhere at once."

" Will you go with us to the masquerade to-morrow night?" cried Miss Newland ; " it will be the last this season."

" Oh, we must all go," said Mrs. Pembroke, " and cannot dispense with your company, Millford."

" And pray," cried Mrs. Newland, " bring your heart with you to the pleasurable scene, for I do not like to see a man's person in one place, while his thoughts are in another."

" And as that is exactly my case at present," said he, " I shall *sans* ceremony bid you adieu."

" Very strange," said Mrs. Pembroke, " very strange indeed, but come, let us look for a vacant table."

Miss Newland played inattentively, and lost the game.

" Your thoughts," said Colonel Dinever to her, " have followed Millford, I suppose ; you have lost three tricks running, and through that the game. I never saw you play so careless before."

" I resign my place," she answered, " for I am weary of play."

" Weary," he retorted, " why, we have only play'd three rubbers."

" Let us change partners."

While this weighty point was being decided, Lady Emma, who had been standing by, joined some ladies who did not seem disposed to play, and they promenaded the suite of rooms together.

Captain Newland followed them, and placed himself by the side of Lady Emma ; it was in vain that she endeavoured to escape from him, for he followed, importuning her to make one at the ensuing masquerade, and allow him the honour of conducting her thither.

" If I go," she answered, " it will be with Millford and my aunt, though I really think I shall not go at all."

" Oh, I had forgotten," said he, " that you were under medical prescriptions, and of course all amusements are interdicted except solitary walks in Kensington gardens."

Vexed at the insinuation, and totally at a loss to guess by what means he attained the knowledge of her having been there, she abruptly quitted the ladies, and placed herself behind Mrs. Pembroke.

Absorbed in thought, and taking very little interest in what was passing around her, when Lord Harry Hazard came forward and proposed her making one at a table for a sovereign each ; the sum was too trifling to be objected to, and they took their seats, when the captain again followed ; one was wanting, they cut for partners, and Lady Emma was paired with him.

Nothing could have been more unpleasant to her in the state of mind she was then in ; however, the attention the game required in some degree kept him silent.

At rather an early hour the party separated.

Early the next morning Lady Emma entered the breakfast room ; it was empty, she rang the bell for her servant, and bid him follow her to Oxford-street, where she was going to sit for an hour to a miniature painter in order that he might finish a likeness he was taking of her previous to the departure of Montague.

On her return she was met by the captain.

"I have been to Mr. Pembroke," said he; "the ladies have not yet made their appearance; suppose you prolong your walk."

This she declined, and they returned together.

On entering the breakfast room, they found Montague seated alone.

"You are an early visitor," said Lady Emma.

"Not the only one" he answered, glancing his eye on the captain.

Before she could reply, Mrs. Pembroke and Lady Lucy entered the room; they were followed by Lord Millford; the former inquired of her niece where she had been, "for I heard," she added, "that you went out early."

Lady Emma hesitated; she had no intention that they should know she was sitting for her miniature.

The countenance of Montague was clouded.

The question was repeated when she answered,—

"I only went out for a little air."

Montague's countenance cleared up, but an ill-natured observation of Lady Lucy's clouded it again.

"This," said she, in a tone of raillery, "is a very pretty excuse for an assignation, as if this morning's walk was not planned last evening."

The captain laughed, and Montague frowned, and Lady Emma coloured deeply.

"Nay, child, do not blush," cried the persecuting Lady Lucy, "there is so much of *mauvaise honte* in it that it quite shocks me."

The captain then produced the masquerade tickets, and presented one to Lady Emma, who declined it.

"You will go," said he. "You must be persuaded to decide on a character."

"I hope," said Montague, gravely, "that Lady Emma will not be prevailed on to undertake a character; she is not in health for the exertion it would require."

"But if attended by the doctor," said Lady Lucy, "there could be no danger."

Here Lord Millford interposed, saying,—

"I have promised the duchess that Emma shall spend the evening in Portland-place, if she was not otherwise engaged, as the whole of her family are going to the Haymarket, and she will be quite alone."

"Then I will be early in Portland-place," she replied, "and thank you for the engagement."

The important business of the masquerade settled, the captain took his leave, and the ladies retired, leaving Lord Millford, Montague, and Lady Emma, who instantly explained where she had been.

"Then I must go without the miniature," said Montague, "for my arrangements for leaving London are all made."

"When do you go?" said Lord Millford.

"To-night, or at the latest to-morrow morning, and you must promise to inclose it in the next packet."

Lord Millford then asked his sister if she knew that Mrs. Newland had sent Caroline from the manor.

She answered in the negative, and observed she was uneasy at not having heard from her.

"Poor girl! how she is persecuted," said Montague.

"And how unfortunate was your meeting her in the park," said Lady Emma, speaking to her brother.

"I have never yet," said Montague, "heard that meeting satisfactorily accounted for."

"Do not play the inquisitor," returned his friend.

"In justice to an injured woman's reputation," replied Montague, "you should at least be explicit with your friends."

After a pause, Lord Millford answered,—

"It was to Miss Millbourne an unfortunate meeting; and on my honour she is innocent. It was all my doing. I was not just then in a humour to bear contradiction, and thought I would see her if possible, in spite of Mrs. Newland's caution. I knew she was an early riser, and fond of walking, and took my measures accordingly."

Montague shook his head; the other continued,—

"I rode to the park, gave my orders to the groom, and walked about till I was weary, and just on the point of giving up my project, when the yelping of the spaniel directed me to the spot. The fan I had purchased on purpose for Caroline, I suppose I drew out with my handkerchief, and, by falling on the ground, it escaped my observation; and this is all and everything from which such a tale of scandal has been fabricated."

"Then I shall not hear again from her," said Lady Emma; "it is a subject she will not write on."

The conversation was then dropped by Montague, who requested his friend to take Captain Newland's debt on himself, and free Lady Emma from an obligation he presumed so much on. "And on my return," he added, "I will be responsible for the same."

"And if you should be detained longer than is expected," replied his lordship, "Emma must pay me, for I am horribly in debt myself."

This point settled, Montague took his leave, promising to call once again before he left London. Lord Millford went out, and Lady Emma retired. When left alone, she reflected very deeply on the conduct of her brother, and most severely condemned him for the disgrace he had brought upon her friend. At dinner they met again, when she inquired before the ladies entered the room, whether the invitation to Portland-place was of his own invention. He answered in the affirmative, saying,—

"I did it to save a duel; for I thought Montague looked as if he had some inclination to affront the captain; but, to save appearances, you can go to Portland-place, and return when you think our gay aunt and her friend are out for the Haymarket. I will order my chariot, and wait your return hither; or if Montague comes first, detain him till your return."

When the ladies entered, the subject was dropped; during dinner nothing was talked of but the masquerade.

"You will be there, Millford," said Mrs. Pembroke.

"I shall look in before daylight," he answered.

"Perhaps you are engaged too for Portland-place," said Lady Lucy.

"It is very likely I shall call there during the evening," was the reply.

At the usual time the carriage was at the door, and the ladies set out for Grosvenor-square, where the party was to meet previous to their resorting to the Haymarket, and Lord Millford's carriage at the same time conveyed Lady Emma to Portland-place. The duchess was fortunately alone, the marchioness and Lady Rachel being in reality gone to the Haymarket.

The little stratagem, invented by Lord Millford, was explained; the departure of Caroline from the manor lamented by both ladies, and the duchess greatly condemned the flighty conduct of Lord Millford, while she did ample justice to that of Caroline. From her, Lady Emma heard that his devotion to the Countess of Maybank was the reigning topic of scandal in the gay world, and that it was generally expected serious consequences would result from it.

"Her profuse style of living cannot," her grace added, "be supported, either by her own fortune, or that of the general's."

Lady Emma sighed heavily as she listened to her venerable friend, for her own observations had led her to conclude that her brother had for some time provided her with the money she squandered, and she had also noticed that the countess had ceased to visit in many families where, at the commencement of the season, she was frequently seen. She now seldom met her anywhere except at home or in Grosvenor-square; at the former place, she was still Lady Lucy's dear friend; and at the latter, Mrs. Newland's elegant countess; while Miss Newland's manner was distant and reserved.

The duchess told her fair visitor that the marquis had been informed from high authority that no opposition would be made to his claims on the dukedom—the estates that had escheated to the crown, it was expected might be redeemed—and the Moncrieffs again possess their ancestral patrimony.

"The plans for the future," her grace observed, "were not exactly decided on, but it was in contemplation to pass some months in the west of England, and if the business which had brought them to England should be satisfactorily concluded, it was probable the family would spend the winter at Edinburgh previous to their setting out for the Highlands."

When Lady Emma rose, in order to depart, the duchess, taking her hand, intreated her, if she should by chance hear where Caroline was secluded, to assure her of her unabated affection, and anxious desire of serving her in any way that could be pointed out.

"But never, I entreat you," she added, "let Lord Millford become acquainted with her retreat; for his imprudent attachment to a depraved woman may have given birth to principles injurious to the safety and happiness of your friend."

Lady Emma assured her grace that in her inquiries she would be particularly cautious, and that through her Lord Millford should never hear of Caroline. On returning to Bedford-square, she found Montague was there before her.

"Now," said he, on her entering the drawing-room, "I see you can resist entreaty; act ever thus, my own dear Emma, and let your own judgment decide for you; neither be lured by persuasions, nor seduced by example, into pursuits injurious to your health, and at variance with your reason."

"I shall leave Emma to profit by your lecture," said Lord Millford, "for I must be at the masquerade by eleven, and I have, besides, to meet a party previous to going thither."

Then wishing his friend health and success, he took his leave.

Montague was thoughtful, and Lady Emma spiritless, yet she endeavoured to appear cheerful, but there was a weight upon her heart that resisted the attempt; she spoke of her brother, of Caroline, of the countess, and found her lover's opinion of that dashing belle of high notoriety similar to that formed by the duchess. Montague presented her with his miniature, again and again he bade her adieu, yet still he lingered, unwilling to quit her. At last he cried,—

"Would to Heaven you had consented to our union, and was now going with me; but let me, on my return, find you but in good health, and kind as I leave you, and I shall have no other boon to ask of Heaven."

Then, entreating her to pay particular attention to her health, he hurried to the chaise that was waiting with his portmanteau, intending, as it was moonlight, to travel one stage on his journey. After his departure, Lady Emma sat for some time, lost in a train of unpleasant reflections. At length she retired, and sought, but in vain, for repose upon her pillow.

CHAPTER XI.

God made the country, and man made the town;
What wonder, then, that health and virtue, gifts
That can alone make sweet the bitter draught
That life holds out to all, should most abound,
And least be threatened, in the fields and groves.—COWPER.

AFTER Caroline had passed many anxious hours in the hope of seeing Mr. Meanwell, he one morning made his appearance at the rectory; he had a few days before called at the priory, and heard from Mrs. Bennet the particulars that have been before related.

Miss Lewson had retired to dress, and the doctor was gone out for a ride; he therefore lost no time in executing the commissions he was charged with. In the first place he had seen Mr. Newport, who had been privately to the priory, and commissioned him to give Caroline a thirty pound note, not knowing she had left the manor, and thinking she might want a trifle for immediate use. Caroline was not without money, yet she gratefully received the note as a token of Mr. Newport's friendship and consideration for her. She heard, too, that his residence in Surrey had been disposed of, and that he was gone to reside near London. Lady Emma, he informed her, had written privately to him on the subject of her removal, and that occasioned his call at the manor. Mrs. Bennet, too, had commissioned him to say that Mrs. Newland had requested her to continue at the manor till the family left it for Brighton, which would not be till the beginning of September; he advised her not to write to any one before she heard where Mrs. Newland would place her, when the family arrived in the country, for he observed, "It is not likely that she will let you continue so near the priory."

"I think," said Caroline, "that I had better go privately away, and never let any one hear of me again."

"Not for the world," was his reply; "such a proceeding would strengthen the vile tale they have fabricated, for it would instantly be reported that Lord Millford had planned your departure."

Ever alive to the rules of propriety, she admitted the truth of his observation, and the subject dropped. He awaited the return of Miss Lewson, and soon after departed.

In the evening an invitation came from a lady, who had taken what was called the lodge, at the extremity of the park, a rural and convenient house; it had been built by the late earl, as a residence for his countess, in case she survived him; after his decease, it had been let to a West India merchant, who had disposed of it to the present occupant.

"Is the invitation for dinner?" said the doctor.

Miss Lewson replied in the affirmative.

"But Miss Millbourne will be very dull alone," she added.

This the latter assured her would not be the case, and the invitation was accepted.

As it was a first visit, Miss Lewson determined on being very smart, and Caroline's taste was exerted to make her so. About three o'clock an elegant but plain chariot drove up to the door, into which the doctor handed his sister, and left their inmate to her own reflections. Unwilling to indulge painful recollections, she sat down to her embroidery. On their return home, Miss Lewson was in high spirits, delighted with Mrs. Clareville; and the doctor was no less pleased with his dinner, which he described as excellent.

"Mrs. Clareville has been very handsome!" said Miss Lewson.

"Ay," replied the doctor, "but she has seen her best days."

"And do you know she inquired who was my milliner," cried his sister, "for she admired my cap very much."

"Ay," said the doctor, "she suited her conversation to her company. She thought the outside of your head better ornamented than the in."

"How provoking you are to-night, brother. Well, I think it is the easiest carriage I ever rode in."

"Well," said the doctor, "I will go and smoke one pipe while you describe your visit, for I perceive you must do it before you must go to rest."

On his quitting the room, Miss Lewson entered into all the particulars of the day.

"Mr. Meanwell was there," said she. "I find he has been very serviceable to Mrs. Clareville, for settling everything for her with the person she took the house of; and though you were fearful of trusting me with a secret, Mr. Meanwell explained everything to us; for Mrs. Clareville seemed quite interested about you. Indeed, we thought Mrs. Newland was fearful that the captain was going to be married to you, when she sent you here, and I said so, when Mr. Meanwell said, he disliked everything like mystery when a lady's reputation was at stake, and then he told us what a vile tale had been circulated about you, for he had heard it all from Mrs. Bennet; in short, he said so many things in your favour, that Mrs. Clareville expressed a great desire to see you; and then I was obliged to tell her that you did not go out. Then she said she would 'call to-morrow morning if it was fine, and steal a look at you.' So, pray, be very smart, that you may do credit to all the fine things Mr. Meanwell said of you."

"I am extremely obliged to that gentleman," she answered, "for the interest he has taken in this affair, and I am sure every generous mind will acquit me of impropriety."

"To be sure they will," answered Miss Lewson; "for I am sure I do; and you might have trusted me with a letter, even if it had been to Lord Millford himself."

"I do not in the least doubt your inclination to serve me," replied Caroline; "but I never did write to Lord Millford, and it is not likely I ever shall do so."

The next morning about twelve Mrs. Clareville's carriage drove to the door, and the doctor, with great ceremony, conducted her to the parlour, where Miss Lewson and Caroline were seated at the work table; easy and lady-like in her behaviour, she fell into conversation with them on the common topics of the day, and very particularly heard Miss Lewson describe the *fete* that had been given at the priory, and the entertainment at the manor. This, naturally, drew Caroline into conversation, and led to different subjects, on which she displayed her taste and judgment. Mrs. Clareville spoke of books and music, and found the recluse well informed on both subjects.

"Oh," thought she, as she looked at the beautiful being that sat opposite her, "that such a flower should waste its sweetness on the desert air!"

While she was musing on the strange caprice of fortune, which had placed her in so secluded a situation, Caroline was secretly pleased with the hope of being better known to her. Charmed both with her ease and conversation, she thought the visit very short, though it had lasted two hours.

Knowing the restrictions Mrs. Newland had imposed, Mrs. Clareville did not distress Caroline by an invitation she could not accept, but said at parting that she should soon see them again.

During her ride home, her mind was wholly occupied in thinking if it would be possible to attach such a being to herself. The plan of life she had marked out on taking possession of the lodge did not afford her the satisfaction she had expected from it. Her life was solitary, her situation isolated, her health declining, and her spirits at times very languid. The canker-worm of sorrow had deeply corroded her heart, and in the language of an admired poet had " stolen nerve by nerve, and pulse by pulse away." Much of the gay world she had seen, but found nothing in its frivolties congenial to her feelings. Her physician had recommended her to try the medicinal waters of the Jessop's wells, which are similar to those of Harrogate. This once celebrated though now neglected place was within a few miles of the lodge, and the road to it was at once both rural and luxuriant. Yet in this ride, to which she was extremely partial, she had no companion, and her gentle heart sighed for some congenial mind, on which it might repose in safety. The person, the manners of Caroline, the accomplishments she was evidently mistress of, seemed to point her out as the very being fitted to share her retirement, and soothe with sympathy her solitary hours. In short, she determined, if possible, to gain her confidence, and free her instantly from the control of those who seemed so little sensible of her real value.

To accomplish her desire would, she perceived, require both address and delicacy, as she did not intend to visit any of the gay folks in the vicinage. She had no wish to address Mrs. Newland on the subject, as letters might lead to a personal interview, a thing to her by no means desirable.

After reflecting some time on the subject, she sent for Meanwell, in order to consult with him on the best method for obtaining the subject she had in view. The knowledge he had of the family that had hitherto protected Caroline induced her to think he might be a proper agent in the business for her.

Mr. Meanwell obeyed the summons to the lodge, and Mrs. Clareville instantly explained to him the subject on which she wished to consult him. Their tete-a-tete was long and uninterrupted, and from Meanwell Mrs. Clareville learned all the particulars he knew of Caroline, and her connection with the Newland family.

"It was a brother of Mrs. Newlands," he said, "that saved her from drowning, and afterwards supported her."

"Do you know his name," inquired Mrs. Clareville, with no small degree of agitation.

"Newport," answered the other.

"Newport!" repeated Mrs. Clareville, clasping her hands together, and sinking back pale and languid on her chair. "Gracious God," she cried, "how inscrutable are Thy ways; but let me," she continued, "collect my hurried thoughts—names are nothing."

The questions that followed elucidated a chain of strange events, for it appeared to demonstrate that Mrs. Clareville was the very person spoken of as the aunt of Caroline, who had been under her care for England, and was supposed to have perished with the rest of the passengers.

"But if this young lady is really the child of my brother," said Mrs. Clareville, "of which, in fact, I have little doubt, her name is neither Caroline nor Millbourne, but Emmeline Lesley."

"There is," Meanwell replied, "great probability in favour of the supposition; yet permit me, madam, to observe, that in the investigation of this business, be the result favourable or otherwise, great caution will be necessary, as you will have to combat with persons possessed of wealth, power, and influence, and well versed in all the arts of legal litigation."

"I see it all," Mrs. Clareville answered, "and will take no effective measures till the arrival of my brother, Baron Oreumburg, who was Colonel Lesley. He is now on the continent, but I expect him home within three months. My present object is to get this young lady under my own care. It would be most agreeable to me to have Mrs. Newland's approbation for her removal. If I cannot obtain that, I will endeavour to prevail on her to place herself under my care, and let them bring an action against me for her detention; and if I defend it, it must bring the whole subject fairly before a public tribunal."

Mr. Meanwell advised that the former measure should be first tried; "and I see," he added, "but one difficulty to be overcome in any proposals you may make for taking Miss Millbourne to reside with you."

Mrs. Clareville inquired what that difficulty was; and her adviser then stated, as far as his information and observations bore him out, the views of the Newlands. "The earl," he added, "has a very great predilection for Miss Millbourne; this has been viewed with a jaundiced eye by the Newlands, who are anxiously wishing to place the coronet on the head of their daugher; it i s not wealth they want, but honours. Mr. Newland's political influence, too, which is at present very great, would be infinitely increased, if an alliance between the families could be effected.

"Is it likely so to be?" Mrs. Clareville inquired.

"Too much so," was the answer, "as the expensive habits of our present race of nobility in general render it necessary for them to seek for wealth in their marriages, and I regret to say, that I fear Lord Millford will not be an exception to the reigning custom."

"But how?" inquired Mrs. Clareville, "would this interfere with this young lady's residence with me?"

"Only," he answered, "as she would be too near the priory; far from hence, depend upon it, madam, they will remove her before they come to the manor."

Mrs. Clareville paused for a few minutes, and then said, "I have some thoughts of going for a short season to Sidmouth; suppose Mrs. Newland was given to understand that I want this young lady as a travelling companion?"

"The very thing; I have no doubt but the proposal will be acceded to," replied her companion.

He then suggested that it would be better to send for Miss Lewson, and make her the principal in the business, "for," he continued, "I am no favourite, I know, with any of the family."

Mrs. Clareville remarked that she had no opinion of Miss Lewson's abilities as a negotiator, "for," she added, "the invitation I sent them was meant to discover

if there was anything about the lady that would render an intimacy desirable, but I soon perceived that she was not the person to my taste, and I am srue I should not be the one to her's."

"She has good nature about her," was the answer, "and is, I really believe, very partial to her lovely visitor."

"To that I readily give credence," said Mrs. Clareville. It was then agreed that the carriage should be sent the following morning to the rectory for Miss Lewson—and Meanwell soon after returned home; after his departure Mrs. Clareville.

No. 13.

ville sat down to reconsider all that had passed, and had scarce a doubt left on her mind of Caroline being the only child of her brother; she well remembered Newport, he was the companion of their voyage; in the moment of danger, when the ship struck, she put the child in his arms and begged him to save her, and bear her to her anxious mother, who was then in England, hourly expecting their arrival; she saw him descend into the boat with the child in his arms, and a small portmanteau, which was safely secured being packed in skins, lashed to his shoulders; her terrors for their safety exceeded her own; the boat was tossed on the boisterous ocean; loud and terrible cries were heard between the pauses of the storm, and in a few seconds it was too fatally discovered that the boat was upset and all hopes of safety for the crew entirely annihilated. By what miracle Newport had escaped she had yet to learn, her own preservation had been strangely accomplished, so too might his have been : but for his conduct afterwards there could be but one motive assigned, and that was avarice, the contents of the portmanteau were invaluable; he know in part what it contained, and to obtain possession of it he had sacrificed his faith to his friend, and his conscience to his God. It may be supposed that these reflections blended with many others produced in a frame so delicate as that of Mrs. Clareville great perturbation of spirits; suspense and anxiety deprived her of sleep, and in the morning her attendant found her languid and feverish; she, however, though strongly opposed by her affectionate old nurse, insisted upon rising, and, with some difficulty wrote a few lines, requesting Miss Lewson to come immediately to her. When the carriage arrived at the rectory, and the note was delivered as directed, Miss Lewson was thrown into a most agreeable hurry of spirits.

"Dear me," she cried, as she entered the parlour, where Caroline was reading to the doctor, "here is Mrs. Clareville's carriage come for me; she wishes to see me directly; I wonder what is the matter."

"Perhaps she is ill," said Caroline, "and may want some one to sit with her; oh, that I were at liberty to attend on her, to watch by her as I did by our dear Lady Acrimony,' to soothe her hours of sickness and enliven those of health!"

Miss Lewson departed as soon as she had changed her dress, and Caroline continued to read till the hour of dining; the day seemed long, for she thought, at least, or she hoped Miss Lewson's visit to Mrs. Clareville was in some manner connected with her situation at the rectory; her suppositions were most agreeably realised on that lady's return, who, with an air of vast importance, answered her brothers abrupt inquiry of "Well, what was the business?" with an "Oh! Mrs. Clareville wished to consult me, that is to ask my opinion on the best method of applying to Mrs. Newland for her consent that this young lady, pointing to Caroline, may go with her to Sidmouth."

"To Sidmouth," said the doctor, "umph?"

"Do you think such a proposal will be rejected," said Caroline.

"I do not see why it should" was the answer, "but who is to make the inquiry?"

"I promised that you would write to Mrs. Newland," replied his sister.

"And will you, sir, so much oblige me?" said Caroline.

"To be sure I will," he answered. "I will write the very first thing in the morning if you remind me of it; but what have you got there, Hetty?" seeing a paper parcel in the hands of his sister.

"Why, some newspapers; I borrowed them for you," she replied, "there is to-day's among them. Mrs. Clareville made me bring it, for there is, she said, a strange paragraph in it, which seems to imply that Lord Millford has fought a duel."

"With whom," said Caroline, struggling to suppress every painful emotion.

"Look for the text," cried the doctor, "and we shall soon elucidate the mystery."

Miss Lewson took the paper and pointed to the paragraph, which the doctor with much composure prepared to read; he wiped his spectacles, took a pinch of snuff, drank a glass of wine, and read as follows :—

"We regret to state that a meeting took place yesterday morning in Hyde-park, between the Earl of M———, and Captain B———, of the Royal Navy; the latter is the nephew and presumptive heir of General B———, husband to the fair but, it is, said, frail Countess of M———; the former, we are informed, is severely wounded, having received the captain's ball in his right shoulder, which is not yet extracted." Caroline trembled, for her worst fears were realised.

Miss Lewson, perceiving her agitataion, said good naturedly,

"It may not be true, or it may allude to some other persons."

Caroline shook her head, and as many past occurrences rushed upon her memory, she answered

"I fear it is Lord Millford that is meant, and from my heart I feel for the sorrows of his sister."

The doctor railed at the depravity of the times, and Miss Lewson condemned without mercy the insincerity of one sex, and the levity of the other.

Caroline was silent, her heart was too much oppressed to enter further on the subject; and as soon as possible, she retired to her apartment, where the first thing that met her eye was the very fan Lord Millford had given her.

She took it in her hand, pressed it to her heart, mentally sighing,—

"Too dangerous emblem of what I once thought affection, I must, I will forget the giver."

She laid it down, took it up again, and at last laid it in the usual place beneath her pillow. Sleep was a stranger to her eyes; she dozed, 'tis true, but her slumbers were unrefreshing, and in the morning her pallid looks afforded ample scope for the sympathy of Miss Lewson. She, however, reminded the doctor of the letter he had promised to write, and he instantly set about the task; when completed, he presented it to Caroline for her perusal. The style was stiff and formal, but the meaning was clear; and without a single comment, she thanked him for the trouble he had taken, and begged that it might go as soon as possible to the post-office.

Her request was complied with, the doctor went out for a morning walk, and poor Caroline had to bear Miss Lewson's condolence, and listen to her conjectures. The day, on her part, was one of extreme anxiety, yet the suspense she must necessarily feel till the arrival of Mrs. Newland's letter was considerably lessened by reflecting on the danger of Lord Millford, and the distress of his amiable and affectionate sister. In the evening she was in some degree relieved by the arrival of Meanwell, but he could state no other particulars than those already related. His visit was short, and only paid to announce his intention of going the next day to London.

"I shall, most likely," he said, "return in the evening, and if I do, you may depend on seeing me the following morning."

This seemed an age to Caroline, yet it was one she felt she must bear with patience. The next morning, Mrs. Clareville called at the rectory, the doctor was engaged, and Miss Lewson was gone to D———, in the chaise, to make some necessary purchases for family use; and thus Caroline had the satisfaction of enjoying her company uninterrupted.

Mrs. Clareville availed herself of the opportunity that had so unexpectedly occurred, and hoped the proposal she had made to Miss Lewson met her willing accordance. Caroline, with great feeling, expressed her gratitude for Mrs. Clareville's consideration, and her hopes that Mrs. Newland would not refuse her consent to so polite a request. Mrs. Clareville's visit was long, and the conversation various; and the elegant ease and familiar tones of her voice soothed, though they could not dissipate, the anxiety of her companion. She spoke of the duel—that morning's papers had given more particulars—Lord Millford was considered out of danger, and the captain had quitted the kingdom.

"Thank Heaven!" she cried, "my dear Lady Emma will not lose a brother she so dearly loves."

Encouraged by the interest Mrs. Clareville expressed for the safety of Lord Millford, and the happiness of Lady Emma, she ventured to expatiate on the worth, the beauty, and interesting sweetness of her friend; the lustre of her mild blue eyes, and glossy ringlets of light brown hair were not forgotten. Mrs. Clareville listened with great pleasure to her description, as the energy she spoke with

proved her heart superior to the baneful influence of envy, and alive to the sympathies that adorn the character of woman. Mrs. Clareville at length bade her
a most affectionate adieu, and added,—

"I hope, shortly, to receive you at the lodge, and the sooner the better."

Caroline bowed her thanks, and the carriage drove away. The next day
brought the anxiously expected letter; it was addressed to the doctor, and was
perfectly satisfactory. Mrs. Newland had added a postscript to Caroline, in which
she observed :—"I hope your future conduct will not disgrace either Mrs. Newland's selection, or my approval of her very polite offer." She added, "my
poor brother is very ill, therefore I have not consulted him on the subject of your
removal."

"I will take a ride to the lodge," said the doctor, "and report Mrs. Newland's answer."

His sister thought Miss Millbourne had better write a note, and send it by the
boy, "and perhaps," she added, "Mrs. Clareville may wish me to go with our
young friend, for I know she will send the carriage."

This proposal was complied with, and as Miss Lewson had anticipated, an invitation was returned for the next day, for all three to dine at the lodge.

The carriage was at the rectory at the usual time the following morning, and a
note from Mrs. Clareville to Caroline, requesting her to bring with her whatever
she wanted for immediate use, and leave her trunks for another opportunity.

This agreeable mandate was cheerfully complied with; their reception was
friendly, and Mrs. Clareville's heartfelt welcome of Caroline brought tears of gratitude into her eyes, and feeling her heart too full for verbal expression she kissed
the offered hand of her new friend, and glided to a seat. Before dinner the
whole affair of the duel was talked over, and Miss Lewson was quite at home,
for it was a subject on which she could display her conversational powers.

"Mr. Meanwell promised to call on us, when he returned from London, to let
us know the exact state of the business," she said, "and I left word at home
that we were come here, so I dare say we shall see him in the course of the day."

"Mr. Meanwell will be a very agreeable addition to our little circle," Mrs.
Clareville answered. "He is a sensible, well educated man."

"Oh, yes, and very much of a gentleman," said Miss Lewson.

"Had he been otherwise than a gentleman," her brother replied, "he would
have been unfit for the station he has so long held at the priory."

After dinner the ladies retired, and left the doctor at leisure to finish his bottle
of Madeira; the day passed in great sociability, and in the evening the carriage
conveyed the doctor and his sister home. After their departure Mrs. Clareville,
leaning on the arm of her young companion, entered an elegant bed-chamber which
opened into a light dressing-room.

"From these windows," she said, "my dear Caroline—for I shall not use the
ceremony, when we are alone, of calling you Miss Millbourne—you will have a most
delightful prospect of woodland scenery; this apartment is your own, and in it I
hope you will enjoy many tranquil hours. My life," she continued, "has long
been saddened by painful recollections of early misfortunes, but I will not depress
your spirits, and I think you will endeavour to restore mine."

"Oh, what would so much add to my happiness, my dear madam," replied
Caroline, "as being the humble means of restoring yours."

As she spoke, every emotion of her feeling heart was visible on her expressive
countenance. Mrs. Clareville gave her a look at once affectionate and penetrating,
as she answered,—

"If I did not fear to distress you, I should inquire if"— she paused.

"Proceed, madam," cried the other, "nor fear distressing me, on any subject you
wish to be acquainted with."

"Did you then never hear if any inquiries were made after your family?"

"Never, madam," she answered; "it was a subject Mrs. Newland never entered
on, if it could be avoided. I have heard great pains have been taken to represent
me as the illegitimate daughter of Mr. Newport, yet his behaviour does not

indicate any such relationship, for if I am the offspring of affection, why does he avoid me ?"

" Then you have seldom seen him ?" said Mrs. Clareville.

" Once, and but once, for several years," she answered, "and then I did not know him ; but Mr. Montague Acrimony discovered him, through the disguise he had assumed. All I have ever heard, is that Mr. Newport, at the hazard of his own life, saved me from drowning, and adopted me as his own child."

Mrs. Clareville sighed deeply, and appeared much agitated. " We will drop the subject, for the present," she said ; then in rather a hurried tone she added, " it was from shipwreck he saved you. Oh, that word vibrates to my brain and almost touches a note of insanity, but yet, my dear, my interesting girl, we must speak of it again but, not to-night ; so pleasant dreams attend you. In the morning, if my nerves are quiet, we will renew the subject, when left alone."

Caroline could not avoid reflecting on the strange coincidence there appeared between Mrs. Clareville's and Mr. Newport's horror (as she had heard it described) of her strange though providential rescue from the pitiless deep.

" They are both strangers to each other," said she, mentally, " and yet the same chain of ideas corrode the peace of both."

In the morning, when they met at the breakfast-table, Mrs. Clareville seemed tranquil, but there was a visible dejection on her spirits, that she strove in vain to conquer ; on seeing Caroline looking earnestly at her, she said,—

" You must not, my dear Caroline, notice my being sometimes inattentive to passing events. I suffer most severely from nervous affections, though I endeavour, as much as possible to control their violence ; I do not expect you to devote more of your time to me than may be agreeable to yourself. Think that you are at home, and at liberty to do as you please ; here you will find many sources of amusement even if I am too indisposed for conversation, which I hope will not be the case ; my collection of books is not equal perhaps to the splendid libraries you have seen at other places, but it consists of the best authors in our language, and I receive from my bookseller most new publications, and in the music-room there is a fine-toned harp and a pianoforte in excellent order. Will you favour me with a specimen of your performance ?"

She instantly complied, and had the satisfaction to perceive that music had a most exhilarating influence on the spirits of Mrs. Clareville, whose countenance lost much of its sadness, while now and then a faint smile irradiated her fine features, and gave them an increased expression of softness, placidity, and benevolence.

When Caroline rose from the instrument, she expressed her admiration at the science she had acquired both in voice and execution ; this led to a morning's conversation on subjects our readers are already acquainted with, such as her leaving Mr. Bellamy's, and introduction to the duchess, and abrupt dismissal from the manor. " For one so young," said Mrs. Clareville, " you have experienced many perplexities, but in future I hope your days will pass with more serenity, at least with me you will be shielded from slander and spared unmerited mortification, and to one possessing so many sources of amusement, retirement can never be irksome."

The entrance of Mr. Meanwell gave a turn to the conversation.

" Feeling for your anxiety," said he, addressing Caroline, " I rode early this morning to the rectory, where I was agreeably surprised on hearing of your removal."

To a question from Mrs. Clareville of " How did you find Lord Milford ?" he answered. " Out of danger, but very weak from loss of blood ; yet, of the two, I think Lady Emma looked worse than her brother,"

" Ah, that I anticipated," said Caroline, " for she feels so acutely for every one she loves ; did you see any other part of the family ?" Caroline asked.

" None," he answered, " they were gone for a few days to old Windsor."

" What unfeeling women," she answered, " to leave Lady Emma at home under such circumstances."

" They think only of themselves," said Mrs. Clareville, "for dissipation chills the heart."

" Not always," Caroline replied, " for in the midst of folly, Lady Emma is still herself."

" Did you hear any particulars beyond what we have before heard," said Mrs. Clareville.

Her visitor replied that Lady Emma had followed him from the sick chamber, and, from her, he had heard that Captain B—— had long suspected the irregularities of the countess, and in consequence had narrowly watched her conduct; when it became too flagrant to escape general observation, he acquainted the general with the statement of facts that were in his possession; the very infirm state of the general's health prevented him from seeking personal satisfaction, which had led to the captain's taking the affair upon himself.

During this part of the conversation, Caroline retired to dress for dinner, and then Meanwell inquired of Mrs. Clareville, if she meant to acquaint Miss Millbourne with her surmises of their affinity to each other.

" Not at present," she replied, " as all inquiries would be useless while Newport is not in a state to be brought forward."

Meanwell shook his head, saying, " I fear they will take advantage of his infirmity to confine him for life."

" And in that case," said Mrs. Clareville, " all hopes of justice will be frustrated."

" Not entirely, I trust," he answered, " for I think the cause of truth and justice will at length prevail."

At the request of Mrs. Clareville, Meanwell stayed to dinner, and during their afternoon's conversation, Caroline discovered that Mrs. Clareville had some knowledge of the family at Firr Grove.

" Sir Timothy had a sister," she said, " some years younger than himself."

" So I have heard," replied Meanwell, " but I never knew her, though I have frequently heard her spoken of by the late countess."

" I knew her well," answered Mrs. Clareville, " and to know her was to love her, for she was all that could be expected in woman; she married unknown to him, and he never forgave her."

" Is Sir Timothy so very inflexible," said Caroline, in visible emotion, secretly trembling for the fate of her friend.

" He is very positive," Meanwell replied, " and when he has once imbibed a prejudice, seldom abandons it."

" Not a character either to esteem or imitate," said Mrs. Clareville.

" The baronet is not generally beloved," Meanwell answered, " yet I venture to assure you, madam, that there are traits in his character worthy of admiration; he was a good husband, and an affectionate parent, and is without doubt an honest man."

" And as that is said to be the noblest work of God," said Mrs. Clareville, " we will leave the baronet in full possession of the honours he deserves."

Soon after tea, Meanwell took his leave, and Mrs. Clareville finding herself rather indisposed, retired early, and Caroline amused herself with a book till bed-time; when, going into Mrs. Clareville's chamber to bid her good night, she found her very ill, having just recovered from a fainting fit.

" Why did you not call me?" she said to the attendants.

" My lady is often so, miss," said an aged woman, called Martha, who always slept in Mrs. Clareville's chamber, " and I thought it would be a pity to disturb you."

" Never think of me," she answered, " under any circumstances in which I can be serviceable to your lady."

A sense of consciousness seemed to return, for the patient sufferer extended her hand towards Caroline, and by a look indicated that she wished her to retire.

" Not till you are more at ease, my dear madam," she said, pressing the offered hand as she sat down beside her.

A refreshing slumber followed; and after an hour's rest she awoke collected, and then Caroline at her earnest request, retired to her own chamber. The following morning she was early up, and heard that Mrs. Clareville had some degree of fever, and was unable to rise, and that a servant had been despatched to London for her physician. With an aching heart, she presented herself at the bed-side, and found the invalid supported by pillows, who said, on seeing her,—

"My dear Caroline, you must not be alarmed. I am very much subject to these fits; mental exertion is sure to bring them on, and during the last few days my mind has been very much hurried; but as soon as I am able, I will explain to you the source of my anxiety. You are deeply interested in it—but more of this another time."

Caroline was astonished; yet, after a moment's recollection, she thought that through weakness, Mrs. Clareville's mind wandered, and therefore did not reply, but retired to a distant part of the room, where at her desire breakfast was prepared, and there she continued till the physician arrived. On his entrance, Mrs. Clareville seemed perfectly composed.

"This air," he said, "is too sharp; I always thought it would be so, though the gentlemen with whom I consulted thought differently; yet my judgment was always in favour of a milder air."

"It is the last resort," she answered, "and tells me truly that you have nothing else to propose; however, as I, like all the rest of Adam's race, cling to life, I will adopt the means you propose for its preservation."

Mrs. Clareville continued for some time very languid; but as soon as she thought herself sufficiently recovered to bear the fatigue of travelling, she gave the necessary orders for her journey. Previous to its commencement, an agent in London had taken for her a convenient furnished house at Sidmouth, the place she had before fixed on during her confinement. She one day said to Caroline, who seldom left her room,—

"I have heard you speak of the Duchess of Moncrieff; it has occurred to my recollection, that a maternal aunt of mine married into that family. I do not know if she ever arrived at the title, for I left Scotland in my childhood; and never after heard (except by chance) of my mother's family."

Caroline replied that she had a small M.S. in her possession, which the duchess had permitted her to copy. "It will most likely, madam," she said, "afford you all the information you may require."

"Well, then," she answered, "to-morrow you shall read it; at present, I should rather hear you sing some little plaintive song, for your soft notes always soothe my spirits."

Caroline instantly complied, and commenced with "Oh, Nanny, wilt thou gang wi' me." She had finished the first verse, when, hearing the door softly open, she beheld Martha standing in an attitude of astonishment.

"What is it that frightens you?" said Mrs. Clareville. "Come in, and hear Miss Millbourne sing one of your old favourite songs."

"Oh, gracious me, my leddy," she replied, in her broad Scotch accent, "I could have sworn that I heard your ain dear mither, Lady M'Gregoire, singing when I opened the door."

Caroline said the duchess had more than once made the same observation.

"I shall now indeed be anxious to hear your M.S.," cried Mrs. Clareville, "for the duchess must certainly have known Lady M'Gregoire, or she would not have made the observation. But, you were saying, you wished to write to her grace before we commenced our journey, and as there will be no time to spare, Martha will stay with me while you are so engaged, but do not name my curiosity about the manuscript."

"Certainly not," she answered; and immediately set about the pleasing task, happy to think that the restraint on her correspondence no longer existed. She wrote also a few lines to Lady Emma, but cautiously avoided naming Lord Millford, confining herself to the description of her own situation with Mrs. Clareville, and the preparations that were making for their journey to Sidmouth, at which place she hoped to meet a lettter from her ladyship.

To both these she received immediate answers.

The duchess congratulated her on her change of circumstances; she touched lightly on the duel, and stated that it was generally supposed a divorce would be sued for; and that an action against Lord Millford was actually commenced.

Lady Emma wrote in a very dejected style, said she was going to old Windsor with her brother; but it was expected that Mrs. Pembroke and Lady Lucy would accompany the Newlands to the manor, and it was thought they would spend the remainder of the season either at Bath or Brighton. "The Christmas," she added, " will as usual be kept at the manor, and after that period I sincerely hope I shall quit these gay circles for ever. One thing," said her ladyship, "has given me great perplexity, and that is, that I have most unaccountably lost Montague' miniature. I never wore it, never told any one but Millford that I had it. I remember leaving it one morning on my dressing table; there were many trinkets there of more value to any one but me, yet that is the only thing missing."

The morning after the letters had been written, Caroline introduced her manuscript, and at Mrs Clareville's request read as follows.

CHAPTER XII.

All nature is but an unknown to thee,
All chance, direction which thou canst not see,
All discord, harmony not understood,
All partial evil, universal good.—POPE.

"THE DUCHESS OF MONCRIEFF TO THE HON. MRS. BYRON.

"AGREEABLE to the promise I made you when we parted at Edinburgh, I transmit you the little history you were so desirous of possessing. The memory of my dear sister's beauty and misfortunes is yet fresh in the memory of many of our contemporaries; and the little you have heard, I conclude, induced you to wish for more particular information. You must, my dear madam, retrograde full forty years. At the time I am about to speak I was young and beautiful, now I am infirm and old. But to be brief:—

"Emmeline and Rodolpha were the daughters of Sir James M'Donald of Clydesdale Emmeline was by two years my senior. Our father died when we were in our infancy, leaving us joint heiresses to his fortune. Our mother was a most exemplary character, and amply supplied the loss we had sustained, by the death of her husband. When Emmeline was in her eighteenth year, she went to pass the winter with an old friend in the northern capital; there she formed an acquaintance with a Captain Lessley, a young man of good family, but small fortune; to whom, without the consent or knowledge of her family, she was privately married. The friends on both sides were at first very angry with the young people, for in the eyes of the sage and experienced, it seemed a most imprudent step. The captain's fortune was next to nothing, and Emmeline had only five thousand pounds, till the death of Lady M'Donald; when the entire property was to be divided between us. I, too, was to receive the same sum if I married with the consent of my mother, there was also the same clause annexed to Emmeline's fortune; but she knew our dear mother would take no advantage of that circumstance. After some time the elders of the two families met, and wisely agreed to make the best settlement they could for the young people. Lady M'Donald advanced the five thousand pounds which she might have retained; it was in consequence secured to my sister and her heirs. The interest of that with Lessley's income, and the money he obtained by the sale of his commission, (for at Emmeline's request he consented to give up the dangerous profession of arms,) produced a genteel income; they took a romantic and retired abode, and for some years enjoyed all the happiness that refined and congenial minds were capable of receiving. In that time, Emmeline became a mother, her first child was a son, her second, a daughter, and they were named after their parents, James and Emmeline. This scene of harmony was too soon interrupted; a severe malady attacked poor Lesley, and he was ordered to the capital for medical advice,

Alas, it was fruitless; he languished a few months, and left my poor sister a monument of sorrow. After spending a short time with some friends at Edinburgh, she returned to her once cheerful habitation, indulging herself with the melancholy pleasure of thinking that she should devote her future life to the dear children of her beloved Lessley. The illness of my mother prevented me from going to her, but it was agreed that she should pass the ensuing summer at Clydesdale. In

No. 14.

the meantime, one of her former admirers again made proposals; he was rejected, for nothing could wean her heart or divert her recollections from the husband she had lost; but Lord M'Gregoire was not easily repulsed, while his rank and fortune induced her friends to wish he might succeed. For many months he pursued her with increasing earnestness, but without advancing in the least degree in her favour. He was a man of turbulent and vindictive passions, over which reason had but little controul, and as he could not gain Emmeline by entreaties, he determined on gaining possession of her person by fraud. Knowing of her dear mother's illness, he availed himself of that circumstance. A messenger was sent to her, who stated that Lady M'Donald lay at the point of death, and that he came on purpose to inform her that no time was to be lost if she wished to see her mother alive. Justly alarmed for the life of a parent so deservedly dear to her, Emmeline requested the messenger to hasten his return, and send a postchaise from the nearest town for her immediate conveyance. The distance from our residence to Mrs. Lessley's was about twenty miles. Lord M'Gregoire had one in the road between us. That part of Scotland was then very uncultivated, and the space between us was a barren heath, with the exception of a few gentlemen's seats, and here and there a scattered village. When the chaise arrived, poor Emmeline kissed her dear children, and resigned them to the care of a most affectionate domestic."

At this part of the narrative, Martha betrayed evident emotion; but a look from her lady kept her silent.

"Without the least apprehension of personal danger, Emmeline performed the first part of her journey, and was within ten miles of its conclusion when evening came on, and on looking from the window she perceived a carriage standing in the road side with two men on horseback close to it. Scarce had she made the observation before the men advanced, and informed her the other carriage was waiting for her; then it was that the dread of treachery first dawned upon her mind; she hesitated and inquired by ' whose orders the other chaise had been sent?' No answer was returned; she was forcibly placed in it; the other was paid and dismissed, after her portmanteau was taken from it; she was placed between them, and the chaise drove off with great velocity. Alarmed at so singular an occurrence, Emmeline implored them to inform her by whose orders they acted, and to what place they were conveying her, for from the feeble light left by the receding sun, she perceived they had quitted the usual road with which she was well acquainted.

" To these questions they returned no answer, but to quiet her apprehensions assured her no injury was intended.

" Distracted at the thoughts of Lady M'Donald's danger, and the distance to which she, by the rapidity of the chaise, found she was being conveyed from her dear children, she burst into an agony of tears, and in tones almost inarticulate, implored them to let her return home. To this no reply was made, and finding entreaties useless, for the remainder of the journey she remained silent.

"About midnight they stopped at an old stone building, which, from the light the moon threw over it, appeared more like a prison for the guilty than a habitation for the innocent. Almost lifeless, she was conducted to a large gloomy chamber, the windows of which were barred with iron, and the furniture appeared coeval with the building. An old woman soon after made her appearance, with some warm wine and coarse brown bread, and told her the bed was well aired, and advised her to go directly into it, and endeavour to recover from her fatigue. This she declined, and requested to be left alone. The woman seemed concerned for her, and told her she was in perfect safety, for that no person would intrude on her privacy.

" Somewhat consoled by this assurance, the trembling and exhausted sufferer threw herself on the bed. A lamp was left burning on the hearth, that only served to make darkness more visible. For some hours sleep was a stranger to her eyes, but at last its refreshing influence afforded a short suspension from sorrow. As soon as the morning light appeared through the thick cloth curtains that shaded the windows, she arose, and looking out, perceived the sea at a distance, while all around seemed heath and mountain. The building was evidently one of feudal construction, for its battlements still frowned majestic in decay. Then it was that she felt assured by whom this act of treachery had been planned; for she had frequently heard this old castle spoken of by Lord M'Gregoire; and when the female attendant entered with breakfast, she enquired if the castle did not belong to him, and was answered in the affirmative, with the addition that the laird was come, and begged permission to see her.

" Feeling she was now so completely in his power, she thought it would be imprudent to incense him by a refusal. She therefore said, when she had changed her dress, which she had not before taken off, she would attend him. In about an hour, there was a knock at the chamber door, and on her opening it, M'Gregoire presented himself. He took her passive hand, drew it under his arm, and conducted her to a small parlour, more modernly furnished than the chamber she had quitted. He then condescended to apologise to his trembling and agitated companion for the violence his unbounded love had compelled him to practise.

" Emmeline entreated him to let her return home, or consent to her sending word of her safety to her friends.

" Both these requests were haughtily refused, and he candidly informed her that, unless she consented to be his wife, she would never see again either her children or friends.

" ' You will not—cannot act so cruel,' said the weeping Emmeline.

" ' You were ever cruel to me,' he answered, ' and my determination is unalterable.'

" ' But my mother—is she really so very ill?' said Emmeline.

" ' She is no worse than when you last heard from Rodolpha,' was the answer. ' And in one month from this time you shall see her if you consent to my proposals; if not, you must abide the consequences of your own temerity, for I am resolved not to live without you.'

" Several days passed in angry conferences, in which poor Emmeline found she gained nothing; for the inflexible M'Gregoire would not concede a single point to her. At length, finding he became more importunate in his addresses, and fearing he might, from being an honourable lover, be driven by resistance into less justifiable measures, she most reluctantly yielded her consent, and gave her hand to one her heart rejected, and her judgment disapproved. He then allowed her to write to Lady M'Donald, and also condescended to write himself. He entreated she would pardon the measures he had adopted for securing the hand of her daughter, and concluded by saying his future life should be devoted to the promotion of her happiness, and that of her family. Though the contents of these letters were far from agreeable, yet they relieved us from such intense anxiety as induced us to overlook, though we could not approve, the measures he had practiced. As Emmeline was his wife, he could not be made amenable for the outrage he had committed, and both his rank and fortune placed him almost beyond the reach of censure. I would have written as my heart dictated, and upbraided him with the treachery of his conduct, but my dear mother restrained my pen.

" ' Write cautiously,' she cried, ' and do not wound the peace of Emmeline, by offending her lord.'

" I did so; and for once disguised my sentiments under the garb of dissimulation. My mother, more collected and less guided by feeling than myself, wrote a particular statement of the alarm we had felt for her safety. ' Your valued Martha,' she said, ' was fearful that my death occasioned your silence, as you had promised to send to her on your arrival here. She waited near a week, and then sent the man servant on horseback to inquire after my health. Judge of our surprise, anxiety, and consternation. Your letter has restored our serenity—the dear children are with me, and shall continue here till your lord permits me to restore them to your maternal bosom.' This letter, we afterwards heard, soothed the spirits of Lady M'Gregoire, and his lordship also appeared satisfied with th one addressed to him. After a very few weeks our dear Emmeline discovered that her so late passionate lover was changed into an imperious and domineering tyrant.   The visit he had promised she should make to her mother had been on many frivolous occasions postponed, and at last his almost constant ill-humour prevented her from naming it to him.   Her letters were short, and betrayed by their brevity the restraint they were written under.   He had removed his beautiful victim to a seat near the capital, where his eldest daughter presided (he had a family by his first lady of four daughters).   She received Lady M'Gregoire with apparent civility, but concealed dislike.   Lady Beatrice possessed few advantages, either personal or acquired ; and the narrowness of her heart made her look with an eye of envy on the beauty and accomplishments of my sister.   Many were the mortifications she had to support, and many the quarrels she had to appease between her lord and his daughter, whose violent spirit opposed itself even to him.   At length, anxious to see our poor Emmeline, and vexed at M'Gregoire's neglect of his voluntary promise, my mother wrote to request he would allow her to spend a few weeks with us and the dear children ; and in a short time after the receipt of the letter, he sent her to us in a most elegant carriage, attended by three livery servants.   Lady M'Donald wept over her daughter, who drooped like a fading flower beneath the costly trappings that surrounded her. I admired the jewels that decorated her person—the equipage that she reclined in ;   yet I thought she did not look half so happy as when she used to ride on her little Shetland pony, by the side of poor Lessley.   Most thankful was the sensitive and sorrowing Emmeline for the opportunity of pouring her sorrows into the bosom of her friends without interruption.   She would sit for hours with the children—weep over them and lament the fatal elevation that had so long separated her from them.   During such times she would describe the caprice and violence of M'Gregoire's temper, and contrast it with the mild, forbearing, and affectionate behaviour of her lamented Lessley.   On such occasions, Lady M'Donald would reason with her in the most endearing manner ; and endeavour to impress upon her mind the necessity of submitting patiently to a fate that could not be altered. 'It is in vain,' she would say, ' to contend with persons who are guided only by the dictates of passion.   If they have not reason on their side, they commonly have power, and that is, in such hands, a more destructive weapon ; therefore, as you value peace, avoid, if possible, all altercation.'   As for me, I was for open rebellion.

" ' Hush, my dear Rodolph,' said Lady M'Donald, ' remember that Emmeline is bound, by her own vow, to obey her lord.'

" ' Well,' said I, ' it may be so, but I should take that word in a very limited sense, and act on my own definition of it.'

" ' So I thought once,' answered my sister ; ' but then I was a happy wife, and it was pleasure to yield obedience where none was exacted.' As she was speaking, a letter was presented to her ; it announced that Lord M'Gregoire was on the road, and would be with us in the evening.   He came, and on his appearance, the serenity poor Emmeline had in some degree regained, vanished like a sun beam. He paid his compliments to Lady M'Donald and myself, and then taking the extended hand of Caroline, he inquired if she was ready to attend him home on the following day.   She bowed an assent, and he then asked after the children.   They were instantly sent for.'

" ' They are grown,' said he, ' and seem less troublesome than when with you. I think you had better settle with Lady M'Donald, for their continuance here.'

" ' My lord,'' said she, turning pale and trembling, ' I hoped—I understood they were to reside with us.'

" ' Then you deceived yourself,' he answered, ' for I never intended any such thing.   Children disturb me ; I cannot bear their noise, and, besides, I should not like to be continually reminded of their father.'

" ' I should never remind you of him, my lord,' she answered, tears trembling in her eyes, ' though I shall never forget him.'

" ' That I well know,' he replied, ' and your continual fondling of the children would be disagreeable to me, for I should think that you thought more of their dead father, than you did of your living husband.'

" Here Lady M'Donald interposed, and said she would willingly take the care of them upon herself.

" ' I have,' he said, ' ordered my house, at Edinburgh, to be got ready for your reception. Beatrice will meet us there, and, perhaps, Miss M'Donald will favour us with her company for a month or two.' To this proposal I willingly acceded, and Emmeline, grateful for this little act of civility, became more tranquil. The next day, before our departure, he requested a short audience with our mother; she led the way to an inner room, and Emmeline and myself were left to conjecture what the subject could be, that we were not to be hearers of. Before our departure, however, Lady M'Donald related the substance of their conference to me in private, that I might prepare my sister for the trial that awaited her.

" ' I was but trying last evening,' he said, ' how Emmeline would take the separation from these children.'

" ' Then you intend taking them with you, my lord ?'

" ' No, madam,' said he, ' I mean to send them to England, to their father's uncle, Sir Malcolm Lessley, to whom I have written on the subject, and he has consented to receive them, and if Emmeline consents to this arrangement cheerfully, she will much oblige me; if not, you may dispose of them and their trifling pittance in the best way you can.'

" Shocked and surprised at this strange proposal, she implored him to have some consideration for the feelings of her daughter, and not to separate her so great a distance from her children.

" ' The further off the better,' he replied, ' and then I shall not be importuned with solicitations for her seeing them, which, I perceive, will be endless, if they continue here; besides, she may have other children, and I should not choose them to have any rivals in her affections. Will your ladyship inform her of my intentions ?''

" ' Indeed, my lord, I cannot undertake so unfeeling a commission; the thought of it would destroy her.'

" ' Then,' said he, impetuously, ' I will do it myself, for I am not to be diverted from my purpose.'

" ' Leave it to Rodolpha,' cried my mother, ' and let her prepare Emmeline for this unnecessary measure.'

" This, after some little demur, he consented to, and added,—

" ' I expect this winter to conclude a marriage I have long had in contemplation for Lady Beatrice ; my younger children I have provided for with their mother's family ; they will never trouble me, and when they are marriageable, I shall dispose of them. They shall never intrude either on the time or convenience of Lady M'Gregoire, and as I have given up my children, she can have no plea for not resigning hers.'

" ' This is a subject on which we cannot all think alike, my lord.'

" ' My wife, Lady M'Donald, must fashion her thoughts by my directions.' " So saying, he quitted the apartment, and, on returning to us, the hurried tones of his voice betrayed evident marks of irritation. Little Emmeline was on her mother's knee.

" ' Come,' said he, ' let us have no long ceremony of leave taking I think you have had time enough for fondling ; be quick, the carriage is in waiting.'

" He left the room, Emmeline retired to bid her little boy farewell, and then Lady M'Donald vested me with my painful commission. Oh, how I hated the monster that could exact such a sacrifice.

" Our journey was very unpleasant ; Lord M'Gregoire was out of temper, he quarrelled with the servants, railed at poor Emmeline for turning pale as we passed the cottage where she had passed so many happy hours with her beloved Lessley, now desolate and abandoned—the furniture having previously been sold by his directions—and the servants dismissed.

" On our arrival, we found Lady Beatrice ready to receive us—I was at that time a pupil of Lavater's, and gave full credence to many of his observations. I did not like the countenance of Lady Beatrice ; her mouth did not please me, her nose was too prominent for the rest of her features, while her little sunk grey eyes spoke everything but good nature. In her figure, too, she was tall without being graceful, and her arms seemed to dangle on her shoulders, rather than suspended from them. However, in a few days we got tolerably sociable, and dashed together into all the gaieties that Edinburgh afforded; but Lady M'Gregoire took no pleasure in the festivities that surrounded her, for she was languid, melancholy, and dejected; and I could not gain sufficient resolution to tell her of the trial that awaited her.

" I wrote to Lady M'Donald, and informed her of my inability to perform the task she had assigned me. I told her, too, of Lord M'Gregoire's splendid establishment, and of a conquest I had made over the heart of Reginald Raithsay, presumptive heir of the Duke of Moncrieff, and the intended husband of Lady Beatrice. Emmeline wrote by the same post, though I did not then know the contents of her letter, I afterwards perused it, and it cost me many tears. Lord M'Gregoire had informed her of his determination of sending the dear children to their uncle, and a little to soften the agitation of her spirits, he added,—

" ' You may return with Rodolpha,' and spend a month with them before they commence their journey to the south.'

"She added, 'I shall be happy to restore my sister to you, for I can perceive she is no longer a welcome visitor here; her wit, her vivacity, her beauty and fascination of manners, so totally eclipse poor Lady Beatrice, that the hopes my lord has so long cherished respecting her marriage with Raithsay will, I think, entirely fade away.'

" These letters did not raise the before languid spirits of Lady M'Donald; the inflexibility of M'Gregoire's temper excited her indignation; and she saw, too plainly, that Emmeline was slowly sinking under the severity of her splendid lot. She feared that the conquest I had made would only increase the misery of my sister by irritating the irascible passions of M'Gregoire. Besides, she thought a union with Raithsay would not be sanctioned by the duke. In family, I was his equal, but not in fortune; and, though the Moncrieffs were possessed of very ancient honours, they were, from causes connected with the history of their country, much reduced in circumstances; and Lady Beatrice would have carried with her a most ample fortune. She, however, concealed her uneasiness, and answered in a general way, saying she should be happy to receive us at our own time. She also wrote to Sir Malcolm concerning the children, and he answered by saying he would receive them with pleasure, and consider them as his own. He rather indignantly rejected an offer Lord M'Gregoire had made him of adding a trifle towards their support, saying the children of his brother should never be indebted to a man that could cruelly insult the feelings of their mother. He desired a female attendant might be sent with them, and at Lady M'Donald's appointment they should be met at Edinburgh by his steward, who would conduct them safe to his residence. Martha cheerfully agreed to accompany them, for, as she was separated from her dear lady, she determined to devote herself to the service of her children. The time for our departure was expired, but a heavy snow had fallen, so as to render travelling unsafe in that part of the kingdom. I did not much regret the delay it occasioned, as it kept me nearer Raithsay, though I was thoroughly disgusted with the imperious and turbulent behaviour of M'Gregoir who was constantly tormenting his angelic wife. Raithsay came but seldom to the house, but he contrived to see me most days at the places he knew I frequented, and a correspondence was carried on between us through the agency of a friend, and entirely unknown to Lady M'Gregoire; but the demon jealousy discovered it. Lady Beatrice intercepted a letter from Raithsay to me, in which he had pressed me to consent to a private marriage before I left Edinburgh, saying he had written to the duke to break off the treaty he was engaged in, as Lady Beatrice was a woman he could never think of marrying. This letter she gave the earl, who, infuriate with rage, rushed into his lady's apartment, and reproached her most bitterly with being the contriver of a scheme calculated to destroy the plan he had been so long maturing. Surprised at hearing of a correspondence she did not know of, she firmly, though mildly, defended her own conduct. I was passing by the door, when I heard M'Gregoire loudly denouncing vengeance on his weeping wife. I entered, and inquired the cause of his anger.

" ' You are the cause, my confident lady,' he answered; ' how dared you presume, while under my roof, to carry on a clandestine correspondence with Raithsay? Here is the proof of it,' said he, holding the letter up; 'have you the effrontery to deny it?'

" ' I have no intention of denying it,' I answered; ' but I should like, my lord, to know by what means you became possessed of that letter, and what right you had to open it.'

" ' By the right of being the protector of your character,' he answered, ' at least while you remain here.'

" ' I will spare you any further trouble on that account,' I replied, ' for I will quit your house to-night, and Edinburgh to-morrow morning, if the roads are passable.'

" ' Perhaps,' said he, with a sneer, ' you may intend travelling towards Moncrieff Castle; it is a long journey, and will require more money than you are mistress of to gain admittance there.'

" ' If I ever undertake that journey, my lord,' I cried, ' I shall travel in my own carriage, and send my husband there before me, to have the gates opened.'

" ' Insolent,' he answered; ' but observe, Miss M'Donald, I shall apprise both the duke and your mother of this improper correspondence, and the ungrateful return you have made me for marrying her handsome beggar.'

" ' You married to please yourself, my lord; it was no compliment paid to us, and the method you took to accomplish it, no credit to yourself; and if you can persuade Raithsay to marry Lady Beatrice, I do assure you that I shall be no obstacle to the union.'

" ' Weak girl!' replied the mortified peer, ' do you think Raithsay is seriously inclined to marry you?'

" ' I cannot answer for his thoughts, my lord, and but seldom for my own—yet, I believe he has too high a sense of honour to profess a passion he does not feel, and too much spirit to be dictated to by any lord on earth.'

" ' You will not,' said Emmeline, who sat almost motionless with terror, ' leave me so soon as to-morrow?'

" ' Miss M'Donald,' answered Mr. Gregoire haughtily, ' has fixed her own time, and I expect she will keep it—but observe, Emmeline, I forbid your journey.'

" ' Oh, do not,' she cried, ' in pity, do not recall the promise you so freely made me.'

" ' I have already recalled it,' he answered sternly.

" ' Then I am not to see the dear children before their departure for England,' said Emmeline, mournfully. ' Oh, my lord, as a father, surely you will have some pity for a mother's feelings.'

" ' I have,' he replied, ' and therefore forbid this journey; the fatigue in your present situation would be too much for you.''

" ' The fatigue,' she said, ' would be nothing compared to the pleasure it would afford me.'

" ' You must find your pleasure,' he replied, ' in obeying my commands; and not in devising means to counteract them.' So saying, he quitted the room.

" ' Rodolpha, my dear Rodolpha,' cried Emmeline, ' why did you venture on this dangerous correspondence.'

" ' Emmeline,' said I, ' Why did you marry Lessley?'

" ' The case,' she answered, ' is widely different, our marriage involved none but ourselves in difficulties.''

" ' Well, Emmeline,' I answered, ' I regret from my heart that this affair should have occasioned you one moment's uneasiness—and yet I will be a duchess in spite of Lord M'Gregoire and his envious daughter.'

" ' Rank, Rodolpha, does not always ensure felicity,' was her reply.

" ' I see it does not,' was my answer; ' but what station in life does insure it? And if I consider precedence one of its auxiliaries you cannot blame me for endeavouring to obtain it.'

" ' The next morning I prepared for my departure; neither Lord M'Gregoire nor

Lady Beatrice attended the breakfast table. I despatched a short note to Raithsay, relating the circumstances that had occurred, and after a most affectionate leave of my agonised sister, set out on my return home, with no other attendant than my own woman. My reception from my dear mother was a warm and tender welcome, mixed with sorrow unfeigned, for the splendid misery of Emmeline. A few days after my arrival at home, I received a letter from Reginald, it was dated from Edinburgh, and informed me he was sent for by express, and then was on the point of setting out for Moncrieff Castle, and that he should call at Clydesdale House on his way thither. He came, and had no occasion to complain of his reception; candid, sanguine, and ardent in his love for me, he explained, without the least reserve, to Lady M'Donald, his present state and future prospects, who delighted with his sincerity, and flattered by the encomiums he lavished on her daughter, made no objection to the proposals he made; yet she regretted on Emmeline's account that he had broken off the marriage with Lady Beatrice.

" ' If I had never seen Miss M'Donald,' said he, ' I could never have been the lover of that lady; besides, I never gave my consent to the articles being prepared. I once told the duke when speaking on the subject, that if I found her ladyship less disagreeable than fame reported her to be, that I would, to oblige him, allow the treaty to go forward—as it was so much pressed by Lord M'Gregoire—but on my introduction to her, I found her more repulsive than rumour had reported.

" ' And who,' added he, gallantly, taking my hand, ' could this fair mountain leave to batten on that moor.'

" ' But there is a mighty mountain between us, Raithsay,' said I, ' no less a one than the duke's consent.'

" ' Does my presumption lead me too far, if I calculate on that being the only mountain I have to remove?'

" I smiled, and told him, ' if I should travel to Moncreiff Castle, that it must be in my own carriage.'

" ' Then so it shall be,' he answered, while his animated looks spoke his gratitude, for the feelings of his noble heart beamed upon his manly countenance; ' and I will hasten, my own Rodolpha, to ensure you a kind reception there.'

" The dear children were then inquired for, and while caressing them he joined me in execrating the conduct of Lord M'Gregoire. He soon after took his leave, and promised to return with all possible expedition to report, he predicted, the success of his application.

" The next day a letter arrived from Lady M'Gregoire, who wrote ' that she had sustained a most violent contest with her lord, on account of Raithsay and myself; that he had at last consented that the children should spend a few days with her previous to their eternal separation from her; if you can but come with them, my dear and honoured madam,' she added, ' it would indeed be pouring the balm of comfort into a wounded heart.'

" Lady M'Donald wrote in reply, ' that as soon as the days lengthened, and the weather improved, she would conduct the little ones to Edinburgh, and there wait the arrival of Sir Malcolm's steward.'

" In the mean time, poor Emmeline endeavoured to appear cheerful, and to bear without resentment the contumelious behaviour of her lord, whose elegant and expensive entertainments filled his mansion with all the fashionable idlers of the northern capital; through whom the beauty, the taste and manners of Lady M'Gregoire, were become the theme of public admiration. His lordship's pride was gratified with the unequivocal approbation that followed the conduct of his lady, and treated her with more consideration than he had before done; but the envy of Lady Beatrice was a constant scource of vexation to her.

" In the interval, letters arrived from the Highlands, in which Raithsay stated, that an important change had taken place during his late absence from the castle. In the first place, his Grace had answered Lord M'Gregoire's angry letter, saying—' It was never his intention to place any restraint on his nephew's inclinations.' ' I regret,' he said, ' that Raithsay should not have taken the same view of the subject as we did; but at all events I am pleased to find that he had made choice of a lady allied so nearly to Lady M'Gregoire.' This was the first article : the next was of more importance.

" When Raithsay entered Moncrieff Castle, he found the duke in deep mourning, as well as all the attendants ; on expressing his surprise, the duke said,—

" ' I have sent for you, Reginald, on very unpleasant business ; we have lost Mrs. Umphreville, or, more properly speaking, my wife.'

" ' You astonish me,' was the answer.

" ' I shall more surprise you,' the duke returned, ' when I tell you that Edmund is my legitimate heir, whom on her dying bed she implored me to acknowledge as such. ' I have lived,' she said, ' to oblige you, my lord duke, an object of at least doubtful character. I cannot die so. Promise me to clear my conduct from reproach, and by so doing, you will legitimise my son.' I hesitated, Reginald, for I always wished you to be my heir ; but I was not proof against her tears and

No. 15.

entreaties, and in that hour of awful responsibility, in the presence of her physician, the chaplain, and others, I solemnly declared she was my lawful wife, and Edmund her son and mine. She lived but a few hours afterwards, and died perfectly tranquil. It was an act of justice I deferred too long; from me she merited more consideration; but in youth passion governs us, and in age, prejudice. She was not my equal in rank, and I never could bring myself to think that she would fill with dignity the station I must have elevated her to, had I owned our marriage. Yet she was everything, Reginald, that is good and amiable in woman, and most severely do I lament her loss.'

" ' To her worth,' I answered, ' I bear willing testimony, for to me she supplied a mother's place. But where is Edmund? Let me congratulate him on his good fortune.'

" ' Noble, generous fellow,' cried the duke, grasping my hand; ' can you with so much ease resign a title you have ever been considered heir to ?'

" ' The loss,' I answered, ' does not deprive me of that I value much more— your grace's good opinion.'

" ' No, Reginald,' he replied, ' you more than ever merit that, and as far as my fortune will allow, you shall be made happy with the woman of your choice.'

" ' Then I have your grace's free consent to my marriage with Miss M'Donald ?'

" ' Yes, Reginald,' replied the good old man, ' and my blessing too, and if she does not love you better for the good humour you have shown in resigning a title, she never deserves to wear one.'

" Edmund entered; he looked abashed and confused when I advanced towards him. I expressed my sorrow for the death of his mother, and congratulated him on his title; he is now Marquis of Raithsay.

" ' It is an honour,' he said, ' I did not covet, and one I shall not long wear, and I deeply regret that my dear mother should have been so solicitous about obtaining it, for to me it is of no value, only as connected with the goodness and condescension of the duke.'

" ' I am glad you are come,' said his grace, interrupting the emotions of Edmund, who spoke with difficulty, ' for we have been very dull without you; but how long can you stay ?'

" ' Not above a fortnight this time, but if I can prevail on the lady we have been speaking of, to be satisfied with plain Reginald Raithsay, though no longer the heir to a dukedom, I will, with your grace's permission, bring her back with me.'

" ' Nothing,' he replied, ' can be more agreeable, if she will take up her abode here during my life; it will greatly improve your fortune.'

" ' But I have promised her one thing, that I cannot conveniently accomplish without your assistance, my lord duke.'

" ' What is it ?' said he.

" ' Only that she may travel to the castle in her own carriage.'

" ' That,' he replied, ' she shall do; you may write to-night and inform her that the necessary orders shall be given for a carriage and liveries.'

" ' No, my honoured uncle,' I replied, ' all but the carriage can be dispensed with during your mourning, and that shall be ordered by Miss M'Donald.'

" This he instantly assented to; in conclusion Reginald said,—

" ' If I did not know that the excellence of your heart equalled the beauty and grace of your person, I should tremble for my future happiness; but confident as I am that Rodolpha M'Donald is every way superior to the generality of her sex, I rest with perfect confidence on her generosity and good faith. I shall be with you, my own Rodolpha, within a very short time, and hope soon to introduce you to my honoured uncle, as the happy and adored bride of your ever-devoted Reginald Raithsay.'

" The duke wrote by the same post to Lady M'Donald; his letter was long and circumstantial, and in it he severely blamed himself for letting Raithsay remain so long ignorant of Edmund's claims. ' But the truth is,' he added, ' that I never meant to own them, for I saw plainly that continued ill health had in some degree impared his understanding, and I thought a private station, with a moderate fortune, would afford him more tranquillity than he would acquire by the possession of a dukedom. Reginald is the orphan son of my only brother ; his spirit, activity, and strength of understanding render him worthy of exalted rank, and he seemed formed by nature to support with dignity the honours of his family. But this change will place them on one who has no desire to wear them ; but as the act has been my own, I must bear the disappointment that has followed. I am now anxious to make Reginald every compensation in my power. I will add all I can to his fortune, and shall be proud to receive Miss M'Donald as the mistress of Moncrieff Castle, whenever she chooses to honour my nephew with her hand.'

" ' Well,' said Lady M'Donald, " what is to be done now ? You are a little disappointed, I see, Rodolpha.'

" She smiled as she spoke ; I did the same, as I answered,—

" ' I am very much disappointed, madam, but I am pleased with Raithsay's confidence, and one would not be outdone in generosity, and if I am not a duchess, I shall have a duke for my uncle ; and, above all, travel to the castle in my own carriage. So duke or no duke, Reginald Raithsay is the lord of my future destiny."

" Her ladyship was pleased with my decision, and wrote instantly back to the duke to inform him of my acquiescence : I wrote also, and shortly after Raithsay arrived at Clydesdale with full powers from the duke to arrange everything relating to pecuniary affairs ; this was soon done, and Raithsay set out for Edinburgh to hasten the progress of settlements, and to order the new carriage.

" In the interval, Lady M'Donald took her journey to Edinburgh with the children, where she was received with unfeigned affection by Lady M'Gregoire, and with studied cold politeness by his lordship and Lady Beatrice, in whose presence Emmeline was constrained to repress her fondness for her own children. Sir Malcolm's steward was already arrived, and waiting at an inn for Lady M'Donald's orders, who fearing delay would only increase the irascible feelings of M'Gregoire, prevailed on Emmeline to consent to their immediate departure, who sustained the shock with more firmness than was expected from her. Lady M'Donald seeing that she was not a welcome guest, prepared for her return home, only waiting to hear from Sir Malcolm of the children's arrival in London ; this satisfaction was not long delayed, for Sir Malcolm wrote that they were well and happy in their new situation ; he expressed his entire satisfaction at having them under his care, and assured her ladyship that nothing should be neglected by him that would conduce either to their present comfort or future advantage.

" With this assurance, Lady M'Donald was perfectly satisfied, and their suffering mother patiently acquiesced in a separation she had not the power to prevent.

" Though Lady M'Gregoire was so near her hour of trial, her mother was not invited to continue with her through that painful period. She returned to her own residence, and was soon followed by Raithsay, who stayed no longer than to conclude the necessary preparations for our marriage, which took place soon after his return.

" In the meantime, as we heard from a friend at Edinburgh, my dear sister was smarting under the irritable temper of her lord (much increased by his addicting himself to the bottle), and the cool malignancy of his unfeeling daughter, whose dislike to her beautiful mother-in-law was increased by the prospect of her presenting an heir to the family. As the time of Lady M'Gregoire's confinement approached, her spirits greatly failed her, and this was by Lady Beatrice insinuated as evincing a total disregard to his lordship's happiness. There needed very little to fan the embers of distrust into a flame in the rancourous breast of M'Gregoire.

" ' She is lamenting the absence of Lessley's children," he cried, ' at the hazard of destroying my hope of an heir.' "

" Impressed with this baneful idea, a sullen gloom hung over his impenetrable brow, and he never met her but with a frown of anger, or a taunt of reproach. When the, to her, dreadful hour arrived, she was, after the most acute and lingering sufferings, delivered of a male child.

"M'Gregoire was wild with joy, and Lady Beatrice bursting with vexation; but the joy of the one was evanescent as the vexation of the other, for the dear Emmeline died in a few days, and the infant did not long survive her. Thus she sunk, in the very prime of womanhood, a victim to the vindictive passions of her unfeeling husband. This heavy affliction most severely affected the before declining health of Lady M'Donald, and Raithsay, in compliance with my wishes consented to my remaining with her; and the duke, though anxious for his return to the castle, kindly approved of his considerate conduct. She lingered a few months, and died perfectly resigned to the will of her Creator, leaving the whole of her property to myself and the children of Emmeline. The house at Clydes-dale was soon after disposed of; we took with us to the Highlands such things as were most valuable, and Raithsay commissioned a confidential friend in London to settle with Sir Malcolm for the security of the children's property, and as both parties acted on liberal principles this, was easily arranged. Thus, the children of my dear sister were placed in easy, though not affluent, independence, for they inherited the joint property of their mother's parents. I should before have observed that Sir Malcolm Lessley was a widower with only one son, then com-pleting his education at Cambridge. To Moncrieff Castle I travelled in my own carriage, and was most cordially welcomed both by the duke and his truly worthy son, whom I do assure you I did not in the least envy the honours he had so un-expectedly attained. After the melancholy impressions that the foregoing events had left on my mind were in some degree obliterated, my spirits recovered their usual tone of cheerfulness, and I was, I think, one of the happiest of human beings. Yet, as nothing here is stationary, my happiness was alloyed by some severe afflictions. The good, kind, and inoffensive Raithsay died three years after our marriage, sincerely regretted by all who were sensible of his worth—for a purer spirit never winged its way from earth to heaven. Death was busy amongst us, for the duke survived but a few years; and out of seven dear pledges of mutual affection and unabated love, Lady Ann alone was spared us. To consolidate the interest of the family, an union was proposed between her and the young Marquis of Randolph, who was distantly allied to the Moncrieff family. The proposal met the entire concurrence of the duke and myself; but it was stipulated and agreed to by both parties, that Lady Ann should be at liberty either to accept or reject the marquis if she felt any repugnance to the proposed marriage. Perhaps her being left so entirely free operated favourably in the marquis's behalf, for, after a twelvemonths' acquaintance, part of which time on her account we had passed at Edinburgh, she cheerfully consented to give her hand to her kinsman. They returned with us to the castle, where they continued for some time, and then left us for their own residence in the Lowlands; but part of every summer they usually spent at the castle. I have now, my dear madam, brought my little narrative nearly to a conclusion; the former part was written many years ago—what remains, I have dictated to a young lady, who has kindly undertaken to be my amanuensis. The duke lived to see the marchioness the happy mother of a large family, and fondly anticipated the hope of obtaining the title for the marquis, who was lineally, though remotely, allied to the eldest branch of the family; the hand of inexorable death defeated the long-cherished expectation; he died before he had completed his fifty-fourth year, honoured, lamented, and beloved—blessed in his life, and happy in his end. On this melancholy occasion I left the castle soon after the solemn obsequies were over, and passed some months with my family, in order to wear off the heavy impression that my incalculable loss had left upon my spirits. When I viewed the increasing family of my daughter, and reflected how comparatively small a portion of the Moncrieff property would devolve to her after my decease, I consulted with the marquis on the propriety of endeavouring to recover the Northumberland estates, to which my sister and I were undoubted heiresses; the suit had been commenced during the life of my father, but at his decease it was dropped, for Lady M'Donald feared to injure our fortunes by continuing the contest after my marriage; at my earnest request Raithsay wrote to Sir Malcolm Lessley on the subject, who declined interfering, and observed that he did not consider it advisable to hazard the fortunes of the children in a suit that might be long protracted and eventually lost, as the present possessor had all the advantages of wealth and influence in his favour, and had, to strengthen his claim, taken the arms and name of M'Donald; there the matter rested, and would have rested for ever had not the interest of my grandchildren induced me to renew the claim. During the time I have been speaking of, I heard annually from Sir Malcolm; he always spoke affectionately of the young people, but the correspondence ceased suddenly on his part, and though I wrote several letters, I never received an answer to them. The duke, the elder one I mean, was offended at such contemptuous treatment, and to oblige him I wrote no more, and some years after I saw Sir Malcolm's death announced in an Edinburgh paper. I then set an inquiry on foot, through a professional gentleman, after the children of my dear sister, and was informed that my nephew held a commission in the army and had embarked for the East Indies accompanied by his sister and her husband; this was all the intelligence that could be procured, and the suit was therefore commenced on my account only, and at my sole expense; it lingered long, was expensive; and vexatious, at length it was thought advisable I should come myself to England to accelerate its progress, especially as I stood sole and indisputable heiress to my father. Certain intelligence having been obtained that my nephew died in India, and that his sister was lost on her passage home, this long-protracted suit is now brought near to a favourable conclusion, my claims have been admitted, and some minor points only remain to be adjusted; when this act of justice to my descendants is completed I shall return to the solitude endeared to me by many tender recollections, and prepare myself to meet that awful hour which will resign me to the same tomb with my dear and honoured husband; in life we were united, and in death we shall not be separated." Here the MS. ended.

CHAPTER XIII.

" No peace nor ease that heart can know,
   That like the needle true,
   Turns at the touch of joy or woe,
   And turning, trembles too."

WHEN Caroline laid down the MS. she turned her eyes on Mrs. Clareville, who sat by her side the mute image of attention, while Martha unable longer to repress her feelings, cried,

" Oh, my dear lady, this duchess is our own dear Miss Rodolpha that was so fond of you and our little master James. Oh, I shall never forget how bitterly she cried about poor Lady M'Gregoire, when she returned from Edinburgh to Clydesdale House. I remember, too, she said she would be a duchess, and sure enough she is one. Well, how strange; but I wonder if she would know my lady, who is her own sister's child."

" Aye my dear Caroline," said Mrs. Clareville, " I was the very little Emmeline her grace so feelingly speaks of."

" My dear madam," said Caroline, taking the chilly hand of Mrs. Clareville between her own, " how happy would the duchess be to see the daughter of a sister she loved so tenderly, and whose memory she still cherishes with such unfeigned affection. But you are fatigued, do repose for an hour or two, and I will sit beside you.

" No," Mrs. Clareville answered, " I shall be better alone. Martha will lead c to my dressing-room, and I will lie down on the sofa, not to sleep, but to reflect on the circumstances your MS. has so unexpectedly elucidated. Martha shall return to you, and explain many little points that I have not spirit to enter into."

" I will wait your own time, my dear madam," was the answer, " for I would not willingly lose the interest I shall feel in any communication you may think proper to make.

" You are a dear, considerate creature," said Mrs. Clareville, "and I am glad to find that you can repress that most troublesome of female foibles, curiosity."

When left to herself, Caroline reflected deeply on the many unexpected events that had followed on each other since her quitting Mrs. Bellamy's ; and, though she could not account for it, she fancied her own fate was somehow interwoven with that of the duchess's and Mrs. Clareville's. In crossing the hall, on her way to the garden, she heard an order given for Mr. Meanwell to be sent for, with a request that he would, if possible, come that evening. At any other time this would not have surprised her, but then it occurred to her that Mrs. Clareville had some inquiries to make of him, or something she wished to communicate to him, respecting herself ; she recollected that lady's agitation when she heard that Newport had been the means of her preservation ; also her saying, " We must talk on this subject another time."

" It is not impossible," she mentally exclaimed, " but I may be related to Mrs. Clareville, the duchess, and Lady M'Gregoire ;" yet the cool dictates of reason decided against the flattering idea.

Mrs. Clareville remained all day much indisposed ; she directed Caroline to write for her both to the baron and her solicitor in London, requiring his immediate attendance at the lodge, and requesting the baron to hasten his return to England. These letters despatched, she appeared easier, and conversed on different subjects till the arrival of Meanwell. On his entrance, Caroline left the room, when Mrs. Clareville concisely explained to him the relationship that existed between herself and the Duchess of Moncrieff, and the little doubt that remained on her mind of the interesting young woman she had so accidentally met with being the child of her brother, and the grand-niece of her grace. Meanwell admitted the probability of her being so was strengthened by concurring circumstances, but he begged her not to indulge herself in the pleasing hope too much, lest disappointment should follow the inquiries that she intended making on the baron's return. Much interesting conversation ensued on this important subject, and it was at length decided that to Caroline should be confided the surmises that favoured her affinity to the duchess and Mrs. Clareville, but with strict injunctions of secrecy till the baron's opinion on the subject could be ascertained. It was also agreed that no communication should for the present be made to the duchess, lest, through her family, it should transpire to the Newlands, who would certainly take every method in their power to prevent the discovery of their presumed guilt. This concluded on, Caroline was summoned, and the foregoing particulars explained to her. Her surprise, though naturally great, was not equal to her joy and gratitude on finding the surmises that had floated on her imagination, and which she feared to indulge, were so likely to terminate in her favour. Mr. Meanwell soon after departed, with a promise of calling again the following day. Mrs. Clareville, much fatigued, and not a little agitated, soon after retired to her own room, accompanied by Caroline, whom she directed to open a writing-desk, in which she would find a memorandum that it was necessary she should peruse. This done, she requested to be left alone, and Caroline, with a beating heart, bent her steps to her own chamber. The evening was fast closing, but, being impatient to obtain the information she expected to find in the papers, she rang for lights, and hastily ran over the following statement, written for a friend in the baron's own hand. As Mrs. Clareville had informed her, the person it was intended for had died while the baron was on the continent, and it had been, by his executors, returned to Mrs. Clareville. It thus began :—

" I and my sister were the offspring of two ancient families. We were born in Scotland, where our parents dying when we were very young, we were sent to England, and placed under the care of our uncle, Sir Malcolm Lessley. to whose memory we both owe respect and gratitude. My inclinations pointed to the army, and a commission was purchased for me in a company that was soon after ordered to the East Indies. Some months previous to our departure Sir Malcolm had paid the debt of nature, and his only son succeeded to his title and estate—a man every way unlike his, to us, lamented father. The house soon became a scene of revelry and dissipation that suited neither our inclinations nor fortunes, though the latter had been carefully improved by Sir Malcolm, and consigned over to us before his decease. We therefore took lodgings, where we continued till the marriage of my sister—an event that had been postponed out of respect to the memory of Sir Malcolm. All the arrangements for that purpose had been made by his consent and under his directions. On that occasion a Miss Aubane became an inmate with us in an elegantly furnished house that was taken by Clareville for the reception of my sister. Their residence in England was not likely to be of long duration, as Clareville was attached to the medical staff, and was going out with the company I was in. My sister had no near connections in England, and an utter stranger to her mother's family in Scotland ; for Sir Malcolm, whether from pride or caprice, I know not which, had long declined all correspondence with our only aunt, who had married into the ancient family of Raithsay, and was residing at Moncrieff Castle, in the Highlands. Thus situated, Emmeline determined on going with us to the peninsula of India, and Miss Aubane consented to remain with us till the time arrived for our departure to that place. The mother of Miss Aubane had been twice married—once to the father of the present Sir Timothy Acrimony, and afterwards to a Mr. Aubane, a merchant of extensive credit and acknowledged integrity. To his care, princes might have trusted their revenues, and from his vast and extensive resources many were served in time of actual or impending danger ; but, as fortune is seldom stationary in commercial transactions, a few short years, owing to the repeated failures of foreign houses, and the then distracted state of the continent, nearly annihilated his well-earned fortune. His lady did not live to experience this sad change of circumstances, and the interesting Elianor, then only nineteen, was his constant companion and only consolation. He did not long survive the loss of his good and affectionate lady, and, unfortunately for his daughter, died intestate. Immediately after his decease, she retired, by invitation, from Lady Acrimony to the residence of her brother; but Sir Timothy, who had been offended at his mother's second marriage, unkindly refused his assistance to his inexperienced sister, who solicited him in vain to arrange and investigate the affairs of her deceased father ; and in consequence, on her arrival in town, she was greatly perplexed, and consulted with Clareville in what manner she could act, so as to secure what remained of his once-splendid fortune. By his advice, a gentleman well known to us (he having been for some time employed by Sir Malcolm as a solicitor) was instructed to act for her, and, owing to his vigilance and exertion, they were quickly adjusted to the entire satisfaction of all parties, and three thousand pounds were all that remained of a fortune that was once thought incalculable. Elinor had long expected that the result would be very unfavourable, and was therefore prepared to support with fortitude the disappointment of her early hopes. The equanimity of her temper charmed me, if possible, more than her beauty had done, and I did not cease to importune her till I gained her consent to share my destiny, whether adverse or prosperous ; and within a few weeks she honoured me with her hand, in the presence of Clareville and my sister ; she soon after returned to Sir Timothy, with the intention of acquainting him with our marriage ; but her fortitude was not equal to her intentions, and she continued at his house several days without entering on the subject, even to Lady Acrimony, from whom she had always received undeviating proofs of friendship and affection. An unexpected resident, however, led to an explanation—a gentleman of good fortune, and unexceptionable character, who had long admired Elinor ; but had, from motives of prudence, refrained from declaring himself till her late father's affairs were finally adjusted, and then came forward with such liberal proposals for a settlement, as induced Sir Timothy, without consulting his sister, to promise him her hand—not in the least anticipating a refusal. And, perhaps, the arguments he advanced in favour of the proposals, joined to the entreaties of his amiable lady would have been irresistible, had she not been irrevocably engaged.

"She wrote instantly to me, stating her very unpleasant situation, and I on the receipt of her letter, set out for the baronet's.

"I found the family seated at the breakfast table, from which the ladies soon retired, and then, without ceremony, I explained my business to Sir Timothy, who received my communication with insulting severity, and inquired how I had dared presume to enter his family without first obtaining his approbation.

"My reply was not very conciliating; and high words ensued between us, which were interrupted by the entrance of Elinor, who mildly intreated him to hear the reasons she had to advance in favour of our marriage before he condemned it.

"This was answered by reproof, and a command to quit his house, and never again to enter it.

"'She never shall enter it again,' I answered, 'nor any other house wheres he is not treated with the respect due to herself and me.'

"The baronet left the room, and Lady Acrimony entered it, leading her children, who wept bitterly at the thought of parting with their aunt.

"The ladies took an affectionate leave of each other.

"My chaise was in waiting, and in less than an hour we were on the road to London.

"As my sister was going with us to India, there needed very little entreaty to prevail on Mrs. Lessley to accompany us thither. Had Sir Timothy received my communications with kindness, I should not have pressed the subject, as I could with perfect confidence have left her to the care of his estimable lady; but as we were then situated, there appeared no sanctuary so secure for a lovely young woman, as the protecting presence of her husband.

"Assisted by Mr. Dennison, our solicitor, Clareville and I arranged all our pecuniary affairs, so as to leave our wives superior to the chances of war, or the caprice of fortune. And, at the appointed time, embarked for our Asiatic expedition, and after a very favourable voyage we were landed safely at the destined port.

"Some months after our arrival my sister became a mother; but to the severe regret of its parents the infant died soon after its birth. Nearly at the same time Mrs. Lesley presented me with a daughter. She recovered very slowly from her confinement, for the climate was unfavourable to her health. Mrs. Clareville was soon restored to convalescence, and it was then agreed that she should nurse our little girl, her mother being too weak to continue the pleasing task that nature has so forcibly dictated as the first duty of woman.

"My Elinor's health daily declined, and her physicians ordered that she should immediately return to England.

"Unfortunately a war was on the point of breaking out with one of the native princes, and I could not with honour desert the army, or I should have disposed of my commission, and returned with her.

"Fortunately an opportunity offered of sending her to England with a family of distinction.

"As Mrs. Clareville was in better health, she preferred continuing some time longer; besides it was thought prudent for her to continue, as through her, the communications from England would be regularly received.

"Previously to Mrs. Lessley's embarkation for her native country, I exacted a promise from her never to seek a reconciliation with her brother—a promise I have since severely repented obtaining.

"I shall leave you, my friend, to imagine, for I cannot do justice to the scene of our separation. Suffice it to say that the infant was left under the care of Mrs. Clareville, and that the family Mrs. Lessley accompanied assured me that they would pay particular attention to her comfort, both during the voyage and on her arrival in England. Soon after her departure, active operations commenced—the war raged with incredible violence, with no expectation of an early termination, for we had to contend with a formidable and implacable enemy. I was in many severe engagements, and my conduct was such as procured me the notice of our commander; and on the next arrival I found myself promoted to the rank of a colonel.

This unexpected mark of approbation was a fresh stimulus to valour, and I believe I did not disgrace the rank my services had acquired for me. Soon after, I was ordered up the country with a fine portion of the army, and Clareville was with us on the medical establishment. Previous to my departure on this expedition, letters had arrived from England; from them we learned that Mrs. Lessley had arrived safe in England, and had, for a short time, by pressing invitation, taken up her

No. 16.

abode at Sir Malcolm Lessley's, as the family she had sailed with had taken their departure for Ireland, their native country. I was not exactly pleased at the residence my wife had chosen, yet I knew that the purity of her heart and the rectitude of her principles would effectually secure her from the contagion of fashionable improprieties. In a subsequent engagement I received a severe wound on my head with a sabre, and in a state of insensibility was conveyed to the garrison.

Mrs. Clareville, through many dangers, came to my assistance. Her presence greatly alleviated my sufferings, and the humane care of the principal surgeon accelerated my cure. His name was Newport. He had been some years in India, and his abilities in his profession were universally acknowledged. I felt considerably obliged by the attentions he had paid to me, and he, on his part, evinced a sincere desire to serve me in any way conducive to my advantage or repose.

"About this time poor Clareville died, through the contagion of an epidemic fever, which thus increased the horrors of war.

"The grief of his widow may be better imagined than described. She, however, still continued in India, hoping that within a few months we might return together.

"I was incapable of active service and confined to garrison duty, when letters arrived from England which stated that a maiden sister of my father's, who had always intended Sir Malcolm should be her heir, had suddenly changed her intentions; owing, as she herself stated, to the dislike she had imbibed to the profligacy of his character, and left me the sole possessor of her fortune, excepting five thousand pounds, which she bequeathed to Mrs. Clareville.

"Mr. Dennison, of whom I have before spoken, had made the will, and on the death of Mrs. Judith Lessley, he requested an interview with my wife.

"Sir Malcolm, when acquainted with the business was astonished, and doubted the authenticity of the will.

"'It was legally executed, Sir Malcolm,' was Mr. Dennison's answer.

"'That point I shall not concede to,' replied Sir Malcolm. 'The old woman must have been insane when she directed such an instrument of absurdity. In short, sir, I shall dispute the legality of the will.'

"'And as a point of justice,' said Mr. Dennison, 'I shall defend it.'

"They parted on terms of mutual defiance, and owing to Sir Malcolm's disappointment, which occasioned constant ill humour, Mrs. Lessley left his house, and retired with only one female servant to a furnished lodging, from whence she wrote to me.

"At the same time, Mr. Dennison also wrote the full particulars, requesting that I would send my child to England with proper vouchers of her birth and baptism, should the fortune of war detain or prevent me from taking possession of my aunt's estate and fortune."

"Mrs. Clareville's return to England was now become imperiously necessary, and she embarked on board one of the company's ships, and with her my little darling girl and our old and valued servant, Martha, who had accompanied us to India; my child was then near four years old; to my sister, I entrusted the care of our most valuable effects, intending to leave the peninsula, as soon as I could do so without injury to a soldier's honour; one portmanteau, alone contained jewels of great value, one casket in particular, that had been presented to me by the rajah, whose son I had preserved in the midst of danger from impending death, and restored to him without exacting any promise in return, except that he would be merciful to such of my brave men as had, or might yield to him. He was grateful for the action, and liberated many that had long been prisoners, and by one of them, an officer of distinction sent me the jewels. In this portmanteau, were also the certificates of my marriage, the birth of my daughter, my will, and many things of great value belonging to Mrs. Clareville, and several ingots of gold that we had jointly purchased with merchandize, that had been consigned to Clareville, soon after our arrival in India, whose ventures had turned out very advantageous."

"Newport, the surgeon, I have before mentioned, and with whom I was by that time on terms of strict intimacy, having made a tolerable fortune, proposed returning by the same ship to England. To his care I entrusted my child, my sister, and my property, and he solemnly assured me that he would attend to their comfort during their voyage, and see them placed in safety with Mrs. Lessley; there were several passengers on board, and many superior accommodations, and I flattered myself they would have an agreeable and safe passage; the captain was an experienced officer, the ship in excellent condition, and the crew veteran mariners. Alas, how futile are the hopes of man. I trusted my dearest treasures to the faithless deep, and had to lament that all was lost soon after the departure of the 'Cleopatra,' (the name of the vessel.) Active operations, which had been for some time suspended, again commenced with various advantages; at length a dreadful battle was fought, at the conclusion of which the enemy fled in all directions. The impetuosity of my men in the pursuit, whose temerity I in vain endeavoured to restrain, led them into an ambuscade at a considerable distance from the main army, when they were instantly [surrounded and made prisoners of war. We were, in consequence of their ardour, marched a considerable distance up the country, my horse died under me, and I had to complete the journey on foot over scorching sands, beneath a torrid sky; my brave men had been previously dismounted. I had during the engagement received a dreadful wound in the shoulder, which had only been bound up during the heat of action to prevent the effusion of blood; parching with thirst and greatly exhausted through fatigue, we at last arrived at an Indian fortress, where the men were huddled together like sheep in a pen, and the officers were consigned to different dungeons. Stretched on an Indian mat on the ground, I had leisure to ponder over my melancholy destiny, separated by half the globe from all that was dear to me on earth, in the hands of merciless enemies, agonised with pain, and faint for want of proper necessaries: all these accumulated reflections operating on a frame naturally irritable, brought on a fever which ended in delirium, and thus, happily freed from painful recollection, I continued many months. The first distinct idea I have after my confinement in the dungeon, is of opening my eyes one morning in a spacious chamber furnished in the Asiatic style, though about it I perceived many European articles, particularly some French china, and a small though elegant piano, at which a lady was seated playing a plaintive Italian air. On hearing me move, she instantly arose, and came towards the cushions on which I lay. She spoke to me in French; her voice was sweetly penetrating, soft almost as my own Elinor's; her form was graceful, but as she was veiled, I could not see her face. I attempted to speak, but she prevented me by saying,—

"'You must not talk at present, suspend your curiosity for a few days and I shall be amply gratified; consider yourself perfectly safe, and depend on being carefully attended to.'

" She then left the room, and a little brisk fellow soon after entered, who busied himself in placing the things in order. I spoke to him in English, he shook his head; then in French, when he bowed and smiled, but did not answer. I then concluded that he had been forbidden to speak, so for several days made no further attempts at conversation. The lady I had at first seen sometimes came with him accompanied by one that from her manner of walking, I considered much older than herself; I could not judge from their looks, for they were both veiled. My wound was healed, my health restored, but with health memory returned, and the tender recollections of my Elinor, my sister, and my child, embittered every moment of existence; the physician who studiously watched every turn of my disorder, one day told me that he had taken the embargo off my servant's tongue, and hoped I would make a prudent use of mine. As he left the room Jacques (so the man was named) came to the cushions on which I was reclined.

"'Now my friend,' said I, 'since I understand you are at liberty to speak, inform me by what means I was conveyed from a dungeon hither (for I had a clear recollection of my former sufferings), and how far I am from an English settlement?'

"The latter question, he replied, he could not answer, for he had never heard it mentioned distinctly, but the former part of my inquiry he could satisfactorily explain; but first, he observed,—

"'I must inform you, monsieur, that I am a native of Gascony, I came here very young with a gentleman sent by the French c urt to the rajah of this country as a most experienced engineer. He was accompanied by his sister, who in the common acceptation of the terms came here to make her fortune, and she soon captivated an officer of high rank in the rajah's court, one nearly related to his favourite lady, through whose influence he possessed unlimited power, he offered to marry my young lady after the fashion of her own country ; for a great length of time she was most reluctant to consent to his proposals, as she would rather have married a French merchant than an Indian prince. At length she acceded to the wishes of her brother, who perceived that he should have a formidable enemy in the favourite if she refused to comply with his wishes. It was stipulated that she should be allowed the free exercise of her religion, and live according to the French fashion. This palace was built for her separate use, and no other ladies have ever been permitted to enter into it. Whatever money would procure, was purchased to gratify the wishes of one so deservedly worthy of the favourite's regard, and this accounts for the European elegancies that decorate your apartment. The young lady you first saw, is madame's only child ; her father, fell in that very battle that you, monsieur survived, her mother receives a handsome allowance from the rajah, and continues to live here in security. About two years ago some French officers of an enterprising spirit made their appearance at the rajah's court, and were graciously received ; they brought with them letters of recommendation to madame and her brother, and were, as the French custom is, allowed to visit our ladies, when one of them, a Captain Le Clerc, fell in love with the young lady, Mademoiselle Nerrissa, who had been educated by madame in the French religion and customs, and they were shortly married in the presence of madame, Monsieur Berri (her uncle), and the physician, our countryman, by a priest that had accompanied the French officers to India. In something less than three months Captain Le Clerc received orders from the nearest French military post to take the first neutral conveyance that offered, and proceed to the Isle of Bourbon. The despatches, he was given to understand, were of great importance, and the preparations for his journey would not admit of an hour's delay. Thus situated, love yielded to the imperious dictates of duty, and he left his young bride under the care of madame ; unfortunately Monsieur Berri died soon after the captain's departure, and since then the interest of the ladies has been less attended to ; as he was a great favourite of the rajah, being very serviceable to him in the construction of various defensive engines of war. Madame had long wished to return to France, but was withheld by the entreaties of her brother, who proposed returning with her as soon as his services could be dispensed with. His death increased madame's desire of leaving India, which will take place as soon as the necessary preparations can be made, and a guard appointed us to the coast."

"After Jacques had proceeded thus far in his account, he paused ; the physician entered, and thinking that he would be less prolix than my attendant, I requested him to conclude the narrative. He politely complied, and briefly stated, 'that on the arrival of the English prisoners at the garrison, which was a short distance from the villa I was then in, madame procured permission for him to visit them, knowing that the Indian doctors would pay no attention to their wounds, from the hatred they bore to the white people, whom they universally considered as enemies and intruders. 'But madam's humanity,' he said, 'is not limited to either country, or colour, and is as freely bestowed on the Asiatic as the European. I found you, monsieur,' continued the worthy man, 'in the height of delirium, with a wound on your shoulder on the very point of mortification. At the request of madame, aided by a suitable present of rupees, the other officers were allowed to walk about the garrison, and a decent chamber provided for their place of repose ; thus their captivity was rendered less irksome, as they had the pleasure of conversing with each other. Peace was soon after restored between the English and the rajah, when an exchange of prisoners was agreed on.'

"'Heavens,' said I, 'my good sir, how came I so unfortunately left behind

"'Your case,' he replied, 'monsieur, required more attention than could be paid to it in a prison; this I represented to madame, and she humanely proposed your being brought hither, but there required both address and delicacy in conducting the enterprise. The governor was applied to, he had been raised to his post by madame's husband, and therefore felt desirous of obliging her, but he observed, you must be sensible of the danger I shall be exposed to, if it is known that I suffer a prisoner to leave the fortress. I replied that I would be answerable for his safety, I think, he answered, after a pause, 'that I can serve you, but you must employ none but your own people, or such as you can place implicit reliance on.' 'This, I assured him he might depend on being done.' 'There are,' he added, 'three private soldiers dead; as many have died here, their number cannot be exactly ascertained. I will report that this gentleman is one of them; they will be interred this night in the sands as is the custom of you Europeans. I will give orders for their removal after the other prisoners are locked in for the night; you may then enter the garrison by a private passage, and remove the prisoner.' This was successfully accomplished, monsieur, and you were brought hither.'

"I sighed deeply, and almost wished I had died of my wounds, but I endeavoured to express myself grateful for the kindness I had received, and was much gratified by being informed that madame had fixed on the next month for commencing her journey to the coast.

"At the conclusion of his recital, he expressed a desire to hear the particulars of my captivity, and I briefly related my unhappy tale; he commiserated my sufferings, and by his sympathy lessened them. From him I heard that it was the intentions of madame to stop for some time at the Isle of Bourbon, from whence she hoped her son-in-law would embark with them for France. At this intelligence, hope again visited my heart, for I thought it would not be difficult for me to obtain a passage to England in some neutral ship. The ladies after these explanations frequently visited me, and we conversed freely on European subjects, and I found that madame had learned the revolution had swept away many of those friends with whom she had hoped to pass the winter of her life. She did not, however, damp the ardour of her daughter's feelings, by melancholy anticipations of remote evils, for that lady promised herself great pleasure from being in France. In speaking of these ladies it would perhaps appear disrespectful if I omitted to notice their personal attractions. As I had latterly seen them unveiled, madame appeared to me to be somewhat more than fifty; in her youth she must have been very handsome, for the contour of her countenance was remarkably fine. Most pretty women fade very early, but finely-formed bone will long resist the impressions of time. Madame Le Clerc in complexion approached near the olive, her nose was Circassian, and her eyes quite Asiatic—black, full, and penetrating; her teeth beautifully white, and her lips red as coral, while the symmetry of her form equalled Grecian perfection, her manners were gentle, and heart feeling, for, when speaking of her absent husband, all the energies of her mind seemed pictured on her animated countenance. I spoke to them of my wife, my child, my sister, and their kind sympathy in some degree lessened the poignancy of my sorrows. We frequently repaired of an evening to a pavilion in the garden, built in the Italian style by an architect from the country, the villa was also from one of his plans; in the garden, fountains were continually playing into basins of Parian marble, surrounded by innumerable flowering shrubs and blooming in perpetual verdure. This delightful place was shaded from the rays of a vertical sun by the lofty branches of the Indian fig-trees. The innumerable birds that took shelter beneath their foliage and warbled their wild notes on the ear of evening produced a pleasing contrast to the stillness of the scene; but even this terrestial Paradise could not calm the agitations of a mind harassed by incertitude, and the arrival of the palanquins afforded me exquisite pleasure. Everything relating to our journey had been so regularly arranged that when the time arrived, there was no confusion occasioned by our departure. The humane physician by agreement, took possession of the villa, intending to accommodate such of his countrymen as chose to reside with him.   We travelled in palanquins, guards had been appointed us, and as the ladies took but few servants, our little company kept close together. Relays both of bearers and guards were in advance of us, and thus we experienced neither delay or inconvenience ; we rested frequently during the heat of the day under the shade of lofty trees, or at places appointed for the repose of travellers. After some days our journey was completed, and we arrived on the coast, where as it had been preconcerted through the agency of a French merchant, an American vessel was awaiting our arrival, and we immediately went on board, and except the ladies suffering severely from sea-sickness, we experienced no inconveniences, for our passage was singularly favourable. During our voyage I learned from the captain that the war between France and England raged with incredible violence. I proposed proceeding with him, and offered him a handsome equivalent on my arrival in England if he would undertake my conveyance thither; but he candidly told me that many of his men were English sailors, and that his orders were not to touch at any port where they were likely to be taken from him, for fear of endangering the safety of the ship; but he suggested that there would be but little difficulty in my getting a passage in some other vessel to a neutral port.   Thus situated I had no remedy but hope and patience ; at last we made the desired port, and were received by Captain Le Clerc with all the natural gaiety of a good humoured Frenchman ; my dress was Asiatic, for my regimentals had been left behind me at the garrison, and I had no opportunity of procuring any other, and if I had, the convenience of such loose habiliments in so warm a climate would have induced me to retain it. I followed Le Clerc and the ladies to his house ; he did not at first, in consequence of my dress, suppose I was a British officer, but when the first hurry of surprise and pleasure was over, and madame introduced me by name, the vivacity of his features instantly vanished, and I had a presentiment that I should be again a prisoner ; the ladies alarmed at the sudden alteration in his manner anxiously inquired the cause, which on being explained, confirmed my fears.

" ' Can we not conceal him ? ' said the elder lady ; ' Impossible' was the reply. I dare not venture on so dangerous an expedient.'

" ' Monsieur speaks such good French, that he may pass for one of your countrymen,' said the younger lady.

" To this I objected, saying if I could through any channel send letters to England, that I did not fear but any reasonable ransom would be paid for my liberation.

" ' Then return to the ship,' cried madam, ' and you may be landed in France, and through the American consul get letters forwarded to England.'

" ' It is now too late,' Le Clerc replied, ' your friend should not have landed ; the governor is so strict that he will not be allowed to return ; besides, as he has been seen by the officers at the port I shall be obliged to report who and what he is.'

" Oh, how severely did I then regret my own folly in not foreseeing the dangers I should have to encounter. Le Clerc also observed, ' that it was expected that the English would make a descent on the island, and that if I announced myself a Frenchman I must array myself against my own countrymen.

" ' Report me as I am, captain,' I replied, ' no brave man will in time of danger desert the standard of his country.'

" Le Clerc extended his hand, paying at the same time a handsome compliment to my principles.

" ' Your confinement, I hope, colonel,' he added, ' will only be nominal, and we will do all in our power to make it pleasant.'

" After this, the ladies retired, and a servant conducted me to an inner chamber, where Jacques attended me, and we reposed on couches during the heat of the day.   In the evening we met ; an elegant repast was spread on the table, and the ladies seemed in better spirits than when I left them.   They hoped the governor would allow of my remaining with them, as he had not sent orders for my appearance at the garrison.   This expectation was, however, soon annihilated by the entrance of an officer, who informed the captain that he must attend the governor within an hour, and take the stranger, meaning me, with him. Le Clerc inquired if the memorandum he sent in had been read. The officer believed it had.

"'I offered,' said the captain, 'to be responsible for this gentleman's security, and was in hopes the governor would have dispensed with his attendance.'

"'He must attend,' the officer answered, and bowing retired.

"In consequence we set out for the garrison. The distance was short, and we went on foot. On arriving there, we were instantly introduced to the governor. He was a man of repulsive manners and illiberal prejudices, and, above all, very hostile to the English.

"'I understand,' said he, addressing me, 'that you are an English officer.'

"I bowed.

"'You know, I presume, that we are at war with England.'

"I bowed again.

"'Then I need not tell you that you are my prisoner.'

"This sentence did not require an answer. Le Clerc then inquired if I might be permitted to reside in his family. The reply was a stern negative. He added,—

"'You must remain in the garrison.'

"I bowed, and followed a sentinel that was in waiting, to whom he gave orders for my strict confinement. Le Clerc followed me to the door, and saw it closed upon me."

CHAPTER XIV.

Give sorrow words ; the grief that cannot speak
Whispers the woe-fraught heart, and bids it break.
I cannot but remember that such things were
That were most precious to me.—SHAKSPEARE.

"MELANCHOLY indeed were the reflections that succeeded. I traversed the chamber with an intensity of feeling that defies description. My wife, my sister, my child, all ignorant of my fate, and most likely mourning me as one numbered with the dead. My Elinor, under this fatal impression, might form other engagements, and thus be lost to me for ever ; my mind, long harassed with incertitude, now seemed lost to hope, and my mental agonies brought on loss of appetite and great degree of fever. The sentinel who attended me reported my illness, and on the day following Le Clerc appeared in my before solitary chamber. From him I heard that three English frigates were seen cruising off the island, and that an attack was daily expected ; that, in consequence, the governor had refused him admission to me,—

"'But,' he added, 'his power is over, for another governor has arrived within these few hours with stores, troops, and ammunition, for the defence of the island He has taken upon himself,' he added, 'the defence of the place, and the ex-governor has signified his intention of returning immediately to France. On hearing of your illness, the new governor instantly allowed me to visit you, and I have reason to hope, if no attack is made, that your future restraints will be very trifling.'

"This agreeable intelligence acted like a balsam on my anxious heart, and hope again played round my too often sleepless pillow. To my great relief, Jacques was again allowed to attend me, and the lively interest he took in my welfare insensibly soothed my anxieties. Every delicacy that could be procured was sent me from Le Clerc's table, who frequently visited me, accompanied by the ladies.

"By the advice of my friends, I drew up two memorials ; one was addressed to the superior officer on the Madras station, and the other to the War-office in England. I also wrote to Mrs. Lessley, my sister, and Mr. Dennison ; the first it was found necessary should be sent to England, and from thence to India, as no communication was open between the English settlements and the island. These were by permission of the governor entrusted to the captain of a Danish merchantman; but whether he neglected to perform an agreement he had been by my friends handsomely paid for, or whether any accident occurred after they were out of his charge I know not, though I have since heard they never reached those they were intended for.

"Thus was I situated when a dreadful storm drove an English vessel on the coast nearly a wreck. The governor very humanely lent assistance to the crew, and permitted them to repair the vessel, under the fortifications.

"Before the captain left the island, he sent to inquire if he had anything on board that would be acceptable to the governor, for as he was on a trading voyage to the African Islands, he had with him many articles of English manufacture. I should before have observed that he sailed under Prussian colours, that monarch being at that time in alliance with France. The governor not to appear above being obliged, accepted some articles; and through Le Clerc and by the governor's permission, I wrote again to England, and entrusted the letters to my countryman's care. I endeavoured in vain to obtain leave of embarking with him, but it was objected to by the governor, who assured me that soon after his arrival on the island, he had made a separate memorial of my case, and transmitted it to France; and he had no doubt but the next despatches would bring an order either for my exchange or liberation.

"When Le Clerc went on board with my despatches, he took Jacques with him as an interpreter; for during his attendance on me he had acquired some knowledge of the English language.

"When the captain heard of my long captivity, he said I must be anxious to hear news from England, and therefore sent me some files of English papers as a most acceptable present. He had brought them out as a venture, and my friend would not receive them without remuneration. Jacques brought them to me with a cheerful countenance, and I received them with unspeakable pleasure. Alas! their contents, though years have elapsed since then, I cannot now revert to, without a sensation of horror; for in the first I took up I read a long account of the affairs in India, in which it was positively stated that I had died of my wounds in the fortress of Hyderabad, the capital of the Rajah's dominions. I now blame myself most severely for giving way to my feelings on that occasion, for I certainly might have expected, and indeed had expected, that such would be the report, and that it would gain credence.

"Yet my spirits were oppressed, and I internally lamented the fatal kindness that had separated me from my comrades, thinking that I might have recovered from my wounds, and returned with them to England.

"After some time, however, I recovered my recollection, and turned again to the papers, and in one of them met with an article that vibrated to madness through every fibre of my frame; it stated that the Cleopatra had been wrecked, and every one on board had perished.

"I arose from my seat—clasped my hands in dispair; and had a pistol been near, that moment would have been my last. It was then evening, and Le Clere entered to pay me the usual visit. My frenzied looks alarmed him. I could not speak, but I pointed to the papers.

"He naturally thought that some intelligence they had conveyed to me had occasioned my agitation; but I could not then explain it to him. He stayed with me as long as possible, and left me a prey to brooding sorrow. In the midst of my misery, sleep fortunately visited my beating temples; I slept some hours, and awoke comparatively calm; and though immersed in grief, it was not so violent as that I had before experienced. When more composed, I communicated the melancholy tale to my friend. He reasoned with me, and endeavoured to inspire me with a hope that the account might be exaggerated, and that on my return to England, I should, at least, discover my suffering wife; but I feared she had sunk under the soul-harrowing thought that her husband, child, and friend were lost to her for ever.

"Months rolled on in incertitude—no letters came—the expected attack on the island did not take place, and in consequence, I was allowed to visit my friends without restraint, and to partake of such amusements as the island afforded.

"My health improved, and I again flattered myself that Elinor might yet be restored to me.

"Oh, if it were not for the balsam which hope pours upon the hearts of suffering mortals, how many would sink beneath the weight of accumulated sorrows. My cup was not yet full; but to avoid prolixity I shall briefly state, that in about six months Le Clerc was recalled to France, and the same ship brought an order for my return.

No. 17.

"It was stated, that on my arrival in France I should be exchanged for a officer of similar rank, then detained a prisoner in England. After bidding a friendly adieu to the humane governor, to whose recommendation I was indebted for the opportunity of returning to Europe, we embarked in the same ship that had brought the order of recal; and arrived after a quick and agreeable passage at a French port. Here my friend, who possessed great influence, lost no time in hastening my departure for England; and then set out with his family for Paris. I should before have informed you that during our stay on the island Madame Le Clerc had presented him with two little ones, on which occasion his number of servants was necessarily increased.

"On arriving in London my first inquiry was after Mr. Dennison. I found him where I had left him, and his surprise at seeing me is beyond my powers of description, as he had not entertained the least doubt of my having died in India. And the letters I had addressed to him had not been received. Upon inquiring at Lloyd's, we discovered that the captain to whose care I had intrusted them, had been captured by a French frigate, and carried into Dunkirk, and in spite of her sailing under Prussian colours, condemned as a lawful prize.

"Of Mrs. Lessley he assured me he knew nothing more than that on her arrival in London he had seen her, and given her the full power of receiving the interest of her own fortune, as I had directed him to do, by the letters she took with her from India. After she heard of the loss of the Cleopatra, her grief was excessive, for from letters that she had previously received she knew that my sister and the child would be embarked in her. A violent fit of illness followed the melancholy intelligence of the wreck; the account of my death succeeded; and her mind was entirely absorbed in sorrow.

"Mr. Dennison further added, that he was then obliged to go to a distant part of the kingdom, and that on his return he received a letter from Mrs. Lessley, which stated that ill health had obliged her to seek relief from retiring to Bath; to that place he followed her, and heard from the person at whose house she had lodged that she had left Bath for Bristol, and that they had no further knowledge of her movements.

"The interest of her money had been but twice received, and I had been absent from England full five years. I thus supposed, and with reason, that she was numbered with the dead. Of my sister, however, I received more agreeable intelligence. She yet lived, though her health was greatly impaired; and the worthy Dennison hastened our meeting by informing her of my arrival in London, to which place she came post to meet me, and that meeting seemed to both like a resurrection from the grave.

"It was cruelly embittered by the recollection of our severe losses. Poor Emmeline wept over the early death of Clareville, and I mourned sincerely the loss of Elinor and her darling girl.

"Time, however, in some degree abated the poignancy of our feelings, and we adopted every method in our power to ascertain if my wife still lived. My return was announced in the daily papers, the cause of my detention described, and Mrs. Lessley implored to inform her friends, if she yet lived, under what circumstances my supposed death might have placed her. But all was useless, and we never heard whether she yet existed, or was numbered with the dead.

"I then gave the inquiries up, as being hopeless, firmly believing that my wife had formed other engagements with some more fortunate man, and was withheld, both by prudence and delicacy, from answering my anxious inquiries.

"Mrs. Clareville had informed me that, during the storm, previous to any apprehension of immediate danger, she had entrusted my little Emmeline to the care of Surgeon Newport, who had, during the voyage, paid her particular attentions, and, in consequence, won her childish fondness. The dreadful scene that followed, she did not retain very clear recollections of, except seeing the surgeon, with the portmanteau slung round his shoulders, and the child in his arms, descend into the boat.

" ' I begged,' she added, ' to be allowed to share their destiny, but the boat pushed off, and my prayers were disregarded. Soon after, the ship struck, and went to pieces, and nearly at the same time the boat sunk, and I found myself,' she added, ' with poor Martha, who clung fast to me, sunk into the boundless bosom of the deep.'

"How long they continued in that perilous situation she could not describe, but eventuallythey were picked up by a Dutch fishing-boat, and carried into Flushing. On her first recovery, she found herself in a comfortable room, on a clean bed, attended by her faithful Martha, but robbed of every valuable she had about her person; even her wedding-ring had not escaped the rapacity of the crew. Fortunately before their departure from India, Martha had providentially preserved some gold coin in the lining of her corset, and this enabled them to procure necessaries till my sister could write to Mr. Dennison, who instantly sent out a confidential person to conduct her to England, who, unfortunately, found her too weak to attempt returning for some time.

" It was during this period that the news of my death had been reported, and Mrs. Lessley had so unaccountably disappeared. Sir Malcolm, after paying Mrs. Clareville's legacy, took possession of our aunt's estate and fortune, as heir-at-law. Mrs. Clareville returned soon after to England, and on hearing my death, as she supposed, fully confirmed, retired into the country, giving up all communication with the world. I continued in London only to transact the necessary business, and give directions for Mr. Dennison to commence an action against Sir Malcolm, for the recovery of my property, and retired with my sister into the country, from whence I was shortly summoned by an order from the war office, which had subsequently allowed my arrears of pay, and ordered to join a fine body of troops, then about to embark for the continent.

" I joined the army, and was several years engaged in active service against the indefatigable and ever vigilant Napoleon. I was in most of the engagements that took place on the continent till the war was closed by the eventful battle of Waterloo.

" During the early part of a former campaign, I had the good fortune to render an essential service to a Prussian troop, that were most dangerously placed in front of the enemy's fire, and by a sudden manœuvre I assisted them in repulsing the French forces. For this service I was honoured with particular marks of attention, and the title of Baron Ormsburgh was conferred on me, by which I have long been known, and as such rated in the army list.

After the peace I returned to England, and finding my sister rather improved in health, I proposed going to the south of France, to visit my valued friends, the Le Clercs, who had been fixed there ever since our separation. This intelligence I had received from a French officer during the time I staid in France. At the time I am writing, Mrs. Clareville is preparing for my departure. I wish I could prevail on her to accompany me. I think change of air and scen might contribute to the restoration of her health, but she is averse to the proposal, and I forbear to press it. The tranquillity she has acquired enabled her to bear solitude, for she has formed but few intimacies since her return to England. But I cannot find peace in retirement : though sorrow and regret have both been frequently suspended in the midst of dangers, yet the image of my lost Elenor and our innocent and lovely child embittered every hour of solitary reflection ; but after having paid the debt of gratitude I owe the Le Clercs, I shall endeavour to prevail on my sister to mix again in the world, and partake of its amusements.

" I have only to add that Sir Malcolm finding it impossible to evade my claims, though he had for years disputed them at a great expense, hasagreed to resign the estate ; in consequence of the many acts of kindness, that both myself and Mrs. Clareville had received from his father, I gave up the arrears that had been awarded me.'

Here the narrative ended. And Caroline, who, during the time it had occupied her in reading, had been assailed by various emions, now laid it down to ponder on the variety of incidents it had unfolded to her; no doubt existed in her mind of her affinity to Mrs. Clareville, through being the daughter of the baron. The unknown destiny of her mother excited her sensibility, and she thought with the baron, that other engagements prevented her from returning to the family, though Mrs. Clareville was of a contrary opinion, fully believing that she had died of a broken heart; and this opinion she indulged as more consonant to the character of her friend, than the supposition of her having formed other engagements.

The following day Mr. Dennison arrived, and Mrs. Clareville informed him of the particulars we have related. His opinion on the subject was favourable to the one adopted by Mrs. Clareville, but he thought it advisable that no legal inquiries should be instituted till the return of the baron. Mrs. Clareville observed that he continued longer in France than he had proposed doing on his departure, but that she had written to accelerate his return.

"Her present business with Mr. Dennison," she observed, "was to secure an independence for her young friend, under the name she then went by, should they fail of substantiating her claim to any other, and this deed she wished to be executed previous to her departure for Sidmouth."

Mr. Meanwell came according to his appointment, and in the evening witnessed a codicil attached to the will of Mrs. Clareville, and in less then a week after, the ladies commenced their journey to Sidmouth, where Mrs. Clareville's disorder assumed a favourable appearance, and Caroline flattered herself she would be restored to her ardent and sanguine wishes, but her friend was not deceived, for she knew her complaint would not yield either to medicine or air, though its severity might be abated, and dissolution for a time retarded; yet she did not damp the ardour of youthful expectation. They conversed freely on the subject that so deeply interested the feelings of both, and Caroline frequently sighed in secret, over the reserve she was bound to practise with Lady Emma, whose generous heart she was assured would participate in her now favourable prospects. Perhaps fancy might whisper a hope that on her birth being proved, Lord Millford might regret the ambiguity of his former conduct. Lady Emma wrote sometimes, but not in good spirits; she complained of langour, of her aunt's extravagant dissipation, and losses at play; but above all, of the long and inexplicable silence of Montague; to this Caroline could only reply in general terms, for she carefully avoided naming either the Newlands or Lord Millford. Through the same channel she heard that the two families were at their respective seats, with a numerous party of fashionable friends. The duchess likewise wrote that the marquis had attained the honours of his family, and was now Duke of Moncreiff. This intelligence, as it gave pleasure to the duchess, afforded both Caroline and Mrs. Clareville sincere satisfaction. She wrote her congratulations, and heard in return that the Moncreiff family would not leave England before October, as they intended passing part of the intermediate time either at Brighton or Cheltenham. Mr. Meanwell wrote that no doubt remained of Newport's insanity, as it was publicly spoken of, both at the priory and the manor; this was very unpleasant information, and pressed heavily on the feelings of Mrs. Clareville. The baron's return too was from various causes delayed, but he promised to be in England at the expiration of six weeks. This time was passed by the ladies in anticipating the events that would follow his arrival.

Caroline's feelings, though much regulated by the excellence of her understanding, were on this occasion hurried, by thinking on the strange circumstances under which she must be introduced to the baron, Mrs. Clareville having purposely avoided any communication upon the subject, for which she so impatiently wished his return. Again Lady Emma wrote word from Brighton, where, according to her account, every heart but her own enjoyed or seemed at perfect ease. The Moncreiff family, the Newlands, Lady Lucy, Mrs. Pembroke, and the Dinivers were all there.

"I have many opportunities," said her ladyship, "of conversing with the dowager duchess, and very frequently does our discourse relate to yourself. I have confided to her grace my anxiety on the subject of Montague's si ence, and she has advised me to refrain making any inquiries on the subject till his arrival in England, when she thinks every doubtful circumstance will be clearly elucidated."

I wish it may be so, for I think some strange mystery is attached to it, yet I cannot entirely acquit him of unkindness. If he has formed other engagements, he might have relied on my never disclosing those he had so anxiously solici ted me to enter into with him.'"

" Ah, Caroline," she added, " he has forgotten the commands of his sainted mother, but I shall never forget them—be friends through life should your cease to be lovers—and as a friend, I would have cherished him in my memory, till the last hour of my existence."

Our readers may suppose that with her kind and considerate friend, Caroline had no reserve, and Mrs. Clareville was by description perfectly acquainted with the whole party Lady Emma described as her associates at Brighton, and there was no one among them, the dowager excepted, for whose character she felt any degree of interest. Lady Emma's situation excited her sympathy, and the prejudice of Sir Timothy, as it related to her, had not advanced him in her good opinion.

" Prejudice !" she one day observed, speaking of the baronet's eccentricities, "is a tree that emits most poisonous vapours ; the shrubs of humanity seldom blossom near it, time increases its acridity, and reason seldom opposes its destructive dominion ; " yet I trust," she added, " that your friends, whom you describe as so worthy of each other, will eventually be united."

In this hope Caroline sincerely accorded, and within a short time answered the letter she had received, in which she described some new friendships she had formed at Sidmouth ; the circumstances that led to their introduction to each other were as follows :—Mrs. Clareville had declined receiving visits, partly on the score of indisposition, but more from the dislike she had to the common routine of such company as usually frequents bathing places ; yet she did not, on Caroline's account, confine herself entirely at home ; they took regular airings, and as the weather was remarkable fine, frequently walked on the beach, leaving the carriage at a convenient distance. One evening while leisurely walking and admiring the charming scenery this delightful spot is so deservedly admired for, Mrs. Caroline felt the arm of her friend shrink from hers, and turning hastily, she saw her countenance shaded with the hue of death ; an exclamation of terror which she uttered led two ladies to her assistance, who were but a little distance from them ; they humanely assisted Mrs. Clareville's to a seat that was near, waited her recovery ; and continued with her while Caroline went to order the carriage as near as possible to the spot the invalid was lifted into it, and the ladies departed after receiving the warm thanks of Caroline. On their return home, a medical gentleman who had attended Mrs. Clareville from her first arrival at Sidmouth was sent for, who attributed her illness to the exertion of walking too far at one time, and advised that her future walks should be taken on a morning ; he conversed with them some time. ar.d heard the ladies described who had so humanely assisted them ; the gentleman, who knew them by description ; explained who they were, and spoke of them in high terms of admiration " They are mother and daughter," he added, " and are held in very high estimation by every one acquainted with their worth. He added that Mr. Beriton had been educated for the church, and was well-known in the literary world as a religious, moral, and entertaining writer; he then drew from his pocket a small volume of that gentleman's writing, from which Caroline copied the following description of Sidmouth, with which she concluded her letter :—

" ' In this enchanting spot is to be seen all that can charm the eye and interest the heart, and raise it from human cares to sublime contemplations ; hill and dale, wood and water, light and shade, alternately relieve and improve each other, while many a gurgling rivulet, pouring its tributary waters into the bosom of the boundless deep, forms a singularly pleasing feature in the scene, and powerfully impresses the contemplative mind, serenely gliding into the abysses of eternity vast extended sea views; bounded only by the vault of heaven, the varied landscape melting into the clouds, the healthful beach, the soul-reviving breeze, the salubrity of the air, and general clearness of the atmosphere, altogether render Sidmouth one of the most pleasant places in the kingdom."

As Caroline was obliged to write so cautiously to her friends, she availed herself of every little incidental occurrence that offered, to fill up her letters, and subsequently wrote a more particular account of the Beritons, who, in consequence of the high terms in which Mrs. Clareville had heard them spoken of, were frequently invited to her house, where their conversation soothed and enlivened many a solitary hour; she described Eliza Beriton as a most interesting and amiable young woman, well educated and intelligent. "Her memory," she added, " is retentive, her observations just, and her feelings, though quick, are under the control of reason, while her pure heart beats responsive to every note of humanity; with her," she continued, " I pass part of every day; we read, walk, and ride together."   To promote the comfort of Caroline, and free her from too close confinement, her excellent friend had engaged an assistant attendant, for she was, through the effect of her last attack, unable to leave the house, but, though many sources of amusement were open to her, through her introduction to the Beritons, she seldom quitted the house but for an airing or a walk; and neither of those indulgences were long protracted, for she plainly and with deep regret perceived that her valued friend would not long be spared her.   Mrs. Beriton kindly devoted much of her time to Mrs. Clareville, particularly during the occasional absence of Caroline.   Her manners were mild and unassuming.   In her youth she had been very handsome, and time had not robbed her of many external advantages; her features were regular and pleasing, and her countenance, when speaking, expressive; but, when silent, placidity was its predominant character.   While the parties were thus situated, Caroline, on going one morning into the library in company with Miss Beriton, was greatly surprised at being accosted by Colonel Diniver and Lord Harry Hazard, both of whom she supposed were at Brighton.   The good-natured volubility of the latter amused and interested her, for he spoke freely of the friends, as he styled them, whom he had left at Brighton.   As they were out for a morning's walk, it was impossible to avoid their attendance home.   They accompanied them to the door of Mrs. Clareville's house, and, before they had separated, inquired if they should have the pleasure of seeing them again.   To this Caroline replied that the illness of her friend prevented her from seeing visitors, and it was therefore very improbable that they should meet again.   To this Colonel Diniver replied that himself and friend were out for a tour, being weary of the monotony of the scene, and should probably continue at Sidmouth for a fortnight.   To this she made no answer, and the gentlemen bowed and left them.   On communicating this incident to Mrs. Clareville, that lady proposed that Mr. Beriton should, if he made no objection to the proposal, inquire where they lodged, and in her name give them an invitation to call at her house whenever agreeable to themselves; and, on Caroline expressing her surprise, her considerate friend replied,—

" If you confine yourself entirely to the house during their continuance here, it may be termed either prudery or affectation; and should you meet them when out, it may, through the malignancy of the Newlands, when they hear of it, (which they certainly will,) be construed into an assignation.   If they come here by my invitation, no blame can be attached to you; and, owing to the kindness of our friends here, you need rarely receive them alone, even should I be too indisposed to see them."

Both Mr. and Mrs. Beriton were present, and approved the proposal, and the former politely acceded to the mission assigned him.   There was no difficulty in finding persons of such fashionable notoriety, and he personally delivered Mrs. Clareville's invitation.   It is needless to say it was instantly accepted.   Mrs. Clareville received them the following morning, in company with Caroline and Miss Beriton.   Their visit was short, for they could not avoid perceiving that she was too much indisposed to take any part in the conversation. After their deeparture, Mrs. Clareville expressed herself pleased with the frank and easy manners of Lord Harry, but by no means impressed in favour of the colonel, whom she thought both proud and assuming. During their continuance, they called frequently, but, never remained long, as Mrs. Clareville was too ill to see them any more, and, in consequence, Caroline seldom left that lady's apartment. On their last visit Lord Harry Hazard inquired if she would honour him with any commands, as unexpected business had occasioned their return to London, from whence they intended setting out for Brighton. She declined writing, but sent a verbal message to the dowager duchess and Lady Emma. Soon after their departure, the baron arrived. The meeting between the brother and sister was affectionate in the extreme, and, as soon as the hurry of Mrs. Clareville's spirits were a little subsided, Caroline retired, and then her excellent friend entered into the subject that had induced her so strongly to solicit the baron's return. At first he was incredulous, but after revolving all the circumstances in his mind, he thought there was a possibility that Mrs. Clareville's hopes and wishes might be realised. On Caroline's return to the sick chamber, he received her in evident emotion, and, assured her that every possible inquiry should be made as speedily as possible, to ascertain if his sister's conjectures were well founded.

"If they are otherwise," he added, " I shall receive and protect you, my dear Miss Millbourne, as the daughter of her adoption."

Caroline only bowed her thanks, and seated herself by the side of Mrs. Clareville. The baron drew a chair, and sat opposite them. Martha stood anxiously watching the countenance of her lady, whose cheeks had a hectic on them that vied with the bloom of youth; and it was equally transient, for it soon yielded to the pallid hue of death. She threw her arm round the neck of Caroline, and rested her head on the shoulder of her anxious supporter. The baron's looks indicated alarm; he drew nearer the sofa on which they sat. Mrs. Clareville had one of Caroline's hands in hers; she motioned to the baron, he extended one of his; she placed the hand of Caroline within it, saying,—

" Remember, you have promised me to receive this dear creature as the child of my adoption, be your inquiries satisfactory or not."

" I will," he answered, firmly, " perform every request you have made me."

" It is enough," she answered, " I shall die in peace."

Poor Martha advanced, her dying mistress cast a parting look at her; Caroline turned pale, for she felt to her heart the convulsive emotions that shook the frame of her departing friend. The baron cast on her a look of indescribable anguish; it seemed to implore her not to move. Alas! she was incapable of motion, for she sat the mute image of despair. A short interval succeeded, and Mrs. Clareville was no more.

The baron's grief was strongly portrayed on his manly and expressive countenance; it was at once deep, silent, and dignified. He arose, rang for the attendants, and quitted the melancholy scene. Fortunately, Miss Beriton was in the house, who prevailed on Caroline to leave the lifeless body of her friend.

We pass over the first few cheerless days in which the baron was seldom visible except at his silent meals, during which time Caroline received a letter from Lady Emma, inclosing one from the dowager duchess, which stated that the duke had suddenly resolved on returning to Scotland, that the family would pass the winter at Edinburgh, where she should expect to receive a long and agreeable letter. Lady Emma wrote in plaintive style, and the burden still was Montague's silence, and the persevering and disagreeable attentions of Captain Newland; she added, there was no doubt of the general's obtaining a divorce from his guilty wife, who had recently given birth to a son.

It was some days before Caroline could command her feelings sufficiently to write, and when she did, her letter was short, and merely announced the death of her inestimable friend, and the arrival of the baron. She observed,—" The shock I have sustained will be long felt; for though I never flattered myself with

Mrs. Clareville's recovery to perfect health, I was by no means prepared for so sudden a separation." The duchess's letter she did not attempt answering till her mind was more at ease. Mrs. Beriton was frequently there, and Eliza was an inmate ; and in Mrs. Beriton the baron found a sensible and humane companion, one who diverted the poignancy of his feelings from dwelling with too much intensity on one subject, by imperceptibly leading him to others. The baron wrote for Mr. Dennison, who instantly obeyed the mandate, and continued there till the time arrived for the funeral. With the baron he held long and frequent conferences relating to the promise he had made his dying sister, of endeavouring to elucidate the mystery that enveloped the real name and connexions of Caroline.

When Martha was interrogated, she described distinctly, for her memory was good, all the passengers in the Cleopatra, and positively asserted that there was no other child in the ship ; and that she saw little miss in the surgeon's arms.

Mr. Dennison allowed that Martha's testimony was conclusive ; but advised secrecy for the present, till proper steps could be taken to ascertain the real state of Newport's malady, who must be personally indicted for the detention of the baron's child and property.

On one occasion Caroline was called in, but she had no recollection of any-thing that could lead to a discovery, for the illness she had after her arrival had obliterated from her memory, even the terrors of the storm. She, however, mentioned that Mrs. Bennet could relate some particulars connected with Mrs Newport's return. And though the baron was anxious for a full investigation o-the business, he thought it prudent to postpone it for some time longer, particu-larly as Mr. Dennison took upon himself to see personally, both Mr. Meanwel and Mrs. Bennet ; as from the former, he had hopes of hearing where Newpor. had been placed.

One morning, Caroline, as was her usual custom, entered the room which con-tained the remains of her departed friend, and there for the first time met the baron, who appeared unusually agitated. He paced the room with hurried steps. She would have retired, but he prevented her by saying,—

" ' Do not leave me, I am not fit to be left alone ; this is a last farewell, for to-night the coffin must be closed.'

" ' So soon ?' " she answered.

He replied, " It is necessary : you may think it strange," he added, taking her passive hand which he drew through his arm, still but more slowly walking the room, " that a soldier, who has been for ten years inured to slaughter, should so deeply and severely regret the departure of one solitary individual. But there is," he continued, " a well-spring in the human heart, that will over-flow its bounds when the inevitable mandate of mortality falls on those we love."

" There is, indeed," responded Caroline, while he tears choked her further utterance.

The baron advanced towards the coffin, and supported his trembling com-panion ; neither of them spoke, for their hearts felt grief that was too powerful to admit of words. Silently they retired, and each sought the solitude of their own chambers. They met no more till dinner, when the presence of Miss Beriton and Mr. Dennison relieved in some degree the severity of their feelings

Towards evening, the weather being very fine for that advanced season of the year, it being then October, as the baron and his little party of friends were walk-ing in a small pleasure garden behind the house, a servant came to inform them that a lady had just arrived in a post chaise, who requested permission to see Miss Millbourne.

" It cannot be," answered the baron. " You must tell the lady that Miss Millbourne cannot at present admit a stranger."

Mr. Dennison proposed inquiring her name.

The servant answered, " that he had inquired it, but that the lady declines sending it in ;" but added, " you may say the Duchess Dowager of Moncreiff had given me permission to use her name as an introduction to Miss Millbourne."

"It is strange," the baron answered, "but as it is so, she must be admitted." Then, turning to Mr. Dennison, he added, "will you conduct Miss Millbourne in, it is not proper she should see a stranger alone."

That gentleman willingly obeyed, and they entered the house together. The lady was in the drawing-room before them; she had been seated, but arose on

their entrance. Wax lights were burning at a distance, for the windows were entirely closed, and the light was too indistinct for them to observe each other's features. The stranger was tall, her person graceful, and her voice plaintively impressive; her "I presume I see Miss Millbourne," seemed to strike Mr. Dennison with surprise.

No. 18.

Caroline bowed, and offered a seat, which was accepted ; for the lady really was almost overpowered by contending emotions.

She remained for some time silent, and then said, though in a low and tremulous voice,—

"A strange irresistible impulse has brought me hither. I have travelled a long way, in hopes of seeing Mrs. Clareville, of whose illness I heard through the Duchess Dowager of Moncrieff ; but I perceive I am too late."

"You are indeed, madam," was the answer.

"Will you," the stranger replied, "excuse my present intrusion, and admit me again in the morning, and tell Baron Ormsburgh that Mrs. Lessley has not forgotten him."

"Mrs. Lessley!" cried Mr. Dennison, advancing ; "then I am not deceived, for I thought I knew your voice; but where, my dear madam, have you been so long concealed, though so anxiously sought after ?"

"The tale would be tedious now," she answered, "but to-morrow we shall meet again. In the mean time, my valued friend," for she also recollected him, "prepare the baron for my appearance."

"Oh, see him now," cried the worthy man ; "there have been years enough of separation and sorrow."

"No, not to-night," she answered, "for I need both fortitude and recollection, and must endeavour to recover sufficient serenity to support me through the trying scene that awaits me."

Mr. Dennison withdrew, and instantly returned with the baron.

"My Elinor, my own Elinor," said he, "are you indeed restored to me ?"

A faint exclamation from the lady followed, who, overcome by the intensity of her feelings, sank senseless on the shoulder of Caroline. And here we beg leave to pass over a scene that we have not power to describe. The baroness, as we must in future call her, requested leave to retire. This was complied with, and Miss Millbourne conducted her to a chamber, to which she was followed by Martha, who had heard the joyful intelligence from the baron.

"Oh, my dear madam," she cried, "you are come too late ; my dear lady has not been spared to see you ;" then, overcome by her sorrowful recollections, she burst into an agony of tears.

The baroness extended her hand towards the faithful and attached domestic, but was too much agitated to reply.

After some time spent alone, (for at her request Miss Millbourne and Martha both retired,) she recovered her self-possession, and in less agitation than could have been expected, complied with an invitation to the tea-table, where she was introduced to Mr. and Miss Beriton. In the course of conversation, she was distressed by hearing that she was too late to see Mrs. Clareville, the inner coffin having been closed before her arrival at Sidmouth ; but, though this occasioned regret to the baroness, it was a satisfaction to the baron, who thought she had escaped some very severe sensations. The funeral was to have taken place the following day, but, owing to the arrival of the baroness, it was necessarily postponed for a few days longer.

CHAPTER XV.

Alas, by some degree of woe
We every bliss must gain ;
That heart can ne'er a transport know
That never felt a pain.—LORD LYTTLETON.

BEFORE we relate the reasons the baroness assigned for her long seclusion, we must recal the attention of our readers to the letter the dowager duchess had written to Caroline, previous to the family leaving Brighton, who commenced their journey under very favourable circumstances, which continued till they were within two stages of Edinburgh; and at the next post town they were to be met by their own carriages; when, owing to the rapidity with which they travelled, one of the springs belonging to the chaise in which the dowager duchess sat gave way, and she was obliged to alight, in order that it might be in some way made sufficiently secure for her to proceed on her journey. In stepping from the chaise, her foot slipped. She fell, and severely sprained her ankle in the fall. She had only her own woman and one man servant on horseback with her, for the other part of the family were some distance in advance; and this circumstance had occasioned the speed which led to the accident. Her grace was unable to stand, and the servants took the cushion from the chaise on which they placed her, while the driver, assisted by the servant, endeavoured to repair the spring.

During this time the duchess was in excruciating pain, and anxiously inquired of the driver if they knew any house near, where she could continue for the night, for it was then late in the evening.

One of them replied, " that Major M'Irwin's was the nearest place he knew of," and at the same time offered to take off one of the leading horses, and acquaint that gentleman with the accident.

This was acceded to by her grace, for she found it impossible to proceed. In less time than she had ancipated, she was agreeably surprised by seeing a low one-horse chaise approach, in which was seated a female, who drove the horse with considerable dexterity.

When the usual inquiries and compliments were over, the duchess was lifted into the chaise, and her foot placed on an ottoman brought for the purpose, for the accident had been explained by the driver, and safely conveyed to the hospitable mansion of the major, who received her at the door with all the formality of the old school. An easy chair was in readiness, into which she was lifted by the servants and carried into the room, where she was placed on a sofa, purposely wheeled before a cheerful fire.

The evening was cold. The servants belonging to her grace soon followed, conducted by the driver, who reported that he could complete the journey with the trunks as the chaise was secured by ropes.

The major proposed that they should first drive it there, that her grace's woman, for he had from the servants discovered her rank, might select such things as would be wanted for immediate use.

The duchess in reply observed,—

" That as all the packages on the chaise belonged to herself, she would, with his permission, have them unloaded there, that the driver might then return, while her own servant went forward to procure assistance, and acquaint her family with her present situation."

This plan was instantly adopted. The drivers brought the chaise safe to the house, where they were handsomely rewarded for their attention and humanity.

It afterwards appeared, that during the time the duchess was being conveyed to the major's, another chaise had passed, which belonged to the duke's suite, in which two of the female attendants were travelling. To them the driver who had been left with the chaise explained the accident, and informed them that the duchess had been conveyed to the major's. The result was, that the servant who had been despatched, met the duke returning in another chaise with a surgeon.

It is almost needless to say that the duke's reception at the major's was both cordial and consistent with the respect due to his rank and dignity. The surgeon examined the ankle of her grace, and gave his opinion that a few days rest with proper attention would restore the use of the foot. The duke then set forward on his return, first proposing that his own carriage should come for the duchess as soon as she could be removed with safety.

After his departure, the female she had before seen entered the room, and with her an aged lady who rested on her arm, and was supported on the other side by a small ebony crutch-stick. Her figure had been fine, but it was bent by time, while the cheerfulness of her countenance indicated that she was yielding without reluctance to his inevitable mandate. The major met her, and introduced her as Mrs. M'Irwin.

"And this lady," said the duchess, bowing to her companion, "is, I presume, your daughter by adoption."

"She is," replied the major. "We have no children; but allow me to introduce Mrs. Lessley to your grace, as one not unworthy the honour of being known to you."

The duchess returned an obliging answer, and expressed her sense of the attentions Mrs. Lessley had paid her. Tea and coffee were then served, the conversation became general, and the duchess had the pleasure to discover that she was in the society of intelligent and elegant persons. A chamber on the ground-floor was prepared, to avoid the pain and difficulty of a removal up stairs; and within a few hours she found herself as much at home as she would have been in her own residence. In a short time the duchess, with the assistance of her woman, was sufficiently recovered to join the family, and partake of their social meals. She expressed herself much pleased with the manners and conversation of Mrs. Lessley, whose voice was particularly soft, sweet, and impressive; and she one day took an opportunity to inquire of the major if he knew anything of her family, for by her conversation she was convinced she was not a native of Scotland.

The major replied, "That she was an English lady, of good family, and but small fortune. She lost her husband," he added, "when very young; we met with her several years ago in England, and finding her unhappy and unprotected, prevailed on her to return hither with us. She seldom leaves Mrs. M'Irwin, whom your grace may perceive is most affectionately attached to her."

This the duchess had perceived, and observed with pleasure her constant attentions to the comfort of her aged and infirm friend. In less than a fortnight she was so much recovered as to propose sending to Edinburgh for the carriage, but at the earnest request of her entertainers consented to continue with them another week. In the meantime, letters had arrived from Edinburgh, which informed the duchess that the family were all well, and anxious for her arrival. On opening her writing-desk to answer them, the last letter she had received from Caroline met her eye, and being in a writing mood, though her last remained unanswered, she wrote again to Caroline an account of the accident that had prevented her from being with her family at Edinburgh. Her grace concluded with saying, "I shall be seriously offended if I do not shortly receive a very long and circumstantial letter from you, which I promise to answer very speedily, if the gout does not prevent me." This she sealed and left on the table, with another addressed to the duchess, her daughter. Before her grace quitted the room she had been writing in, Mrs. Lessley entered it, and glancing her eye on the letters, in a tone of surprise, said,—

"Mrs. Clareville! is your grace acquainted with Mrs. Clareville?"

The duchess replied, "That she was not personally known to Mrs. Clareville, but that she corresponded with a young lady who resided with her."

After the pause of a moment, Mrs. Lessley apologised for the inquiry; but added,—

"The name struck me, for I once had a dear friend whose name was Clareville, but I have no hope that she yet lives, for I have for many years mourned her as one departed to another world."

The duchess answered, that "Similarity of names frequently deceive, and often surprise us, for yours is familiar to me; though before any introduction here I was a stranger to your person; and," continued her grace, "as you have made one inquiry of me, will you permit me to make another of you?"

Mrs. Lessley bowed, and her grace continued,—

"I know that you are a native of England, but your name is of Scottish origin."

Mrs. Lessley bowed again.

" Can you tell me, if any of your deceased husband's family were related to the late Sir Malcolm Lessley, of Lessley, Inverness?"

" Sir Malcolm," she replied, " was the uncle of my husband."

" Gracious Heaven!" cried the duchess, " how strange an event has produced our introduction to each other, for, if I mistake not, your husband was my sister's son."

Mrs. Lessley's surprise, it may be supposed, was great, at the sudden development of her late husband's affinity to the duchess, who did not let the conversation rest there, but pursued it till she had acquired all the information Mrs. Lesssley could give, and at the conclusion felt no doubt but that the stranger to whose kind and humane attentions she was so much indebted, was, in reality, no other than the widow of her nephew.

The M'Irwins were soon informed of this strange discovery, and the major, who had frequently heard Mrs. Lessley speak of her sister-in-law, as one whom she had every possible reason to suppose lost near land, on her return from India, would not suffer her to indulge in the vain expectation of her being yet numbered with the living. That lady herself confessed that her reason disapproved the supposition, yet she said the name so forcibly struck her, that for a moment she could not avoid yielding to the delusion. The duchess then said that probably at Edinburgh she should meet letters from England, which would, perhaps, throw some, light on this interesting subject, as Baron Ormsburgh, the brother of Mrs. Clareville, was, she thought, by that time arrived in England.

" Ah, then," Mrs. Lessley answered, " all further inquiries are useless ; for of Baron Ormsburgh I never heard before."

" At all events," the duchess answered, " I will not send this letter," taking up the one she had written to Caroline, " till I hear again from some of my friends in England. It will then be time enough to inquire if Mrs. Clareville is, by marriage, related to the husband of my deceased niece."

So saying, she threw the letter into the fire.

At the expected time, the carriage arrived, when the duchess left the hospitable mansion of the M'Irwins, and joined, without further accident or inconvenience, her family at Edinburgh. After her departure, the subject her arrival had given rise to was frequently agitated ; and sometimes, spite of probability, Mrs. Lessley would indulge the fond hope that Mrs. Clareville might have escaped the dreadful horrors of shipwreck, and was still numbered with the living. But then again she had no brother ; and who was Baron Ormsburgh ? Independent of this subject, the duchess had left another to reflect on. The excellent Lady Acrimony was no more ; Sir Timothy yet lived, and Montague, whom she had so often caressed as a fine and noble boy, was now in the prime of manhood, and richly endowed with all the advantages of person, improved by a highly cultivated and superior understanding. Mrs. Lessley had always intended that he should inherit her fortune, and was highly gratified on hearing that he was so worthy of her regard. The duchess had promised to write, on her arrival at Edinburgh, and her letter was expected with some degree of impatience. In the mean time, Mrs. Lessley determined on writing to her nephew, Montague, intending to invest him with the power of settling her dividends, and transmitting her a specified sum, to repay the money that the major had at different times advanced for her use, as Mrs. M'Irwin would never listen to the frequent proposals she had made of going herself to England on that business.

" Your fortune," she would say, " will accumulate, and afford you an elegant sufficiency for the decline of life, when we shall, in the course of nature, be taken from you ; therefore share without reserve the little we possess—it is sufficient to procure us all we stand in need of."

But, as Mrs. Lessley knew that the major had some relatives that stood in need of his assistance, she wished him to have the means of serving them. She knew the money he had advanced her would then be particularly serviceable. An end was, however, put to these intentions by a letter from Edinburgh. The duchess wrote as follows ;—

" I have a strange piece of intelligence to impart to my kind and obliging friend s at ——, and to Mrs. Lessley in particular ; I heard it only last evening at Genera F——'s, whose lady is one of my most particular friends.   The general having been in actual service during the late contest, and several military officers being present, the discourse naturally turned on the hair-breadth 'scapes they had run, through fire and flood.   When a lady present inquired if he knew Baron Ormsburgh,—'

" Perfectly well,' he answered, ' I left him but a few days ago. We came from France tog'ether : he had been there I believe on a visit to a family of distinction.

'Is he' said, another lady, 'a German, for I do not think it is an English title ?' ' He his an English officer of distinguished reputation—his title was conferred on him some years ago, by the king of Prussia, as a mark of respect due to his military character,' was the reply ; I paid particular attention to the conversa- and observing the first pause, inquired the baron's family name.

" ' Lessley,' he answered ; ' Colonel Lessley, he formerly served in India.   I was there with him.'   I then answered that I had been positively informed that Colonel Lessley had died in India.

' It was so reported and believed,' he replied, ' but that mistake has long since been rectified.'   I then made some other inquiries respecting his family, and the answers I received induces me to think that Mrs. Clareville is in reality his own sister, and that there must also have been some mistake in the statement of her death ; now my dear Mrs. Lessloy if you think it advisable to go to Sidmouth you are at liberty to make use of my name as an introduction to Miss Millbourne ; lose no time if you resolve on going, for when I left Brighton Mrs. Clareville was said to be very seriously ill."

The variety of emotions the letter occasioned Mrs. Lessley to experience, we shall not attempt to describe, but the pleasure she felt in the prospect of being restored to her husband and her friend was considerably diminished, when she reflected that she must leave, perhaps for ever, those dear friends to whom her attentions were becoming more than ever necessary, owing to the increased infirmities of Mrs. Mc'Irwin ; that lady, however, would not suffer one selfish thought to interfere.

" Go, my dear child," she cried, " and enjoy that happiness that I trust is yet reserved for you.   You have borne trouble with resignation, and will I am sure, support joy with proper equanimity, and view with gratitude and admiration the wonder working ways of Providence, that has thus thrown the rays of hope round your long widowed heart.'   Let me but hear that you are happy,'' she continued, " and I shall die in peace. Yet come again, Elinor, come once more, that we may bless you before we die.

Mrs. Lessley could not answer, but she wept her adieu.   The major could not speak ; he kissed most affectionately her offered cheek, and followed her to a chaise that was in waiting for her ; which conveyed her to Edinburgh, from whence she travelled in the mail to London ; and from thence went post to Sidmouth, where, to the baron and their little sad, though friendly circle, she gave nearly the following reasons for her long seclusion, understanding that Mr. Dennison had explained her sudden departure from London.   She stated that after her recovery from her long and severe illness, that she set out for Bath, attended only by her own maid servant.   At Bath she had expected to meet some ladies that she formed an acquaintance with during her stay at Sir Malcom's, but they had left the place before her arrival at it.   One of them thinking how uncomfortable she would be in so gay a place, without some one with whom she could associate, left a request with the major, with whom she was on terms of intimacy, that he would inquire for her at a lodging she had previously taken for her, and consider her as one that stood in need of consolation ; this was sufficient for that worthy man, who delighted in doing good.   He waited on Mrs. Lessley, the day after her arrival, and invited her to his lodgings, as Mrs. M'Irwin was too much indisposed to leave the house.   A particular intimacy followed this introduction, and if Mrs.

Mc'Irwin was charmed with the elegant manners and lady-like deportment o
Mrs. Lessley, that lady was no less interested in favour of that patient and severe
sufferer. Fom Bath the M'Irwins removed to Bristol, where Mrs. M'Irwin
found herself much relieved by drinking the waters, and during their continuance
there, Mrs. Lessley confided to her her tale of sorrow.

" Her sympathy," said Mrs. Lessley, " soothed my mind, and her unceasing
kindness inspired my gratitude. She had possessed herself of my entire confidence, and I could converse with her without reserve, on the events that corroded
with sorrow every hour of my existence. After some time my anguish sunk
into a calm and settled melancholy ; frequently, however, relieved by long fits of
unavailing tears. On such occasions, Mrs. M'Irwin would weep with me, reason
with me, and point out the only solace for a troubled heart ; namely, resignation
to the will of Heaven.

" I listened with reverence to her maternal counsels ; my mind became less
agitated ; happy I never expected to be, but I endeavoured to be patient under
what I then thought irremediable misfortunes ; and I listened with complacency
to the proposals she made me of going with them into Scotland. The major joined
his entreaties to hers, and painted in strong colours, the impropriety of my living
alone, he added,—

" ' If you retire to solitude, it will only be to brood over sorrow ; if you mix
with the world, you will be encompassed with dangers. Go home with us, my
dear Mrs. Lessley ; we have no children, old age requires society ; be a daughter
to my suffering wife, and she will be to you a maternal friend. Change of air
will improve your health ; change of scene will revive your spirits ; and you will,
I am certain, feel happy in administering to our comfort as we tread together the
down-hill path of life.

" What could I oppose to such kind and considerate arguments ? I consented to set out with them for the north ; I wished very much to have taken my
farewell of Lady Acrimony and her dear children, but was withheld by the promise I had given Colonel Lessley, of not attempting to renew my correspondence with Sir Timothy or the family, a promise I frequently regretted had been
given, and it was one I contemplated the breaking of.'

" Years rolled on in calm and settled serenity ; we saw but little company, and
seldom went far from home. Mrs. M'Irwin had long been lame, and, in consequence, a low chair was purchased for her use ; the major instructed me in the
management of the horse, and I frequently drove her short rides for the benefit
of the air—and then it was that I in some degree repaid the kindness I had received from these generous friends.

" Mrs. M'Irwin had lived in the great world ; her amusements, her sentiments,
and her manners were refined. I read to her, I wrote for her, for she had some
correspondents in distant parts of the kingdom ; she was fond of music, and had
been in youth much admired for her performance on the harpsichord—and I
have sat for hours at the instrument to amuse her mind and soothe her sufferings,
for they were frequently very great.'

" These kind friends were pleased with my attentions, and I was thankful that
I possessed the power of being useful to them ; we seldom saw any English newspapers, and I at last ceased to be solicitous about them. Thus I remained ignorant of the events that have been related, and thus I should in all probability
have remained, but for the accident that introduced the Duchess of Moncrieff to
our remote and peaceful dwelling.'

Our readers will imagine the entire satisfaction this communication gave the
baron, and likewise the pleasure it afforded his lady, by the prospect of having
their daughter restored to them, or more properly speaking, her natural claims
to their affections legally substantiated. The duchess had, in frequent conversations with Mrs. Lessley, mentioned that young lady in terms of high admiration and sincere affection ; but all that she had reported of her, fell far short

of what the baroness found her. The pensive character of her fine countenance was most interesting ; but when enlivened by a smile, it became irresistbile ; and sometimes, particularly when her feelings were acted on, it would assume a glow so bright, a lustre so indescribable, that even the pencil of a Titian might have failed in imitating it. On such occasions the baroness would say,—

" Dear Lessley, if this exquisitely interesting being is not the offspring of our early affections, she is—she must be—the daughter of our adoption, the support and comfort of our future days."

Once in particular. when the various events we have been relating, was spoken of in the presence of Mr. Beriton, Mr. Dennison observed,—

" That chance had seldom before produced so happy a coincidence of circum-stance."

" Chance," replied Mr. Beriton, speaking with peculiar energy, " being destitute both of power and intelligence, can create nothing, direct nothing, support nothing ; no well regulated mind can, in my opinion, doubt for a single moment, the government of a universal power, directing, guiding, and supporting ; the world, his wisdom framed, and peopled with the human race ; and these peculiar events prove that a superior agency directs and presides over the affairs of man."

After the funeral was over, which was conducted with due solemnity, the body being conveyed to a vault that had been formed by order of the late Mrs. Lessley, in the church, contiguous to her seat—the baron intending to make that his usual place of residence, and the burial-place for his family—he proposed spending some weeks at Bath previous to returning to the lodge. The baroness made no objection ; the house at Sidmouth was disposed of, and the family set forward, accompanied by Miss Beriton, whose parents, at the request of the ladies, gave permission for her absence.

Mr. Dennison had previously set out for London, from whence he proposed going to the priory, to make inquiries after Newport ; from thence he wrote that Mr. Meanwell had not obtained any satisfactory intelligence respecting the place he had been conveyed to ; but being in possession of Mrs. Newport's address, that he would shortly go to London purposely to inquire of her into the real state of her husband's health.

Caroline from Bath wrote to Lady Emma, the outline of the circumstances we have been relating, but studiously concealing the particular situation she herself stood in, on which for the future so much depended. She, however, mentioned Mrs. Clareville's generous bequest, and stated that her continuance with the baroness was a matter positively decided on.

This intelligence, so pleasing to Lady Emma, was not equally agreeable to those she was then situated with. Lady Lucy observed that it would get the girl a husband ; and Miss Newman said if she did not soar above her station, she would not in future have any occasion to intrigue for one ; but Mrs. Newland was very much disconcerted when Lady Emma stated that Baron Ormsburg was no other than Colonel Lessley. She, however, made no comment, and trusted that her own contrivance would effectually secure the secret she had so cautiously guarded ; yet she felt some fears for the future, and determined on having her brother removed from the infirmary he was then in, to one where she could depend on no one having access to him. One thing gave her satisfaction, and that was that Caroline made no mention of any circumstance having transpired that could lead to a discovery of her affinity to the family she had been so strangely introduced to. The correspondence between the young ladies continued without interruption. Lady Emma wrote freely, but Caroline cautiously. From her friend she heard that the families would return into Surrey, and continue there till the latter end of January, as Mr. Newland's town house was being considerably enlarged. When this was imparted to the baron, he consulted with his lady on the propriety of continuing at Bath, or going to his seat in Kent, where business of importance called him.

The baroness wished to go first to the lodge, thinking from the accounts she had received from Caroline, that her nephew, whom she anxiously wished to see was, by this time returned from Ireland; but on the baronet expressing a desire **to** avoid any intimacy with the Newland family, it was determined that they should immediately commence their journey into Kent. Of this circumstance Lady Emma was apprised by letter, and soon after their arrival Caroline heard from her the following particulars:—

Her ladyship stated that both families were at the manor, where everything was

in a style of superior elegance, preparatory to the peerage which it was daily expected would be conferred on the master of the mansion.

"My minority," she added, "is expired. I have been at Firr-grove with Millford and Mr. Newland. Sir Timothy's reception of me was cold and formal; and at that moment I congratulated myself for not having assented to the proposals made to me by Montague. Had I entered his family clandestinely, how severely I

No. 19.

should then have condemned myself. On our entrance the baronet arose, supported by a crutch. I advanced towards him, he looked angry, but his features relaxed when I spoke.

" 'My poor girl,' he said, 'you look very ill, and you are feverish; come, sit down.'

" Overcome by the tone of his voice, I burst into tears.

" 'I thought,' he continued, 'that a twelvemonth spent in the gay world would have brushed off these weak sensibilities; but it has made, I see, more change in your health than in your feelings. I have heard, too,' he added, 'that your fortune has been considerably diminished; but that is no business of mine.'

" 'From any other person than Sir Timothy Acrimony,' said Millford, reddening, 'I should consider these observations an infringement on the rules of good breeding.'

" 'You may consider them in what light you please, my lord. I shall not trouble Lady Emma with many more of them; yet something may be allowed to an old friend vexed at hearing she has been made the dupe of unprincipled dowagers, titled gamblers, and needy fortune-hunters.'

" 'To business, gentlemen,' cried Millford; 'we have no right to intrude on Sir Timothy longer than is necessary; and our time is short.'

" "I was vexed," said her ladyship, "at his impetuosity, yet in the presence of so many people, was glad to be relieved from the necessity of making any reply.

" The business was speedily concluded. The baronet presented me with the jewels, which he told me were of great value.

" ' Do not stake them on a game of cards, child,' he added, 'nor suffer others to stake them for you. You may find many among your acquaintance that would know how to dispose of them. Remember, they were the jewels that belonged, in her own right, to the late countess.'

" I extended my hand towards the baronet, for I could not speak. He took it between his own, and looked sorrowfully at me; in that moment the composure I been struggling to attain entirely forsook me, and I again burst into tears. I looked round me in vain for the placid smile of benignity, that I had often seen soothe the asperity of the baronet's irritable feelings; but I looked in vain—the chair was empty, the piano closed, and no vestige left of dear Lady Acrimony, but the image that was impressed on my memory.

" Of Montague, no one spoke. I had hoped Millford would have made an inquiry; but he did not, and I feared trusting my own voice with repeating his name, lest it should betray how deep an interest I took in his welfare.

" 'We part friends, young lady,' said Sir Timothy.

" 'I hope so,' was my reply.

" 'I wish you happy,' he continued. ('Ah,' thought I, 'how easily might you have made me so.') 'I did not mean to distress you; my only motive for speaking as I have done, was to guard you against the unprincipled of your own sex, and the designing of ours; and, above all, if it is to be avoided, shun newspaper notoriety. Lord Millford, to you, and you alone, Lady Emma must now look for a guide and protector, till from her numerous admirers she selects a partner for life.'

" 'On that subject,' said Millford, rather haughtily, 'I need no monitor.'

" Before the baronet could reply Mr. Newland advanced. He had before spoken but little, and that merely related to business.

" 'Sir Timothy,' he said, 'you must allow me to state that Lady Emma has many friends who are interested for her welfare, and anxious to promote her happiness.'

" 'I do not doubt it, sir,' was the baronet's reply; 'the young and beautiful generally have, especially if to the gifts of nature are added the advantages of rank and fortune.

Millford seemed particularly anxious to avoid any further conversation; therefore, taking my hand from the baronet's, he moved towards the door. Sir Timothy apologised for not seeing us across the hall. He bowed ceremonicusly, and we left the room. On our way to the carriage we were met by Doctor Maxwell. Of him Millford inquired when Mr. Montague was expected home.

" ' In less than a month,' was the answer.

" Pray, tell him we shall expect him at the manor, where we shall continue till after that period.'

" I did not speak, though I felt much pleased, that the suspense I have so long been kept in would so shortly terminate."

This was the substance of her ladyship's letter. Caroline was happy to hear that her friend had paid Sir Timothy the necessary visit, and would now be enabled to free herself from all pecuniary obligations to the purse-proud Newlands. She also most sincerely hoped that Mr. Montague Acrimony's return would be productive of mental happiness to both families, should Sir Timothy find that his prejudices had been too hastily adopted. The baroness wrote to the duchess and also to her dear friends, the M'Irwin's, who most sincerely rejoiced in her present state of felicity. The duchess hoped to see them the ensuing summer in the Highlands, and the M'Irwin's entreated that she would send some one to them to supply the loss they had sustained by her departure from them. They continued in Kent, till a letter from Lady Emma, dated from London, put them on the alert for their departure into Surrey. On their arrival at the lodge, poor Caroline's spirits were particularly oppressed, for every object that met her eye reminded her of her departed friend. This melancholy was contagious, for the baroness could but think how greatly the presence of Mrs. Clareville would have added to their domestic happiness. Yet grateful for her present enjoyments, she endeavoured to suppress the vain regrets that too frequently assailed her. An interview soon after took place between the baron and Mr. Meanwell. The latter had kept his promise—he had been in London, with Mr. Dennison, but they had both thought it prudent not to call on Mr. Newport, till the baron was with them, when prompt measures might be taken for discovering the maniac; from him, too, Caroline heard that Lord Millford had been cast in what was thought moderate damages, and that a divorce between the countess and her injured husband was then in a state of forwardness. He also hinted that a marriage was spoken of as likely to take place, between Lord Millford and Miss Newland. Caroline felt the colour mount to her face; even her neck and arms partook of the crimson dye. This was not unobserved by the baroness, who had frequently noticed how seldom Caroline spoke of his lordship, though she was frequently talking of Lady Emma and the Newlands. The arrival of Montague was soon after heard of through the same channel, and that he had set out for London within a few days after his return to England.

Here for the present we shall leave the family at the lodge, and proceed with the events that were passing in London. The long expected patent of nobility was conferred on Mr. Newland—his son was also raised to the rank of colonel, and took the seat his father had left vacant in the lower house. The family had nearly attained the zenith of their splendour. The Moncreiff interest in Scotland had been secured by the services the new viscount had rendered the duke. The M'Donald interest in England he was likewise certain of, and there needed only the marriage of his daughter with Lord Millford to complete a scheme of influence he had long aimed at attaining, and this he now felt little doubt of seeing accomplished. The heavy losses the latter had sustained had enabled the viscount to assume an appearance of liberality, in supplying him with the means of meeting many unpleasant debts of honour, and likewise of paying the five thousand pounds that had been awarded the general.

It may not be unpleasant to our readers to learn that Lord Millford felt most reluctant to accept the viscount's assistance; yet was unwilling at once to give up the society of those he then associated with. It is true he frequently thought that he could pass a few years on the continent, and recover his present embarrassments without the disgrace of retrenching his expenses in the eyes of the world.

Lady Emma had settled her debts or rather those of her thoughtless aunt, and discovered that Mrs. Pembroke's lavish expenditure, if she continued to assist her in supporting it, would in a few years leave her only an empty title to subsist on.   Many were the plans she formed for extricating herself from the society of persons she never could esteem; but all her hopes rested on the return of Montague.   In the meantime, Colonel Newland was continually at her side, and by the insinuations of Lady Lucy, and the taciturnity of Mrs. Pembroke on the subject, was in general supposed to be an accepted admirer.   In fact, that lady was so occupied in her own trifling pursuits, that she paid but little attention to the affairs of her niece; and, indeed, was so situated that she could not, had she wished so to do, have made any effectual resistance to the plans of the Newlands; for to that mushroom family, as she had been once in the habit of calling them, she was then under many pecuniary obligations, though this circumstance was known only to her dear friend Lady Lucy and the party concerned.   In this business that scheming woman acted under cover, but she was authorised by the wily viscount to watch a favourable opportunity and speak plainly on the subject to Lord Millford, from whom, previous to this proposal, he had secured a most advantageous mortgage that swallowed nearly half the rental of his estate.   The viscount offered fifty thousand pounds with his daughter on her marriage, and fifty thousand more after his decease.

"Pho," cried Lady Lucy, "you must gild the bait a little heavier for the credit of your family.   Lord Viscount Newland of Newland Manor should let the world see that his fortune is equal to his rank."

The viscount paused a few moments and then replied,—

"Well, it shall be so, if Lord Millford agrees that the marriage articles shall be drawn under my direction."

"Oh, that no doubt will be acceded to," answered the lady, "for Millford is no cool calculator."

Thus commissioned, she first commenced her attack on Mrs. Pembroke; not that she expected any opposition from her, but she wished to soothe down the family pride of that lady before she spoke to her nephew.

One morning, while they were taking their coffee together, Mrs. Pembroke observed that she had heard the preceding evening that Millford had met a severe run of ill luck with the old set, at the old place.

"I wish," she added, "that he would go abroad for a few years, to recover from his embarrassments."

"Why, he can do that and stay at home," was the answer, "if his pride does not prevent him.   Let him make proposals for Miss Newland; I know they will be accepted."

Mrs. Pembroke replied, "There was a time when I should have been very averse to this alliance, though I know it has been long desired by that now noble family."

"Pho," cried Lady Lucy, "what signifies what your opinions once were; a hundred thousand pounds down, with most likely as much money at the viscount's death, is a very good reason for any alteration in opinions."

"I have no objection but the infancy of the family," said Mrs. Pemberton.

"It will be old in time," replied the other; "and what is rank, let me ask you, without money to support it?"

"True," said Mrs. Pembroke, "but I do think the Earl of Millford should at least marry a woman of family, as the world now thinks a good fortune of much more importance."

"I do not see why Millford should not adopt its opinion," cried Lady Lucy.

"He is to act as he pleases, I shall not interfere," was the answer, and the dialogue ended.

CHAPTER XVI.

" 'Tis gold
Which buys admittance; oft it doth, yea, and makes
Diana's rangers false themselves; and yield up
Their deer to the stand o' the stealer.   And 'tis gold
Which makes the true man kill'd, and saves the thief.
*   *   *   *   *
What can it do and undo?"—SHAKSPERE.

IT was not long before Lady Lucy, by unequivocal hints, made Lord Millford understand the commission she was invested with.   He appeared neither surprised nor displeased at her communication, yet he evinced no eagerness to take advantage of her more than half explained proposals.

It was true he had often admired Miss Newland, as an elegant and fashionable woman, but he had never felt for her the least degree of affection; no, Caroline, the absent Caroline, was the sole object of his secret regard, yet pride and prudence both condemned such romantic feelings; for still the world and its dread laugh prevailed.   Lady Lucy perceiving his irresolution, continued the discourse by saying,—

"She is extremely attached to you; besides, you have latterly been so constantly in all their parties, that the world concludes you intend making her Countess of Millford."

"What has the world to do with my conduct?" he replied, rather peevishly.

"Oh, nothing," she answered, "if you choose to have it canvassed over in every club-house and card-table in St. James's, and this last abominable loss must be paid; neither Lord L—— nor the Marquis of D—— are famous for keeping secrets of this kind; excuse my freedom, I only speak from a real desire to serve you."

She omitted to say the viscount had promised to cancel a bond he held of hers, if she could turn his lordship to her purposes.

"It was only yesterday," she added, "that I heard you tell Diniver you was out of cash.   Lady Emma is, I know, seriously unhappy on your account, though no doubt she will assist you; but her whole fortune would not now extricate you."

"I will never touch a shilling of it," he answered, "I will perish first.

"Well, then, what is to be done?   Mrs. Pembroke has not a guinea she can call her own."

"I will borrow another ten thousand on bond, settle with these very honourable and fortunate friends, then retire into the country, and live on my own estate, and, if I can, prevail on my sister to go with me to superintend the dairy."

"I suppose," cried Lady Lucy, interrupting him, "the sylph of Bedford-square is admirably qualified to admire fat oxen, see the immense beauty of overgrown sheep, and vegetate amidst the venerable groves of your ancestral residence; and then you must take your aunt with you, to look after the poultry, and see the pigs regularly fed."

His lordship started.

"Nay," said she, "if you start at the theory, you will tremble when you practice on your own plan."

His lordship did tremble at the picture she had drawn, and after a long conversation agreed to consider of the viscount's very handsome offer.   The same evening, a high dispute arose at the club-house, between the Lords Q. and Millford, respecting a bet.   Colonel Newland being present, related it at breakfast to the family.   While he was speaking, Lord Millford was announced.   Miss Newland left the room by another door.   After the first salutation, the colonel retired, and at the same moment Miss Newland returned.   Pale, languid, and apparently much agitated, she advanced, with an open palm, and at the same time said,—

"Oh, Millford, I am so rejoiced to see you. I have had the most wretched night I ever experienced."

The viscountess, in a tone of sympathy, inquired what had disturbed her repose. The lady explained by saying she had heard from the colonel, on the preceding night, of the dispute between Lord Quaver and their friend, and

"Nothing," said she, "possessed my imagination but that a duel would result from their differences."

Lord Millford felt flattered by the concern she expressed for his safety; he thanked her in language that indicated obligation for her solicitude.

"But you may rest assured, my dear Miss Newland," he added, "that I shall never pay a debt of honour with a pistol."

"I wish," she answered, in a tone of anxiety, "that you would not contract debts of honour; but I beg your lordship's pardon—I have no right to prescribe rules for your conduct."

"It rests," he answered, "with Miss Newland, to decide whether she will for the future take the trouble of thinking for me, who has hitherto thought but little for himself."

The viscountess left the room, and Lord Millford handed the lady to a seat, and placed himself by her side. The conversation became particular, Lord Millford was explicit, and Miss Newland played her part so adroitly, that in less than an hour his lordship really believed that she had a sincere regard, both for his happiness and character. She gave her consent, with tenderness and hesitation, to his request of having her permission for applying to the viscount, though this, both parties knew, was a mere matter of form. Lord Millford, in reply, talked of the honour she had conferred on him, promised future gratitude and devotion, but never spoke of love; indeed, love had nothing to do with the contract. He soon after took his leave, promising to see her again in the evening. Not wishing to leave himself much time to reflect on the business he had embarked in, he made instant application to the viscount, who received the proposal with great satisfaction, offered to draw up an outline of the marriage articles, which he would present to his lordship for inspection, and then place them in proper hands for execution. The bridegroom elect bowed an assent, and the conference ended. The viscountess, when informed of Lord Millford's declaration, exulted in the success of their plans; Lady Lucy was sent for,—

"The day is our own," she cried, as the latter entered her dressing-room; "Augusta has performed her part admirably, and really deserves the coronet she has taken so much pains to acquire."

When Mrs. Pembroke was informed of the preceding circumstances, she offered her congratulations on the projected alliance; while Lady Emma, who had long expected that her brother's enthralments with the viscount would end in his marriage with Miss Newland, offered hers, in a pensive tone that conveyed more of sorrow than surprise. Perhaps she was thinking of one, with whom he would have enjoyed more happiness, could he have dispensed with splendour.

Nothing now was to be heard of but carriages, jewels, dresses, &c.; a townhouse was to be taken immediately, to be superbly furnished at the expense and under the directions of the viscountess; the marriage articles had not been objected to by Lord Millford, and were already in a state of forwardness. His lordship played the lover very satisfactorily to all but himself; yet he hurried the preparations forward as one deeply interested in the completion of the business, though it was a subject he would never calmly think of; yet as it was a sacrifice he had agreed to offer at the shrine of Pluto; he wished it paid with all possible celerity; and amidst all the bustle that was going forward, there was but one pensive countenance, and that was Lady Emma's.

While things were in this train among the parties in London, Montague Acrimony arrived at the grove, where the first news he heard from Dr. Maxwell was, that his friend Lord Millford was on the point of marriage with Miss Newland, and that it was expected (so said report) that the colonel, her brother would at the same time receive the hand of Lady Emma. Montague changed colour ; he paced the room in no very enviable state of feeling, and at length exclaimed,—

" Oh ! my valued friend, my early monitor, my worst fears are verified. Is this the return I am to meet, for years of firm and unabated affection ?"

" It is better," said the doctor, gravely, " to regret the inconstancy of a mistress than mourn over the infidelity of a wife."

Montague did not reply, but he secretly resolved on setting out the next morning for London, and obtaining an interview either with Lord Millford or Lady Emma. This was not difficult to accomplish, as he had business of the baronet's to transact there. In the evening he heard from the doctor of Miss Millbourne's fortunate situation with the baron. Some particulars of that affair he had heard from the rector. At first he thought he would call on Caroline, and inquire of her if there was any foundation for the reports in circulation, but this thought he instantly discarded, thinking he might lose time without gaining satisfactory information.

The baronet, who was seriously indisposed, did not object to his going to London, though he suspected other motives than those of business hurried him thither ; but as his son was silent on the subject, he did not introduce it.

On Mr. Acrimony's arrival in London he hastened to Bedford-square, and unexpectedly made his appearance at Mrs. Pembroke's, just as the company, for it was a public night, were seated at the card table, and saw his still dear Emma opposite Colonel Newland ; at the same table were Lady Lucy and Colonel Diniver. He advanced, Lady Emma started ; she caught his hurried glance, it was indeed one of anger and resentment. She attempted to rise, but was prevented by Lady Lucy, who, following the direction her eyes had taken, cried,—

" Why, Lady Emma, you look as frightened as Hamlet on seeing his father's ghost. Oh ! now I know what has alarmed you. I heard Mr. Pembroke say that you had promised old Caustic never to play any more at cards, and now, poor child, you are detected in having told a fib."

The gentlemen, if so they can be called, burst into an immoderate fit of laughter, which so disconcerted Lady Emma that she continued motionless in her chair, while Montague, unable to account for the burst of laughter, for he was not near enough to hear the provoking observations made by Lady Lucy, bowed slightly as he passed the table, walked suddenly up the room, and abruptly quitted the house. Unforfortunately, Lord Millford was not present, or most likely some explanations might have been entered into, that would have relieved both parties from the inquietude they then laboured under. Of the porter he inquired if Lord Millford was in London, and heard that his lordship had set out that morning for the priory, and was not expected to return before the following day. Vexed and disappointed, he returned to the inn, from whence he wrote a few lines to Lady Emma, entreating to see her alone the following morning. With this he sent his own servant, who had orders to wait for an answer. He did wait for some time, and at length was informed that Lady Emma was engaged, and could not write that evening, and that in the morning she was going out of town for several days. Every hope of an explanation now vanished, unless he should be so fortunate as to meet with Lord Millford the following day. In this, however, he was disappointed, for that nobleman had not arrived in London. Thus situated, he expedited the business he had on his hands, and returned to Firr-grove. On his way there, he called at the priory, and heard that Lord Millford had quitted it for London on the preceding evening. Thinking that he was purposely avoided, he summoned pride to his assistance, and determined on renouncing for ever a woman who had treated him with such unmerited neglect ; yet to resolve was more easy than to execute, for he could not give up, without another effort, the strong desire he entertained of hearing from Lady Emma herself if the report of her marriage with the colonel rested on the basis of her free consent to it. To obtain an answer on this subject, he wrote to her, and enclosed the letter, as usual, to Lord Millford. He complained of her long silence, of her neglect in not sending the miniature of herself, which she had so faithfully promised should be forwarded to him; but, above all, he dwelt on the strange contents of the letter which conveyed to him the unexpected statement of her refusal to continue the correspondence that she had so freely agreed should, on her part, be punctual. A few lines were written, in the true spirit of friendship, to Lord Millford, requesting him to name his own time and place for an interview, as he had a most earnest and anxious wish to see him. These letters never reached those they were intended for, and, in consequence, remained unanswered. Vexed and disappointed, he determined to let the correspondence cease, without making any further effort to renew it. Sir Timothy perceived the uneasy state of mind his son laboured under. He was no friend to what are commonly called love matches, neither was he favourable to mere matches of conveniency; but he was a very great advocate for similarity of character in those who were to pass their days together. Society, such as the gay world exhibited, he had an insuperable aversion to; and he could not bring himself to believe that any person who had been entangled within the toils of dissipation could ever reconcile themselves to the calm enjoyment of domestic life. He thought, too, that his fair ward had erred against conviction; for she had been warned against the dangers she had rashly ventured to incur. The squibs in the fashionable papers continued occasionally to appear. Lord Millford's losses, both on the turf and at the gaming-table, were regularly reported, and frequently exaggerated. This, on his own account, was a matter of indifference to him; but he was much vexed on finding his sister's conduct and connections so often most grossly misrepresented. He tried to trace the fabrication of these paragraphs, but without success. Thus Sir Timothy's prejudices seemed to rest on, at least, reasonable foundation. In the meantime, Montague continued to wonder at and regret the conduct of the, to him, lost, but still dear, Lady Emma. He, however, practised a cautious reserve; her name was never mentioned, either by him or the baronet, and the doctor seldom alluded to it.

Thus were things situated at the grove when a letter arrived from Sir Robert Brinsby, an Irish baronet, informing Mr. Acrimony of his arrival in England with his family, and requesting that he would favour them with his company at Cheltenham. A proposal more agreeable could not have been made him; he was weary of his own solitary situation. Few persons had access to the grove, and he had but little conversation with either the baronet or the doctor, except such as related to business or politics. Before he commenced his journey, he called at the priory, thinking that by chance he might meet with Lord Millford; there, he was, however, disappointed: no one was there, except the usual domestics. He inquired for Mr. Meanwell, and was directed to a distant part of the building; there he bent his steps, and found him surrounded by workmen, who were employed in fitting-up the apartments of the countess elect. She had been there to make choice of those most agreeable to her, and had given directions for very elegant and tasteful decorations, and the whole was to be completed with all possible expedition. Meanwell returned with his visitor to the parlour, where a long and confidential conversation took place; and from Meanwell's discourse, Mr. Acrimony thought there was little doubt, but the Newlands would carry their point, and unite the two families by a double marriage; he heard also Miss Millbourne's residence at the lodge confirmed, with an account of the genteel provision the deceased Mrs. Clareville had bequeathed her. This was heard with great pleasure by one who sincerely admired her character; but on one point Mr. Meanwell was silent, and that was, the solid hope that was then entertained of proving her legitimate claims to the protection of the baron and his lady; neither did he say that Baron Ormsburgh and Colonel Lessley were one and the same person; but he offered, if agreeable, to Mr. Montague, to introduce him to the family at the lodge. This proposal he politely declined at that time, but expressed a wish of being known to them at no very distant period. He mentioned his intended journey, left a message of congratulation for Miss Millbourne, and took his leave. His suspense on Lady Emma's account was then ended, for he thought her in reality the destined wife of another.

Montague Acrimony was not one that could love moderately; his heart was generous, his temper sanguine, and in spite of appearances, he had indulged the fond hope, thnt on his return to England he should convince Lady Emma she had decided too hastily, or been prevailed on too easily to close her correspondence

with him; besides, as the business he had been engaged in had been most satisfactorily concluded, he knew fortune would be only a secondary consideration, and above all, Sir Timothy was not an avaricious character. Judge then, reader, how severely he must have felt the disappointment of his long-cherished hopes, yet the goodness of his understanding pointed out to him the folly of unavailing regret; and he purposed on his return from Cheltenham to seek for some one, in whose

No. 20.

tenderness and affection he might find a solace for the infelicity of his first and ill-requited passion.

The baronet made no objections to his journey, and within a few days after his call at the priory, he found himself comfortably domesticated in the family of Sir Robert, from whom, during his stay in Ireland, he had received many polite attentions. Here then, for the present, we leave him, to return to Lady Emma, whom we left surprised at his sudden appearance, and subsequently vexed at his abrupt departure. The moment she could escape from the card-table she did, which she thought was fortunately broke up by Lady Lucy, who complained of head-ache, and retired from the company; but Lady Emma lingered in the rooms, and with a beating heart traversed the spacious apartments, wondering that Montague did not return, and fearing, at last, that some sudden indisposition had seized him, she inquired of Mrs. Pembroke if she had seen him before he left the house.

" Seen him," she replied, " yes, and that is as much as I can say, for he passed me with only a slight compliment, never inquired after a single being amongst us, and left the house, I suppose, for I have not seen him since." Lady Emma on seeing him walk from the table had no doubt but he was offended at finding her engaged at the card table with a party she knew that he had a decided dislike to, yet she had yielded to the solicitations of Lady Lucy to make up the set with them, in preference to remaining disengaged, for she knew that Colonel Newland would take advantage of that circumstance, and be the whole night at her side; the game, in compliment to her who recently declined playing deep, was only five sovereigns the rubber. This, totally through inattention she lost; the colonel was out of humour; Dinever, satirical; and Lady Lucy, peevish and discontented; thus the breaking up of the table was a relief to all parties. Before Lady Emma had received Mrs. Pembroke's answer, Newland was again at her side. Vexed at his persevering and irksome attentions, she quitted the company and retired to her dressing-room, hoping that if she did not see Montague again before the morning that she should at least hear from him; in this too, she was disappointed; she then consoled herself with the thoughts that Millford would see him, and through him that she should hear Montague's long silence satisfactorily accounted for; but here again disappointment met her, for those who had so far acted against her had not yet completed their nefarious purposes. After a sleepless night she arose pale and spiritless. Miss Newland had, at the request of Lady Lucy, continued in Bedford-square. During breakfast she observed, " that as Millford would probably not return till evening, she thought a drive to old Windsor would be of service to all present."

" The very thing I was thinking of," said Lady Lucy, " for nothing but air will relieve me from this abominable nervous head-ache, but perhaps, she added, Lady Emma may expect Mr. Montague, and it may not be agreeable to her to leave town."

" I think," replied Mrs. Pembrooke, " that young man's behaviour last evening, was too strange to be lightly passed over, and certainly does not merit much consideration. I hope my niece knows better what is due to herself, than to wait his leisure for a visit.'"

" But I particularly wish to see him," was the answer.

" It is evident," cried Lucy, " my dear Lady Emma, that he is no very anxious for an interview, or he would have waited your leisure last evening, and not have flown off with disdain because his important appearance did not obtain your immediate attention. I should not speak thus plain if any were here but friends; besides, I am sure he only means to make you the dupe of his vanity, and your predilection in his favour has been seen by many with pity and concern."

" I wish the many your ladyship alludes to would think more of their own affairs and less of mine," answered Lady Emma.

" Well, do not be out of humour, my sweet sister that is to be," cried Miss Newland; " oblige us with your company to-day, and most likely Millford will bring Acrimony down with him in the evening."

" Nothing so likely," answered Lady Lucy, " if he has a particular desire to see Lady Emma; at all events, we shall return to-morrow evening."

At length overcome by the dread of ridicule, she most reluctantly consented to go with them. The following morning the Colonels Newland and Dinever made their appearance early, and before dinner Lord Millford arrived, but no Montague with him; every circumstance contributed to the uneasiness of Lady Emma, for there was no appearance of an immediate return to town. One of the horses fell lame, and Lady Lucy's illness confined her to her bed, while the ladies would not think of leaving her to the care of servants, and the gentlemen found amusement for themselves in the billiard-room.

Lord Millford heard from Mrs. Pembroke of Montague's appearance and sudden departure, which, considering his long silence, he thought very unaccountable. To Lady Emma he applied for her opinion on the subject, who answered, she was incapable of forming any reasonable one; but inquired, in her turn, if he had heard of Montague, in Bedford-square. He replied that he had not been there. The fact was, that, before the party left town, Lady Lucy had despatched a servant to the priory, to acquaint him with their departure, and desire that he would meet them there the following day. In consequence, he travelled direct from the priory to Mrs. Pembroke's villa. A strong suspicion of treachery rushed on the mind of Lady Emma; again she thought of her lost miniature, of Montague's long silence, of the pains that had been taken to get her from London, and the method that had been adopted to bring her brother there, before he could have had any chance of seeing his friend. Her mind, thus tossed on a sea of uncertainty, was incapable of action; she dreaded expressing her real feelings to her brother, lest she should involve him in an unpleasant altercation with her ungrateful lover (for such she then thought him). Besides, she feared the ill-natured wit of Lady Lucy, and the affected condolence of Miss Newland. Lord Millford had some thoughts of writing to his friend, but was withheld from so doing by the consideration that Montague should make an apology for his neglect in not writing, before he could, consistently with the respect due to Lady Emma's character, seek any explanation with him. Thus were all parties situated, when a slow fever, which had long preyed on the spirits of Lady Emma, seriously alarmed him, for her health was visibly declining. He then hurried her to London for medical assistance, where she continued a long time in a very languid state. The preparations for Lord Millford's nuptials were nearly completed, and nothing was talked of but the festivities that were to follow that joyful event; but, in the midst of gaety, Lady Emma sat silent and abstracted. During the time we have been speaking of, Lord Millford went again to the priory, to inspect the alterations that were making there, and heard from Meanwell of Mr. Acrimony's call and departure for Cheltenham. When this was told Lady Emma, she struggled to regain the tranquillity she had long lost; and, though she could not be happy, she endeavoured to appear so. And here we will leave the expectant bridal party to their own enjoyments, while we recal the attention of our readers to the artifices of those who had so cruelly destroyed the happiness of two persons so deserving of each other.

It may be in the recollection of those who have attended to our tale, that the uniting of the two families was a primary object with the Newlands. The mutual affection that existed between Lady Emma and Montague was easily discovered, and the getting Lady Emma to London was the first step towards their machinations. Lady Lucy soon discovered that the correspondence, after Montague's departure for Ireland, was carried on through the medium of her brother. The first packet that came she saw by chance on the breakfast-table. Being alone, she made no difficulty of concealing it. On retiring to her own room, she examined the seal, and, perceiving that it was the Acrimony crest, she feared to break it; but, carefully marking the size with a pencil, she determined on getting one speedily engraved like it, before she ventured to open the inclosure. This was soon effected, and the packet was opened in the presence of Mrs. Newland. It confirmed all they had conjectured, and more than they anticipated. He spoke of the future union, as a thing certain of taking place on his return, lamented that she had not consented to the plan he had proposed to her before his departure, as it would have snatched her from the dangers he feared she would be exposed to during his long and tedious absence. He spoke freely of the Newlands, of Lady Lucy, and implored her not to injure herself in Sir Timothy's opinion by putting it in the power of the former parties to report her imprudence to him. He added, "My father is not mercenary, but he is a decided enemy to a wanton waste of money." In short his letter convinced them that he had made a true estimate of their characters, and feared their machinations. Hatred now operated on the minds of both, and they determined to take severe revenge on one that had sufficient penetration to discover their real characters. Finding that the baronet was really prejudiced against Lady Emma, through their former practices, which they had not before exactly ascertained, and that Lady Emma made his consent a positive preliminary to their union, they determined it should never be obtained. For this end the newspapers teemed with the mischievous paragraphs we have before alluded to, and which so unfortunately succeeded in the quarter they were meant for. Mrs. Newland advised that the letter should be resealed and left for the owner, but Lady Lucy more daring proposed stopping the correspondence at once. This was after much consultation agreed too, but in this business Lady Lucy wanted a confident, and found one in her own woman, who had long been in her service, and well trained to mischief. She was employed to watch the letters daily, and secure all that came, from or were directed to Ireland. Montague's second letter breathed complaints blended with reproaches at not having heard from Lady Emma—he also spoke of her neglect in not sending the miniature she had promised him, and bade her, when she looked at his, not to forget the anxiety the original was suffering through her silence ; but Lady Emma had written and inclosed the miniature. She spoke also with regret of her brother's flighty attentions to Miss Newland, and of her own dislike to the whole family. This letter was inclosed and directed by Lord Millford—this precaution was taken that their correspondence might not be suspected, and most fortunate it was for Caroline that she was not at liberty to disclose her real situation to her friend ; had it been otherwise, those whose interest it was to have stopped the course of justice might have done it most effectually. The next step was to obtain the miniature of Montague. Lady Emma never wore it; no one had seen it but her brother. Unfortunately, she left it on her toilette, and never saw it after. It had been long sought by Lady Lucy's emissary, and was at last purloined. When in possession of this, Lady Lucy resolved on a bold measure ; among her other acquirements she had one of the most dangerous tendency, when accompanied by an unfeeling and malignant mind ; she could copy with the most minute exactness the handwriting of any one, and this she frequently made most mischievous use of. On the present occasion their talent was replete with misery, for she availed herself of it, to write in Lady Emma's name to her lover, stating that she repented of the promise she had given him of being a regular correspondent, having heard from undoubted authority that Sir Timothy would never give his consent to their union, and that whatever violence she might do her own feelings, she was resolved never to enter any family, whose principal thought her unworthy their alliance. In this curious document she enclosed the miniature. She sealed her letter with the Millford arms, having borrowed the seal, under the pretence of having mislaid her own, and despatched it without delay to Dublin.

Surprised and mortified, Mr. Acrimony wrote back requesting some solution of this, to him, incomprehensible inconsistency ; but he wrote in vain, for his letters were regularly intercepted.

He expedited his business in Ireland, hoping on his return to obviate Lady Emma's objections to a correspondence, and gain her consent to a private marriage, should the baronet continue his unfavourable sentiments of her.

During the time we have been speaking of, it may be recollected that Captain, now Colonel Newland was paying her the most devoted attentions. It was not love that induced him to follow her, for of that passion, as it affected the heart, he knew nothing; it was not wealth, for in the estimation of himself and family her fortune was next to nothing; but it was vanity, ambition, and revenge, that led him on, if possible, to secure his victim.

Lady Emma's indifference had wounded his pride; her connections, being the daughter and sister of an earl, stimulated his ambition; and the manner in which he had heard, from Lady Lucy, he had been spoken of, both by Montague and Lady Emma in the intercepted correspondence, excited his revenge, and he secretly determined, at whatever risk, to gain possession of her hand. He, therefore, waited patiently the working of events, and saw with pleasure that the losses and embarrassments of Lord Millford, which he privately abetted and publicly opposed, would add to the union of that nobleman with Miss Newland, from whom he expected to meet every necessary assistance in the completion of his designs.

When the Millfords paid their last visit to Firr-grove, they left it before Mr. Newland, who continued some time after them in conversation with Sir Timothy. The former was not a man of many words, but he knew exactly how to time what he had to say; he spoke of Lord Millford's losses, of Lady Emma's folly in assisting her thoughtless aunt, and expressed himself extremely hurt at seeing the estate which the late earl had left unincumbered, now, of necessity, so deeply mortgaged.

The baronet in reply observed, " That a double marriage, if report was to be credited, was likely to take place between the families; and that," he continued, " will set all to rights."

The other replied, " That he did not intend to lay any restraint on the inclinations of his children, and that nothing but a marriage with a lady of very good fortune could enable Lord Millford to support the dignity of his family."

" Well," said the baronet, " but the poor girl that has just left us, is she inclined to the marriage that is talked of?"

" I leave that entirely to the ladies," replied the wily lawyer; " but I have never heard that Lady Emma had made any objections to the proposal, though I assure you, Sir Timothy, that my son, if he was not so greatly enamoured of her, might marry a lady with many more thousands than our late ward has hundreds."

" Oh, I do not in the least doubt it," was the answer; " but as you want honours, and they want money, I think it will be a fair bargain on both sides."

At the same time Mr. Newland heard from Sir Timothy that Montague was hourly expected home; this he reported to his lady, who instantly determined on shortening her stay at the manor, and leaving it before the period of his return, thinking it would be much easier to prevent the meeting of the parties in town, than in the country.

We have before related the success of their infamous projects as far as they related to Lord Millford; and there remained but one stroke more, they thought, to draw Lady Emma into the snare they had long been laying for her, and that was to convince her that Montague was become indifferent to her proceedings.

CHAPTER XVII.

Oh, say not woman's love is bought
With vain and empty treasure;
Oh, say not woman's heart is caught
By every idle pleasure.
When first her gentle bosom knows
Love's flame, it wanders never;
Deep in her heart the passion glows,
She loves—and loves for ever.—BYRON.

THIS visit to Cheltenham afforded an excellent opportunity for the consummation of their plans. Lady Lucy wrote a short note, imitating his hand, as she

had before done that of Lady Emma. A slight apology was made for not calling again in Bedford-square, and an angry reproach expressed at having found her
engaged at cards, with a party he so much disliked. "Anxious," it said, "for your
future welfare, and to save you from the whirlpool of dissipation, that will eventually overwhelm you, I instantly applied to Sir Timothy for his consent to our
immediate union, but found him inflexible to the measure. Knowing that without his sanction I had little hopes of success, I did not presume to trouble you
again on the subject. The miniature your ladyship formerly honoured me with,
I return, and leave you at full liberty to present it to some fortunate man, and
one less susceptible to female impropriety.

"There," cried Lady Lucy, as she presented this vile fabrication to the viscountess; " if this does not cure her of her love for Montague, I have no knowledge of the female heart. Her wounded pride will take the alarm, and the colonel's success will then be certain."

"That is now only a secondary consideration," the viscountess replied, " for
the marriage of Augusta will accomplish all we want, namely—the political influence of the family."

"True," cried the other, " but you must own that it will be more concentrated
if kept entirely to yourselves. Lady Emma has great influence over her brother,
and she may marry some one who may share the interest you have long desired
to keep to yourselves."

"Admitted," said the viscountess. "I resign all further interference, and
leave the whole to your management."

After this, a trusty emissary was chosen for the purpose. The viscountess
found money, for Lady Lucy had none to spare. The letter was sealed with the
Acrimony crest, and sent to Cheltenham, and there put into the post-office for
London.

It now only remained to see what effect it would produce on the conduct of
Lady Emma, to whom it was delivered at the expected time. Her ladyship coloured as she took it from the breakfast table; she knew the crest, and had not
the least suspicion but that the writing was Montague's. She put it in her bosom,
and seated herself at the table.

"Read it, my dear," said Mrs. Pembroke, " we shall not interrupt you."

This was declined, and after swallowing one cup of coffee, Lady Emma, with a
beating heart, retired to peruse it.

The contents both surprised and distressed her, yet resentment almost subdued
regret; and she thought she would banish her ungrateful lover from her thoughts
for ever. One thing above all she was sorry for, and that was the loss of his miniature.

"If I had that," she sighed, mentally, "I would convince him that I could
resign it with as much indifference as he has returned mine. His letters, however,
shall go—all I have ever received I will return to him, with every vestige of what
I once thought fond, sincere affection."

A locket that contained a lock of his hair was the first thing that presented itself. She remembered the time he had given it to her, the look, and the words
that accompanied it. On his first setting out for Ireland, he had implored her
never to forget him.

The recollection brought tears of sorrow to her eyes, and she sat down to
indulge them, and while weeping, almost to agony, her brother entered. Mrs.
Pembroke had told him that her ladyship had received a small packet by the post,
and Lady Lucy added,—

"I think it was from Cheltenham."

In consequence he sought her to inquire if the conjecture was correct. Surprised at her agitation, he anxiously inquired the cause, which she explained by
pointing to the letter; the miniature lay by it. His lordship was indignant at what
he termed Montague's ungentlemanly behaviour.

" I expected," he added, " that a fit of jealousy had occasioned his silence, and thought whenever you met he would satisfactorily account for his long neglect. I will go to Cheltenham, and insist on his giving me a more particular account of his reasons for deserting you."

" Not for the world," said Lady Emma, in reply; "he shall never know the anxiety I have felt at his silence, nor the torture that the suspense he kept me in has occasioned; but that is now over, and I will in future only think of him as he is, not as he once was, when hope fondly whispered to my heart, that he would be through life my guide, my husband, and my friend."

Her tears again flowed, and Lord Millford felt too much distressed to offer consolation; both agreed, at length, to conceal the contents of the letter from the family, and on the propriety of returning Montague's former letters.

" Send back his picture," said Lord Millford.

" I have lost it," returned his sister."

This circumstance she had not before revealed to him.

" There must have been treachery," he cried. " Whod have taken it ?"

" I know not," she answered, " nor is it now worth while to inquire. This is conclusive," pointing to the one she had then received. " This is Montague's writing; the miniature is the one I sent after him to Dublin, and there is the Acrimony crest; and let that set the subject at rest for ever. To seek for any further explanation would but sink me in his opinion, and lessen me in my own."

Finding her so determined, he did not press the subject, but reverted to his own immediate affairs.

" The marriage articles," he informed her, " would be ready for signature the following week, and in less than a month," he said, " I suppose the ceremony must take place."

" Do you go to the priory after it is over ?" she inquired.

" I had intended to do so," was the answer; " but Augusta had determined on a tour into Wales. By our return the alterations she has ordered to be made in the interior of the priory will be completed, and the town-house ready for our reception. I hope change of air and the bustle you will necessarily be engaged in will renovate your health, and restore your spirits to serenity. Do not agitate yourself at present by looking over Montague's letters; collect them when you are more composed, and I will send them to the grove, where he will be sure to receive them."

This advice was adopted, for Lady Emma really had not then spirits to complete the task she had assigned herself.

Lord Millford left her to pay his usual morning visit in Grosvenor-square, and her ladyship dressed for dinner, at which a little conversation passed. Lady Lucy was out, and Mrs. Pembroke merely inquired who the letter came from, and what the packet contained.

"The letter came from Mr. Acrimony," Lady Emma replied. "What the inclosure was I would rather not explain."

" Very strange, indeed," said Mrs. Pembroke; " but you are your own mistress, and certainly I have no right to inquire into anything you may choose to conceal. Apropos," she added, without waiting for an answer, " you must get ready for a ball and supper, that is to be given at Newland house early in the next week. The viscountess means to have a select party; at twelve the refreshment rooms will be thrown open, after which masques are to be admitted, and the company before invited will assume their different characters. I shall want you to assist me with a little money. We must appear in new dresses, for the viscountess and Miss Newland, I know, expect that we shall do credit to their entertainment."

Lady Emma in reply said she had but little money in her possession, and she thought new dresses unnecessary on the present occasion.

Mrs. Pembroke was of a different opinion; she appeared offended, and Lady Emma left the room.

In the evening Mrs. Pembroke went to the Opera.

Lord Millford who had business to transact with Meanwell, proposed setting out the next day for the priory ; and fearing his sister would be dull alone, h^e pressed her to make one in a party that was formed for the evening. This sh^e declined, saying,—

"She preferred being at home, as she wished to write both to the dowager duchess, and her long neglected Caroline."

Her apology was accepted, and she was left to pursue her own designs. She wrote to those she intended, apprising them both of the occurrences that had happened. To the duchess she spoke in general terms, but to Caroline she wrote from the heart. Her letter was long and circumstantial ; she complained of Montague's strange and unkind conduct, in terms of real sorrow ; she observed, too, that she thought Mrs. Pembroke seemed to have adopted Lady Lucy's opinions, and appeared to consider her acceptance of Colonel Newland as a thing that would follow her brother's marriage with Miss Newland, while Lady Lucy insisted that by allowing his attentions, she had given him encouragemeet to solicit her hand.

"It is in vain," she continued, "that I insist on never having encouraged his irksome attention, and that I have no intention of ever receiving his addresses. They laugh at my assertions, or ridicule my uneasiness. Such is my present unpleasant situation," said her ladyship, in conclusion, "and such it must remain for the present ; but as all hopes of happiness for me have vanished, I shall conceal as much as possible my real sentiments, and mix with the bridal party, though the canker of disappointment is rankling at my heart."

Our readers will doubtless conjecture what we should before have stated, that it was through Lady Lucy's contrivance that Montague's last note was stopped, and also, that on the same night the jaunt to old Windsor was planned to prevent the chance of a meeting in the morning.

Though she thought the message she had sent would prevent his calling, yet she was too cautious to trust to that alone

The success that followed her scheme has been already related. Miss Newland was in her confidence, and helped to support the deception she was practising.

For some days preceding the viscountess's expected entertainment Lady Emma was continually distressed by her aunt's constant application for money. Lady Lucy, too, observed,—

"That it would be a downright insult to the vicountess, who that night expected a most brilliant assembly, if they were not dressed in a very superior style. Let Mrs. Pembroke," she added, ' take five hundred pounds of Colonel Newland, and let Millford pay him after he is married.'

"Not on my account," she answered, vexed at their unprincipled importunity ; "if he chooses to oblige my aunt, I have nothing to do with it."

Mortified at her refusal, Lady Lucy reproached her with want of feeling, and Mrs. Pembroke had an hysteric fit, which produced the end intended, for her ladyship agreed that the money should be advanced, if Lord Millford would go with her the following morning to the bank. This point carried, both ladies were in perfect good humour. The money was advanced, and new dresses bespoke.

Lady Emma would have left herself without money ; but her brother observed that he wished her appearance to be equal to her aunt's, and insisted on her retaining one hundred for her own use.

Mrs. Pembroke could not object to the proposal, though she could have disposed of as many thousands. Her jewels were out, and must be redeemed ; her milliners' bills had been long standing, and her new finery must be paid for ; but this she did not think it necessary to explain, fortunately for her, for she began to fear she should not get her finery together by the time. Mrs. Newland postponed her ball for another week, as she heard the Duchess of Bloomfield gave one the same night, and she feared it would draw many from her party that she expected to grace it.

Lord Millford took the opportunity that then offered of going to the priory, having business to transact with Meanwell previous to his marriage.

We must now return to Caroline, who enjoyed all the felicity her heart could entertain in the society of those who so sincerely loved her.

Mr. Denison managed to discover the asylum in which Newport had been placed by the Newlands. He visited him in company with two physicians of eminence who held out hopes of his entire recovery, if he were immediately removed from so dismal an habitation, and had the benefit of change of scene and agreeable

society. On this being communicated to the baron, the requisite steps were taken, and the prognostics of the medical gentlemen were very shortly verified by the much improved condition of the invalid. In his most lucid intervals, he was informed of the baron's identity with Colonel Lessley, and he expressed an ardent

No. 21.

desire to do everything in his power to elucidate the mystery hitherto hanging over the parentage of Caroline, whom he declared most unequivocally to be the baron's long-lost daughter. He also informed Mr. Dennison where he had deposited a portmanteau which contained a number of documents and other matters which would confirm his statements. The portmanteau was obtained, and as it was considered necessary to open it in the presence of a magistrate, application was made to Sir Timothy Acrimony, who was the nearest gentleman who was in the commission of the peace.

The baron, accompanied by Mr. Meanwell, Mr. Dennison, and the aged domestic Martha, accordingly waited on Sir Timothy, and in his presence the portmanteau was opened. The first thing taken out was a pearl necklace with gold clasps. "This," said Martha, "Miss Emmeline had on the last morning I dressed her." The next article was a gold coral cyphered "E. L.," and a superb pair of pistols that had been presented to the baron on his promotion, by the officers of the garrison ; they were richly wrought in gold, his name on them, and the date of the year in which they had been manufactured. There were also found a sprig of pearls, and also a pair of bracelets, very valuable, that were intended as a present for Mrs. Lessley, and had been made by Mrs. Clareville's order ; in the centre was a device, with that lady's hair interwoven with a lock of the baron's ; a few more trifling articles of jewellery, which were recognised at once by the baron as his property, was all that remained, except a number of papers. There was a letter addressed by the repentant maniac to Miss Lessley, stating the injuries she had sustained, expressive of his deep remorse, and anxious desire to make atonement for his dereliction from rectitude. His will, written by himself, was inclosed in the letter ; he had left her the half of his funded property saved from his annuity, as a small return, he said, for the fortune she had so unjustly been deprived of. In another paper he described his escape from the wreck, with the child and the portmanteau in his possession, and how, on his arrival in London, he yielded to the persuasions of the Newlands, and determined to keep the child's existence a secret from her friends. Mrs. Newland had given her the name of Caroline Millbourne, and her husband disposed of most of the jewels which the portmanteau had contained, through the agency of a foreign merchant.

After the perusal of these documents and examination of the other contents, the party took a friendly leave of the baronet, and returned to the lodge.

About the same time a waiting woman of Lady Lucy's who had been concerned in the abstraction of the miniature and letters from the Lady Emma, was discharged by her mistress, and out of revenge made her way to Lord Millford and informed him of all the trickery that had been contrived to create a coolness between his sister and Montague Acrimony. Millford was too generous to keep the matter secret, but immediately wrote a detail of the circumstances to Montague, who was overjoyed at the intelligence that his Emma was still true to him. He lost no time in hastening to her presence, and soon every cloud was removed which had threatened to mar their happiness.

One morning, the baron wishing for a conference with Meanwell, who was, in the absence of Mr. Dennison, his principal counsellor, proposed walking through the park to the priory. His lady instantly assented ; but Caroline turned pale, and remained silent.

"Courage, my dear girl," said Miss Beriton; "why should you shrink from this trial, who have supported so many with fortitude ?" For Caroline's predilection for Lord Millford had not escaped either her observation, or that of the baroness.

The latter, however, did not seem to notice her hesitation, for she really wished to see her subdue, what she thought, a hopeless and unfortunate attachment.

Their walk commenced, and in the park they met Meanwell, who conducted them to the mansion.

Most severe were the conflicts that fluttered in the heart of Caroline, as she traversed, leaning on the arm of Eliza, the spacious apartments she had before trod with Lady Emma. Every step recalled to her mind the scenes that were passed, and with those scenes were blended the images of Lord Millford and his sister. Yet she preserved her composure through the stately apartments, which the baroness had expressed a wish to see, till she came to the picture gallery.

"Here are two portraits," said Meanwell, "lately come down, and I think them most excellent likenesses."

She followed, and her eye soon rested on the sylph-like form of Lady Emma.

"It is a good likeness," said the baroness, on being informed who it represented.

"It is all that painting can express," Caroline replied, with energy; "but the nameless graces that play about her person, and the sweet, fascinating smiles that I have seen fleet, like a stream of moonlight, on her generally pensive countenance, is beyond the reach of art to imitate."

She considered it for some time in fixed attention, which Meanwell interrupted, by saying,—

"Miss Millbourne, here is Lord Millford's portrait."

"This," she said, "is a more striking likeness than the other."

"That," replied the baron, "is easily accounted for, as the features being stronger, are more accurately defined."

"Oh, it is very like him," said Caroline, thrown a little off her guard by concurring circumstances; "so much so, that I should almost think it was himself, such as I have often seen him."

"Hear him, then," said a voice, which she instantly recollected. "Hear him congratulate himself on this unexpected, unhoped-for pleasure." His lordship had entered by a side-door, ahd heard her last observations. "Ready to receive your commands, and honoured in obeying them."

"I have none to give, my lord," she answered, assuming a dignified reserve, that both pleased and surprised the baroness, to whom she instantly introduced him. The ceremony went round, and they proceeded through the apartments usually opened to visitors. At length they came to those that were preparing for the expected countess, and here Caroline's sensations, though painful in the extreme, were far inferior to those experienced by Lord Millford. He hurried through them without waiting to hear the praises that were lavished on the elegant decorations that were in part completed; and offering his arm to the baroness, he conducted her to a drawing-room, rung for refreshments, and entered into conversation with the baron, of whom he inquired if he intended to continue at the lodge.

"That," said the other in reply, "depends on circumstances. I prefer Lessley House to the lodge; but I think we shall continue here, at least, part of the summer."

"Then," said Lord Millford, "I may hope for the honour of being better known to Baron Ormsburgh."

The baron bowed, and Caroline inquired after Lady Emma.

"She is not well," he answered; "but have you not heard from her?"

"Not very recently," was her answer.

Lord Millford looked surprised as he observed that he thought his sister had written to her a few days since, and he inwardly surmised that Lady Lucy had been here also at work.

"I have not received any letter, my lord," was her answer, "for some time past."

"Will you allow me the honour of calling on you for one to her?" he answered.

"I am sure she will be happy to receive one from you."

Caroline looked at the baroness, who said,—

"We have not yet seen any company, nor do we intend to admit visitors for some time to come; but an exception to our general rule has been made on Miss Millbourne's account, and as the brother of Lady Emma Millford, we shall be happy to receive your lordship."

He bowed.

"Caroline and Eliza," said the baroness, "it is five o'clock—we are early folks, we dine at six—we have no time to spare, and I fear we have already trespassed on Lord Millford's."

The baron arose, and Lord Millford advanced to Caroline, saying,—

"Such moments as these make up for ages of inquietude."

Then suddenly recollecting himself, he offered his hand to the baroness.

The baron stopped to engage Meanwell for the evening, and the young ladies proceeded towards the park. When the baron overtook them, Lord Millford quitted the baroness, and would have bade them adieu; but the former prevented him, by a friendly invitation to dinner. This was accepted, and placing himself between the friends, he conducted them to the lodge.

It would be difficult to describe the various feelings this unexpected meeting occasioned in Lord Millford and Caroline; some months before it would to him have been one of pleasure. Then, it was mingled with retrospection and regret. Caroline's reserve, fortunately as he thought, left him at liberty to converse freely with Eliza, who feeling no embarrassment, chatted freely on the passing events of the day.

During dinner the conversation became general. The baron was a most entertaining and instructive companion; and his lady knew exactly how to blend freedom with politeness. Caroline occasionally spoke, but with less ease than usual; but Miss Beriton, who saw and felt for her uneasy situation, exerted herself with so much success, that Caroline's frequent silence was not noticed. Before the ladies retired, the baroness expressed a very great desire to see Lady Emma.

"You say she is not in very good health," she continued. "Send her to us, and we will endeavour to improve it."

Lord Millford looked and spoke his thanks, and shortly after took his leave.

Lord Millford now found the proposed union with Miss Newland so utterly repugnant to his feelings that he determined, even at the last moment, and at every risk, to decline the alliance, much to the chagrin and annoyance of the viscount and his ambitious lady.

At the moment he had come to this determination, the viscount and viscountess Newland, with their amiable daughter Augusta, and their intriguing friend Lady Lucy, were assembled at Newland House, and hourly expecting a visit from Lord Millford, who had recently been chary of his attendance.

"Doubtless," said Lady Lucy, "he will be here presently; go, dress your face in smiles, to welcome him."

"By no means," cried the viscountess. "Augusta cannot look too indignant, or too languid; she must appear very much depressed, and had better lie down on the sofa. I will ring for a smelling bottle, and do you sit" to Lady Lucy, "down beside her."

"I am weary of so much fatigue," said Miss Newland, "and if it was not to oblige your ladyship," addressing her mother, "I would absolutely end the farce before the curtain dropped."

"Impossible!" cried both ladies, "you must proceed—you know the importance the viscount attaches to the Millford interest. It will place him, as I have frequently told you, in the very first rank of those legislators who are serving themselves while they are obliging their friends."

"I am perfectly satisfied," said Miss Newland, "and will therefore enact my part with all possible dexterity, but mind Lady Lucy, when I am Countess of Millford, I shall expect your friends to play fair with my lord."

"It will be in your power then to put him on his guard," said Lady Lucy.

"True, and there must be no more intriguing with ladies of *haut-ton*," cried the other, "for the earl will not have many thousands to spare for disappointed husbands. I declare I fear we shall find it difficult to support the two establishments under thirty thousand a year; the viscount thinks it may be done for five-and-twenty."

"Oh, never perplex yourself about that," cried Lady Newland, "if five-and-twenty is not sufficient, the viscount must assist you; besides, he will doubtless devise some other effective means of increasing your income. Millford has very good abilities; nothing but energy is wanting to make him a conspicious character."

While the ladies were thus amusing themselves in perspective views, fortune was preparing for them the severest mortification. Twenty times in the course of the day Miss Newland changed her position on the sofa, then ringing for her harp, tried the effect of sound, but nothing could soothe the rising tempest of her soul, for no Lord Millford came. Lady Lucy set out again for Bedford-square, and returned to report that Lord Millford had not been there, and that he was much lately in the company of Mr. Meanwell.

"Meanwell," cried Miss Newland, "I hate the blunt familiarity of that man; his activity bodes no good to me. I know he is a sly old Syphax, and is in his heart an enemy to us."

At dinner they met the viscount still much out of humour; he inquired if there was any message from the earl; the answer was in the negative.

"There is more, I fear, in this business, ladies," said he, "than I am acquainted with."

Just then a letter was delivered to the viscount; it came from Lord Millford, and was written in firm, though respectful, language; and, in conclusion, stated that various circumstances had obliged him to decline the honour of receiving Miss Newland's hand, and that the viscount must from that time consider all correspondence on the subject between the families broken off for ever.

The impenetrable features of the viscount for once betrayed the inward workings of his mind; his lips trembled, his eyes rolled wildly beneath his contracted brow, as he exclaimed,—

"It is all over, and my best hopes are blasted."

"And pray," cried Miss Newland, who had been reading the letter the viscount threw on the table, "what recompense am I to receive for the ridicule and mockery that I shall be sure to meet with after being so long treated as the expectant Countess of Millford, to be in a moment discarded with as little ceremony as a milliner's apprentice?"

"Let me advise you, my dear creature," said Lady Lucy, "to think no more of this affair. Your beauty is undiminished; your fortune great; and"——she would have proceeded, but Miss Newland interrupted her by saying,—

"Cease your croaking; you are like a screech owl. I shall think of nothing else till I have convinced the world that I despise the ruined spendthrift, his title, and his family." So saying, she quitted the room in an agony of passion.

Lady Lucy followed, and remained a considerable time with her, and at last returned to say she had left her more reconciled.

"How did you pacify her?" the viscountess inquired.

"Oh," replied the confidante, "I penned a short paragraph, and sent it off to the old quarter, in which I have stated that a certain peer, of high consideration in the political world, has found it expedient to break off a treaty of marriage he was engaged in transacting for his daughter, owing to the very great embarrassments that the Earl of * * * was involved in, brought on himself, it appears, from his great predilection for the turf and the gaming-table."

"Excellent," said the viscount, who had in some degree recovered his own composure. "I do not," he added, "see much to regret, except the loss of the title, and that I must have paid a most extravagant price for. The political interest the marriage would have consolidated between the families was my only object for promoting it, and indeed the only one I considered of any consequence."

"Oh, certainly," his lady replied, "that was all that would be considered of any consequence by persons of understanding. However, the turn Lady Lucy has given to the affair will save Augusta from the mortification of being either pitied or laughed at; and let these poor, but proud Millfords see that they have sunk beneath the scorn and pity of those they no doubt presume to despise."

"Lady Lacy," said the peer, in a tone of solemnity, "I have to observe that as the treaty we engaged in is become nugatory, I cannot cancel your bond."

"It is hard, my lord," she replied, "that I should suffer for the folly of others; I did my best to promote the interest of all parties."

"That may be," he answered; "but as our plan has so unaccountably failed, I must consider the bond still in force against you."

This was spoken in a tone that did not admit being answered, but though the lady did not speak, her sharp features betrayed visible disquietude. This being perceived by Lady Newland, she instantly diverted the storm that she feared was rising, by saying,—

"You must stay with us to-night, Lady Lucy; and in the morning we will prevail upon Augusta to go out of town for a few days till this unpleasant business is forgotten; and perhaps you will make a few visits this evening just to hear how the affair is likely to be represented."

"The very thing I was thinking of," replied the other. "I shall borrow your carriage, and be off immediately."

This was assented to; and the officious confidante set out on her mission, in which we shall not follow her progress, but briefly state, that when Lady Lucy returned to Newland house, she found the viscountess alone, who informed her that Colonel Dinever had been there, and that Miss Newland had quite recovered from the shock she had received in the morning.

Having by the step he had taken eased his mind of a load of anxiety, Lord Millford set out with his sister and Montague to the lodge; they received a cordial welcome from the baron and the ladies, and the earl immediately sought a private interview with Emmeline. We cannot undertake to relate the conversation of the lovers, but we must not omit relating that Lord Millford did not leave a single doubt on the mind of Emmeline of the fond affection that she had early inspired in a heart that really never loved another woman.

"I have," he said, "dearest Emmeline, forborne renewing the subject till I heard in what manner Mr. Dennison would advise my proceeding with Lord Newland for liquidating the mortgage. I have an estate in Sussex that he is of an opinion I can alienate, but I am unwilling to leave the title poorer than when I came to it. Besides, Mrs. Pembroke has an annuity on it for her natural life." These perplexing considerations, he added, had prevented him from applying to the baron before, who, he feared, would object to an early union on the ground of inexperience. "Should he even consent to my proposals," continued the earl, "but procrastinate my happiness till some future period, to hasten that to me anxiously desired event, I must leave England on a small stipend, and leave Meanwell and Mr. Dennison to arrange my affairs in the best way they can. I have been the cause," he said, "of my own anxieties, and I merit the punishment they have brought on me; yet," he added, in conclusion, "I think I could be happy even in exile, if assured that you, my dear Emmeline, would cherish the affection I should leave with you, and promise, at no very distant time, to honour me with your hand."

Emmeline, in reply, entreated him to come to an explanation with the baron.

"He is generous," she said, "ingenuous, and affectionate; let us, then, leave our destiny in his hands."

"Then I have your permission to speak at once to the baron on the subject."

"Not only my permission," she replied, "but my commands, if your lordship thinks them worth obeying; for I anticipate a favourable answer to your application."

So assured, the earl said he would the next day introduce the subject to the baron. This confidential conference, in which, without reserve, their mutual sentiments for each other were fully explained, relieved the mind of Emmeline from many perplexing surmises, and in some measure restored the serenity of the earl; for his companion had informed him of Lady Ormsburgh's desire of assisting to promote their mutual happiness by every means in her power. In the meantime, the baron was engaged in conversation with Meanwell. The subject led to a fortunate conclusion, for Meanwell had explicitly informed him of the earl's anxious desire of obtaining the hand of Miss Lessley.

"He must ask for it," the baron replied, "for I cannot give it unsolicited even to Lord Millford, of whom I really have a very high opinion."

In fact, the baron, when he considered the whole of Lord Millford's conduct as it regarded his daughter, and compared it with that of most other young men, who, if gifted with the alluring advantages of rank and fortune, leave no means untried to gain the object of their wishes, though it occasioned the future misery of the devoted victim; felt there was more in his character to approve than condemn; and, when the party met at supper, there was not a brow shaded by a single cloud.

At the appointed time, the baron and Lord Millford met, when the former gave his free consent to the earl's marriage with his daughter; and all pecuniary concerns were to be adjusted without delay. The baron proposed giving his daughter twenty thousand pounds. "And at the decease," he added, "of the baroness and myself, she will inherit our whole fortune, except the estate in Kent; and, as that came from the Lessleys, I propose it shall return to them; for it would be injustice in me to make the son suffer for the errors of his father."

In this sentiment the earl sincerely accorded.

"And may you," continued the baron, "be as happy in your married life as I have been in mine, without experiencing the miseries of protracted separation; but observe, you are not to reside abroad."

To this prohibition the earl cheerfully agreed; all his wishes, he said, should be regulated by those of the baron, who then left him, and in a few minutes returned with his lady and Emmeline, whose hand he put into the earl's, saying,—

"There, my lord, I present you with one of Heaven's best gifts—the hand, and I believe the heart, of a virtuous woman."

The earl took the little trembler between his own, pressed it to his lips, and led the blushing yet happy Emmeline to a seat. Lady Ormsburgh said a few words on their future prospects, and ended by wishing they might live long and happily together.

"And may you, my dear, my honoured mother," cried Emmeline, recovering from her confusion, and throwing her arms round the neck of the baroness, who was sitting beside her, "be spared to witness our felicity."

"Here is nature," cried the earl, taking a hand of each; "thus, my own, my dearest Emmeline, may I ever see you, confiding and confided in by the best of mothers; and believe me, madam," addressing the duchess, "that every future moment of my life shall be devoted to the happiness of your inestimable Emmeline."

"If we had entertained a doubt on that subject," returned the baron, advancing, and presenting his hand to the earl, "your lordship would not so easily have obtained the prize—and now, Ellinor," taking the hand of the lady, "we will leave these young folks to kill time by themselves."

"I must dress for dinner," cried Emmeline.

"No," said the earl, gently detaining her, "you need not dress; at least, you need not leave me so soon. I have a thousand things to say to you—do indulge me with one hour's conversation." Superior to affectation, she suffered him to lead her back to a seat, and heard with a beating but confiding heart, his vows of constancy and love. He drew from her, too, the fond confession of her long concealed regard, with the struggles she had had with herself to repress the innovation of helpless love. Warm was his gratitude for her ingenuous communication, and pressing her fine form, for the first time unreluctant, to his heart, he said, "I will not detain you one moment longer from the toilet, we shall meet again at dinner. One hour," looking at his watch "is all the time I can allow for your absence from me, on this fortunate, this happy day."

"Will you promise not to exceed the hour?"

"I will," she replied, with a fascinating smile, "but I think you exact obedience very early."

" No, Emmeline," he replied, " it is love that solicits, not Millford that exacts."

" Well, then, to love I yield," she returned, " and I will meet you in the shrubbery at six, we dine at seven. He led her to the bottom of the stairs, and walked into the plantations."

At dinner they were joined by Montague and Lady Emma. Previous to their arrival, Emmeline kept her promise, and was resting on the arm of the earl in their return to the house, just as Montague handed Lady Emma from the carriage.

" Ah now," she cried (when informed by her brother of the successful termination of his conference with the baron), " I can with pleasure congratulate you on your future prospects. The friend of my heart will become the sister of my affections." On the countenance of Lady Emma there was a serene impressiveness, that for a moment alarmed her friend, who inquired into the cause of it with real solicitude, and was informed that it proceeded solely from the great kindness of Sir Timothy, who had been talking to her of his late lady, in terms that had renewed all her sorrow for her loss. He had also proposed that she should make her principal residence at the grove after her marriage, which he wished not protracted beyond the time necessary for the preparations, and had on that subject appointed a time for meeting her brother, to consult on the means of arranging her settlement. Doctor Maxwell, who had been absent, returned while she was with the baronet, who informed him of the then situation of the parties.

" I shall leave, Montague," he continued, " to explain the snares that have been laid, both to destroy the peace, and injure the fortune of this dear creature, whom I have so long thought unworthy of my son."

They soon after set out for the lodge. The fulness of joy, it has been said, is frequently pensive, and so it was with the party there ; the contemplative mind of Emmeline was revolving the almost inexplicable circumstances that had led to her then enviable lot, blessed beyond her most sanguine wishes in the affections of friends so onoured, and a love who had been so long, yet so hopelessly dear to her. The dinner was nearly a silent one, and the baroness, to the relief of the ladies, proposed adjourning to the music-room. They were soon followed by the gentlemen, and in the concord of sweet sounds, the sombre shade of pensive thoughts were banished from the social circle. During a walk in the evening, Lord Millford drew from Emmeline the cause of her seriousness during dinner, and heard, delighted, a full confession of her feelings, which were so much in unison with his own, that their hearts seemed blended into one, and so animated were his expressions of gratitude, so ardent his assurances of everlasting love, that the tears of sensibility flowed freely from the eyes of Emmeline, and spoke her feelings more forcibly than words could have expressed them. A long conversation ensued, and the smiles of satisfaction and confidence illumined every feature of Emmeline's expressive face.

CHAPTER XVIII.

There is a power
Unseen that rules the illimitable world,
That guides its motions from the brightest stars,
To the least dust of this sin-tainted world,
While man who madly deems himself the lord
Of all, is nought but weakness and dependance,
This sacred truth, by sure experience taught,
Thou must have learnt when wandering all alone;
Each bird, each insect, flitting through the sky,
Was more sufficient for itself than thou.—THOMPSON.

DURING the incidents we have been recording, Mr. Dennison had been e _
ployed in bringing a charge regularly forward against the viscount ; who, on hearing

that Newport had made a full confession of their united treachery, thought it advisable to solicit an amicable adjustment. He endeavoured to lay the whole blame on the former, and declared that he believed the property disposed of, for which he confessed having received a considerable sum, belonged solely to the former. The evidence of his being a party could not exactly be proved except by Newport, who earnestly implored the baron, through Meanwell, to settle the busi-

ness privately. Proper persons were accordingly appointed, and the whole train of evidence gone through—Mrs. Clareville had placed in Mr. Dennison's hands an affidavit that there was no other child on ship-board but her niece; and this was fully corroborated by the testimony of a servant who happened to be at Newland's when Newport brought the child there, saying, he had preserved her from the reck. The baron swore to the property found in the portmanteau, and New

No. 22.

port's confession was likewise produced; and altogether formed a mass of evidence too satisfactory to be for a moment disputed. The award was in consequence given in the baron's favour; and the viscount agreed to refund ten thousand pounds. This the baron added to his daughter's fortune.

Another mortification yet awaited the viscount. A bond had been discovered respecting some money he had once borrowed from the late Lord Millford; it was found in a secret drawer of an ebony cabinet in the late earl's bed-chamber, at the priory. This bond was for twenty thousand pounds; there was found likewise a good collection of scarce coins, and some valuable family jewels. Notice of this discovery was the next day forwarded to Mr. Dennison, who instantly waited on the viscount, who assured him that the money had been returned, and that he depended on the late earl's honour for destroying the bond. This subterfuge did not answer the end intended, for Mr. Dennison informed him that the mortgage he held on Lord Millford's estate would be redeemed, and that the money on bond must be taken in part. After a little demur, and many complaints on the part of the viscount, the proposal was finally agreed to.

This important point being decided on, the law business went regularly forward, and during the negotiations, the lease of the manor was sold by auction, the New-lands not choosing to reside any more at that splendid mansion, and it was purchased by Lord Hazard, and finally transferred to its former owner. The house was pulled down, and the costly appendages disposed of—all vanished like a vision, for no trace was left of Newland's manor, save the ground it had stood on, and in its stead arose a neat and regular village, where cheerful industry took the place of pride. It would take up more space than we can spare to enumerate the plans and regulations laid down by the baron, whose active mind was fully occupied in promoting general good.

During the time the young people had been waiting for the forms of law to be completed, Newport had seen the baron in company with Meanwell. The agitation of the former was visible at first, but by degrees it wore off. On the baron offering his hand, he said,—

"Reproaches I could have borne, for I knew them merited; but this unexpected kindness quite oppresses me."

The baron soothed him by saying,—

"All is forgotten, for we have found our daughter such as the fondest parents must be proud to own, and I shall ever consider you the preserver of her life; and that to you we owe the blessing of having her rights so unequivocally proved."

Thus restored to health and hope, he no longer shunned society, and soon after returned with his wife to their former habitation, but not before he had bespoken, as the retreat of his age, a neat cottage in the projected village.

During this interval Lady Ormsburg and Emmeline had both written to the dowager duchess a full account of past transactions, and received in return letters of sincere congratulation. Her grace requested that as soon as circumstances would admit, that they would meet her at Edinburgh, where she would wait their arrival, as it was necessary that she should see the baron respecting his joint claim to the Northumberland estate. But this, as the expense and trouble had been all her grace's own, and her journey to the south had been productive of such important discoveries, he declined taking any part of; and at a future period formally resigned all claim to it in favour of the duchess's grandson, receiving at the same time a small sum, solely to prevent future litigation between the families.

The M'Irvine's, too, had been written to, and in return requested once more to see the daughter of their affections. A journey to Scotland was therefore decided on, and fixed to take place immediately after the marriage of Lord Millford and Emmeline.

Montague and Lady Emma first received the nuptial benediction, and set out immediately after the ceremony on a short tour; and on their return, Emmeline gave her unreluctant hand to the enraptured earl in the old chapel of the priory. From the chapel the Earl and Countess of Millford, followed by the baron and his lady in their own carriage, set out on their journey to the north, and as had been agreed on, met the duchess at Edinburgh, who received the whole party with sincere cordiality, and the blushing bride with the tenderest emotions of affection.

"Oh, my dear lassie," she cried, "I rejoice to see you placed above the malice of your enemies, and raised to the rank you was born to do honour to ; and, my lord, I am proud to tell you that you have not disgraced your noble lineage by an alliance with the ancient families of Lessley and M‘Donald."

To which the earl made a suitable answer.

The party continued a month at Edinburgh, and from thence visited the kind-hearted M‘Irwins, whom they found in tolerable health, and much pleased with the visit. Towards the end of October, they returned to the priory. Lady Emma had taken up her abode at the grove, to the great pleasure of Sir Timothy, where she realised by her conduct every wish that her grateful and happy Montague had ever formed. The village, which was named Millford, throve apace, through the united energies of those concerned in its progress. A cottage was finished for Newport, where he passed the remainder of his days in serenity and peace, happily relieved from that severest of all feelings—a wounded conscience.

Lord Millford, through the judicious arrangements of his friends, was freed from all his pecuniary difficulties, and had still an income sufficient to support his rank, and allow of a provision being made for a rising family. The first winter was spent in Bedford-square, the house being sufficiently commodious to admit all the united parties, who formed but one happy family, over which, by the desire of Lady Emma, the baroness presided. Numerous were the visitors that poured in upon them to offer compliments of congratulation ; but, as the ladies had decided on a plan which united elegant amusements with domestic comforts, few were the visits they returned. On the return of spring (for our rational characters did not spend the summer in London), they divided for a short time—the baron and his lady went into Kent, the Acrimonys to the grove, and the Millfords to the priory.

We have little more to add ; but, to gratify the curiosity of our readers, we will just revert, for a few minutes, to the less amiable characters that have appeared in our story. Mrs. Pembroke, after rejecting an offer made her of residing at the priory, became an inmate with a fashionable dowager of quality, to whom cards and scandal were the stamina of existence. The viscountess went to reside on the continent—principally at Paris. The gaiety of that capital, and the manners of its inhabitants, exactly suited her disposition and pursuits. She was severely mortified by the neglect of her children, who seldom troubled her with letters, unless they wanted pecuniary assistance. Her son had married the divorced wife of a French count, whose extravagant pursuits involved him in endless perplexities, which far exceeded the very handsome income assigned him by the viscount. To meet present exigencies, he had disposed of his commission, and by so doing greatly offended the sordid peer. Miss Newland eloped with Colonel Dinever, soon after her rejection by Lord Millford, and her father never forgave her, though he allowed her an annual stipend for her own use. The colonel, soon disgusted with her imperious temper, left her to her own pursuits, and she fixed her abode with Lady Lucy O'Leary, and in the same house was the divorced countess, lately returned from abroad. The characters of this trio were so very equivocal, that they were universally neglected by most of their former associates, and indeed by every one that valued themselves either for reputation or consistency. The sordid accumulation of money was the principal pleasure left the viscount, and though he had no one with whom to share it, for he had considerably lessened the sum he had promised to allow his lady when she left England, yet he continued to add hoard to hoard in joyless seclusion. It is true he did not suffer his family to want ; but he greatly abridged them of their former splendour, and they sank as low in the estimation of the fashionable world as they had long been in the opinion of such as preferred moral excellence to guilty greatness. The viscount's political importance declined, younger men opposed him, and old ones were weary of his avaricious pursuits.

Sir Timothy was as happy as his temper and infirmities would allow him to be, and Lady Emma delighted when she saw the smile of satisfaction play round his furrowed brow, which never failed calling the glow of gratitude into the animated countenance of Montague; while Lord Millford, happy beyond his most sanguine wishes, in the society of his intelligent and interesting countess, resigned without a sigh all the gaieties he had before so largely partaken of. Meanwell continued for some years at the priory, where Newport was a frequent visitor, and there, too, the ector was frequently entertained with his favourite old port.

Miss Lewson was often invited by the ladies to their social circles, and at last became, from copying the manners of the baroness, a very useful old woman, for the ladies raised her in her own opinion, by making her the distributor of their donations to the poor and friendless; and when the village was peopled, she had so much employment for her time, that she left off studying the fashions.

Sir Timothy lived to see his descendants multiply, and was pleased on reflecting that his name would not be lost in the annals of his country; for his son took a just and firm part in every measure calculated for the general good of society, and he had no doubt but his grandsons would be guided by their father's example.

Martha did not long survive the marriage of her young lady. The dowager duchess lived to a very advanced age, and the tears of grateful affection were shed over her memory by her surviving friends. The baron and his lady continued to make the lodge their usual place of residence, making, however, occasional excursions to their estate in Kent.

At the conclusion of our tale, the most perfect harmony prevailed among the concentrated families, whose pursuits were in union, and their enjoyments satisfactory, for the goodness of their hearts accorded in the general diffusion of human happiness, and often did the baron and his lady, when contemplating the felicity of their children and friends, bend with hearts full of grateful adoration before the Supreme Disposer of all events, for the blessings so unexpectedly bestowed upon them, through the fortunate concurrence of circumstances produced by Newport's just remorse and eventful atonement.

THE END.

HELEN HALSEY:

A

TALE OF THE BORDERS.

A ROMANCE OF DEEP INTEREST.

LONDON:

HELEN HALSEY

A Tale of the Borders.
CHAPTER I.

THE unwise licence and injurious freedoms accorded to youth in our day and country, will render it unnecessary to explain how it was that, with father and mother, a good homestead, and excellent resources, I was yet suffered at the early age of eighteen, to set out on a desultory and almost purposeless expedition, g some of the wildest regions of the South-West. It would be unnecessary

and, perhaps, much more difficult to show what were my own motives in un.. dertaking such a journey. A truant disposition, a love of adventure, or, possibly, the stray glances of some forest maiden, may all be assumed as good and sufficient reasons, to set a warm heart wandering, and provoke wild impulses in the blood of one, by nature impetuous enough, and, by education, very much the master of his own will. With a proud heart, hopeful of all things if thoughtless of any, as noble a steed as ever shook a sable mane over a sunny prairie, and enough money, liberally calculated, to permit an occasional extravagance, whether in excess or charity, I set out on one sunny winter's morning from Leaside, our family place, carrying with me the tearful blessings of my mother, and as kind a farewell from my father, as could decently comport with the undisguised displeasure with which he had encountered the first expression of my wish to go abroad. Well might he disapprove of a determination which was so utterly without an object. But our discussion on this point need not be resumed. Enough that if "my path was all before me," I was utterly without a guide. It was, besides, my purpose to go where there were few if any paths; regions as wild as they were pathless; among the strange tribes and races; about whose erring and impulsive natures we now and then heard such tales of terror, and of wonder, as carried us back to the venerable periods of feudal history, and seemed to promise us a full return and realization of their strangest and saddest legends. Of stories such as these, the boy sees only the wild and picturesque aspects,—such as are beautiful with a startling beauty—such as impress his imagination rather than his thoughts, and presenting the truth to his eyes through the medium of his fancy, divest it of whatever is coarse, or cold, or cruel, in its composition. It was thus that I had heard of these things, and thus that, instead of repelling, as they would have done, robbed of that charm of distance which equally beautifies the moral as in the natural world, they invited my footsteps, and seduced me from the more appropriate domestic world in which my lot had been cast.

With a light heart, full of expectation, a free steed that seemed rather to swim along through space, than tread monotonously over the rugged ground, the day passed away with an almost unnoted flight. My eyes had been charmed in the observation of trees and groves, picturesque objects of sight in hill and dale, wood and water, and such occasional more worldly matters, as were provoked by long ranges of whitened cotton fields, or yellow corn yet bristling in unbroken rows. At the close of the day, I had reached a cabin where I found shelter for the night, and at early dawn, I again set forth, with the promise of another day of generous sunshine. This day was consumed like the last, and with equal satisfaction to myself. The buoyant spirit of youth rises in exultation in any exercise, which seems to impart equal freedom to soul and body; and there is something of the same triumphant pulse in the heart, galloping over the prairies, over the hills, or through the long cathedral ranges of gigantic pine forests, which one feels on the deck of a fine ship, careering over the billows of the broad Atlantic, with a breeze that sends the foam flying at every plunge, from the bold prow of the imperial vessel. The man is wonderfully lifted with the consciousness of having at his command, and being able to command, such a noble animal as the horse, and rapidity of motion is the source of an intoxication, of a sublime sort, of the character of which we can form a good conception from the interest we take in a race, whether of steeds or steamboats; the danger of being hurled down by the one or blown up by the other, being, in both cases, absolutely and entirely forgotten. Mine was a nature particularly to exult in such exercises, my temperament being wholly sanguine, and the indulgence of my parents having left it to an unrestrained exercise, which rendered it feverishly irritable when not engaged in such performances as were grateful to my excitable imagination. After the close of the second day of my journey, it seemed to me as if both my horse and self could have begun anew, with a more buoyant spirit than before,—as if the toil itself refreshed us, and as if no more grateful object lay before us, than just to be permitted to wander on, and on,—"the world forgetting, by the world forgot."

Certainly, the true secret of perpetual life, is perpetual motion. Find the one, and we secure the other. Alas! the want of daylight is the great drawback to our progress and discoveries. We have just begun to make them when the curtain falls upon us.

The close of the second day brought me to the foot of a long range of hills, the lower steps possibly of the great Apalchian chain, inclining to the Mississipi. It also brought me to the very borders of what was in that day, known as the region of doubt and shadow, I had reached the confines of civilization—even such imperfect civilization as belongs to our thinly settled frontiers. I was now ninety miles from Leaside, and only seperated by a narrow wall of hills from that strange region of forest mystery and romance, about which so many surprising stories had been told me. This also was the Indian country—here the red men still lingered, mixed up with reckless, renegade whites, who preferred the wild priviledges of savage, to the more wholesome, but seemingly less attractive pleasures, of civilized life. As I thought over this taste, I could not but shudder to discover that such also, to some extent, was the feeling in my own bosom. But I was too young to encourage unpleasant reflections, and for these but little time was allowed me.

Just on the edge of this neutral ground—this debateble land—neither savage nor social—stood a house that has since had more than one remarkable history. It was a miserable shell of logs, roughly hewn, of two stories, to which, in the rear, was appended a long shed of framework, intended to contain some three chambers, or, upon a press of company—passage way included—possibly four. It was a public of notorious resort—standing almost astride the area, from which diverged four roads, leading to as many different quarters of country. It was consequently much frequented, and the landlord, who will probably be well remembered by many as Jephson Yannaker, was, at the time of which I speak, doing a thriving business. There were many witless lads like myself, travelling for same regions and many more, not so witless, but more reckless, travelling in the their humors, —at our expense I had not much time allowed me to examine the. exterior of this establi shment, before a stout, shock-headed, burly, red-faced, but kindly looking personage, whom I soon learned to be Yannaker himself, advanced from the door-way to the head of my horse.

' Come, light, stranger,—you're just in time to shake a leg with the best of them Light I'll see to the critter,'

His words were explained a moment after, as the discordant twang of a half-tuned fiddle smote my ears from the interior, In entering, I had just time to discover that several horses were hitched to neighbouring trees, and on one side of the premises, but rather nearer to the house, there stood a sort of travelling carriage of rude structure—a strong. unwieldy vehicle, to which two able draught horses were still partially attached. From a few bundles of fodder at their feet, it seemed to be the design of their driver, who was busy in the carriage, that they should enjoy their forage where they stood.

But the sight within made me forget every thing without The hall ran nearly the whole length of the building, and it was comparatively a large one. A bright fire was blazing in the chimney, and a matter of thirty persons, or even more, were strewn around the apartment. Of these, though less than half, a fair proportion were women. Near the fire sat the fiddler, the croakings and creakings of whose crazy instrument had assaulted me on my first arrival. He was still busy in the seemingly hopeless task of screwing its strings into something like symphonious exercise and utterance. He was a plain country lad, in homespun, with a cap of coonskin still clinging to his head, which swung pendulously over his fiddle, as he now jerked at the ke s, and now jostled with the bow.

But there was nothing in his appearance calculated to detain my glance. This now roved about the assembly, which promised to be as interesting as it was certainly promiscuous and picturesque. The men were stout fellows all, of the true farm-yard breed, famous at the flail, and with fists, whose seeming efficiency re minded me mo e than once of the powers ascribed to those of Maximin, the   G who could fell a bullock at a blow. It did not seem as if they had prepared themselves for the festivities they were about to enjoy. Their costume was that of the farm-yard. Plain blue or yellow home-spun, rough shoes, and, though the winter had fairly set in, many were the bronzed and naked breasts displayed by the open shirt of coarse cotton. The frolic, so far as they were concerned, was evidently extempore. They had been suffered no time for the toilet. But this did not seem greatly to abash them. The unconventional world in which they lived, had rendered them somewhat insensible to that feeling of *mauvaise honte*, which would have been sure, in such a case, to have distressed the half civilized lad to an immeasurable extent. They showed no concern at the matter, but dashed forward, each to his favourite lass, as coolly and confidently as if fashion had received her dues, and the toilet all the necessary sacrifices. And there was, in this very freedom, a sort of savage grace, which greatly tended to lessen the rudeness of its general aspect. Most of the fellows were well formed—rough, but erect and easy—and having that use of their limbs, boldly flexible, which the life of the hunter and the horseman is very apt to impart in the case of a well made person. Where had these lads come from? From a space of country twenty miles round, through which the very whispers of a fiddle make themselves heard, Heaven knows how, and whose attractions among such a people are felt, Heaven only knows to what extent. Some of them were professional hunters; some, idle ramblers like myself; and some few might have been gathered in the immediate neighbourhood. But, as I could give no very good reason for my own presence in such a place, it would be unreasonale to expect me to account for theirs.

The girls,—but here the case is very different. When did ever damsel find herself in such a situation without contriving some of her secret graces before the toilet? Though she mirrors her beauties in the stream, she will yet manage to give them some of those helps of art, a knowledge of which she seems to have caught by instinct. There were some twelve or fourteen damsels in the room, and a profusion of ribbons—and of these a country girl must have the gaudiest. Fancy, gentle reader, the picture for yourself. See Mary with her bandeau of Hibernian green—her belt of golden yellow—her neckerchief that seems to have been dyed in summer rainbows, and her dress that might have been made out of their skirts. And there is Susan in her head-dress, and Sally in her blue and scarlet, and Jenny in her " Jim-along-Josey," without ever dreaming that her style of body garment would ever become a fashion in the great city, and be known by such an imposing name. I am not good at such details, and you must conceive them for yourself. It is very certain. however, that with all their superior pains-taking at the toilet, the women lacked the graces—however inferior—which distingushed the deportment of the men. They sat stiffly and awkwardly, like so many waxen figures, each on her stool, as if troubled with a disquieting apprehension that any unwise movement would overturn the fair fabric of her present state, and be equally fatal to head-dress, handkerchief and happiness. There was one exception to this uniform display of ostentation and awkwardness—of whom more hereafter.

But the waxen images were made to move. The fiddle began to speak in tolerable tune, and the brawny boys sprang across the ocean of floor that separated them from the green beauties on the sunny banks, and appropriated them, I suppose, according to previous arrangement. In the twinkling of an eye they were upon the ground, every mother's son of them, and busy in the mazes of the country dance, Such a shuffling of the feet, such a tearing of music to very tatters, by that crazy violin, and the inverate musician, who scraped away as if catgut could bring about the noble catastrophe—would require the creation of a special muse to describe, and until that event, we leave the affair to the quick conception and conjecture of the reader.

CHAPTER II.

I KNOW not why, but the whole proceeding, with all its whirl and excitement , its odd merriment and grotesque display of art, produced in me a feeling of dis-quiet, approaching even to melancholy. Perhaps, this was, because it reminded me of Leaside, and the fiddling of old Ben, our venerable butler, when little Mary Bonham was my partner, and we wandered down together in the same sweet primitive movements that now seemed to be desecrated wantonly before my eyes. The whole scene of home grew up before me as I gazed and mused. The stately hall, hung with pictures, nicely curtained, with the massive piano on one side, and the equally massive book-case on the other; the one a treasury of the sweetest sounds, the other of the noblest sense. My father, with his white hairs, on one side of the fire-place; my mother, with her stiffly-starched white cap on the other;—the one with his huge Shakspere on the little table beside him,—closed, with his silver spectacles peering out between the leaves;—the other with her knitting apparatus in her lap, the work dropping to her feet, as she watched our movements while the kitten, lying on its back, was disen-tangling with mischievous pains-taking that which had tasked the ingenuity and industry of the good old dame, to put together, for the last half dozen evenings. That passing but sweet glimpse of the dear old homestead, with all its holy asso-ciations, was the first mental image which crossed my mind, reproachful of my wanderings. You may be sure that I did not encourage it, but, anxious to re-move it, I hastened round the dancers, to the opposite side, intending to make my escape at the doorway, and go out beneath the skies; but I was interrupted in this progress, and diverted from this purpose, by finding the narrow way occupied. I looked down at the person who thus obstructed my pathway, and almost recoiled in pleasurable surprise. Before me sat a young girl of fifteen or thereabous. She certainly could not have been more than sixteen. The first thing that struck me about her was the exquisite but dewy brightness of her eye, which was as dark of hue as the coal may be supposed to be on the eve of that moment, when, under the force of heat, it becomes a brilliant. The face was small, very small, when you turned suddenly from the blaze of the large expanding eye to note the accompanying features;—but it was also very beautiful. The skin was singularly clear and transparent for such black eyes and hair. The forehead, about which was bound a narrow braid, was high and broad, and constituted fully one half of the face. The hair was parted, Madonna fashion, as if art, after long ex-perience, had become assured that, in the present case, her best policy was to obey the laws of simplicity. Her neck, which was only half bared, seemed very white and beautifully rounded. Her figure, which was evidently slight, could not be distinguished by reason of the huge travelling cloak in which she was still wrapped. The whole appearance of this young creature, so unique, yet so little like the rest in the assembly, fixed my regard, and would have done so even had the excessive brilliancy of her eyes and beauty of her complexion not enchained it. Her seeming isolation, too, so much like my own, was another circumstance to commend her to my sympathies. A scene like the present, in a frontier country, I need not say to my readers, is apt to set at defiance the more restraining laws of society in the obviously social world; and, assuming the exercise of one of the most understood privileges of the place, I did not hesitate to accost the stranger. She was evidently a stranger like myself, and I jumped at once to the conclusion that she was one of the inmates of the travelling carriage that I had seen at the door.

"You do not dance," I said to her, bending down beside her, and speaking in those subdued tones which seem the properest when addressing the young, the timid and the artless.

She looked up, then around her, with something of the expression of a startled fawn, away from its dam, and trembling at the approach of some strange monster of the wilderness. There was an air of anxiety in her glance, which made me more cautious in my approaches, and at the same time, more earnest in my interest. As she did not answer, I put my inquiry in another shape.

" Will you not dance with me?"

" Oh, no!" she answered, still looking anxiously around her, and particularly at the entrance. " Oh, no! I do not wish to dance. I am a stranger here, I know nobody."

" I too am a stranger here," was my reply, " let us therefore know one another, let us be friends."

She allowed her eyes to rise for a moment to the level of mine, and when they encountered my glance, a deep crimson overspread her cheek.

" Shall we not be friends?" I repeated, as I found she did not design to answer.

" What can I do?" she answered, and the question struck me as remarkable for its simplicity. It seemed to indicate a higher standard of duty, in the matter of friendship, on the part of this young creature, than was customary among mankind in general. I contrived, however, to reply, though her question was evidently one not easy of answer.

" What should a friend do, but love his friend, and think of him, and pray for him, and be glad to see him, and sorry to lose him."

" Ah! but I shall soon be gone."

" Gone! where?"

" To my own home—you to yours."

" And why should we go different ways?"

" I don't know," she said, in low subdued tones, which so far flattered me, as they seemed to be regretful ones.

" There is no reason why we should not go together, at least for a little while. For my part, I have set out to travel, and it does not matter much whither I go. Where do you live!"

" Miles off—very far. Close by the river—"

" River—what river?"

" Far—far! You cannot go. No, no! You cannot go there."

I observed, as she replied, that her glances sought anxiously the entrance, before which I now discovered, in the dim light of evening, that there stood a group of persons three or four in number.

" You little know how far I am willing to go for my friend—for those whom I love;" was my reply, and my hand rested, while I spoke, unconsciously on my own part, on hers. I felt hers tremble beneath it—withdrawn—and only then was I conscious of the trespass, which, had I been in a highly civilized world, had been committed by this presumption. I proceeded:

" If one's friend is true and worthy, one follows her to the end of the world, follows nobody else, thinks of nobody else, cares for nobody else, loves her over all the world."

" Ah! that is friendship;" she answered with a sigh.

" I would be your friend—I will follow you;" I continued impetuously, encouraged by her words.

" No! no!—I have no friend. I live very far,—by the river—the road is hard to find—bad swamps—you cannot follow me."

Her answer was made with some trepidation, and an increased anxiety of expression, as her glance was directed towards the door.

" And why should it be hard to find, and why should the bad roads and the swamps prevent me, when it does not prevent you? Why can't I follow you. I will follow you."

" No, you must not!—as a friend you must not."

This was spoken with singular emphasis; then she paused abruptly, as if disquieted at the degree of empressement which she had given to her utterance. But she had also given peculiar force to the word " friend," and that pleased me. It seemed to say that she herself was not displeased with the appropriation. But there was a mystery in the whole matter. Her strange mode of speech—so artless, yet so reserved—her evident anxiety, if not apprehension,—and the secrecy—could it spring from ignorance—which she resolutely maintained as the whereabouts of her abode? I was resolved not to give the matter up. But, for that moment, this resolution was made in vain. We were interrupted, and, as I thought, rather rudely, by some one thrusting himself in between us. I turned to meet the intruder, in a mood prompt enough to punish the intrusion, and was confronted by the stern glance of a man in middle life—perhaps a little beyond it—such seemed the testimony of thick masses of grisly beard which stood about his cheeks and chin. His keen inquiring glance, fixed upon my own face, rather tended to increase the disposition which I felt to resent what I esteemed his impertinence: but the momentary reflection that he might be the father of the damsel, moved me to tolerate a bearing which, under any other circumstances, would have moved me to do battle, and which, in the opinion of the country, would not only have justified, but called for it. While I was meditating what to say—for he still kept his glance fixed upon me—the girl rose and took his arm. He turned from me at this instant, and led her off to an adjoining apartment, followed by Yannaker, the host, who seemed to be busy in no worse office than that of showing the parties their several chambers.

"My game is up for the night," was my muttered reflection, and, so thinking, I dashed out of the hall, and with hot brow and excited spirit stood, unknowing where to turn, beneath the cool and mantling starlight.

CHAPTER III.

THE sounds of that crazy violin, which I now began again to hear, sounded a worse discord in my ears than ever, and gave an impulse to my footsteps which they seemed to need. I dashed forward, following what seemed the open grounds, and soon found myself ascending a little range of hills. The night was very clear and very beautiful—of that sombrous sort of beauty, when the light just suffices to enable you to distinguish objects, but helps, at the same time, to magnify their aspects by its own vague medium. The trees stood up—those stately pines which maintain, day and night, one unceasing murmur, which is more dear than song to the imaginative spirit—in frowning and vast magnificence beside me, like so many gigantic wardens of the land, marshaling the entrance to some wondrous palace. Under their guidance, as it were, and through their ranks, I hurried on, musing over the thousand fancies which, I suppose, would be natural enough to any youth under the same circumstances—newly enriched by a sense of liberty—a feeling of manliness—which the very privilege of roving at that hour, and in new scenes, would be apt to inspire; and, anon, reproached by the stern internal monitor within for filial disobedience—remembering with sinking heart the tears of my mother, and the frowning farewell of my father—all of which was, in another moment, to be banished from thought by the intrusive image of that strange, sweet maiden, sitting by herself, wrapped in her heavy cloak, yet looking out with such bright, diamond-like, heart-conducting eyes. I might have wandered thus for hours—perhaps all night, (for what youth, with such feelings in his heart, and such ferment in his brain, ever cares for the dull sleep of ordinary mortals?) had I not been roused to other thoughts by a sudden and startling sound, which reached me from the range of dark hills opposite. I could only liken this sound, with which I was unfamiliar, to the bay or howl of the wolf, or, perhaps, a dozen of them; and, though the idea of a wolf-hunt struck me the next moment, as being among the most famous of all ideas, it

was some qualification, just then, to any such desire, that I was horseless, weapon-
less, without company, and totally ignorant of the habits of the animal, and the
country in which I stood. That domestic virtue, discretion, interposing at this
juncture, persuaded me to retrace my steps to Yannaker's, which I reached in
reasonable time, after once measuring my length over a stump that very impru-
dently stood in my way on the slope of a little hillock. The violin was still at
work, and, though I felt apprehensive that until it slept I should not, I persuaded
old Yannaker out of the circle, where he himself shook a leg, in order that he
should show me the way to my chamber—a measure to which I was induced by being convinced that the fair stranger would not again emerge from hers that night

I slept soon and soundly, in spite of my convictions – slept to dream, precisely
as I had mused, of home, and strange woods and adventures, with ever and anon
that fair young face, and those dark lustrous eyes, peering downward, as if from
heaven, into my very heart. This image so completely filled my brain, that it
was the first to encounter me at my waking; I started up, with a bright sun blazing through a half-opened window upon me. There was a stir below, and, half
vexed with myself for having slept so late, I jumped out of bed, and ran to
the open window. As I feared, the traveling carriage had disappeared, and in
it, as I concluded, my fair incognita. I dressed myself with all dispatch,
and hurried below. Preparations for breakfast were in progress, though the
room still retained some of the traces of last night's exertions. Part of
an antique frill lay in one place at my feet, and at a little distance I detected, beneath the breakfast table, a piece of red stuff, most like red flannel, in
conjecturing the uses of which I was reminded of the apocryphal story of the
Countess of Salisbury, and the now proverbial sentence of the courteous monarch :
" Honi soit qui mal y pense." The worst evil that I was thinking of, was my
mysterious damsel, and the timely entrance of Yannaker enabled me to make the
necessary inquiries.

" Gone, sir—gone as fast as a pair of the best horses in Massassipp could
carry her."

" How long, Mr. Yannaker ?"

" Don't mister me, stranger ; I'm plain Jeph Yannaker to travellers, and Yannaker to them that knows me. I'm agin making a handle for a man's name
before you can trust yourself to take hold of it."

" No offence, Jeph Yannaker ; I only speak as I've been accustomed."

" No offence, to be sure, it's your teaching, stranger, but here in our parts, where
people's scarce, and the sight of one's neighbour does the heart good, a handle to
his name seems to push him too far out of the reach of a friendly gripe. It's a
stiff, cold sort of business, this mistering and squiring—will do well enough among
mere gentlemen, and lawyers, and judges, and such sort of cattle, but out here,
where a look upon the hills and swamps seems to give a man a sort of freedom,
it's God's blessing that we have few such people here. Here we've nothing but
men, just as God made us,—not to speak of a little addition, in the shape of jacket
and breeches, made out of blue or yellow homespun."

Those who have had the good fortune to know Jeph Yannaker, will give me
credit for having reported him correctly. His life was an eventful one, and one
day shall have its history, though it come from no better hand than my own. But
to return. After some little time, taken up in disclaimers and other matters, for
it seemed to me as if the worthy publican was wilfully bent on avoiding the topic
to which I sought to confine his attention, I at length gathered from him, not only
that the damsel had taken her departure, but that she had been gone ever since
midnight ; that she never slept in the house at all, but had only retired with her
uncle from the crowd ; that, as soon as the moon rose, the latter had geared his
horses, and just when I was enjoying the sweetest dreams of the treasure so newly
found, she was spirited away by her grisly protector—whom I rejoiced to find was
not her father—but in what direction Yannaker either could not or would not say.
I immediately declared my purpose to pursue, and requested that he would have
my horse brought out. He looked at me with open mouth, and a chuckling

"haw! haw! haw!" that promised to correspond with the boundless dimensions of his distended throat. I became impatient, and with some peevishness demanded the occasion of so much unreasonable and unseasonable merriment.

"What!—go?" he asked.

"Yes, sir,—go! and what is there so very laughable in such a determination?" He composed his muscles instantly.

"Not before breakfast—oh, no! I am sure of you till then. Why, breakfast is a good thing, the best of things on an empty stomach—breakfast is a warm thing, the warmest of things for a winter day. Why, stranger, no man's brains do good service, unless breakfast has warmed his belly; and, I tell you, even the horse, besides, knows when his master is well filled and sensible, and when he is not. Let a good horse alone for that. Why, lad, the best horse I ever knew or

No. 2.

crossed, would always cut capers when a man undertook to straddle him who happened to be hungry; no horse of mine should ever be crossed, if I know'd it, by a man who hadn't had his breakfast."

"It so happens, Mr. Yannaker——"

"Plain Yannaker—plain Yannaker," he said, interrupting me.

"Well, then, plain Yannaker——"

"Ha, ha, ha! That's it. You're right—I like you the better for it. Say 'plain Yannaker,' if you please, in preference to Mister Yannaker."

"I say, then, plain Yannaker, that my horse is not yours, and neither knows nor cares whether I have had my breakfast or not."

"Wouldn't have such a horse, stranger, as a gift. By the Lord Harry I wouldn't. But don't be wolfish at Jeph Yannaker. Here's your breakfast, and your horse shall follow it, as soon after as you please—only, let me tell you, you're clean mistaken. Never was a horse yet that didn't know whether his master was fed or not—unless he was an idiot beast—a clear senseless animal—and I reckon there may be idiot beasts as well as idiot men. There now, sit down to your breakfast—the old woman's poured out the coffee, and all's ready. I'll see to the critter."

Jeph Yannaker had a way of his own, as most who knew him know, which there was no resisting. He had the most good-humoured cast of countenance, the most benevolent smile, the most kind solicitude of manner; yet, if tales speak true, he could cut a purse, and a throat, too, upon occasion, as promptly as the Pacha of Yannina. Of this, however, in another history. Enough, for the reader, that I, a boy of eighteen, found it impossible to be angry with such a person, and he forty-five or fifty. He quieted me in the most persuasive manner, and, seeing me safely seated over my eggs and hominy, in equal good humour with them and himself, he sallied forth to put my nag in readiness. My breakfast was soon discussed, and my horse at the door. My host, however, did not seem willing to part with me. I had dropped the usual *quid* into his hands, saying good-humouredly,—

"There, plain Yannaker, we are quits for this time."

He laughed.

"You are a clever chap, and I somehow like you. We takes a liking for a human being every now and then, jest the same as we takes for a fine horse, or a speaking hound; and I've got a notion that when you give yourself time, you're a raal good fellow! Aint you?"

"'There's more than you who think so," I answered with boy sharpness.

"Oh? git out," said he, "nobody beside yourself. But where away, lad? You're not a guine running after that gal you seed last night?"

"I am though," I answered doggedly.

"No, don't. Take an old fool's counsel for once, and save your horse's wind. In the first place you can't find her."

"I'll try for it."

"And in the next, it'll be much worse than shaking hands with a hungry bear that aint willing to be friendly at no time."

"Indeed! But what know you of her? You told me you knew nothing."

"Well, in one way, that's true enough; and when you gets to be as old as me, you'll find out for yourself, that a girl child is about the hardest critter in the world to know entirely. But I wasn't speaking of any danger from her, by no means.—but of them that, may be, you'll find along with her."

"Ha! that old uncle of hers?"

"Perhaps,—and a rough colt, I tell you, to deal with, take him at any turn. Bud Halsey is all bone and gristle, I tell you, from tooth to toe-nail."

"Is his name Bud Halsey?"

"Yes, when he comes to Yannaker's,—but I can't answer for it anywhere else. All I can say is, that your course lies in any other part of the world than where he is. I say so, lad, for your good,—for, as I told you, I somehow likes you."

"But what is he, friend Yanneker?"

"He! He's nothing, as the world goes,—but something, I tell you, when he works his grinders. Keep clear of him, that's all. It don't become me to be talking behind the back of a man that pays his way in good money,—and I never axes such a man how he gets his money. That's no business of mine. But, to begin agin, and to end, lad, at the same time—keep clear of that gal's track ;—it can't be that you've got so deep into the mire at one sight, so there's no reason to go deeper. Go home, and let Bud Halsey's niece marry somebody else."

Yannaker was evidently no sentimentalist.. His phraseology, which likened love to a bog, and the lady to a wild beast, or angry cur at least, seemed to me nothing to the purpose, and strangely savage and unpoetical. I answered him in a way intended to be conclusive, as I flung my leg over the saddle.

" Thank you, friend Yanneker,—you no doubt mean me kindly, but if Bud Halsey were twice the monster that he seems, I'd take his track."

" Well, it's cl'ar lad, that, you've been pretty much used to having your own way, and such people are never made wise, but by a little worry—so go a-head, as quick as you please, only keep your eyes busy, believe nothing that you hear, be scared at nothing that you see, and be ready to treat a man with two legs as if he was an animal with four—for, if you go after Bud Halsey, there's no telling whether man or beast will sprawl first. If you must have the ways of a man, be sure you have the heart of one. There's no telling how many dangers a stout heart will carry a fellow through."

Something piqued with the tone of this discourse, I struck spurs into my steed, and sent him through the gateway, as I replied,—

" Thank you, thank you, friend Yannaker—I have no fears, so do you have none. I trust your eggs won't give out before I return. I shall be back by Christmas for my egg-nog."

" Go a-head !" was all his response which reached my ears—but I could hear him mutter something more, as, shading his eyes with his hands, he watched my progress along the road.

CHAPTER IV.

My reader, if he still has in his veins any of the hot blood of his early manhood, will easily understand how the exhortations and warnings of the landlord, so significant and forcible as they were, should have awakened in me the spirit of curiosity, and prompted into activity my natural passion for adventure. My damsel became, in my eyes, the heroine of romance, to be rescued from the bearded giant —to be won by feats of arms, and the most reckless audacity. I began, the moment I was fairly out of sight of Yannaker's, to examine the neat silver-mounted pistols—the property of a dear departed brother—which had long been my favourite possession, and which I now carried in the pocket of my overcoat. It will amuse, rather than alarm, the reader to describe these mortal weapons. They were of the smallest calibre, capable of carrying only a buckshot, and useless for any purpose unless with their muzzles, fixed upon the very bosom of an enemy. But I had little experience which could test their value. Like other boys, I had been taught by a tender mother that lead and powder were horridly dangerous things, and that pistols were pistols. As I gazed on the pretty playthings which I carried, and saw that the priming was dry and grainy, I was inspired with as much confidence in their efficiency as ever had that famous knight—I forget his name—who wielded *Excalibar*—in that spell-endowed weapon. A dirk-knife of more respectable dimensions which I wore in my bosom, completed my equipments in this respect.

I need not say that I pursued my way almost at random. I have said that four roads diverged into different regions of country, from the area in which the house of Yannaker stood. I had dashed on that which had presented to the casual eye the most obvious carriage track, and with all the ardour and the hope of youth, I followed this route till sunset, when I found myself in front of a wigwam, in the door of which stood a haggard woman, scarce able to move, bearing in her countenance all the proofs of a severe visitation of autumnal fever. From her I learned that no carriage had passed that day, and, indeed, before I made the inquiry, I had lost all fresh traces along the road of the vehicle, which I had set out to follow. Here was a quandary. To return then was out of the question. My love and romance together failed to inspire me with any desire for riding back over such a road, and on a night which promised to be equally cold and starless. To go farther was idle, considering my objects, and I gathered from the woman of the house that her dwelling was the only one on that road within fifteen miles. I was perforce compelled to remain where I was,—a necessity which, when I saw the cheerlessness of the interior, was felt to be even heavier than the protracted journey. But for my faithful horse, I had taken the back track, and seen "plain Yannaker" by the next day's dawn.

I must hurry over the next three days. They were unmarked by any event of importance. Nothing had occurred having any bearing on my purpose, nor did I feel or find myself, up to this time, one step nigher to the fair object who was still the warmest and most vivid presence in my imagination. I had, meanwhile, retraced my course to Yannaker's, heard more of his warnings with as little heed, tried another of the roads diverging from his house with as little profit, and now, in a third direction, was labouring at the close of day among the swamps of Choctawhatchie. That night, the brown heath and dried leaves formed my bed ; my canopy was the tree and sky, while a rousing fire at my feet, and in front of my horse, served to keep at a distance any beast of prey which might have been disposed to disturb us. I confess I slept little. I had not so much faith in the effect of fire upon wolf and tiger. I was in a region where they still were found, and what with seeing to the comforts of my horse, gathering brands, and trying to keep warm, the morsels of sleep which I caught were equally small and unsatisfactory. It was more refreshing to me to get fresh glimpses of another day.

I was once more afoot, with the dawn. My brave steed had borne the privations of the night better than myself. At least he wore a more cheerful aspect in the morning—and this encouraged me. I dashed forward with that neck-or-nothing philosophy which feels itself prepared for whatever may turn up, though with a lively hope that it may take the shape of breakfast. No man can endure long the want of hunger as well as sleep. One or other he may stand with tolerable fortitude for thirty-six hours, chewing the cud of his reflection, in the absence of tenderer meats,—but denial of both, for such a period, will go nigh to unnerve and undo the bravest. Just then, however, I felt very sure there was no standing hunger half so long. The idea of a smoking breakfast, I modestly confess, had put to slumber, for the time, certain other far more sublime ideas.

I had not to ride far—perhaps some eight miles—before I found my breakfast. This was at an Indian cabin, as miserable a mud hovel as ever engendered vermin, and reduced humanity, a willing victim to their ravages. My host was a half-breed,—one of those dark, untamed, surly savages, such as the Indians, with a white cross, invariably become. He placed my food before me as if it was poison. His looks, indeed, seemed to defeat its alimentary properties, for I ate with suspicion, and it did little help to my digestion. Fortunately, my horse found no such fault with his corn and fodder, probably because he looked at them, rather than the hands by which they were furnished. My host eyed me in silence, took my money with the air of one who would just as lief take my life, and watched my departure from his door with the indifference of one who is assured that it must be taken wherever I may go. My reflections owing to sleeping in the woods, starvation, bad food, and sulky savages, had become far less audacious, knight-errantlike, and consolatory than usual. There was but one remedy for them, and that lay in the spur at my heels. I touched up the sides of my horse, whom a hearty breakfast had rendered somewhat dull, and on we went, dashing through a region that not only grew more wild, but more water at every step. The conviction that a river was at hand reminded me that my incognita had said that she lived beside one, and this memory, with the increased rapidity of my motion, served to disperse in some degree, by disquieting reflections.

It was towards midday, when I was suddenly startled by sounds, like those of a horse, at some little distance before me. This led me to prick up my senses a little, and feel in my pockets for my pistols.

But, just then, I had no need of them. A moment more showed, and dissipated, the occasion of my alarm. Man and horse came suddenly in sight, wheeling out from a little Indian trail, a little a-head, and on the right hand of the path which I was pursuing. The horse was a miserable hack, driven to the top of his speed—which was no great matter,—by the unrelaxing application of whip and spur. The rider was evidently engaged in a race for life. He was a small person, well wrapped up in clothes, with a brand-new beaver on his crown, and a smart whip with an ivory handle in his grasp. His boots and unmentionables, originally of city make and good cloth, had been in close acquaintance with the tenacious yellow mire, which was abundant enough at every turning. His face was sharp and his eyes vigilant; at an ordinary time, and under ordinary circumstances, it is probable that their expression was sufficiently shrewd and sagacious, but just then, it was pale with fear, and expressive of no other quality. The man was evidently half-scared to death. I drew up and faced him. He would have dashed aside in consternation, regarding me as an enemy; but my voice arrested and somewhat quieted him. Besides, having unconsciously planted my heavier steed directly across the track, no spurring or whipping that he could use, could force forward the feeble animal he rode. He was accordingly, breathless and looking back, compelled to stop.

To make a long story short, he had been robbed, most civilly, according to his own account, some three hours before. His business had been to collect certain monies, in which object he had succeeded. The money—a considerable amount—had been promptly paid him by his debtor, from whom he had taken leave and gone upon his way rejoicing. But he rejoiced not long. An hour had not elapsed ere he was accosted by the rogues, two in number, and they—women.

"Women!" I exclaimed with equal astonishment and mirth. The pitiful fellow shrunk beneath my glance, and made a stammering explanation which half excused him. According to his belief they were women only in costume. Like the worthy Welshman, in the case of Falstaff—he "liked not when a 'omans has a great peard; he spied a great peard under her muffler." One of the rogues, it seems, had been so indifferent to propriety of costume, as to make her toilet without shaving; and a grisly beard a month old, had made the pistols which she presented to the breast of the collector, doubly potent in his eyes. The pistols were clearly masculine. Having relieved him of his pleasant burden, they laid a hickory over his own and horse's back,—a mode of objurgation which horse and man seemed equally prepared to comprehend. He heard but the one comforting assurance that they gave him at parting, that if he only dared to look back for an instant, like Lot's wife, they'd salt him for ever. He had ridden some fifteen miles since leaving them, taking care to incur no such penalty. His farther information was of some colour for my own prospects. He gave as his opinion, that the whole region, which he had fancied a *quasi* wilderness, was alive with rogues—that the settlement was quite a numerous one—that they occupied every fastness and place of cover, and retreat—hammocks and islets—in the swamps and river

> "And every alley green,
> Dingle, or bushy dell, of this wild wood,
> And every bosky bourn from side to side."

They were a vast community, kept together by the common object and necessity, roving always in concert, and sworn against all laws and all honesty. He did not scruple to declare his conviction, though this he did in a whisper, and with an eye cast furtively around him, that even his debtor, who had paid up so promptly, was of the very same fraternity, who had only paid so readily because he well knew that his associates would very soon put him again in possession of the same money.

"And who was your debtor?" I asked with some indifference, as a matter of course, and almost heedless of the answer.

"His name's Bush Halsey."

"I felt my cheeks glow again.

"Bush Halsey?—are you sure it is not Bud Halsey?"

"Oh, yes! He's got a brother named Bud Halsey."

"And where's he? Is he here in the swamps?"

"No, I guess not. I heard of him night afore last, down to'ther side of the nation, but he's gone below."

"Gone below! where?"

"I can't guess."

"And how shall I find this Bush Halsey?"

The poor fellow was unwilling or unable to give me directions. His fright revived when he recollected some threats that were thrown out, of future treatment, if he dared to reveal anything in relation to the robbery, and my anxiety to get intelligence, and my determination to go forward,—expressed in spite of his counsel to the contrary—now seemed, all on a sudden, to impress him with the belief that I was one of the gang, and no better than I should be. An attempt which I made to get some further information touching the Halseys only rendered him more anxious to shake off an acquaintance who might think proper, at any sudden moment, to finish those feminine proceedings which had begun in the swamps; and, seeing his disquiet, I wheeled my horse out of his path, and bidding him God speed, boldly turned into the dark, narrow avenue out of which he had emerged.

CHAPTER V.

I WAS certainly about to pursue, with sufficient audacity, a career, which, with sufficient boldness, I had begun. The romance of the thing was still uppermost in my mind. The truth is, that youth, unaccustomed to trials of its own, is not always persuaded of the realness of danger. There is always a hazy indistinctness about the wild events of which it reads or hears, which touched by the warm rays of an unrestrained imagination, becomes a glory in its sight, and effectually hides from view the cloud and storm from which it has arisen. I was moving forward as one in a dream. Accustomed to a life of security, and to the even progress of the day, unbroken by anything unusual, and secure from any evils which are not common everywhere to life, I could not and did not yield my belief to the strange stories which I heard. That they were commended to my fancy was natural enough, as they came clothed with the hues of the picturesque and novel. But that they were real, actual, living and daily occurring things—that here, in America—in our matter of fact, monotonous, prosaic day,—there were *bona fide* brigands, such as we read of in Italy,—was a matter not so easy to be brought within the compass of belief. Thinking from my feelings, I judged the affair of the fellow with whom I had just parted, to have been some clever practical joke of some dare-devils, exaggerated by his unmanly terrors, and hereafter to be explained when the trick had been sufficiently played. Then the robbery had been committed by women. Only think of my being bid to stand by my own little incognita! The fancy made me laugh outright, and I felt very certain, that, in such an event, I should take to her arms, with the full purpose of using my own. I did not actually wish to encounter her in the character of a footpad, but I felt that such an event would not be entirely without its pleasant accompaniments.   A wrestle with her did not seem an affair to inspire terror; and laughing at the conceit, I dashed forward, muttering from Dick, the apprentice,—

> " Limbs do your office and support me well,
>   Bear me to her, then fail me if you can."

Filled with such pleasant musings, I had ridden probably three quarters of an hour, after parting with the collector, and in this time I had overcome an interval of four miles—not more,—for the road, originally an Indian trail, was broken by numerous bottoms,—mucky places, of which the reader will form a sufficient idea from the distich written with coal, upon the blaze of a tree, which stood fronting a place of similar character, called Crane Tructa, through which I once had to pass :

> " Here's h—ll, and it
>   To go through *yit*."

The citizen would only need to gaze upon such a spot and acknowledge the same necessity, to feel the force and propriety of such an inscription.   The poet was worthy of the subject, and that is no mean praise.   I had gone through some three or four of these miry gulphs, which the most reverent nature would be very apt, involuntarily, to liken to the infernal regions, Acheron and Styx—though none of them was so bad as *Cane-Tructa*—and had at length emerged upon a high and beautiful knoll of green, the sloping edges of which were fringed with dense barriers of cane, their feathery tops waving gently, like the plumes of so many gigantic warriors, and was advancing, in an easy lope, into an area, about two hundred yards round, on which trees seemed never to have grown, when my horse suddenly stopped short, and shyed half round, while his elevated head and ears attested some occasion of alarm.   I raised my eyes, and discovered, directly on the path in front, squat upon a log, the butt-end of which was thrust out from the opposite forest, a man in a grey overcoat, with slouched hat, and a huge rifle which lay directly across his thighs.   The suddenness of the encounter a little staggered me ; but remembering my fanciful philosophies, and the ludicrous plight of the collector, I soon recovered myself, and determined promptly to yield myself to any mirthfulness which the mischievous nature of men, in such situations, might be disposed to practise.   But as soon as I got nigh enough to notice the exact features of the man before me, I arrived at the conclusion, instinctively, that he was no amateur. He was one of those men, whom we know at a glance, as persons of downright serious business, who never laugh, who know nothing in life but its necessities, and regard all things and all persons with that hard-favoured earnestness which looks directly and only to the most slavish calls, whether of a hunger that needs, or an appetite which lusts.   He neither moved limb nor muscle as I approached, yet I could see that his eyes observed me keenly.   The reader will be pleased to remember that I am of the sanguine temperament—a temperament which acts promptly, without much reflection, from a spontaneity, the result, it would seem, of a corresponding and equal activity of mind and feeling.   The truth is, such persons think with as much rapidity as they move, and if rightly trained to habitually just thinking, their impulsive movements are very apt to be quite as correct in their tendencies as if they were made under the most deliberate exercise of thought and will. This is said to account for my conduct on this occasion. It did not appear to me that I thought at all of what I should do.   But the resolution and the performance were one. As I approached the stranger slowly, I threw my left leg over, so as to sit entirely upon the right, thus facing him fully as I drew nigh.   This is a favourite mode in the southern country of sitting a horse, when the rider meets with a friend, or with any one in whom he has confidence, or with any one he is disposed to linger and converse. It shows that there is no trepidation and no desire of flight.   Sitting thus, I approached the fellow, and stopped my horse directly before him.   He looked up at me with a savage sort of inquiry in his glance, as if to say " what next ? "   I did not suffer him, however, to put the question in words, but proceeded in the following manner :

"I have but one question, stranger, before I begin, and that is, am I safe here from a sheriff? Be quick and tell me, for I must ride until I am."

"And what makes you afraid of a sheriff?"

"You're not one, I hope?"

"Rather guess not."

"Very well! Now then—do you ever see one here?"

"No! They take root here but never grow. A deputy came here once, from somewhere below ; they planted him, but he never come up."

"Good! I need go no farther then, " said I, dropping from my horse, and taking a seat beside him on the log.

"Whar' are you from ?" he asked.

"Tennessee."

"What's brought you here?"

"This! " said I, jerking my horse's bridle as I spoke. The fellow lowered upon me, with looks that showed he was no joker, as he responded—

"You mean to say you come on him?"

"Not exactly, though I did come on him. But the horse caused my coming here. I made a swap, giving that nag, which you see is a fine one, with a fellow at muster, who traded me a creature that had spavin. We didn't see it at first, for he was warmed with riding. But going off from muster I stopped at a friend's house, where I sat an hour. Meanwhile the horse had cooled off, and was as stiff in her joints as if they were made of ridge poles. I had got on a mile further, hardly able to get along, when who should come by but Backus, the fellow I had swapped with. When I saw my own fine animal that he was riding, and felt that I could hardly hobble along with the one I rode, I got down and stopped him, jerked him from the beast, and we got to blows. Somehow he got a knife in him, and I got my horse back. People would have it 'twas my knife did the mischief, and there was an inquest, and a warrant—and all that sort of thing,—and so I sloped—but look you,—you're sure you're not a sheriff or a deputy ?"

"And if I was?"

I grappled him by the throat in an instant, and drew my dirk, which flourished his eyes before he could say "Jack Robinson!"

"Hold off, stranger!" he exclaimed, grasping my arm. "I'm no sheriff—and no deputy. D—n the breed, I'm just as much afraid of 'em as you."

"Well you spoke in time!" I said with half subdued fierceness of look—"it's no time to play with a man when his neck's in a plough line."

It required no small effort, I assure you, to compose my muscles and carry on this game without laughter. But I felt that it was now necessary. If my neck was absolutely in a halter, it was very clear to me that my life was not in a state of absolute security. One glance at the ruffian at my side had served to dissipate all my romantic fancies.

CHAPTER VI.

Thus far I had carried out my assumed character, with tolerable success. I had certainly lied with a natural grace and readiness that did not need a prompter, and I had the satisfaction to see that my new comrade, in his own mind, took me to be as great a scoundrel as himself. I somewhat blushed for myself, as I became assured of this, but blushing then was no part of my policy. I was in for it, and had to go through. I remembered the counsel of old Yannaker at parting, and salved the hints of conscience by reflecting that I was in the rogues atmosphere. Every step I took with my companion left this matter less in doubt. Though by no means a garrulous fellow,—really a fellow of few words, he contrived, in those few words, to give me insight into many and very strange things. As-suming that the circumstances under which I had sought refuge in the swamp, and my own inclination, had already made me one of the fraternity, he gave me a brief but comprehensive history of their doings and ways of life. What had been told me by the collector was fully confirmed. The region in which I wandered was possessed by a community of rogues. They were numerous and extensively

connected throughout the country, some of them had absolute wealth; and children born in this American Alsatia—so long had it been a realm of outlawry—were now grown to manhood. What aristocracy was here. I asked myself, while my cheek glowed again,—was my beautiful unknown one of these? Had she drawn her infant breath among such scenes, such rogues—had such always been her connections,—and in what degree had she escaped the contaminating influence of such an atmosphere of

No. 3

crime. The robbery of the collector, by persons in female garments, now struck m^e
—as it did not, when I first heard of it—with a sort of horror. I could feel the
enormousness of the crime, committed by women, when I thought of her, as one
who might be in training for like practice. But when I thought of her more particularly—when I remembered that night—her shy and timid air—her subdued
and gentle accents,—and the tenderness that spoke out equally in eye and voice,—
I was re-assured. I felt happy in the conviction that no sort of human training
could pervert such an exquisite work of Heaven.

Enough of this,—let us hurry forward. We were on our way together into the
recesses of the swamp. This was an admirable receptacle—a retreat, in which pursuit of one, familiar with the region, would be undertaken by a thousand men in
vain. Pursuing a zigzag and continually changing course for several miles, I yet
conjectured that we were not more than one mile from the spot where we started. A
long dim avenue, led, as through some lonely corridor, into a spacious area, or chamber almost surrounded by water, opening only upon one defile, which might be guarded
by a single man. Here and there were nooks, closets, as it were, of forests, which one
might select for studio or dressing-room, and be secure from passing interruption;
—and anon, you had a larger field of operation—halls fit for courtly audience—vast
parlours, of green wall and azure ceiling. But the reader must conceive for himself, what the rapidity of such a narrative as this, will not suffer me to describe.
Enough, that love could not easily contrive such a labyrinthine bower, for the
safety of the beloved one, with all the appliances of art at his bidding, and all
the resources of imperial weath at his command. Woodstock was a fool to the
swamp city of Conelachita!

By little and little I made new discoveries. Here was art as well as nature.
Sometimes little tents of bush would appear,—snug cottages for a single sleeper.
Anon came a more permanent if not a more pleasing hovel, made of logs and clay.
Here a horse would be fastened—his saddle and bridle hanging to the tree above
him; now a face would peer out from the copse beyond us, as the trampling of
our steeds would become audible; and now a whistle, or the bark of a dog, would
announce our approach, which to distant echoes, would be sure always to be on
the watch, to take it up, and repeat the signal to others yet beyond. All this
was so much romance, which made me half forgetful of the risks I incurred,
and of the policy I was to pursue, in order to escape them.

At length, my conductor came to a halt.

"Here," said he, "let us hitch—we must take boat here."

I stopped, got down, and followed his example. We fastened our horses to
swinging limbs, and set forward. I discovered that we were on a sort of islet, on
the edge of a river—a dark, deep, but narrow stream, which whirled by us with the
rapidity of a foaming current, carrying along with it reeds and branches, and sticks,
the tribute of numerous shores, on the several creeks above. A neat little dug-
out, capable of carrying two persons only, was fastened at the landing.

"You can paddle your hand, I suppose?" said my conductor. Could I not?
I could have paddled both hands. It was one of my favourie exercises, from my
my own noble river, the Alabama. I answered him by taking my seat in the little
bark, that danced like an egg-shell n the whirling current.

"She's a clean critter," said my companion with evident satisfaction.

His praise was deserved, A better balanced canoe, of better proportions for
such a stream, I had never beheld. It was a pleasure to send her forward, and
we found no difficulty in crossing the river;—but, having made the opposite
shore, we followed it up, until we passed into the mouth of a creek, a broad but
sluggish stream. This we ascended for half a mile or more, when we drew up to
some tolerably steep banks, jumped ashore, and hauled the canoe into a crevasse,
which might have been the work of hands.

We had not gone far when we heard a voice. The person did not appear, and
he language used was short and gibberish beyond my comprehension. It seemed
o be understood, however,, by my companion, who turned aside at once, and
ntered upon another path. Here we met another person who regarded me

attentively, but went forward without a word. The next moment we encountered two women, possibly the very feminine rogues who had robbed the collector, but if they were. they had taken care to shave themselves since they shaved him,—for their chins,—and I examined them heedfully as they passed—were quite as clear as his pockets. They did not pass in silence, however, but had a few words on common-place things, and a nod and a smile to me. They were young too, the jades, but quite ugly enough to have frightened the collector, without renderingjaries-a sary the show of pistols. A whistle, once, twice, thrice, repeated, at stated 🙰 odss and places, now notified our approach of higher personages, and emergin p from the avenue into an area, we came upon a group of five men, who seemed te be busy about a canoe of considerable dimensions, which was yet in the log, though the burning and hewing had been begun. One oi them, who was stooping over the log, seemed to be engaged in describing the outlines. He rose from hisg stooping posture as we approached, and discovered to me a person not only ol large frame, but of imposing presence. He was over six feet in height, broad breasted, sinewy and muscular, with limbs of admirable symmetry, which his costume, which was all of buckskin, made Indian fashion, showed off to great advantage. His coat was a hunting shirt thickly fringed; no longer fresh in its original bright yellow, but subdued by exposure to the weather, to an uniform umberous aspect. There was no covering on his head, the hair of which, though, thick and long, was white as cotton. His beard, which spread over his bosom in thick curling folds and masses, was such that, if I had not felt sure that he was only a great rogue, would have led me to suppose that he was a great patriarch. His eyes were large, deeply set, and of a clear dark blue. His nose was Roman, his mouth small and expressive, and the whole expression of his face that of benignity, and a conscience quite at rest with his fellows and the world. I may add that, as he wore neither stock nor neckcloth, there was scarcely anything in his costume or appearance, to remind me of civilised life, and yet, even with his habit borrowed from the Indian, there was quite as little of the savage. The picturesque in his guise, and its noble simpilcity, according so happily with his features and his frame, effectually relieved his appearance of that which might otherwise, in my sight, have seemed strange and unnatural. He extended his hand at my approach, a slight change of expression from interest to civility, being apparent in his countenance, then, after giving some directions to the workmen, he drew aside with my late companion. A few moments only had elapsed when he returned, having, as it would seem, in that time, gat hered from the latter all the knowledge which he had respecting me. He again gave me his hand, and drew me aside from the rest.

" You have been unfortunate, young man," said he—" and I am sorry for you. There can be no greater misfortune than taking life, particularly at your age. But Fry tells me you had provocation. Pray, how was it ?'

I had to begin anew the work of invention. Of course, my story, in substan- tial particulars, must be the same as I told before. But there was a difference, which I soon discovered, between my present and former companion,—while, to the latter, I appeared reckless; to the former, as a man evidently better acquainted with human nature, I adopted another tone. He had himself indicated my cue, when he spoke of the provocation which I had received. He knew enough of the superior nature and education—which I felt that I could not, and did not wish to, conceal—to be aware that no such crime is ever committed by such in wanton- ness, or from the mere brutal instinct of passion. There must be provocation and hot blood, in the case of the educated man—with very few exceptions—before ke will do murder. I framed my story accordingly. He heard me patiently, and I was particularly careful to say no more than was necessary. This is the great secret in lying successfully. When I had done, he took me kindly by the hand.

" Here you are safe," said he, " as long as you choose to remain. You know what we are, and must abide by our laws. We ask you for no participation ir our practices, unless your own will inclines you that way,—which I would no encourage. This affair may blow over—your friends may succeed in hushing it up, and then you may return in safety to your family. Nay, even we may do something towards this result, however strange you may think it. Outlaws ourselves, we have friends not only among those who obey, but those who administer the laws. What is your name, and from what part of Tenessee do you come? Let me know these particulars, that we may institute an inquiry, and see what can be done for you at home."

Here was a dilemma. But there was no time for delay. It was necessary to answer promptly. I gave my name as Henry Colman, of Franklin County, West Tenessee. It was fortunate for me that I knew something, personally, of this region, for it appeared so did my examiner, and he subjected me to a keen scrutiny, in which I did not dare to falter. My answers seemed satisfactory. He pressed my hand, and bade me go along with him. and we rejoined the persons we had left.

To these I was not introduced, and he only remained with them long enough to give some directions on ordinary subjects. This done, he bade me go with him, and we pursued our way together through a long wood, occasionally crossing branch and creek, upon a rude log or fallen tree. My companion was free of speech, and his conversational resources, I soon found, were equally admirable and ample. He was deeply versed in books—he had seen the world, and was not insensible to its refinements. His eye was evidently one accustomed to seek out and discriminate the forms of beauty in external objects, and he frequently drew the regards of mine to this or that point of view in the surrounding landscape, which was either picturesque or fine. All this, while it increased my respect for him, lessened the impressions which I had received of his objects and associates. I found it more and more difficult, at every moment to believe of his outlawry. It was all some pleasant jest—some queer contrivance of clever people, to produce a laugh at the expense of the credulous;—and with this notion, I was more than once provoked to blurt out the truth in my own case, and my convictions in theirs, in order to show that I was a little too sagacious to be fooled further than I thought proper. But a lurking grain of prudence at the bottom of my brains prevented me from so precipitate a proceeding. Besides, had I not an object—was not this Mr. Bush Halsey and was not Mr. Bush the brother of Mr. Bud Halsey, and did not Mr. Bud Halsey have in charge my beauty of the cloud—my fair unknown—the dark-eyed, mysterious damsel of whom I was in search? But where was she and that grisly personage? Except in size there was no resemblance between the supposed brothers. I confess that when I recollected the rude stare and deportment in the latter, I was in no way anxious to meet with him—but my desire to see her rendered me comparatively indifferent even on this head. I was soon to be relieved on some of my doubts. We had now got into a region of upland swamp, which bore some of the marks of a more civilised settlement. A corn-field opened upon right and left, and cattle were lowing down the lane, wigwams appeared in sight, and a troop of barn-fowls were strutting to and fro in all the consciousness of corn and company. Beyond, might be seen a tolerable log-cabin, from which the cheerful smoke was arising, in a long spiral column, through the patriarchal branches of a clump of oaks.

"Here, sir, is our wigwam. A little rough, but not without its comforts. If we have not the laws among us, we are not without those things which the laws were intended to secure. Here, too, you will find a few books, and if you are a musician, there is flute and violin. I keep them, still, rather as proof of what I have been, than what I am now—though the enjoyment of music is not absolutely inconsistent with the most desolate of human conditions."

I had observed, prior to this, that, on more than one occasion, the remarks of the senior had run into a melancholy tone; and I now discovered that there was a sudden expression in his countenance that looked like a settled sorrow. Ther was no unmanly whining, however, in what he said; but the incidental and unforced utterance of an habitual feeling which, at such moments, was an appropriate echo to the thought which he had occassion to express. We entered the house together. It was the ordinary log hovel of the country. The room, or hall, upon which we entered was a small, snug apartment, fourteen by sixteen. Its chinks were all neatly covered with clapboards. Its tables were of common pine—its chairs of domestic fabric also, seated with skins, Several tiers of rude shelves on one side of the apartment contained the books of which he had spoken which were certainly numerous for such a region. There, too, were flute and violin. The window—there was but one in the apartment,—was glazed and hung with calico, and my eye was fixed upon a slender rocking chair which was cushioned with calico, and stood very near the fire-place. Such a chair could not have supported the huge frame of my host for ten minutes. By whom could it be occupied ? I looked round and listened in vain. The dwelling had evidently no tenants but ourselves. Here was a disappointment. But, the rocking chair was a promise in which I put some faith, and there were other proofs of a female presence around us. There was a band box, speaking volumes of itself ; and on one of the tables I discovered a little open basket full of squares of calico, for quilting ; and there was an unfinished stocking, with the bright needles sticking in it, peering out from a corner of the aforesaid basket, and these were all signs of a feminine presence, which would not allow me to despair. But let us hurry through the day. Mr. Bush Halsey, for I soon discovered that it was he, indeed, treated me with the most marked attention, He played the country gentleman to perfection. A servant came at his summons, a neatly clad old African dame, who proceeded to set the table, and get us refreshments. At times, Mr. Halsey disappeared, leaving me to myself. And when he came in, it was always to renew some interesting conversation, and display his own proficiency in all its topics. I began to be very much pleased with the man, and, but for a natural anxiety which I felt, as to my situation and the result, which gave a little dulness and restraint to my manner,—I should have shown myself quite as happy and as much at home, as I had ever done at Leaside. That I was dull, Mr. Halsey ascribed to my feelings on the subject of the crime I had reported myself to have committed ; and though he did not discourage such feelings, he addressed himself more than once to the task of strengthening me under them. His kindness was such that, even on his account, I half repented of the game I was playing. But I had not the courage to stop where I was. Indeed, there was no stopping. The cards, so far, were in my hands—but whether the prize deserved or justified the venture, is a question to be solved hereafter. Day passed, the night waned, and my host showed me my apartment. For an hour after I had retired, I heard him playing upon the flute, and in such mournful caprices of sound as I never could have conceived before. It seemed to me that, if a heart could ever speak in music, such would have been the strains poured forth by a breaking one. This ceased, and I must have slept a little. I was certainly in a doze, when I was startled by an unusual noise. A door was grating, there was a bustle, the tread of several feet, then boxes or trunks were hauled over the floor, and there was a murmur of tongues,— subdued, as if to avoid unnecessary disturbance. This was followed by the opening of another door, and the voice of Mr. Halsey. " Ah ! Helen. Is that you." Scarcely had he spoken, when other accents succeeded, which thrilled through my very soul.

" Yes, dear father. May I come in ?"

" To be sure !" was the reply.

I could fancy the kiss and the embrace which followed. I could have sworn to that voice among a thousand. The bustle ceased, the sounds died away. There was no further stir that night. But my sleep was gone. Thought was too busy in my head for sleep ; and with the first peep of dawn I was out of bed, but not sooner than my host. I saw him from my window, moving off towards the swamp, accompanied by the grisly guardian of my fair one. The tripping of light feet in the adjoining hall drew my attention thither. Hurrying my toilet, I entered the apartment, and as I expected, discovered the object of my search. She sat in that very rocking chair which had so much interested me the night before. Her back was to me, and she only half looked around as I opened the door. When she saw me, she started to her feet with an exclamation of equal apprehension and surprise.

" Ah ! you here !" she exclaimed. " Oh ! wherefore have you come ?"

" Did I not tell you that I could find you out—that I would follow ?"

" Oh! why have you done so?" she spoke, in manifest alarm, clasping her hands imploringly as she did so.

" And why not ?"

" There is so much danger."

" I do not care for danger."

" But why risk it ?"

" Because I love you."

" You love me ? oh, no ! you must not. I am not for you to love. I am a poor girl of the woods. Go—leave me soon. There is danger if you stay. You know not—you cannot guess the danger."

" No! There is no danger where you are."

" I—I, myself, am danger," she exclaimed, with a pretty energy. " The people will not love you here—go home to your own. Fly—leave us. You cannot go too soon."

" Your people shall be my people."

" It cannot be. You have your own father, your own mother."

" They shall be yours."

" No, no—my father is here."

" He shall be mine!"

" Alas! you know not what you say. You know not me—you know not him. If you knew! If you only knew!" and she clasped her hands despairingly, while she spoke.

" Nothing could make me love you less. I know you—that you are beautiful and very dear to me."

" Say not so ! Leave me. Go your ways while there is yet time. Alas ! I know not if it is not too late already."

" It is not too late! I know where I am—among whom I am. Helen, I know all."

" Alas, alas !" She covered her face with her hands.

" But I would sooner be here with you, loving you as I do, than among the civilest people in the world. Only suffer me to love you—say that you do not hate me—that, were it with yourself, you would not have me leave you."

" Why should you think that I could hate you ?"

" I do not think so."

" Do not—do not."

" Ah, Helen, could you grant me more. Could you but say that you would receive—return my love."

" I know not what it is to love."

" Let me teach you."

" No, no—you must go. I am a child—I must not listen and hear you talk such things. You do not, cannot know the truth—all the truth. Hear you, stranger——"

" Call me not stranger—call me friend—call me Henry Colman."

" Henry, is that your name?"

How sweetly did she speak the word ! With what interest ! I could almost have renounced my real name for ever after that.

" Yes."

" Well, Henry, hear me, and believe me. There are bad men here, very bad men—they will do you hurt. Go home to your people while you can. You are not safe here."

" What ! not with your father ? He is good—he will protect me."

" Yes, he is good. He will do all that he can for you, Henry; but he cannot do all. My uncle is a fierce man—very violent—and it is not always that my father can keep him from doing wrong. Besides, Henry, my uncle likes you not—he saw you at Yannaker's."

" True; but there's no reason why he should dislike me, because he met me there."

" No; but when he frowned, you frowned too; and he didn't like that. He spoke of you. Oh! if he comes back and sees you here!"

"I shall not fear him, Helen."

"Beware of him—do not make him angry."

"Let him beware of me!"

"Hush! You know not what you say. He is the master here—he rules in the swamp. It is he who has brought my father here. Hark! They come. Oh! Henry, that you were gone—gone away—a thousand miles from this."

"You with me, Helen, and your prayer should be mine."

She cast upon me but one glance; but that was sufficient. I felt, from that moment, that I was the master of her heart.

CHAPTER VII.

THE moment after, the father and uncle entered the room. The latter looked at me with a keen, stern, searching glance.

"Who's this? Who have we here?"

He was answered by his brother.

"The young man, Colman, of whom I spoke to you!"

"Colman, Colman! I have seen his face before."

It was then time for me to speak.

"You have, sir; at all events, I have seen you. We met a few nights ago at one Yannaker's."

"Your memory is good, I see," was the reply, with something of a sneer in his accents. "But what brought you here? You followed us!"

"Scarcely, I think, else I should not have got here before you. My horse had very much the selection of the route to himself. In every respect he may be said to have brought me here."

"And who are you! What is your name?"

"My name is Colman—Henry Colman, sir. I am from West Tenessee. I have related to this gentleman all the facts in my history necessary to be known."

The tone of my speech was intended to show a proper degree of resentment at the abruptness of his, and to check the sort of cross-questioning to which he was disposed to subject me. His brother interposed.

"Yes, Bud, you have already heard."

"True,—but what of that. I have no objection to hear again. Truth never suffers from twice telling. I know the young fellow has killed a man about a horse, and flies here for shelter from the sheriff. All very well, and very straight ;—but what's the upshot of it. Does he expect to remain here for ever—or does he propose at some convenient day to return, and blab everything that he has seen and heard among those who give him protection."

"As a man of honour,"—I began.

He interrupted me.

"Hark ye, lad, were you a spy upon us, you would still insist, if questioned, that you are a man of honour. Perhaps, it is not men of honour that we want,—but bondsmen. We deal with our men as the devil is said to deal with them. We take security for their good will to us, by requiring of them the performance of some evil deed to others. Will you commit another crime? You see I do not mince the matter. Will you join us?"

I gave a single glance at Helen Halsey. I shall never forget the appealing expression of her dark and dewy eyes. Her hands were clasped—her form bent forward, as if waiting for my answer. That was tolerably prompt.

"What if I say 'No'?"

"Ha! you dare then?" and his brow grew black; the heavy muscles corrugating in little knots above his eyes, like so many young serpents coiled together, while his feet advanced, and his shoulders seemed to work convulsively, as if preparing for a mighty struggle.   I receded a step, and put my hand into my bosom, as I replied :—

"I will not be driven by any man."

Here, Bush Halsey, Helen's father, interposed, and drew the other aside. His words, which were those of entreaty and expostulation, only reached my ears in part ;—but the reply of the other was fierce and loud.

"You are a fool, Bush, for your pains, and I am a greater fool for submitting to you, as I do.   You should not meddle in these matters at all.   You have nothing to do with them."

Here some words escaped me.   Bush Halsey again spoke, and his reply was entirely lost.   He spoke for several minutes, interrupted now and then only by some single expletive, uttered sometimes in scorn, sometimes in impatience, by the lips of the other.   The final speech of the latter, set me at rest for the moment.

" Have it as you please.   But let him not leave your own premises.   If I find him prowling where he should not be, let him bewae."

This was intended for my ears, for the glance which accompanied the word, was bestowed wholly upon myself.   This said, he took one step towards us, then, suddenly wheeling about, without a farther syllable to any, he strode from the apartment.   A moment before, and Helen had retired to her room.   Her father then approached me.

" You hear the terms of your stay among us.   It makes your retreat a prison yet this is favourable to your circumstances.   No reproach can be urged against you, for remaining where you are, under a sort of duresse.   For your sake I am glad that it is so.   My brother is a violent man.   We differ, as you may see, materially in temper.   He has been rendered more violent, and perhaps unjust, by frequent injustice.   Indeed, we have both suffered from a like cause ; but it is my fortune still to remain somewhat human—possibly, because I have been left one human blessing which was denied to him.   I am still a father.   But come. Walk with me now, and I will show you your prison limits.   You must not suppose yourself without privileges.   Your bonds are not too close for sport and moderate exercise.   The island which I occupy is free to you in every quarter, and it is not so small as you might imagine.   Come, I will show you my dominions."

Our ramble was a long but pleasant one.   My prison was a spacious one, well wooded and watered, completely insulated by creeks, and admirably chosen for the residence of a recluse.   My companion carried me to his favourite walks— pointed out his fishing traps—his choice fishing grounds in spring and summer— a delectable bathing place, and more than one ample area, in which could be seen the implements of exercise, the quoit, the bar, &c., all convenient, and all arranged with the eye of experience and art.   At certain points of view, I could see men on the opposite side of the creek, engaged in various duties, some sawing or choping, others busy about boats and other matters, and now and then, one might be seen peering through a copse, as if engaged in no better business than that of seeing what his neighbours were after.   The redoubtable Bud Halsey was no where visible. After all, my prison limits were not without their attention.   Every moment with Bush Halsey proved him to be more and more a man of thought and observation. He was full of anecdote, sometimes indulged in a little fit of broad humour, and was at all times the most intesting companion.   And when I thought of Helen, I smiled at the thought which could suppose that I could feel any privation, in the same prison bonds with her.

CHAPTER VIII.

I PASS over the events of a week—a period in which I suffered no annoyance, not even seeing for a moment the person of Bud Halsey.   No doubt he was busy at his usual operations. His absence gave me no concern. Never was man happier than myself. Never did time pass so pleasantly. I began to love my venerable host, as well as his daughter. He certainly showed himself a most excellent man. Thoughtful, tasteful, philosophical, his nightly conversations were a rich treat that sometimes made me forget that Helen was by my side. Then, he had a most excellent skill in music. His flute, after I retired at night, seemed the voice

of some complaining angel. It was so mellow, so wild, so sweet and spiritually sad. Sometimes, at evening, when Helen would be absent, he would give me glimpses of his life, and the causes of his present situation. So far as I could gather from him, his worst crime was bankruptcy. He owed money which he could not pay. His person was threatened, and, with a morbidly keen sense of freedom that shrunk from the idea of a gaol as from degradation, he fled to the

No. 4.

uncultivated forests—still in possession of the heathen—seeking safety. His child, meanwhile, remained with an aged relative. His brother followed him, but with a less innocent conscience. His hands were stained with blood, without hope or excuse, the doom of outlawry—outlawry or death! But on this subject Bush Halsey said but little. That he should remain where he was, and in contact with a brother, whose deeds he certainly ventured to disapprove, is only to be accounted for by assuming for him a certain degree of phlegmatic irresoluteness of character. His temperament possessed nothing of the energy which distinguished that of his brother. He was mild, playful, and persuasive; the other harsh, impetuous, and commanding. I need not add that, save by his presence, he had no participation in the doings of the banditti in the midst of whom he dwelt. If the father improved upon acquaintance how much more did the daughter. She was, indeed, a wondrous treasure of the wilderness—not simply beautiful, but sagacious beyond her years and sex—disguising, under the harmlessness of the dove, the wisdom of the serpent; under the simplicity of the child, the forethought and mature mind—on all subjects not conventional—of the high-souled, intellectual woman. In merely worldly matters, she was a child. She had no concealments. The thought spoke out in her eloquent eye, ere her lips could utter it; the feeling glowed, with a speech of its own, upon her cheek ere yet her mind could embody its character in thought. How soon did she show me that I had won her heart, and how confidingly, then, did she walk with me, speak with me, let her fancy have its utterance, though every syllable and look betrayed her soul's dependence on my own. We rambled and we read together—she sang and I listened—as if we were both of the same household. We made every foot of our island limits our own. She knew the restraints set upon my footsteps, and when in the delight of my heart, and the buoyant impulses of my spirit, I would have launched into the canoe, or borne her across the tree that spanned the creek, and conducted to the opposite territory, she caught my hand and restrained me.

"Do you think I fear, Helen?"

"But for my sake, Henry."

For her sake, it seemed to me, as if I could have done or forborne anything.

Thus we lived and loved—need I say how happily, with how few qualifications. Yet qualifications there were. How was this to end? The question forced upon me a sort of self-examination, which, as it never resulted in my own acquittal, I never allowed it to be a protracted one. My conscience smote me for the game I was playing with this dear young creature. I really had no purposes. It seemed as if I could have lived with her, and her only, all my life; but the idea of living all my life in that swamp retreat was unendurable. And to carry home with me as my bride, the daughter of an outlaw,—or, at all events, the niece of one,—was not to be thought of. I had lived too long in the world of conventionalism not to have acquired certain laws and lessons which were fatal to the philosophies of any being so purely unsophisticated as Helen Halsey. Her heart was mine, but not her philosophies. Yet, truth to speak, I meditated no evil. did not meditate this matter at all. Life was simply passing away in a delightful dream, and I was too much the boy to be willing to disturb its pleasant progress before the necessary time. But there were other qualifications to my enjoyment besides my own reflections. I discovered that my steps were closely watched. On the occasion when I first made this discovery, I had been standing with Helen on the bluff of a creek, admiring the proportions of as lovely a cockle-shell of a canoe as ever danced over an Indian-water. I had been trying to tempt her to enter with me. She had resisted and dissuaded me, and while we were discussing the project, my eye had suddenly caught the glimpse of a living object directly before me, on the opposite side of the creek. In that quarter the copse was exceedingly dense. Canes and water-grasses grew down to the very lips of the stream, and in the rear was a thick hedge of evergreens, shrubs and brambles, slightly sprinkled by heavy timber. A second look betrayed to me a pair of eyes keenly fixed upon our movements. In a moment they had disappeared. I quickly conceived the necessity of saying nothing on the subject of my discovery, an.

showing nothing in my deportment which could make it apparent to the spy himself. But the circumstance left me less at ease than formerly. Another day within the same week turning suddenly a little lane, with Helen, we passed three men, who observed us very closely. One of these men, particularly struck me as one whom I had seen before, and the manner in which he eyed me, disquieted me, as tending to show that he too was striving in the work of recognition. Bu he passed on, and, with so many objects to divert and interest my thoughts, it was not likely that this should linger very long in my memory. I am very sure it would not have done so, but for other events of like nature, which kept the recollection fresh.

Meanwhile, where was Bud Halsey, that formidable and fierce bandit? I had seen nothing of him since that parting which had been so nearly a meeting. was not sorry at his absence, and Helen shared my feelings.

"I'm so glad," said she, one day, as we loitered through as close a copse as ever favoured the wishes of two foolish hearts; "I'm so glad Uncle Bud is gone. Somehow, Henry, I tremble when I think of him, on your account. You have defied him, and he don't l ke you."

"Nay, he can scarce be offended with me because I showed a proper manliness! Besides, what care we? So long as I do not pass the boundaries there can be no chance of our quarrelling; and I'm sure, Helen, unless you go with me, I do not care how long I remain in them. I could remain here for ever."

"Ah! you say so, but——"

"Truth, Helen. Have I not told you—how often—how much I love you? But you, Helen, have not spoken once. Will you not tell me, dearest, that you love me, too?"

"Oh, no! I do not feel as if I could say the word."

"But you feel it, Helen?"

"Oh! yes; I feel as you could wish me;" and she turned and threw herself into my arms, burying her face upon my breast, and weeping unrestrainedly. Reader, were you a boy once?—have you a heart?—did you ever love? If yea to these, you understand what I cannot describe—that moment of happiness! Until then I had regarded that verse in which Coleridge speaks of a similar event as an exaggeration. In my silly conceits of convention, living among artificial men and women, I had thought it wholly out of reason and all natural laws, that an innocent girl should be so audacious. But that scene convinced me; I could neither doubt the love, the truth, or the innocence, of that dear child of the wilderness; and sweet and sacred to me now are those nature-prompted lines of the Bard of Genevieve :—

> "Her bosom heaved—she stept aside,
>   As conscious of my look she stept,—
> Then suddenly, with timorous eye,
>   She fled to me and wept.
>
> She half enclosed me with her arms,
>   She pressed me with a meek embrace,
> And bending back her head, looked up,
>   And gazed upon my face.
>
> 'Twas partly love, and partly fear,
>   And partly 'twas a bashful art,
> That I might rather feel than see
>   The swelling of her heart."

And thus we stood, thus we clung to each other, forgetting earth, almost forgetting Heaven,—if such forgetfulness were possible, at a moment when we were in the enjoyment of that bliss, most like heavenly, the dearest known to earth—the full, precious acknowledgment, in the heart that we seek, of that passion which is flaming triumphant in our own!

CHAPTER IX.

How long we remained thus, for how many moments she clung thus passionately to my bosom, I cannot tell. The sense of enjoyment seemed to blind and render obtuse all the ordinary senses. I saw nothing, heard nothing, felt nothing, was conscious of nothing, but her sobs, her glistening eyes, upturned and seeming to melt in the intense gaze of my own, and that beating heart, which seemed bursting to yield itself to the custody of mine. In that moment we were torn asunder. A strong grasp was laid upon my shoulder, and I was hurled to the ground, half stunned, with a heavy knee upon my breast. In the same instant, the savage tones of Bud Halsey told me but too truly whence came the assault. It was under him I lay, with two of his myrmidons at hand, busy in preparing the ropes which were to bind me. Recovering from her first terror and surprise, Helen clung to his arms, imploring my release. But he repulsed her with rude hands and bitter accents.

"Away, you are bold, wanton—do you not blush—do you not hang your head in shame? Have not my own eyes surprised you in the embrace of this traitor?"

"Traitor!" was my exclamation.

"Ay, traitor—traitor and liar! We have discovered you. You are found out."

I did not speak. I struggled, but I need not say how fruitlessly. I was in the arms of a giant, and while he held me firmly, his two assistants passed their lines about my wrists, securing my arms behind my back. I was then permitted to rise.

"There," said my enemy, with a bitter laughter, "there, Helen Halsey, behold your lover. Oh! shame—shame upon you, Helen! What will your father say?"

"My father! He is here!" she exclaimed with an accent in which delight and suffering seemed equally expressed. "Oh, father! how glad I am that you have come. Save him! Do not let them hurt him—he is innocent!"

It was at this opportune moment that the father made his appearance. She darted forward as she beheld him, caught his arm, and drew him forward. His countenance was marked by doubt and inquiry, and was grave to sternness. He gave me but a single glance.

"Bud Halsey! what is this? Why have you bound the youth?"

"The serpent! You have been harboring a serpent in your bosom."

"What mean you?"

"'Tis as I thought. This fellow is a traitor— a spy upon us. He shall die the death of one."

"Oh, no! no! He is no spy—no traitor."

Such was the exclamation of the maid. The uncle turned upon her like a hyena.

"As for you, miss, you should be silent for shame. Send her away, Bush Halsey, she has no business here. I found her in the arms of this fellow—close hugged—lip to lip! Ha! did I not?"

"Helen!" exclaimed the father.

The girl's face was covered with her hands—her head drooped—she seemed ready to sink into the earth.

"Go home, Helen!"

She looked up timidly.

"Oh, father, you will save him? He is no traitor! He is innocent!"

"Are you?" he demanded in freezing accents.

"Oh! my father!" she cried in tones of mingled agony and reproach, as she threw herself upon his breast, and hid her face in his bosom. For a moment he seemed to press her there, then suddenly pushing her from him, uttered sternly but the single word—" Home !"

She receded from him, looked at me with a glance of deepest apprehension, then clasping her hands, as if in prayer, moved slowly out of sight.

—————

CHAPTER X.

WHEN she had disappeared the father spoke.

" Now, Bud Halsey, what is all this?"

" It seems to me plain enough. Have I not told you ? This fellow is a spy upon us—a traitor. He has lied—his whole story is a lie !"

The old man looked at me with a stern but sorrowful glance.

" It is false ! I am no traitor." I had uttered this assurance before—had spoken several times, particularly when the rude assault was made upon Helen by her brutal uncle ;—but, in my excitement, though I very well heard and understood what was said by everybody else, I knew not well what I said myself. My asseveration now seemed to have little effect—upon Bud Halsey at least.

" Oh, my good fellow, we expect your denials. We look for no admissions from you,—no truth, as long as a lie will serve your purpose."

" A lie !" I exclaimed, writhing furiously in my ropes.

" Ah, a lie ! Look not so indignant at the charge, my lad,—we have made the discovery, that a lie comes easy to you. Your invention is good. But you will pay for it. You hang, by all that's powerful, to-morrow morning !"

" Hang !" said Bush Halsey.

" Even so !"

" Pshaw, Bud !—you cannot mean it. You are not serious?"

" As a judge ! as a judge—the supreme judge, without appeal, in all this region —I have doomed him. He dies by sunrise."

The affair was looking serious. The ruffian continued,—interrupting the expostulations of his brother.—

" The long and short of the matter is this. I have discovered that this youth fo his own purposes, has come among us with a lie in his mouth. Suspecting him at first, I despatched Monks to Tennessee, to make inquiry as to the truth of the story which he told us. He has been all through Franklin county, and finds that the sheriff has no process against any person named Henry Coleman, that nobody of the name of Backus has been murdered there, and the whole affair is a mere invention of this chap to find his way among us. Now what can be his object but treachery. He is a creature of the sheriff. He would betray us. Well ! he probably understands the conditions of his venture. He must abide them. You know our laws. He too shall know them."

" I cannot think the youth an enemy, Bud Halsey,—and you recollect he is my guest."

" And you are mine. You have no right to harbour a spy. Our safety makes this necessary. As for his being no enemy, that is possible, but I think him otherwise. Besides, as your guest, he has proved himself unworthy of trust, since he seeks the first opportunity to dishonour your daughter."

" You are a foul mouthed liar !"—I exclaimed, "I love Helen Halsey. Never was mortal love less free from taint than mine. This, indeed, brought me here. I met her for the first time at Yannaker's—was pleased with her, and set out to find her. Circumstances helped me in the pursuit, and prompted the story which I told. It is true I am no murderer—no outlaw. But motive beyond what I have told you, I had none. Nothing but an honourable passion has prompted me in what I have done. This alone has brought me here."

" An honourable passion prompt a lie !" said the outlaw, with a sneer. " But," he resumed, "if this be true, you are ready to marry Helen Halsey ?"

His keen eye seemed bent to search me through. The eye of the father appeared on a sudden to watch me with a new interest. At that moment the idea struck me that the whole affair was a piece of practice—a conspiracy among them—to force me into marriage; and, with this conjecture, indignant that I sould be thus hampered, and forced into an engagement of the sort, I forgot the claims of poor Helen—nay, connected her with the scheme—suppressed her own strong yearnings for the prize thus proffered me, and replied doggedly :—

" I would not be compelled to marry an angel."

" Nor shall my child be forced on any one, Bud Halsey."

" Pshaw, Bush, you are a child yourself. How know you, man, that the measure is not neccessary for her safety. Ay—look not so black scowling—do you not suppose I feel like yourself?—but I say it again—to save her— to save her from shame !"

The frame of the old man was violently agitated. His lips were blanched to perfect whiteness ;—for an instant his eyes glared on me with an expression akin to that tiger-look which his brother habitually wore,—and he exclaimed :—

" Speak not of this to me, Bud Halsey. I will not hear it even from your lips. Could I think it true, I should do murder myself. But it is not true—it cannot be true. Helen is as pure as any angel !"

" She is!" I exclaimed, fervently.

" Very well! I am glad to hear it—I am willing to believe it. You surely cannot be unwilling to marry an angel ?"

The old man interrupted the outlaw.

" I tell you, Bud Halsey, that my child must not be named again in this business."

" And I tell you, Bush Halsey, that unless this traitor weds with Helen Halsey by sunrise to-morrow, he sees the last sunrise of his life. He dies an hour after. Take him away, men, and keep him safe in the new den !"

CHAPTER XI.

I was seized by a couple of stout ruffians, who lifted me, head and feet, as if I had been a mere stack of straw, and bustled off upon their shoulders to the edge of the creek where a boat lay, into which I was tumbled with as little remorse as was shown to Falstaff, when they emptied him out of the wick-basket into the Thames. They pulled down with me something like a mile, then landed on a sort of island, which seemed to be covered with an almost impervious forest. Once more lifted upon their shoulders, I was borne through narrow avenues of the wood a distance of some three hundred yards or more. Our course seemed to be a winding one. We at length reached a very strong log-house, consisting of a single apartment, probably twelve feet square. The logs were hewn and fitted closely. They were of the heaviest kind. There was no window, and but a single, and that a very low door, into which I was thrust headlong. Here I was left—the door fastened behind me, in a darkness that was rather increased than relieved, by an occasional gleam of sunshine that stole here and there through chink or crevice—to brood over my condition, and reconcile myself to the future prospect with what philosophy I could command. That prospect was no ways encouraging, and my philosophy was not of the most composing or consoling nature. I confess it, boy-like, I fell into very ridiculous and childish furies, the recollection of which, to this day, brings the blush into my face. I raved, and swore, and flung myself about upon the damp earth until I was tired. A few hours brought me to my senses. Darkness and silence are great subduers of passion—great promoters of reflection. Why will not our legislators discover this, and substitute imprisonment for life in place of that code, equally barbarous and ineffective, which violently tears away the sacred life principle, from the temple made after the image of God, in which he has enshrined it? In the darkness of the scene—a gloom, thick and seemingly solid, and tangible—which was spread around me,—and that awful stillness which seemed to breathe in slumbers of the grave—I began to recover my half-banished senses. I began to consider my situation. What was that? What was I to do? What was my hope? It was now clear to me that, in spite of the kindness of Bush Halsey's nature, he was powerless to save me. He himself lived but upon terms with his outlawed brother, who, I was now persuaded, was as reckless in his ferocity as he was unscrupulous as to all moral restraint. That Bush Halsey would try, as he had already tried, to save me, I had no question, even though he might have entertained some of the loathsome suspicions which his brother had tried to thrust into his mind. But I had marked too well the natural and enforced expression of defiance which the outlaw had shown towards himself, not to feel very sure that there was no hope from his interposition. And, as for the sweet, suffering Helen! She would pray, I knew—she would be sleepless in the toil in my behalf?—but what would it avail? I had already seen, in her frequent deportment, how much fear she entertained of her brutal uncle, and though she might acquire greater courage in approaching him than usual, having my danger in view, yet I could not deceive myself into the notion that much good would result from any of her entreaties. Well,—the substance of my reflections led me only to this. I was in the meshes—in a den of thieves and murderers doomed to death and hoping nothing either from their mercy, or their dread of legal vengeance. But there was one alternative,—one outlet—allotted to me of escape—to wed with Helen Halsey! Well, could I stickle to avail myself of the alternative? Nay, was not this my own desire but five hours before? Would I not have esteemed such a prize, a treasure beyond all price, but a little while ago—the sole, great object of my desire? Strange, indeed, what perverse mortals we are. My pride revolted at the idea of being forced into the possession of that which I desired beyond all other objects. I now persuaded myself that uncle and father, were both in a scheme to force me into these nuptials—that it was a cunning device to restore to society some of her outcasts—one of those petty, dirty little tricks of a base and cunning nature, of which I was to be the victim. I need not say with what loathing I revolted at the suggestion—how indignant it made me, to think that they could fancy me so dastardly, or so blind—and I resolved rather to meet my fate than dishonour my father's family, by so connecting myself. In justice, however, I never for a moment suspected Helen of any consciousness of their design. No—felt that she was pure and true. I did not think it. My heart prevented my thoughts in her case, and every feeling within me rose in arms against the slightest suggestion of my reason to this effect. Her heart had been pressed against my own—her face, covered with mingling tears and blushes, had been buried in my bosom, and that sacred pressure had been enough, not only to endear her to me for ever, but to make me confident in her truth and loyalty. Ah! that first press of heart to heart, when both hearts are young and ardent. What a volume does it teach! What a life does it embody!—how full of assurances and inquiries, and promises and hopes,—sweet regrets,—and pleasures, so acute, as almost to be akin to pain! That first kiss of love—that first dear, stolen embrace,—the keenest joy of life, to which all other joys are dwarfed! Still, quivering in my whole soul with the rapture of this embrace, I could not think of the dear girl, with whom I shared it, but as a victim like myself. Yet, so thinking, I would not stomach the necessity of being forced to wed her, by the imperious will I despised. The ore I brooded on this threatened necessity, the more I revolted from it, and against it.

"No!" I exclaimed bitterly, in all the heroics of boyhood, "sooner let me perish!"

Having reached this conclusion, I found composure. I stretched myself at length upon the ground, which I had now leisure to see was strewed pretty thickly with dried leaves, and was surprised by sleep; and, dreaming of a fierce and deadly struggle with the outlaw, Bud Halsey, I was awakened, somewhere about midnight, by a rough hand laid upon my shoulder, a rough voice, which I too well remembered, in my ears—and, flashing in my eyes, a huge torch, by the blaze of which I was half stupified and blinded. The intruder was Bud Halsey. He stuck the torch in a crevice of the wall, and calmly seating himself before me, regarded m e with a glance of the keenest inquiry. I need not say that I returned it with one of scorn and defiance, and we looked upon one another in this manner, in a silence which lasted for several minutes. At length he said,—

"You do not seem to understand your true condition, young man. Did you suppose that I was trifling with you when I sent you here?"

"If you were," I answered, "it is a sort of trifling which I should be very loth to forgive, should the moment ever arrive when resentment would be to any purpose. I cannot suppose you were trifling."

"You are a lad of more sense than I had given you credit for. The rest ought to be easy. You see your condition. You have heard your fate. You have had time for reflection. Are you prepared? Will you choose? Will you hang, or marry the foolish girl you have dishonored?"

"You dishonour her by your foul breath, and foul imagination. She is pure as Heaven."

"Pshaw! young man! Do you suppose me as unread as yourself in the history of human nature? Do I not know the weakness of woman's nature, and the recklessness of man's nature, when occasion serves, and opportunity invites? But be this as it may; I give you an alternative. If you have not wronged Helen Halsey, and you love her, as you profess, so much the less should be your reluctance to marry her. If you did not design to marry her before, as I suppose from your unwillingness now, there is every reason for suspecting you as I do, and taking for granted all the worst that one evil nature can imagine of another. On this subject we need waste no words. The simple question is before you. Will you marry her?"

"Where is her father? I would see and speak with him."

"You cannot."

"Why not? He will not refuse me."

"But I will! Look you, young man, Bush Halsey is, in some respects, as great a simpleton as yourself. If he had a voice in the matter, he would send you home to your mother, perhaps fill your pockets with ginger-bread, pat you on the head, bid you go on your way rejoicing, and shed a flood of tears at your departure. But I am the master here! I am the outlaw! I do and counsel the robberies, and, if you please, I command and execute the murders. You know enough to make the task of confession on my part a very easy one. You know too much!—And this is the true reason of your predicament. You came here of your own free will, knowing among whom you came, and practising deception and falsehood to wind yourself in among our secrets. You are a spy, and our situation is such as to render us rather unscrupulous with that sort of persons. But I am willing to please my brother, and to gratify my niece. They are pleased with you, and I have not scrupled to say, and I repeat, notwithstanding your denials, that I think it necessary that you should marry her. It is for this reason that I propose to you this alternative, grant you this time for reflection, and seek you out at midnight to enlighten you more fully on the necessity of the thing. Had it not been for this, I should have had you knocked on the head without a word of parley; and, sure that we should have no further trouble at your hands, should be now comfortably asleep, instead of sitting here, at midnight, endeavouring to make you sensible of your danger. There now—you have the whole, and what is your answer?"

The whole manner of the outlaw was so contemptuous, his tones so cold and sneering, his suggestions so unfeeling, and everything about him so offensive to my feelings, that I forgot my own danger, and replied promptly:—

"Nothing! I have no answer."

"Nothing! You have no answer?"

"None for *you*."

"Very good! I leave you! You may look for me at sunrise, when you may probably be better able to find an answer. Good night."

Coolly detaching the torch from the wall, he waved it around, so as to take in at a glance the entire apartment, and without further word, left the dungeon. The door was carefully fastened behind him, and the sound of voices without, led me to the conclusion that he did rot omit the precaution of placing a guard upon the premises. In a few moments more I was left in darkness, and to my own reflec-

tions. These were not so gloomy. They were of a stern and angry sort. I had been irritated, not subdued, and, to confess a truth, I could not bring myself to believe that the case was so desperate as the outlaw made it appear. I could not think that Bush Halsey was so powerless, or that I should be abandoned to such a cruel fate. It was all a contrivance to terrify me into certain measures, and it was only a test of manliness which was to hold out longest. I was resolved not to show the white feather, and, after a while, fell asleep, as if nothing threatened in the mourning.

No. 5.

CHAPTER XII.

"No! No!" I exclaimed at waking, which I did early,—"my neck was never made for an halter." I tried to raise my hands to it, as if to assure myself that there was not one already around it, but the ropes with which I had been bound, and which, for the moment, I had forgotten, checked somewhat the exulting nature of my thoughts, as they checked the movements of my arms. I had been dreaming of the events which had taken place, and my exclamation was probably due to the character of my dreaming thoughts. I now repeated it, as if to assure myself, but it called up as unnatural an echo, as ever was heard in Killarney. The voice of Bud Halsey, speaking outsi'e, replied.—

"That's a matter about which no man is sure for thirty minutes. In fifteen a cord may be adjusted, and where the woods are convenient, the affair may be all over in twenty. In your case, it still depends upon yourself whether you escape the present danger. You have still a few minutes to sunrise!"

The suddenness of the response, its character, and the character of the man by whom it was spoken, all combined to send a chill through my body, which it had not felt before. The next moment the door opened, and he appeared before me. You have already had a description of the man, but now there was a sly grin upon his features which they did not usually wear, and which seemed to betray a sort of satisfaction which he yet laboured to discourage and keep down. The effort of a man passionate by nature, to subdue the show of impulses which are yet grateful, will usually result in some such conflict upon the features, than which, perhaps, there is nothing more unpleasant to behold. I had much rather have seen him furious.

"Well, young man," he said, entering, "the time is at hand for your final answer. You have still till sunrise. It will not be ten minutes before you see his red streaks on the top of that pine. Bring him out, men, that he may see more easily."

His orders were obeyed, and I found myself, still bound hand and foot, laid down before the door of the dungeon which I had just occupied. I now felt the cold, which I had not experienced to any unpleasant degree during the night. But now I was chilled and uncomfortable, and with the rigid position in which my limbs were fixed, and the effect of the keen morning breeze upon me, coming out suddenly as I did from one of the closest log houses, my teeth almost chattered. I fancied that the outlaw perceived my discomfort, and that he probably ascribed it to another cause, for his features put on that same expression of satisfaction which he yet laboured to conceal. It was with some effort of will, that I succeeded in keeping down my tremours. There were some four persons, stout ruffians, loitering about. One was busy in building a fire, two others stood apart at some little distance, conversing in low tones together, and looking occasionlly at me, while, directly a my side, sat a fourth, coolly disentangling a plough line, the probable uses of which I did not venture to conjecture. But it did not help much to lessen my shivering tendency.

"Step back a moment, Warner," said the outlaw to his assistant. "The lad has little time for talk."

The fellow did as he was bidden. He looked upon me as he moved away, and I fancied I knew his features. I had seen him gazing at me once before, while I walked with Helen, and it then seemed to me that I had seen him elsewhere. I was now sure of it, but where? At all events, if he ever knew me before, there was every reason to apprehend that he also would remember me. But I had not time to think of him. When he had withdrawn, Bud Halsey began, as he always did, with sufficient abruptness.

"Well, young man! the time is at hand for your final answer. You may not know me—you may think me jesting—anything, but serious—but look yon, as I live, and the sun shines—by heaven, or by hell, there is but one escape for you from death, and that is by marriage with my niece. Nothing else can save you ; and, but for what I suppose to be her situation, her feelings, and those of Bush Halsey, who has very much the feelings of a girl—but for them, even this choice should not be allowed you. Nay, to show you how large is the concession which I make, I tell you that I now know you to be the son of one of my deadliest ene- mies, one of those men who have made me what I am, and to whom I owe nothing but undying hate. Your father, in his official capacity, as Judge of the Supreme Court of Alabama, robbed me, by an unrighteous decision, of lands and fortune. Enough, Master Henry Meadows, otherwise Colman, you see where you are, what is known of you, and expected, and what you have to expect. You see the men are waiting, the cord is ready, and you are already under the tree from which you may be suspended. It has borne as stout a man before.''

He turned from me as he spoke, and joined the two men who were conversing at a little distance, said a few words to them, pointed towards me, then disappeared in the wood. But a few moments had elapsed, when he again came in sight, and approached me.

"Your answer, Henry Meadows !''

The smile had disappeared from his features. The face was savage and stern in the extreme. There was nothing there of encouragement, and during his absence my own reflections were of a confused and conflicting character. I need not say that I could not convince myself of the earnestness and sincerity of the man—I could not persuade myself that such a destiny was really contemplated for me. My pride determined my course. Was I to be made a laughing-stock ? a butt— pointed at as one scared into marriage—led to the altar, through fear of the halter ! even the jingle of the words suggested itself to me at the moment, and the thought that such a jingle would commend the anecdote, in future days at my expense, con- tributed to strengthen me in my resolution of defiance. My answer was ready.

"I defy you, sir. Do with me as you please, but you shall not force me to your purpose.'

He hesitated—gazed at me for a moment, as I fancied with an expression o chagrin, and then replied,—

"Very well, young man,—as you please! I have done all that I could—more than I ever expected to do to save any one caught in your situation. Your blood be upon your own head. Ho! fellows!''

He waved his hand and the subordinates drew nigh.

"Are you ready? Secure your man !''

In the twinkling of an eye, I was caught up and placed upon my feet, while the fellow named Warner, adjusted the defiling cord about my neck, and, with the end in his hand, proceeded to climb the tree under which I stood. I writhed in my bonds—I could not struggle, for hands and feet were equally secured. But my writhing was in vain. Indeed, so well fastened had I been, that but for the support of one of the outlaws, I could not have kept my feet. The moment was one of unmixed horror. I began to fear that the farce was to become a tragedy. I looked searchingly into the face of the outlaw, but it expressed nothing but the most dogged determination. The sun, at the same instant, threw a golden crown upon the brow of a towering pine, some thirty yards in advance of the spot where I stood. I shivered! Where was Bush Halsey? Where Helen? My head seemed to swim. I was growing blind. Father, mother!—could this all be true ! was I thus doomed ! Torn from you to see you never more ! I felt that my senses were insecure—that I could no longer depend upon them,—but I could hear— hear every syllable, every breathing. That one faculty seemed to grow doubly acute at the expense of all the rest. There was a whispering among the acces- sories. Then came the deep but low words of the principal.

"Run him up ! There's no use to wait. He's pluck to the last. He'll die game !''

I felt the motion—my feet were gone from under me. I strove to cry aloud but the words subsided into a husky murmur, and I resigned myself—how—with what grace—with what hope—with what thoughts, if any,—to the last terrible change!—when, uddenly, I neard a cry—a piercing shriek—I knew the tones of that voice—I knew the nature of that cry ! The voice was Helen's—the cry—oh! God! it was the lost woman's appeal—for mercy, mercy, mercy! I too strove to echo the cry, but I was choking. I could hear the hollow gurgling of the breath on my own throat—I could feel it!—That was all!

CHAPTER XIII.

I was conscious of a sudden but not unpleasant concussion. I awakened, opened my eyes, and found myself upon the ground, with Helen clinging to me, and plucking at the cord about my neck,—while the outlaw was contending almost violently with her father. I understood the affair in a few moments. Bush Halsay still held in his grasp the knife with which he had smote the cord by which I was suspended. I had been rescued at the last moment—rescued, it was very evident from what I then saw, without any participation in the act by the outlaw. He still appeared resolute upon my death, and, by the numerous gathering of ruffians by whom he was surrounded, and who seemed only to await his final orders, I felt very certain that the dreadful scene must be renewed. I spare the arguments and expostulations of Bush Halsey. I say nothing of the tears and entreaties of Helen.

"Let him submit—let him obey!—let him act as a man of honour!"—was the final answer of the outlaw.

"He will—he will submit!" was the cry of Helen—poor girl—not knowing what was the requisition.

"Give him time—treat him as a man of honour!" was the answer of her father.

The tears of Helen—her beauty—the passionate and unmeasured interest which she expressed in my fate—no longer restrained by the dread of her uncle,— the awe of her father, or the natural apprehension and modesty of her sex—did more to reconcile me to compliance than did all the violence of the outlaw!

"Hear me," I exclaimed, interrupting the dispute;—"hear me, sir,"—addressing Bud Halsey,—"had you been more reasonable, and less violent at first, all would have been easy. I am willing to marry Helen—nay, should have sought her, in due time, at the hands of her father. It was in pursuit of her that I sought out your retreat in the swamp, and it was in order to obtain more ready admission that I framed the story of a crime which I had never committed. My hands are innocent of blood, and I am no spy upon you. Under the ardent passion which brought me here, I should have regarded the hand of Helen as the dearest blessing which could be bestowed upon me, and I am only sorry that your violence, by wounding my pride, should have prompted me, even for a moment, to reject such a boon. I do not ask for life—I make no such prayer to you—I can die, I trust, like a man—but I am willing to comply with your conditions!"

"Loose him !" was all that Bud Halsey vouchsafed to say, as he turned off.

"Oh! my Henry!" was the exclamation of poor Helen, as she swooned away upon my bosom.

CHAPTER XIV.

But the swoon of joy occasions no apprehensions. My bonds were severed, and Helen recovered, so that we were enabled to return together to the cottage of her father. He was kind to me, but grave. It is not improbable that Bud Halsey had succeeded in filling him with some of the base suspicions which were strong in his own bosom. Helen was happy, with a sort of uneasy happiness. Whether she seemed to doubt the reality of the event, or that she felt that my consent to the marriage with her had been somewhat extorted, in spite of my avowals, I cannot say,—but, though smiling, and declaring herself blest, there was a restless, feverish excitability in her actions and movements which did not usually mark them. For my own part, I was sore equally in mind and body. The latter had not passed through the humiliating scenes just described, without undergoing some hurts and bruises. But these were as nothing to the mental annoyances which the same events had produced. I had been trampled upon—dishonoured—my person degraded by the hands of ruffians, and by the shameful and defiling rope. I felt mean and humbled, and, it may be, that, showing something of this feeling, in my intercourse with Helen, I had caused in her that appearance of inquietude which marred, in some degree, the more grateful appearance of her happiness. But I must not linger on this matter. Bud Halsey was a man to move with all imaginable promptness, and that very night he made his appearance at the cottage, accompanied by a young man, decently clad in black, with something of the outward appearance of a divine. Such he was, if we may be permitted to make certain allowances, of which more hereafter. He was introduced to me as the Rev. Mr. Mowbray—a gentleman of the Episcopal persuasion. He was a fine looking young man, of florid complexion, a bright blue eye, with a restless roving twinkle, which betrayed an unsettled and capricious disposition. His temperament, and the general expression of his features, showed the presence of strong, unregulated passions. Surprised at seeing him where he was, and procured with so much readiness, I was still more surprised to learn that he was a regular resident of the swamp—one of the community—sharing in its spoils, and, possibly, though of this I could say nothing, partaking of its miserable practices. The singular moral anomaly of the criminal, influenced by superstition, and insisting upon having a sort of religion of his own, even while engaged in the grossest violation of all moral and divine laws, is too well known, and of too frequent occurrence, to render necessary here any elaborate metaphysics. Perhaps the wonder is, that such contradiction should be found among a Protestant people. In such countries as Italy and Spain, the anomaly, if still difficult of explanation, is yet, because of our familiarity with its occurrence, of less startling effect and character. There, it has been usual to refer it to the mixed influences of a bad political government, and the habitual training of a priesthood, for ever indefatigable in the maintenance of its powers. The crime is partly the result of necessity and circumstances—the superstition of mixed ignorance and training. The same anomaly in America, and with the descendants of the ancient Puritans, must find some other explanation. Here, it was, undeniably; and I soon found that the Reverend Mr. Mowbray was not only useful (?) where he was, but that there were frequent occasions for his services. The sick had his prayers, and the burial at which he did not officiate was a subject of no little dissatisfaction among the living friends of the deceased. On the Sabbath, when the *business* of the community was not urgent, his preaching was well attended. Subsequently I was given to understand, that it was owing to the expression of some discontent on the part of one the assistants, that I was allowed the ghostly help of this gentleman on the morning of my execution, that led to the delay in carrying into effect the sentence of the outlaw chief, and so, accordingly, to my rescue. Complying with the suggestion of the subordinate, Bud Halsey sent for his chaplain, and thus my danger became noised abroad, so as to reach the ears of Helen and her father, in season to bring them to my rescue. You may take for granted, that, from that moment, I readily recognised the importance of a regular chaplain to a band of robbers. My bride made her appearance in all her beauty, and with all the usual becoming blushes. Beautiful she was, and the simplicity of her costume amply set off and distinguished the peculiarity of her charms. I forgot, as I surveyed her, the painful circumstances which had conducted me to this event. I thought of nothing but the passion with which she now filled me—how lovely she was in my eyes—how precious to my heart. I took her hand with rapture, and, for a moment, had no feeling but one of unalloyed happiness. But, even as the service proceeded, while my lips uttered the sacred responses, a dark cloud passed over my imagination. My eyes ceased to behold the actual, surrounding objects. I was transported to another region. I beheld another and very different sight. The good old, well ordered, well adorned hall at Leaside, with all its images of solemnity, mixed with comfort, rose up before my glance. My father and my mother—the one sternly contemplative, the other sad, but smiling, as if in spite of the numerous apprehensions that struggled about her maternal heart. Ah! could they conjecture where I stood, and how engaged—in what ceremony—so awful, so irrevocable, so important to their son—so interesting to themselves—in which they were not permitted to partake—of which they were not permitted to know! I felt a growing weakness in my eyes, mastered my resolution, spoke audibly the last responses, and clasped my bride to my bosom. With the kiss which I then pressed upon her lips, came a crowd of confused thoughts and inquiries. I was a husband at eighteen. An outlaw's daughter was my bride. Had I left the home of my father for this? What had I become? What was I to become? What was to be the fruit of this affair? What fate was before me? Was I, too, to become an outlaw? Was I for ever cut off from society and my father's home? I could not answer these inquiries, and, which was worse, I could not dismiss them. Was I happy? That was another question, the answer to which must be confided to the future!

CHAPTER XV.

But youth—the youth which has been accustomed to indulgence—lives so much in the gratification of its passions and desires, that reflection, which is the result of training and habit, does not often disturb the enjoyment of the present moment. As for happiness, this is, at no period, a proper question. We have only to live as long as we can, endure as sturdily as we can, and do our duty with our best strength and manhood. A lad of eighteen, brought up as I had been, to be very much his own master, is chiefly considerate of the day, and of what it shall bring forth. With a very different signification and commentary, the scripture apothegm is his—sufficient for the day is the evil thereof—and the good also. In boy language, I was happy, in spite of the momentary misgivings that disturbed me at the altar. I was a husband. I had taken the highest duties of manhood upon me, and this fact was an appeal to my vanity, which thus, in turn, became a minister to my other impulses. My wife was beautiful and accomplished, intelligent and gentle, tender, and full of love for me, giving me hourly proofs, not only that she regarded her happiness as complete, but that she was womanly solicitous of mine. Had all the circumstances of my marriage suited—had it taken place with the family sanction, and had her connections been such as I would have wished them, I could have found no better wife. She, by herself, was all that I could have desired; and, hurt, as I had been, in my pride, stung, mortified, and harassed, by the events which preceded my nuptials, my honey-moon was yet without a cloud. Bud Halsey kept out of sight, and, in our little islet and cottage, we revelled in all the intoxicating delight of a first passion gratified. We lay in the sun like two children, thoughtless of the coming on of night, thoughtless of all things but the dear shady solitude which love had peopled with its own ministering forms, all wooing and beautiful, all sweet and musical, all sympathetic and devoted to the tender mood which prevailed equally over the souls of both. Thus we walked and rode—rambled through silent groves, and, sitting on the trunks of fallen trees, under the shade of their mightier descendants, wove into blossoms, the pretty, petty fancies of a youth, that might well—at that period—have furnished a similitude for the first garden experience of our luckless ancestors. That honey-moon was certainly an Eden, while it lasted, to us both. But it was not to last. Helen, however, was not the one in our case to pluck the forbidden fruit. The error was mine. I have already said, or shown, that I was of an impetuous, impatient character, not disposed to forego my object, yet soon gratified, and restless after novelty. With such a person, the thing once attained is apt to lose its attractions, and it is sufficient to brush away the gold and beauty from the more delicate forms of human enjoyment, that we grasp them rudely to our embrace. The first enthusiastic burst of passion over, reflection followed, and then recurred to me, in all their force, those vexing and unanswerable questions which had disturbed me at the altar. What had I become? An outlaw? No! But next kin to one! Certainly, should the government of the United States, or of Mississippi, ever find it necessary to send a sufficient force into our swamp retreat, for the purpose of rooting out its profligate possessors, I must share their obloquy and punishment;—and, even if this fate were not to be apprehended, was the doom less humiliating and painful to which I was now apparently fated. It was forbidden me to leave the swamp! I had not even the rogue's privilege, but, as I refused to participate in the deeds of the outlaws, I was regarded as one not only not to be trusted, but one to be watched. The melancholy prospect was before me of wasting my days in a region in which I was a prisoner—denied even the indulgencies of the reprobates around me, and with no hope of a change for the better, unless by qualifying myself for the privileges of the ruffian, in the commission of his crimes. There was no outlet to society or ambition. I could neither hope for the external resources, nor for the distinctions of the world. My talents were denied a field of action. I was to rust disused, a sword in the scabbard, a shield against the wall, the blood-steed chafing in the stable, the mountain bird beating his wings against the bars of his cage. These reflections naturally followed, when the delights of my new condition became familiar. Even love is a food that can satisfy few men. It is the blanc-mange, the syllabubs, the comfits in the great feast of life. But we must beware how we make a meal of it. It is to be taken sparingly after other meats, and by way of giving them a relish. The only food that never cloys the human spirit, is the prosecution of our daily tasks, in obedience to the natural tendencies of our intellect and our training. These tasks performed, love consoles us in the shade, binds up our wounds, soothes us in our prostration and defeat, and cheers us with song and sentiment. But as we neither want song nor consolation always, so we may suffer love to wait for us in the shade, while we follow our employments in the sun. By attending to this wholesome rule, we shall discover, that, while the burden of labour diminishes, love undergoes increase; and from a sickly, and somewhat affected damsel, becomes a bright-eyed, cheerful matron, who rears our children with fruitful breakfast, and sees that dinner is ready for us, at the proper hour, when we return from work. But I did not philosophise after this fashion until long afterwards. In that hey-day of my hot youth, and while that first—would it were the last!—struggle was going on, I simply felt and deplored the ennui, without undertaking to ascertain what were its true sources. Had my reflective powers been equal to this, I should probably have been the better for it. But, as it was, seemingly remediless as the condition of things appeared, I was miserable without the hope of redress. The ardency of my love lessened, and, instead of now going forth ever with Helen, I stole forth more frequently alone. I wandered off into the deepest woods, and wearied at every step, with myself and everything around me, I still felt how much more wearisome it was to return. Still I strove to hide from my wife the discontent of which I was now myself fully conscious. I was generous enough, and man enough, to endeavour to conceal from her the signs of that inquietude which I too well knew she would ascribe to my lessening attachment. In her presence I strove to be cheerful, to smile, to meet her eye with the same expression of love in mine, which it had been so easy a task for me to exhibit until now. Nor was it always difficult to simulate this appearance. She was so really beautiful, with eyes of such dewy brightness, so gentle, so yielding and dependent, that really I could not but curse the capricious nature which had grown dissatisfied so soon, with a creature so truly excellent and charming. Still she hung upon my arm, yielded herself upon my bosom, sung to me in deep embowering woods, and by the petty chafing streams that ran through our swamp fastnesses, and still I thought at moments that I ought to be and was, satisfied and happy.

But these gleams were only transient. Love, alone, has no means of continuing its excitements, after conquest. With this event life begins, with all its solemn duties. Unless these duties provoke the fitting performance—unless the man then brings into exercise all the energies of his intellectual nature, and addresses them to the business which seems to be most particularly called for by the tendency of his *morale*—he cannot well be said to live, and none of his enjoyments will be lasting. This must be the fate of all persons brought up in idleness. Life, with such, must be a sort of mill-service, a perpetual rounding of the circle in a beaten track, which, as it demands no mental exercise, furnishes no mental supply, keeps up no mental life, and leaves the intellectual nature as thoroughly blind as horses are said to become, habituated to the same motive service which has afforded us the comparison above. But a truce to these reflections, which I did not then make. My wife began to discern the change in me. What change is there, however light, in the man she loves, which the woman will not discern? I soon saw that she felt the change. Perhaps, it was no small proof of my own continued attachment, that I could so soon discern that she had made the discovery. Of course I did my best to lessen this impression. I renewed my efforts to appear happy—we resumed our walks together—followed the same streams, sat beneath the same shade,—but we both felt that it was now a task to pursue the same life, which was once a pleasure only. The green and the freshness seemed to me to have gone from life—the glory and the gladness—we felt the misery which the departure had occasioned, but knew not, in our ignorance of heart and life, where to look for the remedy. It was soon very evident to me, that her father beheld the change. He looked more gravely when we met—more sadly—but without severity. On the contrary, his endeavours to console and to conciliate me were redoubled; and when in his society, I generally found myself more cheerful, and if not more reconciled to my imprisonment, at least more easily inclined, for the moment, to dismiss it from my thoughts. That he ascribed my demeanour to any change in my regards for his daughter, I did not imagine. He knew me better than I did myself. My own conscience reproached me with such a change. He, more wisely, ascribed it all to the natural impatience of my mind, under the novel restraints to which it was subjected—restraints which not only deprived me of all opportunity for its exercise, but denied me to see those friends and connections in whom I was naturally so deeply interested. As for poor Helen, she was still so loving, so considerate, so desirous to win me to pleasure, to see me happy—and failing, so sad,—that, when not thinking absolutely and only of myself, my heart smote me for its coldness to her. Coldness shall I call it? No! it was not coldness. I had not then any idea that any woman could be half so dear to me as she was, even in those moments when I felt least satisfied. But she was not to know this. My discontent increased, and at length settled down into positive clouds and gloom. I no longer made any effort to conceal it, and it was some consolation to me that my wife, with a prudence which is seldom exercised by wives, never once called upon me to account for it. She was content to do her best to cheer me, to prove that her love for me had not lessened, and she left to the delicate unpremeditated attentions of a fond heart, and tender solicitude, to heal those hurts, which any attempt to probe might only have rendered worse.

CHAPTER XVI.

MEANWHILE, I had become somewhat intimate with Mr. Mowbray, the reve end gentleman by whom I had been married. I had met him in some of my

rambles, and as he was a person of invincible self-esteem, he had contrived to keep with me, in spite of the evident coolness which I manifested towards him. His adroitness finally broke down my barriers of reserve, and I listened to him, ffer awhile, with tolerable patience, the unfavourable impressions of my mind

No. 6

gradually giving way, the more I was brought in contact with the offensive object. This is one of the most fruitful dangers which beset young men. I had reason afterwards to believe that Bud Halsey had instructed Mowbray to throw himself in my way, with the view to bringing me round to his purposes. This young man spoke with a vivacity which was very much akin to wit. He was sprightly, forcible, and pungent in his remarks, frequently novel and always audacious. That he was thoroughly unprincipled, need not be said, when it is remembered what he led and what principles he professed to teach. Perhaps there is no hypocrisy so complete and lamentable as that of the professor of religion, having the care of others, yet daily, and daringly, indulging in the most unscrupulous practices of sin.

"You are cool to me," he said one day, when I was more than usually depressed by the circumstances of my situation. He had joined me when I least looked for, and least wished, any such companionship.

"Why should we not be friends?" he continued, without giving me time to answer. "Here we are, both of us young fellows, neither wanting in stuff for conversation; why should we not be more frequently together? As we have a little world of our own here, why should we not make the most of it?"

"You may—you should," was my answer. "But you forget, it is your world, not mine."

"Make it yours—why not?"

"Thank you, but I have no taste for cutting throats or taking purses."

"Pshaw! I do not mean that. There are enough to do that without requiring either you or me. My taste as little inclines to it as yours."

"Why then are you here?"

"A truant disposition—like your own, perhaps. But now that we are both here, whether from choice or necessity, I am for making the most of the situation. Why should not you? Why, for example, should you mope alone in these woods, when you might have company?"

"Have I not? Are you not with me?"

"Yes; but I verily believe that you would rather have my room than my company."

"You could scarcely believe this, yet continue to give it me."

"You forget my profession!" he answered, with a laugh. "My religion compels me to seek the unhappy—my humility prevents me from heeding their rebuffs. I am for saving you, my friend, in your own spite,—for consoling you when, perhaps, you would prefer to drain the cup of bitterness to the dregs, through sheer obstinacy,—and for giving you my good company, always, when you are most oppressed with your own."

"Do you not incur some risk in this liberality? Intrusion does not always get off with a simple rebuff."

"Ah! you must not suppose that I carry my religion to excess. I do not tell you that I turn the other cheek that it may be smitten also. I have not yet reached that point of patience and forbearance, when it is agreeable to set up for a martyr. I have still a taste of the old leaven in me, and can lay on as well as my neighbour. But there need be no quarrel between us. Time sometimes hangs heavily on my hands here, as it evidently does on yours. If we were to meet oftener, it might weigh more lightly upon both. I have usually been considered a good fellow as a companion, and you seem a lad of mettle. You have sense and spirit. Let us see if we cannot help each other through the swamp—no bad figure for representing the dull days in this quarter. Come, now, let me be your guide for the next half hour, and I will show you some retreats here, which, I suspect, you have never seen before. What say you?"

I suffered him to lead me on. Indeed, I was now not only indifferent to the route which I should take, but somewhat regardless of the character of my companion. The last few weeks had made me tolerably reckless, and setting aside some of my scruples as I proceeded with him, I abruptly asked him for his history. I was anxious to get some insight into a character which seemed so curiously compounded.

"My history!" he answered. "You shall have it. It will scarcely interest you, but will do you good. You smile?"

"Yes!—why should you care whether it will do me good or not?"

"You mistake me somewhat. I have no wish to do you harm."

"What! not to involve in your meshes—make me an outlaw like yourself?"

"Pshaw, no! I care for this neither one way nor the other. My fault, indeed, is want of sympathy with my race."

"Why do you wish society, then—companionship—why seek mine?"

"Simply because I am selfish. Selfishness makes good companionship. I seek you for myself—for my own enjoyment, not yours, though I should have no sort of objection that you should gain by the communion. But you will know me better when you have heard my story. Here, we are secure. We have quite a pleasant shade. The trees arch here in cathedral fashion. The sun scarcely penetrates, except in little droplets of light, and the effect is very much such as we should suppose it would produce through the stained windows of a gothic abbey. The breeze comes up very pleasantly from that water. Your wanderings have brought you here before."

The spot was very beautiful, with an interest derived entirely from the foliage, and the mixed effect of shadow and subdued sunlight. There was no inequality in the landscape. The ground was perfectly level, with a slight slope to the water's edge. The creek wound semi-circularly about us, and along the opposite edges was lined with a thick fringe of canes, from whence shot up the gigantic spire of cotton-wood tree or pine. We sat down upon the shaft of a fallen tree, and, after a few preliminaries, my companion began his story as follows:—

MR. MOWBRAY'S STORY.

You see in me an instance of the injurious effects of endeavouring to force goodness into the heart by a sort of hot-house process. Unless by miracle, by the direct intervention of Deity himself, you cannot make a man a saint before his time. There must be trials and preparations, by which to subdue stubborn tendencies, irregular passions, and a dogged, inflexible will. I do not pretend to set before you the sort of training which should be employed for this purpose. It is enough that I had none of it; and, with just enough of prudence—cunning, perhaps, would be the proper word—I suffered myself to be converted into an apostle, before I had ever thought to overcome the natural desire which every man is supposed to have to be a sinner. I was born of good family, in one of the oldest of our northern cities. I need scarcely tell you that the name I bear is not the one to which I was born. I was tenderly nurtured, and well educated. My father was not only distinguished in the social, but in the intellectual world. He was a man of profound scientific and literary acquirements—highly and equally esteemed for his moral virtues, and mental superiority. It was, perhaps, my misfortune in particular that he died, just at that period when, emerging from boyhood into youth, my training required the firm hand and the calm thought of experienced wisdom. My boyhood gave signs of intellectual promise. My youth had other developments. I was wild and vicious, full of blood and passions—eager in the attainment of my object, and not over scrupulous—speaking within certain limits—of the process by which this was to be done. But the tenderness of relatives, and the sympathies of friends, kindly charged all these developments to the exuberance of youth. I was simply sowing those wild oats, which, I am disposed to think, must be sown by all men, sooner or later, at some period in their lives. The misfortune is, that, in my case, sufficient time was not allowed me to sow my tares, when I was required to enter upon another sort of harvest. It is scarcely to be wondered at if the tares and wheat came up pretty equally together.

Our family was reduced in fortune and straitened after my father's death, to such a degree that it became necessary—painful necessity!—that hereafter the sons should sow that they might reap. We were all required to work for our bread, and the question was, in what way we should encounter a necessity so humiliating without losing the rank and consideration of gentlemen. This inquiry, of course, involved a farther necessity, not only of finding a proper employment, but one neither mechanical nor laborious—one that would neither soil the hands nor lessen the leisure. Two of my brothers were already lawyers, one was a physician, and as both these professions were already crowded, it was unanimously concluded among my friends and relatives, that I was to be a parson. Not that I had shown any of those moral qualities which would naturally incline a devout parent to see a future saint in the son. I was neither humble in spirit, forbearing in anger, nor gentle in my deportment. I had nothing devotional about me. I had the most indomitable will,—I had the most fierce, selfish, and passionate desires. I had no single requisite for the business of the pulpit, but such as belonged to the simple intellect. As I do not scruple to declare my moral deficiences, so I do not hesitate to avow my intellectual adequacy to the work before me. I was warm, animated, fluent—intense in my earnestness to the last degree, and in the employment of illustration and figure, equally forcible and ready. I was destined, so everybody said—regarding nothing but my mental endowments—to figure as a new Boanerges in the church.

But, at first, I was just as unwilling as I was unprepared, to enter upon a duty for which my mind had no sympathy. If I inclined to anything in particular, it was to the law. To the forum I looked as the scene of my future triumphs—as the field of my future eminence and fame. But I was made to see with eyes of others. I was shown the crowded state of the bar. I was shown the struggling and always half distressed situation of my brothers, neither of whom had, as yet, earned the salt for his porridge. They were still an incumbrance on the very little property which the misfortunes of the family had spared to my mother. Nobody seemed to regard the moral requisites of the churchman, as at all necessary. Nothing, at least, was said on this part of the subject. It was chosen for me as a handicraft—a trade—by which I was to jump into a snug living, and have the farther privilege of choosing, as my own pecular property, one of the richest ewes of my flock. These results were continually spoken of, as a matter of course, by all around me. They formed a familiar topic with the community. Religion had become so much of a profession, among laity and clergy, that the trading results were habitually look to, by both parties, as a legitmate subject of consideration. In old communities, which have been, from immemorial time, distinguished for high social tone, the maintenance of social appearances becomes, finally, the leading object with all parties; and all that is then requisite with the individual is, that he should respect his own cloth. It does not matter that he should not deserve to wear it. The only important particular is, that he should wear it with decency. The rule holds with religion as with medicine or law—it is ranked with those as an ordinary means of employment, and by many, as one of the most inferior. Indeed, one of my objections to adopting this profession, arose from hearing it so frequently spoken of as one that required little or no ability. The common saying amongst us, was, "when a fellow is too stupid to be a lawyer or doctor, you must make him a parson." There was room for the sarcasm. We had many boobies in the pulpit. There was little eloquence and less thought. Some of our divines were able men, but they had grown tired of warring against those feminine tastes in the audience, which called for little more than common-places and declamation. Women, of whom most of our American audiences are composed, do no little towards the degradation of the clergy. It requires but little skill and management among them, to win the reputation of great piety; and still less ability, to secure that of eloquence and talent. I have frequently amused myself, during my brief career in the pulpit, in preaching nonsense-sermons, that were simply complicate and high-sounding, larded at frequent intervals, with biblical phrases, with which they were commonly acquainted. I observed that, on such occasions, my preaching always gave the most satisfaction. I have always been applauded for these sermons, and more than once called upon to print them,—but I too well knew that what would be tolerated in the pulpit, would never pass the gauntlet of the press,—though, towards the close of my career,—when I was willing to break with my congregation, I was more than half tempted to comply with their wishes, and put forth a volume to show how easily and admirably they had been gulled. But I anticipate.

It was with considerable reluctance that I was brought to regard the wishes of my friends and family with favour. It was only when it became evident that this was the only way in which I could get my bread, and get it buttered too, that I consented. Promises, assurances the most positive, were held out to me, not only of a church, but of a wife, both of them the most elegant and eligible in every point of view. Then there was the influence, the authority, which the cloth exercised ; and, this was my own thought, and that which rendered the suggestion of my friends more palatable—then there was the distinction, the eminence to be attained by the pressing, persevering and highly endowed intellect. Won by all these considerations, I became a student in divinity, put on the grave suit and demeanour, and went to my studies with the resolution not to forego the cakes and ale, if they were to be had at the expense only of a little hypocrisy. My character was one of great energy, and might have been of great power, had it been less capricious. As it was, I devoted myself to study with that earnestness which distinguished me in the prosecution of all my plans. I was late and early at my studies. Ambitious to a very high degree, the goal immediately before me was one of human distinction. My industry and zeal became the popular theme in our little world. Old men looked upon me with wonder—old women with admiration. I was sought by the grave and the senitors of both sexes. I listened with reverence, and when I spoke, dealt in sententious apothegms. I practised my part with a degree of skill, which, perhaps, was only remarkable for the consistency which my character displayed, in spite of my passions and caprices, during the tedious period of my novociate. I was successful, and the time arrived when I should take orders and be admitted to the priesthood. The ceremony you have witnessed. I need not describe it. It is enough for me to say, that, solemn as it is, terrible as is the trust which the neophyte undertakes, and awful as appear the responsibilities accruing from his obligations, my mind strove in vain to concentrate its thoughts upon the procedings. My heart had nothing to do with them. It was communing apart with its own vanities— yearning with its merely human passions, and canvassing at every interval, the hopes, and fears, and fancies which occupy the spirit of the worlding. But a little distance from me stood a maiden whom my eyes had long singled out as the object of their desires. I saw her not then, but felt that she was there. Pure and meek, she had long efore won the affections of one who was neither pure nor meek. Unknown to erself, I had already made a conquest of her. That I knew. I was no smal! idge of the female heart. I had fathomed the intricacies of hers, and resolving at she should be my prize, I had adapted my deportment to those tastes which, felt assured, distinguished her nature ; and even at that moment when devoting yself, mind and spirit, irrevocably to God and the Redeemer, I thought of either, except vaguely, uncertainly, and without being at all touched by the profound depth of the obligation which my lips had sworn. I thought only of the ortal beauty whose spirit seemed effused about me,—whose presence I felt was ear,—whose eyes, I wellkn w, watched every step in the progress of the ceremony, ith the intensity of the purest human love. I was ordained—I had attained one f the objects of my hypocritical endeavour, and the struggle now was for the rest.)id I attain them ? Did I doubt of their attainment ? You shall hear!

Yet, do not misunderstand me. If you suppose that I did not strive after eligion, when I had once undertaken the study, you will do me injustice. It may e that I did not strive enough,—with all my heart, with all my mind, and with ll my strength, as we are required—but I certainly did not set out to persevere a merely cold system of hypocrisy. I was not unwilling to become what I wished to profess. I strove, I studied, I thought, I asked. It is not improbable that in study, thought, and inquiry, I sometimes forgot prayer. I did not pray enough. I never acquired the first most necessary frame of mind. I had no humility, and this want—had not my congregation been wilfully and beyond redemption, blind—must have betrayed me long before I wilfully betrayed myself. I was myself deceived. I sometimes fancied that my condition of mind was good—was what it should be. This was during my noviciate. I was never deceived in this manner after the assumption of the duties of the priesthood. No! no! I knew myself by this time, and the struggle thence was simply to keep the real nature from any and every exhibition inconsistent with that which I had put on. But of this hereafter.

My friends kept their promises. They procured me a church, and noble congregation. I was at once installed into a good living, and, very soon after, chose from among my flock, the fair and truly good creature, upon whom, for so long a season, my eyes had been set. She did not with feminine subtlety endeavour to hide from me the joy she felt when I declared my passion for her. " She was too, too happy." Such were the words muttered in my bosom, as she yielded herself to my embrace. We were married, and with herself she brought me a handsome property. Was I satisfied? Was I happy? No! I had reaped the reward of my toils,—I had gained all the objects which had been proposed to me, when I first commenced my career of hypocrisy. Station, fortune, fame!—for I had grown famous in our little world—but, I did not deceive myself! I was not only not happy, but I was ill at ease. The constraint upon my nature was a bondage which I yearned to throw off. I was like the captive in the toils! True, I was surrounded by plenty—beauty was in my arms—fortune at my feet—crowds of admirers followed in my steps— troops of friends gathered at my bidding—my voice could still or rouse the multitude—but I lived a lie!—and every moment of breath and being was a pang. I do not say that my moral sense revolted at this condition. No! it was my blood, my passions, which, restrained, in order to the acquisition of an object, threatened momentarily to revenge themselves for the unnatural and uncongenial bondage into which my will had forced them.

Meanwhile, had the theatre of my mind been such as it could have chosen, I should have been content. My mind was fully exercised. In the habit of intensifying on every subject, I was necessarily a most enthusiastic preacher. Never was the vehemence of true zeal and genuine piety more life-like than mine. They attributed this vehemence to my extraordinary zeal and piety, when it was only the natural working of my blood. In a disputation in behalf of atheism, I should have been equally vehement. It was the characteristic of my temperament. But nobody inquired into this. It was enough that I kept them from sleeping;—that, all animation myself, I enlivened them Of course, nobody who goes to church applies to himself the denunciations of the preacher. The simple fact of church-going seems sufficiently to satisfy the ordinary mind; and people fancy they are in a very comfortable sort of trim for heaven when they yield audible responses to the preacher, and never forget to make their genuflexions at the appropriate moment. I saw and understood all this, and was by no means unsparing of the scourge. I laid it on with heavy hand, and, assured in my own heart of my own miserable hypocrisy, this conviction furnished an additional reason why I should cry aloud, and spare not, in dealing with the sinfulness of others. In this sort of excitement I lived—I drew my breath. My blood demanded excitements, and, dammed up in its natural tendencies, was forced to find outlet and utterance through other avenues. Was there a controversy with another sect or church, I headed it;—was there a new mission to be established, I counselled it, urged it, and compelled it. Furious in my struggles, I made a battle field wherever I came, and while all were delighted and wondering at my zeal in the cause of the Redeemer, I brought nothing but religious uproar, and confusion, and disputation wherever I appeared.

Had my congregation been only half-witted, had they but bestowed upon the subject but half the thought which the meanest of them gave to his ordinary worldly concerns—they must have mo:e than suspected my sincerity. The very excess of my fervour, must have made them doubt its purity and source. But a few years before—not five,—I had been notoriously a very vicious youth—noted for excesses, and recognised, with difficulty, any restraint. On a sudden, the change had been effected. Now, it is not denied that this change of heart, can be effected by ruling powers of Providence, at any moment,—in a moment,—in the twinkling of an eye ,—but this change of heart must subdue the heart,—must teach patience, humility, and moderation. The individual must remember, with horror, his own pastoffences, and must, in fear and trembling, approach those of others. If such a change produces any external results at all, it must be in this very particular. It must lead to great toleration. Mercy, not denunciation, will be the language of-the newly reformed—humility, not arrogance,—patience, not imperiousness. There was no such show in me. On the contrary, never did self-appointed legate, more freely use God's thunder. The Pope was not more imperious, when, setting his feet upon the necks of princes, he insisted that the act was done in his two-fold character, of man and father,—than was I in dealing with those very faults and vices in others, in which, but a little while before, I had notoriously indulged myself. But I had no help. My passionate and imperious nature was resolute to speak out, exrcise itself, consistently with the part which I was now compelled to play, to the mockery of God and man alike.

But there was a change at hand. In the midst of my successes—when I stood in the regards of the community as little less than a God—when thousands followed, and, without knowing or suspecting it, hundreds of poor women worshipped me— when my eloquence was most briliant, my exhortations most urgent, my severities and rebukes most pungent and excoriating—my secret was discovered. It could not be concealed from one who had been among the first to follow—to worship me, and to love—my wife! Without being a philosopher, her moral and religious instincts were true ;—there are religious instincts in every nature, to be brought out by education ;—to her my secret was betrayed on numerous occasions. Seeing me at home—in disabille—without those restraints of decorum in which I garbed my-salf for the enconnter with others, she soon had sufficient proof that I was no saint. My passions, my temper,—my real nature—was not to be hid from her, and when the applauses of others filled her ears—when her friends eulogised my virtues, and congratulated her on her good fortune, in the possession of such a saint,—she only wept. She was no more to be flattered into happiness, than she was to be deceived by externals. She could not conceal her convictions and feelings from me. Long did she strive to do so, but her Christian spirit triumphed. She revealed to me the extent of her discoveries, her fears, her wretchedness,—she implored me to repent in sincerity, or, at least, to forbear the profession which could only be dis-honoured by my hypocrisy. She did not use this language, but this was the sub-stance of what she said. She employed the gentlest forms of speech, such as were dictated by a still devoted heart and an ardent passion. But I flung her from me. She had doubly offended me, as she had discovered my secret, and, in doing so, had shown me that the love which she bore for me did not amount to the adora-tion which alone I sought. My desires were of that imperious sort, that would admit of nothing qualifying in the homage which I received. The whole heart for me, or none,—and it must be a thoroughly confiding heart, a perfect faith, never questioning, always submitting, always assured—with the old-time loyality of the serf—that the king could do no wrong. I flung her from me,—it was the Sabbath, —and, proceeding to my pulpit, I made the high ceiling echo again with the intensity of my exhortations. I was never more eloquent. I was stung, provoked, exasparated,—and, at such moments, my vehemence was a torrent that defied all let or hindrance. But my wife went not with me. From that day forth she was never more an auditor of mine. She prayed at home—in secret, and I well knew that her prayers were for me. But her firmness vexed me. Her superiority wounded me. Her keenness of remark annoyed me. She was no longer to be deceived ; and, whatever might be her external bearing—and it was exemplary]

—I felt that, though, perhaps, secure of her obedience,—I was no longer secure of her respect.

Thus passed several months, and, with my domestic relations such as I have described them,—the constraints of my public career became more irksome. The redeeming circumstances by which I had been consoled, the applause and admiration—though not by any means lessened,—began to stale upon my estimation. The field was a confined one—the audience was the same—I had already heard their wonder—it no longer gave me pleasure. It no longer rewarded my eloquence or stimulated my exertions. I felt, more and more, with the progress of every day, the intensest cravings for my freedom. That denied, what was all in possession? The passion grew to morbidness, and, but for one event, the catastrophe which finally happened, would at once have taken place. My wife brought me a child—a fine, fair son, that, for the time appealing to the more ordinary human feelings, reconciled me somewhat to the restraints of my position. Caressing him, I felt how sweet it was to be a father. My wife seized the moment when she saw me most tenderly engaged in fondling him, to renew her entreaties and exhortations,—and, had my passion been less like that of a demon, I must have been overcome. I answered her gloomily, almost fiercely, and left the room. It is not easy for you to imagine my feelings from this slight survey of my position. No man, whatever be his nature, feels quite at ease in daily communion of the most confiding and affectionate character, with those whom he defrauds. Such was the relation in which I stood with my flock. Besides, mine was a diseased nature, and the fraud was one of the most extreme and vital character. Every encounter with my congregation was productive of a struggle, and you may suppose many more struggles of conscience and prudence must have grown out of a position which exposed me to some of the most peculiar temptations. The office which I held is one of peculiar and scarcely limitable privileges and powers. The trial must be a great one, even where the professor is a really good man, conscious only of the best purposes. What was mine? That I yielded—that I did not always struggle,—that I frequently abused my trust, you may conjecture—it is not for me to relate. But, usually, the vicious man, if busy without, in a practice which wrongs his neighbour, is not often met at home with those rebukes and reproaches, on that account, which he does not hear abroad. If he himself does not offend against his wife, she is very apt, readily, to forgive his offences against others. Not so, mine! Her love for me, based originally on her convictions of my piety, was not sufficient to keep her silent when my secret was in her possession. Her love for purity was greater. Her loyalty to God was superior to that which she felt for me ; and for this, I was indignant. Half-formed calculations, plans and purposes, of remedy and relief, began to fill my brain ; and at this time, had my sermons been scanned by a suspicious judgment, they would have been found distinguished by a tone of bitterness and sarcasm, if not contempt, which, addressed as they were to my audience, would have tended, in no great degree, to render them satisfied either with their seats or my eloquence. It was then, too, that I amused myself at their expense, with those nonsensical sermons, of which I have already given you some idea. You may imagine it did not increase my estimate of the value of their judgments, even when shown in my own eulogies, when I found them particularly delighted with these specimens of rigmarole. Having reached this stage, can you not guess the rest? Having gained all that I could gain by the constraints which I had put upon my nature—having found these gains unsatisfactory, if not worthless—what had I to bind me to my home? My wife pitied rather than loved me, and the flock by which I might have been loved, was the object of my own scorn and dislike. I left them,—and, with a sense of joy in my new found liberty, which I should find myself at a loss for language to describe. You cannot conceive the satisfaction which I felt in writing a farewell letter to the heads of the church. I revenged myself in that for long months of bondage. I filled it with passages of most withering scorn. I avowed my own hypocrisy, but reminded them of theirs, and asserted my better claims to God's favour, by the very proceeding by which, in the estimation of the world, I had er-

nounced God himself—namely, my resignation from a station to which, as I alleged, scarcely one of us had any proper pretensions. That I had ceased to be a hypocrite, was a sufficient reason to hope for my final regeneration as an honest man. This step was taken in connection with several others. I renounced home, and wife, and child, at the same moment. It was some proof, perhaps, that I was not utterly reckless, when I felt unwilling any longer to look them in the face. I had means,—I had money,—and, passing to New Orleans, I found an element

of sufficient elasticity for my moral nature, in its various theatres of pleasure and dissipation. I took ample revenge for my long abstinence. I drank—I gamed—and to make a long story short, I am here! You look at me with horror! Hear me! I believe there is a God, and I believe there is a devil. We are the subjects of one or the other, and if one rejects our services, as not worthy of him, it is scarcely possible to suppose that the other will not have need of them. We cannot well war with the direction given us. Miracles may do much, but there is

No. 7.

little wisdom in waiting for them. I would if I could—but I despair. I toil with the conviction that I am a doomed man—doomed from my birth. The appalling feeling is over me, that under this doom I will perish—perish for ever ! That this high spirit is utterly outcast—that this high thought, which I have betrayed, and his glorious mind which I have defrauded of its privileges, and degraded to evil iurposes—will become extinct. I shudder with the thought of annihilation, since it is only the hope of immortality that moves the moral, and satisfies the intellectual nature. You see that I do not exult in this depravation. You see that I relate the story of the past without pleasure ! That I suffer ! That I feel the folly and the sin of all that miserable boy-career, begun in narrow schemes, and finishing in shocking perversion. You ask why I do not change—why I stubbornly live in sin—why I do not regret, repent, retrieve ? What if I tell you of my tears, my prayers, my repentance ? I do weep ! But what is repentance that does nothing but weep ? This is mine ! I do nothing ! My repentance is without results ! I cannot pray—I cannot toil—in any work of good ! There is a terrible power that denies me—that keeps me back from the very first performances of repentance ! I dare not ask what is this power ! I only feel that its presence is upon me, baffling my purpose, and mocking at all my hopes ! It never can be withdrawn ! I am not suffered to approach the throne of God—I am doomed, utterly doomed, of **heaven !**"

*   *   *   *   *   *   *

Thus ended this extraordinary narrative. The speaker had risen, long before he came to the close, under the exciting character of what he said. He now sat down, but, suddenly, again rose to his feet, as if to depart. There had been a very decided and remarkable change in his appearance, during its progress. At the beginning, his features had been marked by a good-humoured indifference, a sort of easy, careless, good-natured recklessness, which half reconciled me to a person, against whom my prejudices were naturally strong at first. But, as he proceeded, he became excited in his narrative, and very soon illustrated, by his example, the characteristic of intensity, which he insisted upon as so prominent in his temperament. At the close, and when he pronounced those scarcely coherent, but very solemn sentences, with which he abruptly finished his narrative, his features grew dark. There was a wild and troubled expression in his eyes, which were sombre and restless, as some deep pool which secret fires are troubling. His lips were parted and the corners drooped, while his breast laboured with emotions, which must have aptly corresponded with those which his words expressed. The awful thoughts which had fallen from him, if really entertained, were well calculated to awaken the most fearful agonies in his breast. To what a dreadful approach had he come ! Upon what a precipice did he stand ; and how wretched and demoniac the sort of reasoning from which he proposed to draw his consolation. We may suppose that when Lucifer broke finally with Heaven, and had no more hope, that he consoled himself by some such philosophy. He was not in the mood, nor I in the vein, for farther conversation. At such a moment, any attempt at exhortation on my part would have been as injudicious as impertinent. We walked together for a space in silence. I need not say how much my respect for this unhappy person had increased, from hearing his story. I say respect—because it was now evident to me, that his position and practices were not such as were agreeable to him. He was wretched, and the worm of remorse was already busy at his vitals. In this was my hope on his behalf, though it was evidently not his own. There is some hope for the sinner who is miserable—none for him who is insensible. As we reached the place where he had joined me and were about to separate, he turned to me—and said warningly,—

"I had forgotten ! Be cool, be cautious, in what you design. Do nothing hastily ! Bud Halsey already suspects you, and he is master here. His brother can do nothing. Be warned. I would befriend you."

"What mean you ?" I demanded.

"Nothing but what I have said. It is what you mean, that is the question

Bud Halsey has noticed your discontent. He suspects its cause. He suspects you, your wife, his brother. He has his eye upon you all! Beware."

He disappeared in another instant, and musing upon what he said, I made my way homewards.

———

CHAPTER XVII.

WHAT were my designs? The last word—the warning caution which Mowbray had suggested, produced a closer degree of self-examination than I had ever before undertaken. I had no designs. I was aware of none; but that it was expected of me that I should entertain some, naturally led me to them. Was I to be fettered in this way all my life; my youth lost; my better energies swallowed up in such a miserable sphere of imbecility as that in which I found myself—release from which seemed only obvious on terms of still worse degradation? The thought was inexpressibly humiliating. From humiliation I got strength—I got resolve. My purpose suddenly adopted, was to fly from my prison—to devote all my energies, all my intellect, to this one purpose. But art was necessary—cunning—I was to foil the devil at his own game—with his own weapons. To this resolve I rushed, ere I reached the cottage of Bush Halsey. There, I found my wife awaiting me. I threw off the air of despondency which had possessed me. The simple determination to be doing something had its effect in relieving me from the mental prostration under which I had suffered. I met Helen with a degree of buoyancy which I had never shown before. My rude laughter, and violent mirth, made her look at me with surprise, but it was a surprise not unmixed with pleasure. She congratulated me and herself upon the change, and, in the belief that I was happy as she wished me, and, quite content with herself—of which my late sullenness had made her somewhat doubtful—she surrendered herself up to the feeling of joy which, for the time, had neither doubt nor qualification. In these feelings of satisfaction, Bush Halsey shared. He had beheld my despondency with dissatisfaction, and readily divined the cause. But he could see no remedy. He knew his brother—the tyrannical nature, by which, himself governed, he governed all others; and, believing that I had no escape from the swamp, he could only counsel me to the sort of resignation by which he himself was reconciled to it. But the change which my deportment had undergone, if it deceived both himself and daughter, did not long deceive the latter, or she began to doubt the purity and propriety of its origin. Women are close observers and arrive, by the keenest instincts, at the truth in all things which much affect the objects whom they love. Whatever might be the success of my practice upon others, its tendency was more than doubtful to her, and, after a few weeks, she was less satisfied with my violent good spirits than she had been at first. These alone, perhaps, would not have disquieted her, but, by this time, I had become rather a frequent associate with the outlaw parson. The flexibility of this man was wonderful. He had left me, on the day when I had heard his narrative, looking more like a maniac than a man. Never could I suppose that the same person would ever smile again. The next day, he met me with a obscene jest. It was one of the characteristics of his temperament to be easily moved by the passing influence, whether grave or gay—a sort of moral character to receive its dark or bright aspects from the colours with which he came in contact. I found him always thus capricious;—at one moment gloomy, even to ferocity, and sometimes touched with a sort of religious fanaticism that would have done honour to the ruggedest Bare-bones of the long parliament. The next day, he was the courtier—

all gravity and smiles, and as loose in his morals as the most reckless cavalier of
the court of Charles the Second—as courtly as Waller, and as licentious as Roches-
ter,—as sentimental sometimes as the one, and again as filthily witty as the other.
He realised the extremes of character more suddenly, in the same person, and frequently on the same day, than any other man I ever met. I confess that I was
not unfrequently pleased with his society—his wit—his eloquence—his sentiment,
He had all upon occasion, and, had he been an adroit man, might, I believe, have
led me as he pleased ; but he was totally devoid of judgment—had none of that moral
prudence which makes the great politician ; and, while he won at one moment, he
too frequently offended all my tastes, and disgusted me at another. I sought him,
however, and this flattered him. I was rather superior as a companion to those with
whom he ordinarily associated, and, in the better capacity which I brought to appre-
ciate his merits, he showed himself very accessible on the score of mine. In the new
pleasure which I occasionally found in his society, in the excitement which it
afforded and offered me, and in the prosecution of the plan which I had hit upon
for extricating myself from the meshes in which I was bound, I sought him frequently. He was not the person to pry very deeply into the sources of the
pleasure which he received, nor to analyse those motives in others, the results of
which afforded him the society which he desired ; he seemed to take for granted,
with that vanity which was a large feature in his character, that I sought him
because of his intellect. I encouraged the idea, made frequent appeals to his
judgment, and, by getting him to dilate upon various passages and portions of his
story, directed his thoughts upon himself rather than to mine. In this way I
brought not only him but others to the conviction that I was fast losing my superior
moral standard, and reconciling myself to such as were paramount in the swamp.
Bud Halsey looked on me with more complacency, and not unfrequently contrived
to join the parson and myself in the long rambles which we now so frequently
took together ; he had occasionally a word for me of more particular favour, and
took care to confirm, by sentences of mingled sneer and compliment, those
impressions, which he fancied had been conveyed by my companion to my
mind.

"You will be a man yet!" was his frequent phrase, as he left us for his other
objects. "Your eyes are opening."

But the circumstances which gave him satisfaction now, afforded none to his
brother, Bush Halsey or my wife. Their attachment to me, as I have intimated,
rather than said, arose in part from the tenacious firmness with which I had held
to my virtues. I have endeavoured to show that Bush Halsey was the victim of
his own imbecility, as well as of circumstances. A good man, meaning well, and
with an excellent mind, he was yet controlled entirely by the superior will of his
brother, a man of inferior intellect, of bad habits and character, but of indomitable energies, and unrelaxing determination. It was his own misery that, unwilling to face bankruptcy and its consequences, in the civilised community in
which he had lived like a nobleman, he was yet compelled to rear up his only child,
a girl, in contact with the wretched profligates among whom I found him. But,
once a slave, such a man always remains a slave. From the moment that he
yielded to the suggestion of his brother, and fled from his creditors to the wilderness, from that moment he yielded himself up to a bondage, from which he did
not now hope to set himself free. But that his child should grow up in such a
situation, with no escape from such a life, was to him a source of perpetual suffering. Elegant, himself, in his tastes, he had tutored hers, with a degree of
watchfulness and skill which can better be conjectured than detailed, and it was
with a feeling of exultation, therefore, that he hailed the circumstance, already
narrated, by which I had become her husband. Still, I do not mean to say that
he counselled, encouraged, or in any wise contributed to those arrangements of
his brother, by which that event was precipitated. Let me do him the justice to
say, that I verily believe the event, as it did happen, was distasteful to him. His
simple wish, as he frankly avowed to me afterwards, was that we should grow
together, by the natural tendencies of a sympathetic passion, and he did not

believe that his brother would seriously oppose my departure from their retreat, when my connection with Helen should become indissoluble. He did not know the despotical nature of that man—he did not conceive it possible that such a connection, as that which Bud Halsey acknowledged with the outlaws, could so completely subdue and set at nought the natural ties of kindred, flesh, and blood. He had yet to learn how terribly and entirely this was to be done hereafter.

It will be easy to understand how, even to him, not less to my wife, the idea that I was about to be beguiled from my virtue, by the subtleties of Mowbray, was of intolerable annoyance. He had indulged himself in the hope, that I was to restore his daughter to society. For himself he had no serious cares on this subject. He, too, would like to run to society. He lived among the outlaws in a sort of Coventry, and distrusting them, and half distrusted by them. But he was no longer so youthful as to feel deeply the privation, except on account of one whose happiness was truly so much dearer than his own. He did not doubt that the time would come, when I should be suffered to go free, and he shrunk with horror from the thought that, meanwhile, I should be guilty of any course of conduct, which should lessen my desire to return, or affect my peace of mind and security when I did so. The changes in my deportment surprised him, and, as in the case of his daughter, at the first blush, gave him pleasure. They had both been disposed to ascribe my previous gloom to a lessening of my regard for the latter—to the staling of a boyish passion in possession of its object ; and a change in this respect in my conduct, was too grateful at first sight, to render them at all desirous of seeking farther into its causes. But when my intimacy with Mowbray was remarked — when, too, it was seen that I betrayed more curiosity, more sympathy—with the proceedings of the outlaws—and when Bud Halsey began to regard me with favour, every apprehension of poor Helen was aroused. The favour of her uncle seemed to her one of the most doubtful and dangerous of signs. The danger seemed conclusive, when, one morning, Bud Halsey sent me my horse. The brave animal had been taken from me, at my first coming, I had not been permitted to see him since, and when, with a sentiment of pride and pleasure which I could not conceal, I went forth, laid my hand upon his neck, and heard him whinny his recognition as he heard my voice,—then all her suspicions seemed confirmed. I was about to leap upon him, with all that gush of unmeasured exultation, which youth feels, confident of strength, buoyant with prospects of assured success, and in the possession of one of those agents of power and speed in the employment of which the impetuous nature feels all that enthusiasm and delight which grows out of the innate union and joint action of blood and brain ;—my hand was on his neck, my foot in the stirrup—when Helen called me to her side.

"Go not yet, dear Henry—come with me first—but a moment. I would speak with you."

I confess to a little reluctance at quitting the animal, even at the solicitation of one so dear. But I followed her. There was nobody besides in the cottage. Her father had gone out on a ramble. When I joined her in the chamber to which she had returned, she at once, and passionately, putting her hand upon my arm, thus addressed me :—

"Oh, Henry, forgive me, but I fear you, I suspect you !"

" Suspect me ?—of what, dear Helen ?"

" This horse, this new favour of my uncle, your intimacy with that Mr. Mowbray, all make me tremble lest they seduce you to their evil practices—lest you should be tempted,—lest you should fall ! Oh, Henry, be not tempted, be firm, go not with them to do evil. Go not,—for my sake, Henry, for your own sake ;—go not, go not !"

I kissed her, oh ! how fondly—pressed her to my bosom—and while the tears gathered in her eyes—while she clung to me with continued pleading,—I begged her to be quiet—to believe me still. It was necessary, however, that I should maintain appearances, and, breaking from her, I hurried to horse, and proceeded to join Mowbray in a canter which he proposed. How I felt myself, once more on horseback! What a feeling of pride it inspires, mounted on a noble steed who knows his own strength, and rejoices in the free play of his majestic limbs. My horse knew his rider, and I him, and as I rode forth to meet Mowbray, I found myself calculating the chances of a long chase, through swamp and through brier, against any, the best mettled, in the camp of the outlaws.

CHAPTER XVIII.

It will be unnecessary that I should enter into the details of the game which I had taken it in hand to play. Of the numerous daily interviews I had with Mowbray, and others of the outlaws, I shall say little. Let it suffice that I flattered myself with having fooled them all to the top of their bent. Even Bud Halsey, I at length grew satisfied, had became convinced that I was ready to thrust out my cold iron, and cry 'stand!' to a true man, whenever he should give the signal. In this, the probabilities favoured me. It was natural enough that a youth of my age and temper, situated as I was at the moment, should soon overcome the scruples of my education, in an anxiety to feel my freedom once more—nay, that my principles should very soon become corrupted, breathing such a rogues' atmosphere, and in daily contact with some of the choicest specimens of scoundrelism. I had striven, in playing my part, not to suffer it to appear that I made the transition too easily from a rugged honesty to a loose indifference to all its exactions. On the contrary, at first, I allowed it to appear that my chief pleasure was in being once more on horseback. I next suffered Mowbray to perceive that his conversation interested me. I laughed heartily at his jests;—he had no small powers of humour, and could hit off a ludicrous picture in low life with the extravagance and felicity of Lover. By little and little, I let myself be led to association with others, and, finally, to partake in their amusements. The outlaws were generally great card-players, and Mowbray himself was an adept. They had other amusements, some of which were even of less intellectual character. Quoits, hurling the bar, and the Indian ball-play, were in common use, at moments of leisure ;—and, for the indulgence of these amusements, they had more than one fine amphitheatre, formed by natural but small prairie spots in the swamp. Pistol and rifle shooting, I readily joined in, for reasons that will be understood. It gave me practice in the weapons upon which, could I secure them, it might be that I should have to depend;—though, when I saw how expert were the outlaws generally with them, I shuddered at the idea of encountering them. I have seen them frequently trim their dog's ears and tails by rifled pistols, at ten or twelve paces; and there was one of them, an Alabamian, by the name of Brewton, that could, at every shot, hit a half dollar piece while falling, which he himself had thrown into the air. I could do nothing like this, but I could lay my bullet at twelve paces within the circle of a man's breast, and I did not care, for such purposes as I had in view, to do better than that.

In these sports Bud Halsey now frequently joined us, and, if you can suppose such a thing as civility in a bear, then was he civil to me. He had a sort of rough, condescending pleasantry about him, when in a good humour, which greatly increased his popularity with the men, but which, as it was a seeming condescension, was more offensive to my pride than had been his insolence and harshness ; but I contrived to keep down my gorge, and to stomach, in some way, what I could not easily digest. It was a severe task, but I toiled faithfully to maintain appearances suited to the new character I had assumed ; I pleased myself with the hope that I had deceived him. He evidently looked with satisfaction at my increasing familiarity with his men, and at my engaging in practices which, if not in themselves immoral, are at least very often associated, among men, with those which are so. I gamed, and drank, and swore, growing worse every day by little and little, and reconciling myself to these excesses by a frequent secret reference to the object which I desired to attain. It was a gratifying thing to me, as it convinced me of my successful acting, that Bush Halsey and his daughter both appeared to take my change of character seriously to heart. At length her frequent sighs changed to expostulations, and it became a task of greater difficulty than ever to keep my secret. I could only evade and baffle scrutiny by putting on an air of levity and recklessness, which usually had the effect of silencing the entreaties which I felt that it might be imprudent to satisfy.

But my change of demeanour and profession involved me in one difficulty, extrication from which was not so easy. Having given a loose on one occasion to my new principles, and very deliberately declared my scorn of the social contract as it existed in legalised society in the hearing of Mowbray, I was confounded by his clapping me on the shoulder, and telling me that a fine chance was now before me for making a beginning—that Bud Halsey had received intelligence of a large sum of government money being on its way from one of the land-offices, which it was his design to make sure of, and, for this purpose, meant to scatter his whole force, in every direction along the possible route of travel. Bud Halsey made his appearance suddenly, a moment after, and confirmed the statement. I fancied I could detect a keenness of glance, an intense and searching expression in his eye, as he listened for what I should say. I did not hesitate. I professed myself pleased with an occasion to try my skill, concluding with the hope that the affair might be a spirited one—that the guardian of the money would find an occasion of fight.

"If you have the stomach for it," said Bud Halsey, "you shall be the first at the gripe. But you are scarcely the man," said he, with something of a sneer, " for such a business. You have not been long enough from your mother."

"You shall see!" I replied, though I did not exactly see the purpose of his sneer, unless it was to goad my vanity.

The movement promised to be an important one with me. What did I propose to do? What did I promise myself by it? It was not until after I was committed to the enterprise that I asked myself this question. Then, the whole results opened before my eyes. What should I aim at but escape? I should be provided with horse and weapons—and a sudden dash to right or left would be only a natural movement such as was to be expected from the events of such an expedition. On the other hand, there was the danger of being suspected, and sped by an expeditious bullet; or of not being able to carry through my design of escape from the lack of opportunity, and of being compelled to countenance, of not assist in the contemplated robery. The affair was no child's play, and it behoved me to consider it with equal calmness and resolution. I had gone too far to recede. Besides, the confinement to which I was subjected had become so irksome that I was willing to encounter any risk rather than continue in it. As it promised to be unending otherwise, I felt that the earliest movement was necessarily the best. I said nothing of my design, however, to my wife. I preferred that she should neither hear nor suspect it, till I was off. Is it asked whether I proposed to abandon her,—no, but I could not bear the torment of my situation, and my purpose was to leave a letter for her, declaring my feelings, the necessity by which I was impelled, and my wish that she should rejoin me at any early moment in Alabama. I designated a spot where I would meet her, and pacified my own doubts with the conviction that when once I had fairly escaped from his clutches, there could be no motive on the part of Bud Halsey, to keep his niece from a situation in life, in which, while he could fear no risk, she would hold an agreeable and honourable station. But I did not know the man.

CHAPTER XIX.

My determination was not suffered to remain a secret. The day previous to our contemplated foray, Bush Halsey, my wife's father, returned to the cottage in no little excitement. His daughter and myself were sitting beside the fire. His countenance was filled with an agitation which he did not endeavour to conceal; and, after a hurried glance about the premises to see that there were no eaves-droppers, he addressed me, in my wife's hearing, after the following manner:—

"Henry, what's this that Bud Halsey tells me? He says that you go forth with him to-morrow night—I need not say on what sort of business.'

"It is even so, sir."

"Henry, dear Henry!" exclaimed Helen, approaching me, confounded, incapable of saying more, yet saying, how much, in that brief, broken exclamation.

"You cannot mean it!" said the father.

"What am I to do, sir?" I asked—"remain here all my life—doomed—a vegetable for ever?"

"Do not this, at least! Better remain the vegetable. Incur not that terrible destiny of my brother, in which, though free from his crimes, I must still partake. For God's sake, young man, think of your parents, friends, rank in society—reputation! Think! think."

I need not detail the conversation. The reader will perceive its tone. The agonised entreaties of my wife—the earnest, pleading exhortations of her father—his tears no less than hers—assuring me of their joint sincerity—left me without any good reason why I should not relieve them from their sufferings, by letting them know the whole truth. I told my story—showed how I had been practising upon Mowbray and his fellows—and what was the particular motive of my present determination.

"It is perilous, but I cannot disapprove of your plan. Go when you will, it will, perhaps, be inevitable that you should incur some risk. I, too, have been thinking of this flight—not for myself—for there is nothing to be gained by me, in going once more into a gentler word—but for you and Helen. Why not work together now? We shall, perhaps, never have a better chance if we wait a thousand years.'

My wife eagerly caught at the idea. I was not less pleased with it myself, but was less sanguine of success in an attempt at escape, burdened with a woman, under circumstances that would require great promptness, and possibly involve the necessity of fighting. But Bush Halsey met all my objections.

"I have been somewhat prepared for such a movement for some weeks past. I saw your unhappiness for a time, and readily understood it. It was then that I planned a mode of operations, of which I should have spoken to you before, but for the sudden change in your behaviour—a change only to be accounted for, by supposing that you had become completely reconciled to your bonds, and, which was worse, not less reconciled to the loose morals by which they were governed. Now that we understand one another, we can act together, and with a better prospect of success. Let me tell you my plan."

Bush Halsey had indeed taken up the affair with a degree of energy quite unusual with him. He surprised me, not less by his activity and progress, than by the plausibleness of his scheme. After giving me the details, he proceeded thus:—

The two plans can be made to harmonise admirably. The boat lies on the Cedar Island—the creek broadens at that point with a quick current, and carries us, without effort, into the main stream. Once let us pass Buffalo Bend, and we are pretty safe. That is the last point of land on which Bud keeps a watch. The difficulty will be in getting to the boat on the Cedar Island. Cedar Island is two miles off. The route is circuitous and well watched. But the watch will be diminished when Bud Halsey takes the road, and you have, to a certain extent, dis-armed suspicion. Now this is what I propose. Bud sets off at sundown—you are to follow with Mowbray, Hard-Riding Ross, and a couple more, who are, in reality, but spies upon you. They will call for you at dark. Your horse shall be in waiting for you at the front door, and everything shall look as if you were getting yourself in readiness within. Meanwhile, you shall garb yourself in my old grey overcoat. My slouch-cap will pretty well cover your brows and hair. Your height

is very nearly that of mine, your bulk is something less; but we have no moon, and, even with a bright starlight down upon you, the difference between our per-sons is not so great as to startle the suspicions of any of our fellows. You shall take my staff, imitate my walk, and find your way down through the pine avenue, along the main trace, which you can keep with tolerable ease, if there be any light at all. There will be three sentries at most, whom you will meet—possibly

No. 8.

but one—and as I have been pursuing this very walk for three weeks past, now giving the word, but most frequently not even accosted, the probability is that you will pass securely in like manner. You will find Helen already at the boat. She must contrive to get there by another route, a full hour before you. As soon as you join her, let the canoe drop with the stream, until you get to Fawn's Point—she knows the place—there you will run into a cove, and at that place, I must join you. You could scarcely get along into, and down the river, unless with a pilot. It is fortunate that I am a good one. Meanwhile, I will keep Mowbray and his dogs in play, until I think you safe on the water, and then get to you as I can. He will probably send or ride after Bud Halsey, to advise him of your flight. He will scarcely think to impede mine."

Much more was said, which it is not necessary here to repeat. But we perfected our arrangements quite as satisfactorily as it was in the nature of circumstances to allow. Meanwhile, the task of dissimulation was doubly difficult. That night I took supper with Mowbray, had a famous *rouse* of it, and listened, for the tenth time, to one of his most licentious stories.

———

CHAPTER XX.

The next day dawned upon us fair and light. The better to disarm suspicion, I spent the morning in company with Mowbray, and in exercise on horseback. I dined at the cottage,—Bud Halsey looking in just before my arrival, and asking where I was. I met him when leaving Mowbray, after our morning's ride. He gave me a smile of peculiar significance, but said nothing. I remembered this afterwards, when it became a question with me whether I had ever, for a single moment, succeeded in deceiving this keen-sighted and suspicious outlaw. Our dinner passed in silence. I had no appetite. Helen's eyes were tearful. Bush Halsey was in better spirits, though his mood seldom rose above that evening serene which had always marked his calm, benevolent disposition. Dinner was scarcely over before Helen prepared to take her departure. She was to seek the island by a route at once unpleasant and circuitous. It was necessary that we should not all be seen on the same route. That which I was to take was assigned me, as the easiest to be found by one so much a stranger as myself to the intricacies of the swamp. We parted with many tears, as if we were never to meet again; —but she was firm, though she wept. When she was gone, the old man and myself went once more through our calculations. Every step we were to take was to be precisely understood by both. This done, I rode to Mowbray's. I had two objects in this visit. I wished, in the first place, to be seen up to the latest moment preceding my flight; and I was also desirous of securing the pistols with which I had been practising. It seemed to be reasonable enough that, on the eve of starting on a perilous expedition, I should demand the weapons which a stubborn cashier might render necessary. Nothing of moment transpired during this visit. The swamp was everywhere astir. Steeds stood here and there, saddled beneath the tree, waiting the rider and the word; and there was an air of general preparation over the encampment, which was equally picturesque and pleasing. I got the pistols without difficulty, and hallooing to me on leaving him, Mowbray reminded me to be in readiness at dark. I did not need his warning. I was very soon ready for the worst. Evening seemed very slow of approach, and when twilight had fallen, which it did at that season, and in that situation, in an instant, I still felt that there was quite too much light. But I dismissed my nervous doubts and made ready. The old grey cloak, the slouch cap, the white cotton neck handkerchief, were soon huddled on, and, with my pistols in my bosom, and a good, stout, silver-headed hickory in my grasp, I went forth, as a hale, heavy man of fifty, with just a slight stiffness in my lower limbs. Fortune favoured me. I reached the canoe in safety, and found poor Helen half dead with apprehension. My coming filled her equally with tears and strength. She grasped the paddle with as much dexterity as an Indian maiden would have done, and as much grace as a princess. Slight and beautiful, she was yet a creature of great resolve, when the moment came of great necessity. This is a striking characteristic of our southern women, as known from the earliest pages of our history. Delicate and feeble as it would seem in make, lanquid and luxurious in disposition, they will yet, when aroused by the pressure of extreme events, sudden danger, and painful necessities, meet the crisis with the souls of men—with souls, in some respects, very far superior, indeed, to those of the most heroic men. Men struggle with the consciousness of strength, but the struggles of women are undertaken with an opposite conviction. It is with a full knowledge of their weakness that they come to the encounter with those evils, to meet which seems to demand the utmost exercise of strength.

On we went! Our paddles were scarcely needed. We swept down with the current as fast as we desired, probably at the rate of four miles an hour. The stars gave us abundant light. The silence of night was upon us—how solemnly. Not a whisper broke from our lips, but, shifting, with the stream, and only plying the paddle to keep us from the banks, our little boat went onward like a spiritual thing, hardly making a ripple on the bosom of the water. Thus we wound, to and fro, in and out, in a progress that, however rapid, did not, in half an hour, carry us far from our starting place. Such was the circuitousness of the creek. At length, Helen broke the silence with a whisper. Bending forward, she said,—

"Here, Henry,—this is Fawn's Point, where father said we must stop. The cove is on the other side, where we are to wait for him."

Our paddles dipped simultaneously, and, slightly changing her direction, the canoe rounded into as beautiful a little cove, as ever harboured the shallop of a Choctaw princess. We run her up beneath some clustering bays, and without making fast, we waited in silence for the signal of Bush Halsey. I never passed a more tedious two hours in my life. More than once I proposed to Helen to proceed.

"Your father is safe," said I,—"he has nothing to fear. It is probable he finds it impossible to reach us. We can get on without him."

She objected, insisting that, as I knew nothing of the route, I must lose my way, and probably fall again into the meshes of the confederacy. There was reason in the objection. To fall again into their hands, after an effort to escape, would have been certain death. But delay was dreadfully oppressive. We were not able to converse, for fear of alarming some unfriendly ears. We could not move about, for fear of disturbing some unfriendly watch, but crouching in the dark, we lay cramped up in our little dug-out, in a situation of constraint and impatience that would have been utterly intolerable, except that Helen was lying in my arms. More than once, while in this situation, we heard noises, or fancied them. The bushes would stir, possibly as some wild beast pushed through them, some bear or deer—the dried leaves would crackle as beneath the crushing tread of some slow, heavy person or animal; and my keen, and just now, suspicious ears, caught up sounds that I could scarcely satisfy myself, or Helen, did not fall from the lips of some whispering watcher.

At length we heard a distinct alarm throughout the swamp. It must be remembered, though we had taken so long a time in reaching it, that we were then only about half a mile, by an air line, from our little cottage settlement. A bugle was thrice heard to sound, followed by the cry of a dozen beagles, faintly swelling upon the breeze, or struggling into echoes from every quarter.

"The alarm!" said Helen, starting from my embrace. "They are on the chase, The beagles are in cry."

"Shall I not put off now?" I demanded.

"No! oh no! We are in the dark here. Let us wait."

The sounds died away, and half an hour more elapsed, without any other alarm except in a single instance, when, it seemed to us, as if a beagle gave tongue not two hundred yards from us, seemingly just on the other side of the creek. At length a faint rustle was heard, not more distinct than had reached us before ; and, when we least expected him, Bush Halsey stole through the copse under the shadow of which we lay. Pushing off as he stepped into our little vessel, he whispered,—

"We are pursued, closely I fear, and possibly watched. I expected to have been overtaken. Why I have not been, I know not. They were ahead of me at one time, and Bud Halsey himself upon the trail."

The words struck me with instant apprehension. His own approach had been made with so little noise, and I had heard quite as much before his coming, that I began to be filled with surmises and misgivings. But not a word was said. In another moment we were out of the cove, and began to feel the full power of the current. Suddenly a voice hailed us from the point of land to which we were nearing.

"Boat!"

A thunderbolt would not have astounded us, falling at our feet in the calm of a winter day.

"Boat!" the cry was repeated from the very island we had left. "Pull in or we fire!" We now understood the whole. The pursuers had scattered themselves along the head lands. Having an intimate knowledge of the route, they had reached the several points before Bush Halsey, who had been greatly delayed in his progress to join us by the active interference of his brother ; and that brother was on our heels! We had every thing to fear. Again the summons, and the distinct clicking of the gun-lock was significant of the coolest determination. Bush Halsey reached forward and pulled Helen down in the boat towards him. I was on the forward seat. Not a word was spoken, and our paddles dipped the water simultaneously, and with the strength of sinews, braced to their utmost tension by the necessity and danger. A voice, stern, keen, superior, struck our ears—a voice that we too well knew.

"Bush Halsey, be not a fool! You cannot pass, and by God, if you try it, we shoot. I mean it. You know me! The treachery of my own brother is his death."

We were visible enough, not as individuals, but as a whole. The boat, like some dark animal, was gliding through the water. We were rapidly passing our enemies. Bush Halsey whispered to me,—

"But a few yards will save us. That point, if we round it, will give us shelter ; a stout pull, now!"

A shot whistled before me, perhaps, meant as a warning, an exhortation to provoke no farther the wrath of him by whom we were threatened. At the sound, Helen started up in terror, and streatched her hands towards me, and, simultaneously with this movement, we received a volley. I felt a slight pricking sensation in my left arm, but forgot it all, as a half-suppressed scream from Helen betrayed either her apprehensions or her hurt. We rounded the point at the same instant, and were thus safe for the moment from our enemies. I turned to Helen, who lay, as before, backward in the arms of her father.

"Helen," I said with a tear, which I could not subdue. "Helen."

She answered with a moan.

"Helen," said the father, huskily, as he listened. "Helen, my child, you are not hurt."

"I am,—father—Henry."

"God! it is not, cannot be true."

She sank the next instant, with limbs relaxed and nerveless, down into the bottom of the boat. Bush Halsey and myself turned to her at the same moment. She had swooned, we sprinkled her with water, but we could do nothing for her where we were. While we busied ourselves about her, the boat grounded. We lay on a muddy ledge, which skirted an island thickly set with fresh trees.

"It is well, Henry. We can take her ashore here. I know the place. I think we are safe."

We landed in silence, the old man persisting in bearing Helen on his own shoulder to the shore. She had come out of her swoon, and now and then she moaned, and strove to speak.

———

CHAPTER XXI.

WE were very soon able to read her destiny. We carried her on shore to die! Her career of youth and happiness was short indeed. The shot was in her breast, and fatal. We spread a couch for her of leaves and bushes, beneath the shelter of a close copse of evergreens, and covered her with the grey overcoat which had disguised me in my flight. We did not need to tell her that we had no hope. She felt by certain instincts that we should have none.

"Henry, I am dying," she said to me, as her father wandered off.

I know not what I said in return—something, perhaps, which I meant to be consolatory—some one of those idle common-places, in which the bystander would deceive others, when he cannot deceive himself.

"No!" she continued; "I have no hope but that we shall meet again. That is my hope and my prayer. Oh! my Henry, pray for it—pray for me! It is not so hard to die with such a hope; but I fear, Henry, I tremble. I am not, I have not been good enough to die—I loved the world too much—I loved you too much, my Henry! God forgive me; but was not this the punishment? It was a short-lived rapture, my Henry—oh! how very short!"

I buried my face in the leaves. I could not speak—nay, I could not weep. The fountain of tears seemed utterly dry. The old man returned and kneeled beside her with me. She was sinking into stupor, with occasional awakenings—awakenings of a higher and more spiritual life. She spoke of things to us, as it seemed, wildly; but no doubt they had meaning for finer senses. How slowly, how sadly went that night away. It was a pure and gentle night—blessed with many stars, that kept trooping overhead in noiseless march, and looking down stealthily above us with their strange eyes. There was a slight breeze, that swayed the trees around us with a not unpleasant and spiritual murmur; and the chafing of the creek upon the little dark beach, along whose slippery edges we had struggled with our precious burden, mingled a most unseemly but faint music with the strain. I remained close beside her all the night, but she ceased after a while to be conscious of my presence. She had sunk into a condition something like sleep. Towards daylight she roused herself.

"Where are you, Henry? I see you not. I feel much better; but I do not see you. Come to me."

"I am here, dear Helen."

"Why do I not see you then?"

"Your hands are in mine—it is my lip that is pressing on your cheek."

"Something is over my eyes—father—Henry—take the cloak from my face that I may see you. I am better now!"

And so speaking, she died! I do think she was better then—better then, and blessed! She was certainly with God!

CHAPTER XXII.

COLDLY the day dawned upon us, and with an aspect of peculiar desolation. The inanimate form of Helen was still clasped in my close embrace. The old man spoke.

"We are alone, my son! We are alone."

Oh! how true, how touching were his words. What a change had the morning brought us—what a change from day to night. But a few hours ago, and I was all buoyancy—nay, in the impetuosity of my mood—in my eagerness to escape from the durance in which I was detained, had I not calmly contemplated flight, leaving it to a doubtful chance whether I should ever meet with her again. Now that it was very certain that we were separated—separated for ever in life, and oh, how completely—I could not well comprehend how life was to be sustained. She had become part of my life; torn from me, I began to realise the vague sensations of a heart from which certain vital sources are suddenly withdrawn. Such a thill as remains—such a tremulous uncertainty of sensation.

But one seldom dreams long over the dead. Death is among the most certain of the things of life. It is no illusion. It is a terrible reality. Its touch palsies —its aspect chills—its stony glare rebukes, and mocks, and warns. Icy lips—I pressed them, but it was with the feeling of one who sought for pain and mortification. Stony eyes! I gazed in them, as one would gaze within his own allotted sepulchre.

The future, as well as the past, lay before me in the present. The unforgotten past, the undeveloped future. Awful volume! my heart was too full to read it. I shrunk from its dreary, dreamy lessons in dismay. I shrunk into myself—into my own littleness; and assured of the great loss which I had just sustained, remembered with a glow of shame, upon what small game my thoughts had been set. How mean and petty were the objects of my eager thirst. How contracted, limited, and worthless, the poor things of the finite upon which I had set my heart. What a precious thing is the love of a pure heart, when it is lost to us for ever.

But what were my woes to his, that desolate old father? What are the sorrows of youth, at the worst, to those of age? Youth has so many resources in youth itself. The soul is still active and impetuous—the blood still ready for new encounters, nay, desiring them; and every pulse and emotion vibrates with a vitality which soon provides recompense for every failure and mortification. The heart still sends forth new tendrils in place of those which have been lopped away, or are withered, and it is seldom indeed that they do not attach themselves to other objects, in the absence of the lost, which partly, or perhaps wholly, supply their deficiencies.

But the heart of the old man, like the aged plant, has no such resources—puts forth no new tendrils. Rend the branches—sunder the close-clinging stems, and the hurt penetrates to the core, and fixes there. The worm follows, and decay. The heart is eaten out and gone, though a few fresh leaves, a little coronal of green, may yet be seen upon its mossy top, in sign rather of the immortal principle of life than of the tree that lived. The saddest sight in nature is that of age tottering to the grave, unsupported by the dutiful arms of youth.

How sterile is such a life—lingering on after the loss of the beloved ones—looking on their tombs, and until it forgets its own. I thought, even at that moment, of these things, as I thought of Helen's father. And yet he looked upon the inanimate form with a strange and most unnatural calmness. He had loved her with a love surpassing the love of woman. He had lost her, at the moment when such a loss was least to be feared; and by what a sudden stroke! It may be he was stunned—that, like myself, he did not realise our privation so completely as I, at least, was yet destined to do. But no! his eye was filled with as much intelligence as calm. Whence did he derive a consolation, of which I knew nothing? I have not said before that he was a religious man—prayerful, truly devout. Such an assurance may amuse the thoughtless. Piety in the abode of outlaws! Prayer, religion, where the hourly practice is crime! But it was nevertheless true. Bush Halsey was a weak man—it was an error in him to continue in the swamp, witnessing what he had not the power to prevent—but his instincts were just—his heart was in the right place, and he kept his hands clean from the sins in which all around him, but his dear child, wallowed freely.

At this hour, struggling, as he did, against his loss, the calm upon his face was no bad sign of that within his soul. It was the calm derived from resignation—a calm which nothing else can give; and, sitting beside the body of the beloved, he at the foot, and I supporting the precious head, with all its weight of drooping ringlets, he conversed of death—its mystery—its sublimity—its repose. Philosophy, in its cold and questioning mood, would have mocked at such discourse as that in which we dwelt. It was either beyond or below philosophy—for, in our belief of the spiritual world, we were both children. But the philosophy of the worldling will never bring him any definite knowledge on the subject either of death or life. Its beginning and ending recognises these conditions, but nothing more. The teaching which can influence us any farther, must be addressed to the heart—to that faith which seems to me equally born of our instincts and some blessed sympathetic influence which favours our aspirations and wishes from without. I believe, if we are earnest in the call, we may evoke spirits now, as in those days when angels walked among men. They walk among us now, as they did in the days of the patriarch :—

"Good spirits are beside us night and day!"

Good spirits are beside us. Helen, oh, Helen! wert thou not beside us, on that day, when thy freed spirit, violently freed, regained its first life, but hung, hovering, on suspended wing, and sanctified to our souls the precious hour that followed. Else, how was it that, lonely as we were, there was such a flood of serenity around us? Thou wert with us, my Helen! thy spirit was upon the scene and in our hearts ; and the skies smiled though we were sad, and we both felt, that in love we were not unremembered, and that if God had ravished the blessed spirit from the frail tabernacle in which it had first found its dwelling, it had not been entirely taken from the world of which we were a part. We still breathed an atmosphere in which floated ever the pure soul of the creature whom we loved.

"My son," said the old man ; "Henry, you must leave this place. It is not for you a place of safety. It is for her—it will be for me. But you will be pursued. You must contrive your flight this very day."

"What mean you, sir? Am I to go alone? Do you not go with me—and these precious remains—shall they not go with us until we can find consecrated ground?"

"All earth is consecrated ground. God has made it all. The uses to which we put the earth consecrates it. What place of city sepulchre is more pure than this? The islet is very lovely to the eye! Trees and shrubs keep it ever green. The waters which bathe it on every side, keep it ever pure. Birds live here and sing throughout the year. Man does not vex the spot with his strifes and follies. Can there be a fitter place for the grave of my child, who was so pure and so lovely? No, Henry ; it is here that we must make her grave."

We searched out a spot for the purpose. The island was generally a flat, but in the centre there was a slight elevation, crowned by a clump of gigantic cottonwood trees. The shade was equally sweet and sepulchral. There was a copse of thick vines and shrubs which partially enclosed it, and which, we knew, would be covered in the spring with the honeysuckle, the jessamine, and other sweet-scented flowers. Here then we brought her. Here, with the paddles of our canoe, we scooped out a narrow grave, and making a bed of leaves, we wrapped her in the thick, grey, close-bodied coat of her father, and laid her down to her eternal rest. Sweet form, so dear to me, shut in for ever from my sight! Sweet spirit, so blessing, still hovering around my own!—my only prayers were my pangs. I could not shovel in the earth upon her—I did not—the old man did it all. How could I cast the earth upon the white, unprotected limbs, which, but a few hours ago, had embraced me with a passion so tender and so true.

We sat beside the grave for hours after, but with little speech from either. What was spoken related to the solemn subjects upon which the old man had already spoken—life and death! These are the great engrossing subjects. Strange how people strive to evade them. How the shudder which follows the first thought of death, makes them recoil from the second, as if it were a subject which we might put by at will—as if it were not, in fact, the only thing in life which is inevitable. The first shudder over, the thought of death is morally wholesome. We should think of it daily, not only of its inevitableness, but as of a thing, the character of which is to be mainly influenced by our daily actions. Could we think thus, religion were easy—it were the next step in the simple process of bringing back the stray sheep to the Good Shepherd.

CHAPTER XXIII.

It was sunset. To this hour we had lingered by the little hillock, which had shut in from our eyes, for ever, the thing that was so precious in our sight. I had given myself up to the feeling of desolation which took possession of me. I lay beside the grave, my fingers penetrated the soft mould, which was soon to become enriched by hers. My brow lay upon the damp earth. A sort of stupo seemed to overcome me. But the voice of the old man aroused me to my duties.

"Henry, my son! it is time to depart. Farther delay may endanger your safety. Come, it needs not that we should remain above the grave to mourn. The sorrow of the living attends him, and cannot be shut out. Happy, indeed, are we—did we but know it—that this is the case. How soon would the feeling of our griefs, did we not strive so recklessly to get rid of them, bring us that perfect peace of the regenerated soul, brought home to God, which we all so much require. We must go, my son. You will not forget!"

"Forget, my father, no! She was too precious for that. Never!—never!"

"Yet the memory of the perished dear one should be a sweet, not a distressing memory. It should strengthen our hearts, while it subdues our passions. Suffering is meant for this. We should grow strong in the prosecution of those duties which are set for us as tasks—duties whether of endurance or of performance,—the reward of which, when done, is life eternal in communion with the beloved ones. Fortunately for me, my son, the duties before me are not of long duration. I shall soon meet with my innocent child. I shall see her first!"

We took our way to the boat in silence. There we found a basket which Helen had brought with her, and which I had not seen before. The provident girl had filled it with cakes, which she had prepared against our journey. We had not eaten all the day,—for that matter, I had scarcely eaten anything the day before. I had no appetite. I could not partake of the cakes of Helen—nay, the basket in my eyes gave me a painful feeling. I thought of her thoughts, her hopes and feelings, as she prepared these little necessaries!—how sweet would have been our feast together, gliding down, night and noon-day, along that lonely river. Now! Oh! that now!—I pushed the basket from my sight.

The old man knew the river well. We glided by raft and snag and sawyer, in perfect safety. Night came on, and we were once more silent voyagers by the dim light of the stars,—those never-tiring ministers of night, those numerous herds of eyes, that spread themselves out, or shrink and cover themselves within her cloudy fold, at the slightest symptoms of her anger. I leaned back and watched them, and wept silently beneath their glance. How much is the love of the young heart associated with, and awakened by, those uncertain periods of time, when twilight, the moon or the stars, are in the ascendant. The affections do not seem

to flourish in the noon-day. There is something in the intense passionateness of the sun's glare, that seems to offend the delicacy of youthful sentiment. But the fainter light, the subdued beauties of evening and night, the pale, insinuating charms of moon and stars,—win their way to the young affections, without startling, and link themselves to all their dearest emotions. Looking up to those bright, pale watchers, I could not well believe that I was alone. I sometimes fancied that two of them, looking more like eyes than stars, drew nigher to me; and, at such moments, the breeze, which came from the woods along the waters, seemed to

No. 9.

whisper in the very accents of a beloved one. I was young,—I could still dream —but that poor old man—who still plied his paddle, now right and now left, with a vigour of stroke that was really wonderful—he had long since ceased to dream! I offered to relieve him of his labour, but he would not. Indeed, as I knew nothing of the river, and as our dug-out depended for its direction upon the paddle, not upon the tiller—for it had none—any attempt of mine would, in all probability, during the night, have ended in mischief. Thus we went—both silent—both absorbed in thoughts which, as we mutually understood them, called for no utterance. Sometimes the silence was broken by the howl of the wolf, the scream of the eagle, or the melancholy hooting of the owl, from one or other of the shores between which we stole, like some fairy vessel. At other times we could catch a moaning sound from the woods, like the far cry of one in distress, which was yet only the effect of the wind, rushing in currents through unlooked-for openings of cane, by which, in some places, the banks were lined—regions of the bear, presenting at times along the shore, a dense barrier fully a mile in depth. How melancholy sweet are thy numerous voices, oh solemn and mysterious night.

I slept! how long I know not, but I was wakened by the boat striking against the shore. I started and looked up. The old man was standing on the land, upon which he had already drawn one half of the canoe.

"Where are we, sir?" I asked. "What time is it?"

"It is nearly daylight."

"I have slept, then?"

"yes,—very soundly! you needed it, my son."

"But you, sir?"

"Ah! I need very little—old people need less than young. The work of renovation is not so necessary in them."

"Do you know where we are, sir?"

"I think I do; but I may have erred in my calculations, as I was anxious not to go too far. We are, I think, about a mile above Baker's Landing. There is a saw-mill somewhere about, which we shall probably see by daylight. I wait for that, to be certain. Here begin the settlements, and here I propose to leave you."

"How, sir, leave me? Will you not go with me, and live with me—my father, mother, all, will be glad to have you."

"No, Henry, I return to the swamp."

"Return! Return to the swamp?"

"Yes! I have nothing now to take me into the world—much to keep me out of t—and here!"

I strove vainly to shake his determination, and finally ceased to attempt it. I could not but think he was right. What had he to do in the world—what was the world to him—or he to it? His world was in the forest, there, with his child. At that moment, I half believed that my world was there also. Certainly, the more I thought of leaving it for ever, the more difficult it became to subdue my emotions.

Day at length dawned upon us. The saw-mill was in sight, and a cluster of cabins running down to the very brink of the stream. The old man pointed them out, and taking from his breast a purse of half-eagles, forced it into my hand. I did not scruple at receiving it; I had no money. What I had when I came into the swamp, had been taken from me, and never returned, when the myrmidons of Bud Halsey took me into custody.

"With this, Henry, you can easily procure a good horse at any of the settlements along the river—most probably at this. There, God bless you, my son—go —go, and be happy!"

We parted—good old man—but not without a hope,—and not for ever!"

CHAPTER XXIV.

I soon found my way to the saw-mill settlement, where I accounted for my appearance by representing myself as left by a raft, having wandered off from one of the landings into the swamp. The story was plausible enough, and occasioned no remark. I had rather more difficulty in getting a horse than Bush Halsey had imagined, and was content to take an old hack at forty dollars, being, indeed, the only tolerable animal to be had. I was enough of a jockey to see that the creature had been once badly foundered, nor was this denied by the owner. His hoofs were scaled, and worn low, and he walked tenderly, as if the quick was ailing. But it was Hobson's choice with me, and I did not look closely to his infirmities. I took for granted that he was good for six days travel, and after that he might be crow's meat for what I cared. Paying for him, I found myself with eight half-eagles, and some small change—more than enough to meet my wayside exigencies; and with a last look upon the river whose contiguous streams had been of such fatal interest to me, I dashed up the narrow Indian trail which as I was instructed, would conduct me into the main track leading homeward. That day I rode forty miles, and slept at the wigwam of a mulatto, who gave his wife—an Indian woman—a sound drubbing in my very sight, and in spite of all my expostulations. I believe the only offence on her part was that she had suffered the fish to burn, which his imperial highness had caught for his own, and which furnished a very sorry portion of my supper. She probably deserved all that she got—was a sulky hag, of fierce, black, revengeful aspect, who in all probability will have a day of reckoning with him on this very account. My interposition saved her from a part of the flogging —at all events, such was his asurance to me while it was in progress; and with this I had to be satisfied.

The next day I started with the dawn, paying five dollars for my night's lodging my own, and my horse's supper. I soon discovered, from the lank sides of my horse, that I had paid for him unnecessarily. Yet had I gone into the stable myself, and seen counted out to him thirty good ears of corn;—this too, after he had been nibbling for half an hour on the blades. But the corn had been withdrawn from the trough after I had retired. The poor animal was evidently suffering from starvation. He bore me feebly, and with tottering footsteps. At noon I stopped on the edge of a field prairie, where the grass was tolerably good, and continued for an hour to "chew the cud of sweet and bitter fancy," while he digested more stable material. This freshened him a little, and at close of day, I reached the hovel of a Choctaw, who, in answer to my first inquiry, replied,

"Yaow!—hab 'nough co'n—'nough fodder.—Plenty co'n—plenty fodder ! Man eat—hoss eat—plenty co'n, 'nough co'n—too much co'n—too much fodder !"

The assurances were thick and substantial, and my Choctaw Boniface promised to be a landlord after the most liberal fashion. He did not misrepresent his corn crib: it was ample. He took me to see it, and then took me to his bear-pen, where he had a two-year old Bruin, of the brownest complexion, taming for a pet, which he was very anxious to sell me at seven dollars, to carry home to my squaw. The quizzical chuckle and wink of the good-natured fellow, as he named the squaw, brought the tears into my eyes. He evidently regarded me as a boy who had as yet no thought of a wife. He had no wife, but he fondled his bear quite as much as if it were one—probably much more than he would have fondled the loveliest squaw that he could have found in the whole bosom of his tribe. This fellow did not spare his corn in my case, but gave me an ample supply of bread stuffs for supper,— together with some well broiled slices of smoked venison, of which his cabin had a tolerable supply. He was no doubt an active hunter, when sober. But the signs of whiskey-worship were sufficiently apparent in his face, if not in his cabin. His nose had the sign manual of strong drink, in the largest car-buncles that human nose ever maintained—a congeries of little red hillocks that half reminded me of a settlement of marmozets, or prairie dogs. Unfor-tunately for me, his liberality in the matter of corn, unlike that of my mu-latto host of the night before, was as much shown to my horse as to myself. In looking at the corn-crib and the bear, I allowed myself to be diverted from the condition of the animal, and the Indian improvidently gave him his corn and fodder together. The half-starved animal naturally fastened upon the corn and surfeited himself; and when, at dawn the following morning, I prepared to mount him, I found him dead foundered, and barely able to walk. Grieved at the event, vexed with myself for my own neglect, I was yet compelled to push forward ; and, paying my Choctaw his fare, which called for another of my gold pieces, I set forward—thinking it probable that, as the animal warmed with walking, the stiffness would diminish or disappear. And so it did ; but not sufficiently to satisfy me, or relieve my anxiety and impatience; and, after dragging along at the slow pace of three miles an hour, for seven hours, I concluded to abandon the miserable animal, and pursue the rest of my journey, or until I could procure another beast, on foot. There was a slight rising of the country on my left hand, which appeared covered with a pretty thick growth of grass,—and into this I rode him. The woods gave him a very good shelter, and the grass would sustain life until he might be picked up by some traveller or neighbour. At all events, I was resolved not to burden myself any longer with the care of a beast whose limbs could scarcely support his own frame, to say nothing of mine. Ascending the hill, I found a beautiful hollow, where the grass, protected from the sharper winds of winter, was still luxuriant and tender. Here I stripped him, and, after some search, having found a hollow gum of considerable size, I hid away the saddle and bridle, for future use, if necessary. I had scarcely done this, and set the poor creature free, before I heard the trampling of horses from above. Here, then, was a prospect of succour and assistance, much sooner than I could have hoped for it. I hurried immediately to the road-side, from which I had been removed about an hundred yards, and when I reached the edge of the hill which looked down upon the road,—from which I was effectually screened by a thick under-growth by which it was edged,—I was about to halloo and spring forward, when a sudden suggestion of prudence persuaded me to stop and first reconnoitre. Accordingly, stooping down, I crawled forwards on hands and knees until I reached the edge of the hill, at the foot of which the road ran, and, at this very moment, the travellers whom I had heard, drew up below. It was well that I adopted these precautions. The very next moment, my ears were struck by the sounds of a voice which grated harshly upon my ears, as that of my worst enemy. I felt a shuddering horror through my whole frame. Cautiously, I divided the bushes with my hand, and looked below; and there, sure enough, stood Bud Halsey, beside his horse, from which he was about to lift the saddlebags. His back was to me, but a glance sufficed to show me that he was the man. I in-voluntarily felt in my breast for my pistols. They were safe. They were loaded, and my nerves, disquieted for an instant, were again firm. I felt that it would be easy to fell the outlaw in his tracks, and I half resolved—but it was for an instant only—that I would do the deed. But I grew wiser in another moment. In the intenseness of my feelings in regard to this man, I had failed, for the first few minutes, to see that he was not alone. Beside him, dismounting while I gazed, were the *soi-disant* parson, Mowbray, and another man, the fellow Warner, of whom I have already spoken, as one whom I remembered to have met before entering the swamp.

Here was a concatenation accordingly. What was I to do ? I could not doubt the intention of these fellows; I could not but believe that their journey was undertaken because of my flight. They were in pursuit of me. That they had no idea of my proximity, I soon felt certain, as they prepared to water the horses, and to take refreshments at the spring which I now perceived to issue from the hill upon which I stood, the water foaming below in a basin several yards in breadth. I was not more than fifteen feet above them, and at one time, as they were about to seat themselves, I might have so tumbled a rock upon them—had any been convenient—as to have covered and crushed the three. I looked about me, as the thought occurred to me, to see if there was no such friendly fragment at hand.

But, if I had any doubt at first of the object of this journey, it was soon dissipated by the dialogue that ensued between Bud Halsey and Mowbray. There had evidently been a good many previous words between them, for they were both very much irritated. The manner of Mowbray was marked by sullenness, and that of Halsey was fully characteristic of his extremest mood of asperity. The first speaker whose words were distinguishable was Mowbray, though the tones of Halsey's voice had reached me as he drew nigh.

"I really never fancied myself a fool, Mr. Halsey; and until it can be shown that I am one, to blame me for my course in this business is, in fact, in other words, to accuse me of treachery. I see no other alternative."

"And do you suppose, Mr. Mowbray, that, if such a suspicion entered into my head, I should tamely sit here palavering with you? No, no, sir; by God! the stroke would have followed the suspicion, as certainly and soon as the thunder follows the flash. I give few words to traitors, I assure you."

Mowbray muttered something which I could not make out, but the harsh accents of Halsey seemed to drown his utterance.

"I am not in any complimentary mood, and therefore do not call you fool either as you seem to insist that I do, or should. I know that you are no fool, and it is therefore that I blame you; but I will tell you what is the matter with you, Mr. Mowbray—you are a vain man, with all your wisdom, and this boy has flattered your vanity until he has bedevilled you. You have ceased to watch him, in listening to him; he has seen your weak points, and, contriving to make you look inwards, you have been able to see nothing that he has been contriving without. Your vanity, sir—it is your vanity, sir, that is your weakness—that makes a fool of you, if anything—blinds you, at all events, to the duties that you take in hand."

"You speak plainly, sir, at all events."

"Ah, ay, it's a trick I have, and as it's plain truth that I generally speak on such occasions, it's not a bad trick. I tell you, Mr. Mowbray, that I have a trick of acting plainly too, upon occasion,—and let me say in your ear, that, when I found how completely you had suffered this chap to slip through your fingers, in a trap of your own making, I found it almost as easy to put a bullet through your ears as to speak to them."

"I should not have been more a sufferer than by the course you have taken. It is not too late, sir."

"Come, come, Mr. Mowbray, this will not do. I must have no sulks! You have blundered—shockingly blundered, and I must be permitted my own way of reproaching you for it. The matter is a serious one. It endangers our whole business, our lives, and the safety of our men. Let us see that there be no more blundering. This fellow cannot long escape us. He will not, if you do not again suffer that d—d petty weakness of yours to blind your eyes and baffle your judgment."

Mowbray was silent—with a silence that betrayed dissatisfaction. The other did not seem to heed it, as he went on:

"By this time every avenue is guarded—every outlet from the swamp. We must be a-head of him; and, if not, travelling night and day for the next twenty-four hours will make us so. What sort of a horse was it that he got from that old fool, Houser? Did you think to inquire, Warner?"

"A regular break-down, a poor, foundered, spavinned critter, not worth skinning. I know the nag well enough. I reckon he's hardly got through the swamp with him yet."

"And why didn't you follow him when you found out that he was so poorly mounted?" demanded the outlaw.

"You forget, sir, I went down to the mill in the boat. I had no horse, and he had a matter of eight hours' start of me."

"Then, be sure the fellow's ahead of us still. He's the chap to push a horse from the jump, without asking how he's to hold out. He's ahead of us, but can't keep so long. At all events we'll push for the 'Racoon Crossing,' and scatter there. We should have him by another sun-rise. D—n him! But for that foolish brother of mine, and the poor girl—I would that her blood were not upon my hands—poor Helen—any blood but hers!—but for them all this would have been prevented. We should have no such trouble. I should never have been so weak—so silly—but it can be mended—at least, it's not too late for that! There shall be no relentings now."

This was spoken rather in soliloquy. The slight touch of a human nature which the outlaw displayed, when speaking of his niece, brought the tears into my eyes. But his expressions with regard to myself in the next moment dried them, and I could have pistolled him on the spot, with a coolness and recklessness like his own.

Their meal was finished in silence. At the abrupt command of their leader, Warner gathered up the fragments, and I saw them mount their steeds, and set off upon their journey, without moving from my position. I caught a glimpse, as they were mounting, of the face of Mowbray, who was the slowest in his movements of the three. I observed that it was almost purple with suppressed choler. He rode after the others in silence, with lips closely compressed, and with the air of a man who could speak daggers, and use them too, if he dared!

CHAPTER XXV.

I FELT my heart grow very chill as I reviewed my situation. My path was every where beset, and Bud Halsey, knowing the country as he did, and being the person that he was, was not likely to leave his work unfinished. The conversation of my pursuers was of a kind to leave me hopeless of any escape, except through the merest good fortune, and the most unyielding firmness. On the very path that I was pursuing, my arch enemy, with his two subtle satellites, was himself upon the watch, and yet, I could not choose any other route. I knew of no other and the very fact that I knew my enemies upon this, who they were and where they were, determined me still to go forward as I had begun. I must take my chance and meet events with whatever courage and conduct I could command. It was evident from what they had said, and from the free rein with which they dashed forward, that there was some certain point ahead, at which they aimed, and where they intended to await me. What was the point? Where was "Racoon crossing?" I was ignorant of every step of the route. I had nothing to do but to go forward with as much prudence as possible—to prepare against all sudden surprises—to keep in the cover of the woods, where they were of a nature to suffer me to do so, and to feel my ground at every change of position before betraying myself. In no other way could I hope to avoid the encounter,—for which, should it be unavoidable, I must only man myself with the most desperate resolution. The determination to sell my life as dearly as possible, seemed to nerve me with strength to proceed, and, cutting myself a stout hickory from the wayside I started forward, with spirits much lighter than seemed to be altogether justified by my situation. A moment's reflection now served to convince me that, what I had lately regarded as a crowning evil—the loss of my horse—was, in reality, somewhat favourable to my hope of escape. It enabled me to keep the cover of the woods, to advance noiselessly, and conceal myself with more facility on the approach of danger. Encouraged by thoughts like these, and by that sort of audacity which comes from one's desperation, I dashed into motion with a sort of defiance, and, keeping along the margin of the road, ready to seek the shelter of the woods at the smallest alarm, I commenced my pedestrian expedition with all the philosophy of which I was master.

I had always been counted a good amateur walker, but walking as a duty, and in a new unopened country, following Indian foot-paths, and fording streams, wading swamps, and "cooning logs," is a very different business. The road was a terribly broken one, crossed by frequent ravine and rivulet—for I was not yet entirely out of the swamp country—and full of obstructions from fallen trees, vines, briars, stumps, and broken branches. But I was sustained by the very difficulties of my situation. I was stimulated by the trial of my strength, and able to get forward at the rate of three miles an hour, which was probably quite as much as could have been done, in his best days, by the miserable beast I had abandoned. But five hours at this pace soon lessened pretty equally my strength and elasticity. Towards evening, I began to feel the approaching gravity of the scene. The trees began to cast a longer, denser shadow across my path, and the sun glimmered faintly, sprinkling the open space with a cluster of beaded gold-drops, which, while they caught my glance, and while I looked for them from side to side, did not very much tend to enliven me. The wilderness seldom has its singing birds, and I failed to hear the chirp of one the whole afternoon. Once a couple of deer glided over the road from one thicket to another, but a sign of living thing beside, I saw not ; and, as the sun disappeared, a couple of screech owls commenced a most gloomy death-duet, from opposite sides of the path over which I was to make my way, and seemed to accompany my progress for a good half hour after. The moon rose, however, almost with the disappearance of the sun, and I gave her, from the bottom of my heart, a traveller's benison. She poured a steady blaze of light across the path, and thus enabled me to avoid its pitfalls and obstructions. Having no place of retreat, and with my spirits somewhat revived by her countenance, I still pursued my way, resolving to continue on until absolutely worn out with fatigue. For three hours more I did so, but weariness began to wrap me as with a cloud. I staggered rather than walked along the path, and, to keep my eyes open, though I felt no hunger, I took from my pockets one of the corn biscuits with which I had provided myself at the hovel of the Choctaw, and commenced eating against time. While thus engaged, I happened to come upon a trail which struck into the woods upon my right, and seemed to lead to an opening, which was partially discernible from the road—the moonlight falling down upon the space, in a body, giving it the appearance of a placid lake. My exhaustion furnished me with sufficient reasons why I should turn into this path, which I did without a moment's hesitation. I followed it for some hundred and fifty yards, when it forked. I took one of the branches at hazard, followed it some fifty yards farther, and found myself suddenly in front of a rude shanty of logs, more like the den of a wild animal than the dwelling of a human being. Prudence would have counselled me rather to find my night's rest in the thicket than in such a hovel ; but the sight of anything in the shape of human habitation, seemed to me to convey the idea of security. Besides, this place was evidently abandoned, and had been long without a tenant. I did not plunge into it headlong, but exercising all the circumspection that I could command, in that general dulling of the faculties that had been produced by weariness and cold, I examined the hut cautiously from the outside, taking care to peer into it from each corner, and without seeing anything to alarm me. The roof, which had been originally a thin thatch of pine boughs and leaves, was half broken in and lay upon the ground below—the ends of the remaining branches still hanging half way down and threatening a further fall. The door which was made of plank, was thrown down within : and such, in short, was the generally desolate air of the place, that I took possession at once, taking for granted that my pursuers were considerably ahead of me, and of other persons I had nothing to fear. I was, perhaps, more readily persuaded to give this preference to the hovel over the woods, as, by this time, I could hear, rising at intervals from the deep recesses of the swamp-thickets, confused sounds, not unlike the hoarse voices of beasts of prey preparing for their nightly orgies. I could not doubt that, among these, the sharp bay of the wolf was a frequent sound ;—and, as it would not be prudent for me to raise a fire, lest, in driving the brute from my slumbers, I should only furnish a conducting signal to a foe equally if not more deadly—I concluded to take my rest in the cabin. The door I raised to its former position so as to close entirely the opening, fastening it in its place by the withes of grape-vine, which I found in long coils conveniently within the cabin. This done, I looked at my inner accommodations. The moon, shining down through one half of the dismantled roof, enabled me to see and to dispose of the mass of pine trash, which had once furnished the thatch above. Of this, I made a very comfortable couch in the covered part of my den, which was still in shadow ; and, having put my pistols within a convenient grasp of my hand, I yielded my farther cares of the night, to the gracious Providence, which had hitherto had me in its keeping, a brief prayer for protection, and a few sad thoughts to the memory of poor Helen, and I was soon lost to the farther troubles of consciousness.

I slept very soundly and satisfactorily. My previous excitements and fatigues had given to my slumbers a rare and delightful relish, to confirm the sweetness and efficacy of which, my dreams were of the most soothing and grateful tendency. The past experience of pain was forgotten in their ministerings. Poor Helen was once more a living and loving spirit in my arms. Once more I found myself roving over the wild recesses of Conelachita in her company—my arm about her waist, and both of us as happy, and as little moved by care, as if there had been no other human beings in the world around us. From this happy state, I was suddenly awakened—I know not how! The moon was shining directly down upon my face. I looked round as if seeking Helen, becoming aware very slowly of the solemn truth of my loneliness. But I soon became aware of other facts in my condition. The door which I so carefully put up, as a defence during my slumbers, was removed, and now partly rested against the passage. I could see one of its angles protruding through the space. In the opening, and upon the sill, crouched a form, which, at my first consciousness seemed to me to be that of a wild animal. I fancied it a bear. Under the momentary impulse, I stretched out my hands to the spot just by my head where I had placed my pistols. They were gone! and the half scornful chuckle of the intruder, as he beheld my movement, at once informed me by what agency. I started up into a sitting posture and confronted the stranger.

"Be quiet," said he, and I then recognised the voice of Mowbray. "Be quiet —keep your temper and your breath, and all may go well with you."

"Where is Bud Halsey?" I demanded, under I know not what impulse.

"Fortunately for you, not within hearing distance. You are lucky in one thing, that he sent me on this route, instead of taking it himself. But for this your sleep had not been so gently broken."

"But how did you find me out?"

"Ha! ha! ha! you are a rare person at hide-and-seek. You remind me of that sagacious bird—the ostrich I think it is—that, when pursued by the hunter, buries its head in a hollow, leaving the rest of its carcase to take care of itself. He's a bad scout who thinks because he can no longer see his enemy, that he himself must needs remain unseen. Why did you hide in the hovel at all—why not in the woods?"

"I was afraid of wolves, and did not dare to light a fire."

"But why not take a tree?"

"I never thought of that! I was, indeed, too much tired, and too sleepy to · think at all."

"Well, that is frank enough, but, when you determined to take the cabin, you should not have raised the door. That was enough to tell me that somebody was within,—and then you slept in the moonlight! I saw your features distinctly—

saw where your pistols lay, and found no difficulty in cutting through grape-vines, letting the door down quietly, and removing your pistols."

This simple statement showed how obtusely I had gone to work, in the stupor caused by fatigue and drowsiness, in rendering myself secure.

"I guarded only against wild beasts—I thought you were far ahead!"—I muttered, as if to excuse my stupidity.

"You thought we were far ahead? Why what did you know about it?" said Mowbray, with some surprise. I hesitated before replying,—

"Why should I answer you? Do I not know you to be my enemy? What need of parley between us?"

I spoke this fiercely. I was now desperate. His coolness—as I conjectured, arose from the feeling of confidence in my capture which filled his mind—incensed me, and I felt the momentary impulse to spring upon him where he stood.

No. 10.

"Be not wrothy!" he said, "keep cool. You forget, my good fellow, that you are defenceless!"

"Are you sure of that?" I demanded.

He held up my own pistols as I spoke.

"What are these?"

"True, but I have this!" and I drew the dirk from my bosom with which Bush Halsey had provided me.

He cocked both of his pistols as I answered.

"And of what avail would your dirk be, Henry Meadows, against these? I have but to draw the trigger of either. I know the pistols, and you know my aim. But a truce to this,—you do not know me. I do not seek your life. I will save it if you will suffer me. As I said before, it is fortunate that Bud Halsey sent me on this route instead of taking it himself."

I interrupted him.

"Speak to me as an honest man—as a man, Mowbray. Do I understand you? Can I believe you? Do you not mean to betray me once more, as you did when you devised the scheme for robbing the supposed agent?"

"How know you that?" he demanded.

In brief I told him of the position I had kept when Bud Halsey, Warner, and himself stopped for dinner at the spring. How, hanging over their heads, I had heard their conversation.

"You heard, then, the insolence of this bearded tyrant? You saw what I had to endure—I, a gentleman born and bred, at the hands of that ruffian. You heard,—you say? you heard!"

"Every syllable."

"And you cannot understand why I would thwart the scoundrel—why I would save you?—nay, why I should show you how to put a bullet through his brains! All this will I do! Are you ready to second me? Will you play a desperate game for your life?"

"Try me! If you speak to me fairly, the thing may be done. They are but two and we are—"

"Wronged—and of equal number. Be it so! To prove to you that I am in earnest, here are your pistols. Sound them—see that they are charged. Take nothing on trust. All right?"

"Yes!"

"Now, hear me! You choose for your place of rest, the very region where we proposed to lie in wait for you. 'Raccoon Crossing' has three tracks, each leading to an old Indian encampment. You happened to choose the one least likely to have been chosen by one seeking concealment. It lies almost within sight of the road, and was probably the only track you happened to see. It was for this reason that Bud Halsey sent me on this route. He took for granted that you would be more likely to be encountered on either of the others. To one of these he sent Warner, the other he pursued himself. The third, and least likely, under ordinary calculations, to have brought you up, he assigned to me, for no better reason that I can conjecture, but that he suspects me. He suspects me of being privy to your flight, and some singular circumstances, which I need not tell you now, contributed to make his suspicions natural and strong. It will probably increase your confidence in my present plan, when I tell you that, being under his suspicion, I am probably marked out as his next victim, and he only brought me with him, from the swamp, that I might be under his own eye, till the proper moment of dealing with me. A common cause unites us. Are you ready?"

"For what?"

"For what?—Why, blood!—Death!—what else? Do you fear? Will you not fight?"

"Fear! no! Be not so violent! I like harsh language as little as yourself. All I wish to know is what is your design—your plan. I have no notion of striking like a blind man in the dark."

"Very good! I understand you. I am a little irritable—half mad, indeed

I feel that I am just sane enough to do mischief, as I certainly am to design it. Here, then, you wait. Keep your den—keep in the dark corner, while I go and bring Halsey."

"Would it not be better to go to him?"

"No! no! it is better as I tell you. I will bring him here. You will keep still —keep dark. I will lead the way into your den, and when he comes, be sure and make your mark upon him. I will be ready to follow up the blow. Only be sure to hit the right man. I am not quite prepared to be laid by the heels—far from it —far from it—yet I have an ugly notion that my time is not far off. Be you sure of your man, that's all. Look to your pistols—have them cocked, and in readiness —and above all things, be cool—be firm—do nothing in a hurry!"

Having thus counselled me, he warned me where to dispose myself, and proceeded to replace my door, which he made me fasten on the inside precisely as I had fastened it before.

" He will probably insist upon the removal of the door himself, for he fancies nobody can do such things half so skilfully. Should this be the case, he may, and probably will, enter the cabin first. In this event, you will act without waiting for me, only taking care that I am not immediately behind him. You will easily know him by his superior bulk. You cannot well confound us, unless you are alarmed beyond measure, which I hardly think will be the case. Be of good heart —you will need all of its strength in half an hour."—With these words, he disappeared.

CHAPTER XXVI.

As all the particulars in my situation were known to himself, I was content that he should have the management of the affair. It is true, some doubts of his good faith occasionally disturbed me, but they were soon dissipated with the reflection that, had he meant me mischief, nothing would have been more easy than to have carried out his purpose while I slept. He had disarmed me of my most effective weapons—had afterwards restored them to me—and. besides, the manner of the man amply denoted the sincerity of those denunciations of his principal, in which he so violently dealt. Still, though resolved to confide in him, I felt very reluctant to await the outlaw in the close den in which I was cabined. Could I have been sure of his route in approaching, I should certainly have gone forth and waylaid him. But the more I reflected, the more I felt the prudence of leaving the matter to Mowbray. At all events, I was weaponed! I could do mischief! I could make my enemy pay dearly for his conquest, if he succeeded in obtaining it. I was resolved not alone to perish; and above all things, not to suffer myself to be taken alive! I had too vivid a recollection of that humiliating half-death, by the rope, which I had already undergone at the hands of this butcher.

A more tedious hour than that which followed, I never passed in all my life. My head, meanwhile, was filled with a thousand doubts, suspicions, and apprehensions; but, as the more manly course, after all, is to give no half confidence to your ally, I yielded myself up to patience with all my philosophy. To keep quiet, in the one position, in the guise of sleep, was the most difficult of all efforts, and required the utmost inflexibility of nerve. This was the last and most urgent necessity, since I was not to know at what moment the enemy would peer into my premises. A thousand times I fancied whispers and approaches from without. The lifting of a dried leaf by the wind, the straining or the sighing of a bough under the same pressure—these would make my heart beat and jump with the liveliest anxiety. But I may say, confidently, that I succeeded in quieting my impatience, so as to maintain a position of the utmost physical inflexibility. I do not think, after the first three minutes succeeding the departure of Mowbray, that I stirred a muscle. I know very well that I did not move a limb. Those three minutes I devoted to stirring the priming in my pistols and putting them on cock—shrouding myself as closely as possible in the darkest corner of my den, and putting myself just in that position which would enable me to command the entrance, with the best possible prospect of doing my work efficiently.

Thus prepared, I endured the hour—for it was fully that—of interval, which followed the departure of Mowbray, before I became conscious of his return. The ears of him who watches for his foe are singularly keen and apprehensive. Miss Baillie, in one of her plays, has a happy illustration of this exquisite nicety of sense, under such circumstances. I cannot say that I heard the approach of Bud Halsey, at the very moment when I yet knew that he was nigh. The instinct of hate or love, is a nicer sense than any which we have in ordinary. It is an instinct—a sort of spiritual sense, which, leaping the ordinary outworks of nature takes in the coming events long before they have cast a shadow over the citadel. I knew that my enemy was nigh, though I did not hear a footstep—not a whisper reached my ears—not a sound disturbed the familar silence,—yet I felt that he was breathing in the same atmosphere with myself. I felt my heart bound—I felt my pulses quicken—but I was prepared for the worst! Fully ten minutes followed, of the most nervous anxiety. Still, not a sound—not a movement! Cautious, indeed, were the approaches of the outlaw, and though, every moment, more and more impatient for action, yet the very caution of mine enemy tended to the increase of my strength. At length I was made conscious of a sound, and, an instant after, the light of the moon glinted from the blade of a knife, which I now perceived to be working upon the wythes which fastened the door. A few moments sufficed to sever them on each side, and I then saw that the door, which was a massive one, was gently, and with ease, lifted from without, and lodged on the inside, resting against one of the posts. The figure of the person by whom this was done, was now partially apparent to me, but, as the front of the house was in shadow, I could not sufficiently distinguish the individual. Could I have been sure of my man, nothing would have been more easy than to have shot him where he stood. But I suffered him to enter, which he did so cautiously, that, though I saw him approach, I never heard a footfall. One more step brought him into the light of the moon, and then, thrusting one of my pistols forward, I pulled trigger upon him. To my utter consternation the weapon gave no report. The flint gave no fire. Before I could present the second pistol, I heard an exclamation from the lips of Mowbray, at the entrance—a single "Ha!" in tones of mortification, and I then beheld him dart upon the outlaw, while he was advancing upon me, and strike him twice in the back. A terrible yell burst from the lips of Bud Halsey, as he turned upon his assailant.

"Traitor!" he exclaimed, "it is you!"

As he turned, with this exclamation, I sprang forward, clapped my remaining pistol to his head and fired—this time with effect. My bullet went through his brain at the very moment when, grasping Mowbray by the throat with one hand, with the other he drove the bowie knife, which had been destined for my bosom, through that of my confederate. Halsey sunk down lifeless, in a heap at my feet; while Mowbray, with outstretched arms, staggered backward, and leaned for a moment against the unhung door, which shook beneath his frame. He spoke but a few words, but they belonged not to the present scene or circumstances.

"Raise my voice, my brethren—cry aloud,—the time is at hand."

"Mowbray!" said I, grasping his body and endeavouring to support him, as I saw that he was about to fall.

"Ah?" said he with a momentary consciousness, "I see how it is! There's no use now! But tell her—tell her all." His lips parted in hurried and frequent murmurs. I let him down gently upon the pine straw.

"Tell her what?—tell who?—name her, that I may know."

"What !" he exclaimed, with a momentary recovery of strength, "have you not heard ?—have you not understood me ?"

"Not a word—not a syllable !"

"Great God !—then it's too late !" and the tears gushed from his eyes. Still he muttered, seemed anxious make me hear, grasped my arm, and with a final effort to lift himself, sunk away, and expired in a faint shriek, the appalling sound of which I sometimes hear in my dreams, even to this hour.

CHAPTER XXVII.

I WAS roused from my musings by the necessity for self-preservation. There was still an enemy upon my track. With the thought, I drew myself out of the moonlight. I stole forth in the shadows of the house, and from tree to tree around it, listening for the footfalls of danger. I heard none but my own. Still, there was danger, and it behoved me to prepare for it. I hurried back to the hovel—repossessed myself of the pistol which had failed me, and which I had cast to the ground when it became necessary to use the other—picked the edges of the flint with the handle of my dagger,—and thus, partially sure of this weapon, I proceeded to make a hurried examination of the dead bodies in order to possess myself of theirs. I found an armoury. Bud Halsey carried three pistols himself and a bowie knife ; while, from the breast of Mowbray, I plucked two more. I secured them all, not so much with the thought that I should need them, but simply to prevent other hands from using them against me. Thus armed, I stole from the hovel, and made my way in the direction of the main trace from which I had departed.

I had two objects before me—to find a horse, and to elude or frighten Warner. In all probability, I should be compelled to effect the latter, in order to secure the former object. Where the horses were haltered, was to be ascertained. Probably, they were in this man's keeping. He and they were to be searched for, and at some hazard. But I gave myself up confidingly to the gracious Providence that had carried me so far through, and went forward with a free but cautious footstep. If he had heard the shot, which—within three miles, in the deep recesses of night, he was likely to have done,—in all probability he would make his way towards the spot whence it issued. Even while I meditated the question, his horse thundered down the avenue. I resolved on the most merciful expedient, and as the steed appeared in sight, I gave him my bullet. The beast dashed aside a huge tree that stood some fifteen steps upon the path, then fell forwards, with a tremendous concussion to the ground. I had no time to lose. I rushed forward, and as I broke through the bushes, Warner cried out to me :—

"Captain—Mr. Mowbray—it's me—Warner—what have you done ? Help me. I'm half crushed under the horse. I reckon he's done for. He don't move "

"Villain !" I cried, bestraddling him, as he lay with one leg and thigh completely under the animal. "Villain !—this moment is your last."

"How ! Who's this ?" he screamed, making at the same time a vain effort at resistance ; one of his hands striving hard to find its way into his bosom, against which my knee was strenuously pressed.

"Do not move—do not struggle—I have no wish to kill you—but unless you a requiet I will do so."

"Is it you, Mr. Meadows ?"

"Ay ! you came too late."

"Who fired before ?"

"I did."

"At whom ?"

"Your master—Bud Halsey—and he lies as stiff and silent as your horse."

"Grim !—you don't say so."

"It is true as gospel."

"And Mr. Mowbray ?"

"He was killed by Bud Halsey."

"I looked for that !" said the fellow, very coolly. "Well, squire, if it's true what you say, I reckon I must give in! But help me out of this fix, for mercy's sake—I'm afraid the leg's smashed."

"Not till I've emptied your bosom of what it's got in it, my good fellow. Let us see."

He offered no objections to my search, and I drew from his bosom and waist, with some difficulty, a pair of pistols, a bowie knife, and an ordinary *couteau de hasse*, for Warner was a " master of the pleasant sports of Venerie."

"What am I to do now ?" was the mournful exclamation of the ruffian.

"I'll tell you," was my answer. "Where have you left the horses of Bud Halsey and Mowbray ?"

He gave me directions where I should find them, and leaving him where he lay, I at once went after them. They were soon found, and choosing the best, which was a noble black of Bud Halsey, I mounted him, and led the other to Warner.

"Now," said I, "there is but one way for you. I will help you to mount the horse of Mowbray, which is a short animal, and as you are a good rider, you can keep on with me to the next settlement, where you can get surgical assistance, or at all events the best assistance that the neighbourhood affords. What say you to that ?"

"Thank you, sir, but I know a better way. Only help me to get on the horse, sir, and then, with your leave, we'll part company. It's not every day that I can visit the settlements, and it may be as much as my neck's worth to go in your company."

"Be it so," I answered. "You have your choice. You are your own master." He signified his readiness to make the effort, and fastening the horse of Mowbray to a sapling close beside him, I threw my whole strength into the effort, and succeeded. In a few moments he was off in a smart canter, while taking the opposite direction, I proceeded also at a similar pace. How my mother blessed me and kissed me, and welcomed me home, how she looked into my face and wondered at its sedateness, how my father pressed me for a narration, which, until this moment, I have shared with none, these call for no farther development. But there was a cloud upon my brow which neither had ever beheld there before, and there was an abstraction in my glance, which was strangely at variance with the imperious and direct gaze with which, before that season, I had met every other eye. In the brief space of two months, I had counted years by moments. I had crowded the events of a long life, into the limits of a single moon.

THE END.

London : Printed by E. Lloyd, 12, Salisbury-square, Fleet-street.